Only Killers and Thieves

Only Killers and Thieves

A Novel

Paul Howarth

HARPER LUXE

An Imprint of HarperCollins*Publishers*

HarperCollins books may be purchased for educational, business, or sales promotional use. For information please e-mail the Special Markets Department at SPsales@harpercollins.com.

FIRST HARPERLUXE EDITION

ISBN: 978-0-06-279209-9

HarperLuxe™ is a trademark of HarperCollins Publishers.

Library of Congress Cataloging-in-Publication Data is available upon request.

18 19 20 21   ID/LSC   10 9 8 7 6 5 4 3 2 1

FOR
SARAH

[He], with his little band of black boys at his heels, inspired the aborigines with such a wholesome dread, that it was only necessary, when on any of their marauding expeditions, to say [his name] and they would go yelling pell-mell into the bush.

—*description of a Native Police officer*
in The Queenslander, *13 February 1875*

Only Killers and Thieves

Central Queensland, Australia

1885

1

They stalked the ruined scrubland, searching for something to kill. Two boys, not quite men, tiny in a landscape withered by drought and drenched in unbroken sun. Vast plains pocked with spinifex and clumps of buckbush, grass brittle as old bone, red soil fine as gunpowder underfoot. There'd not been rain for a year. The whole bush smelled ready to burn. Dust blew in rivulets between the clutches of scrub and slid in great sheets over open ground. No cattle grazing here. What remained of the mob was down valley, closer to the creek, where the water ran in a trickle through a trough of dry mud and the surrounding floodplain offered the last of the feed. Now all that lived in these northern pastures were creatures meant for the terrain: lizards, snakes, spiders; possums, dingos, roos. Often there'd be rabbits but even the rabbits knew to shelter from the afternoon sun. Only the flies were moving; there was nothing for the brothers to hunt.

They paused and stood together with their rifles down, grimly surveying the surrounds, breathing hard, the air too hot and thick to properly fill the lungs. The older of the pair took off his hat, wiped his brow with his wrist, spat. He settled the hat back on his head. It didn't fit him well. The younger's fit him even worse. Tommy and Billy were fourteen and sixteen years old, and both wore their father's old clothes: tan moleskin trousers tied off with a greenhide belt, dark and sweat-stained shirts. They exchanged a weary glance and stood waiting. A light breeze blew. The shrill rattle of cicada screams. Flies covered the boys' shirt backs and crept toward their eyes and earholes, until a casual swipe of the hand flicked them away. That lazy stockman's salute picked up from their old man, or something they were born with, maybe. Flies had been coming at them their entire lives; they'd been fighting them off since the crib.

"Well," Billy said, "I reckon we might as well quit."

"She won't be happy."

"She can please herself. It ain't our fault there's a drought."

Tommy opened his flask, tilted back his head, eyes closed against the sun, and drank. The water tasted stale and metallic and caught in the back of his throat. He winced as it went down, a childlike revulsion against the taste. Still some boy left in him yet: whereas Billy now had stubble and their father's broad frame, Tommy's body was slender, his nose was freckled, his eyes a watery blue. His hair was fairer than his brother's too, tints of red in a certain light, which came from their mother's side. She was Irish, their father Scots, and there was English blood in both lines. If they were dogs they'd have been called mongrels. Australian was a whole new breed.

Billy held out his hand for the water, Tommy passed it across, and as his brother drank, Tommy's gaze wandered over that barren and rubbled ground to the thin blue-gum forest that marked the northern boundary of their run, shrouded in a fine eucalyptus mist.

"Hey," he said, nodding. "Be shade in them trees."

Billy lowered the flask. "I ain't hot."

"Me either. I mean the rabbits. Might even find us an old-man roo."

Billy scoffed, flicked water at Tommy's face.

"Don't bloody waste it," Tommy said, wiping himself down. "That's all there is left."

"Tastes like foot wash anyhow."

"Give it here then." Tommy took back the flask and stoppered it. "So, what about them trees?"

Billy considered it a moment, then set off walking north. Tommy followed. The cicadas fell silent. The only noise out there the scuff of their boots and the whisper of their moleskins as they trudged through the rocky scrub. Tommy checked behind them as he walked. Mile after mile of empty terrain—it was already an hour's walk back to where they'd tied the horses in a stand of ironbarks, might be half that again by the time they reached the blue gums, and then the long ride home. Most likely all for nothing. Neither had fired his rifle since they'd left the house just after noon, or even taken aim.

It was cooler in the trees. Shadow dappled the forest floor. Deadfall and leaves crunched underfoot, a taint of eucalyptus in the air. With their rifles raised the brothers began flushing between the trunks, some tall and white, others gnarled and twisted by the sun. They moved slowly. Scanning side to side, heads cocked to listen, silence all around. With the dogs they might have fared better, but Father had them for work. He never spared them: poor old Red and Blue.

Suddenly something bolted, crashing away through the brush, Billy first after it, Tommy just behind, both of them tearing between the trees, jumping fallen logs and bulging roots, carrying their rifles two-handed, ready to aim, but the thing was always beyond them, never a clear view, a shadow slipping through the sunlight, until even the sound was so faint that Tommy could hear nothing over his own ragged breathing. He slowed and then stopped, his hands on his knees, Billy coming back toward him, calling, "What you quit for? What's wrong?"

Tommy shook his head. "It's gone."

"We might have caught it yet."

"You get a look-see what it was?"

"Dingo, I reckon."

"Dingo would have fought us. That quick, likely an emu."

They recovered their breathing, Tommy leaning against a smooth-barked trunk, Billy peering through the thinning trees to where the forest ended and the next tract of open ground began.

"You know what's over there?"

"Course I do," Tommy said. Broken Ridge cattle station accounted for almost the entire district: excepting their own selection, and one or two others like it, there was not much this side of Bewley that wasn't the squatter John Sullivan's land.

"Want to take a look?"

"What for?"

"You ain't curious?"

"We should be getting back."

But Billy was already moving, weaving through the trees. Tommy let him go. He cleared his nose, took another drink from the flask. Billy called for him to come. He was standing at the tree line, waving like he'd discovered virgin land. Tommy sighed, trudged after him, then stood with his brother looking out over the fringe of a landholding a hundred times the size of their own. Broken Ridge was no selection: Sullivan's grandfather had been the first white man to settle this part of the frontier, had taken all he could defend, no purchase, no lease, and the next two generations had pushed the boundaries farther still. Now John Sullivan owned the entire district—and everyone in it, Father claimed—without so much as a shilling having ever been paid.

The immediate terrain was familiar: bare ochre earth scattered with boulders and scree, termite mounds as tall as a man. But where the land opened out and sloped into the valley, Tommy could see a distant meadow, with what looked to be Mitchell grass growing improbably lush and green, the dark shapes of livestock dotted throughout. Beyond the meadow and the tree-lined patchwork of surrounding paddocks and fields, the jagged red ridge for which the station was named sawed against the sky, the foothills part-shadowed as if wildfire-scorched.

"One man," Billy said quietly. "One man owns all of that. And here's Daddy barely making it still. All these years, and we ain't worth the dags on Sullivan's arse."

Tommy looked at him sideways. "You might not be."

"I mean it. When I get my own run . . ."

Billy drifted into silence, the dream of it, his long-held plans.

Tommy said, "We should go."

"We ain't doing no harm."

"You know what Daddy would say. Anyhow, it's a long ride home."

Billy smirked at him, then stepped deliberately from the tree line, spread his arms, and turned around. "See? What did you reckon, the ground would give out?"

He shouldered his rifle on the strap and swaggered away. Tommy cursed, ran after him, and together they wandered cautiously between rock mounds ringed by snake tracks, more clumps of spinifex, occasional mulga trees and Moses bushes, and the flat-leaf tendrils of prickly pear. The valley opening before them, the pastures running on and on . . . it seemed incredible to Tommy that Sullivan's land could be fed by the same creek that flowed barely shin-high on their own. Unless it wasn't—there might have been another river that Tommy didn't know. It was possible. Broken Ridge was big enough that there could easily have been two.

They'd been walking less than a mile when Tommy saw the first horse coming over the rise. He threw out a hand and grabbed Billy by the shirt and pulled them both down to their knees, his eyes on the horse all the while. It was heading east to west, only five hundred yards away, and was ridden by a very tall man, sitting fully erect in the saddle, wearing a slouch hat and long-coat flapping open at the sides. After him came another rider, this one small and hatless, then a further five horses, seven in all, trotting in a single-file column. Trailing behind them were three native men chained together at the necks, running in the dust thrown up by the hooves and struggling to keep their feet. Whenever one fell the others did too, causing the convoy to halt and the rear-most rider to shout and curse and yank on the chain, hauling them upright in a clumsy jerking dance, whereupon the convoy would move forward until the next man fell, and the dance started over again.

All this the brothers watched wide-eyed, neither of them speaking, barely breathing so it seemed, until finally Billy took Tommy's arm and dragged him in a crouch to a pair of Moses bushes growing side by side. They sprawled on their bellies and crawled underneath, thorns snagging their shirt backs and scraping their skin, wriggling far enough through to see the convoy again. Once more it had stalled. Another of the men had gone down. The rider yelled and pulled the chain, but this time there was no response. The group watched and waited. The rider got down from his horse. He was wearing a kind of police uniform, as were three of the others: white trousers, blue tunic, peaked hat. He walked over to the fallen native and kicked him. The native shifted in the dirt. The trooper slapped the other two about their heads, then kicked the man again. When still he didn't rise, the trooper returned to his horse, pulled a rifle from his pack, and looked toward the front of the line. The tall man nodded. The trooper stood over the native, aimed, and fired.

Tommy saw the body flinch before the sound of the shot came tumbling over the plains. A noise escaped him. A soft and high-pitched breath. He could feel his heart hammering against the ground as the fading rifle report was followed by a muted cheer. The other riders were clapping. The trooper gave a little bow. He bent and uncuffed the body from the neck chain then bullied the remaining men into line. They rose, cowering behind their hands. The trooper shook out the chain and remounted his horse, but the party didn't move on. The front two men were talking. The tall man extended an arm and pointed to where Tommy and Billy hid. Other heads turned their way. Then all but the last horse broke into a gallop and fanned wide across the plain, and Tommy gave out a moan like a just-kicked dog.

"Keep quiet," Billy whispered. "Don't move."

On the horses came. The ground rumbled with their hooves. Billy was edging backward and was almost out of the bush when Tommy realized he was gone. He pawed at his brother's collar; Billy brushed him off and warned him again not to move. "Don't!" Tommy was saying. "Don't!" But Billy was almost out now, shuffling himself clear, the shock in his face like a man falling, clutching at the air.

Through the branches Tommy watched him rise slowly to his feet and lift his rifle above his head, barely the strength to manage it, his whole body wilting as the horses bore down, full gallop still, and not fifty yards away. Billy stepped into the clearing, everything trembling, his legs jagging back and forth, stumbling backward as the riders reined their horses so late they were almost upon him, turning his head against the dust cloud that washed over him on the wind.

Two riders came out of the line, walking their horses slowly on. Tommy recognized both of them—John Sullivan and his offsider, Locke—but the troopers were like no kind of police he'd ever seen. They were black. Three uniformed natives, rifles in their hands, cartridge belts slung across their chests. The tall man in the longcoat was white and very slim; he kept back from the group and began with the makings of a pipe, as Sullivan and Locke drew up directly in front of where Billy stood. Sullivan was plump and red-faced and wore a stained and sodden shirt carved by braces digging into his chest. Thinning hair sprouted wildly from his scalp, and his little eyes pinned Billy in a glare. Beside him, Locke chewed on his tobacco like a cow at her cud, his face in shadow beneath the brim of his hat, stubbled jaw working up and down. A short-blade sword hung at his side; it glinted as he leaned in the saddle and spat a thick string of brown saliva onto the ground by Billy's boots. Billy lowered his rifle. He lifted his eyes toward the men.

"You would be one of Ned's boys, I take it?" Sullivan said.

"Yessir, Billy McBride."

"And the other one? I forget now, which of you's which?"

Tommy's innards quickened. Billy glanced across but didn't answer. Sullivan said, "Either he comes out himself or we'll fetch him—however you prefer."

Tommy's head hung. He blinked into the dust. Dryly he swallowed, then with his rifle in his hand he shuffled out of the bush and walked meekly in front of the group, eyes down, couldn't meet their stares. When he reached Billy's side he stood so close to his brother that their arms and shoulders touched. Fingers brushing fingers; neither pulled away.

"Well, it's been a while," Sullivan said. "You're almost fully grown."

Father kept the children hidden whenever Sullivan came to the house, sent them to the stables, the barn, the sheds. It hadn't always been like that—Tommy remembered the squatter once giving him a small wooden horse, which only years later had Father taken from him and burned.

"So," Sullivan said, dropping the reins and folding his arms, "you want to tell me what you're doing with them rifles on my land? Your old man send you up here? Not duffing my cattle, were you, boys?"

"No, sir," Billy said. "We was hunting rabbits and got lost, that's all."

"Got lost? Missed the tree line when you crossed it, did you?"

"There was a dingo," Billy said hopefully. "Or an emu, we wasn't sure. We chased it and forgot where we was. We wasn't duffing, I swear."

Sullivan sniffed and looked about, as if searching for proof.

"Thing is, son, whether it's a dingo or emu or bloody

kangaroo, once it's this side of the trees it's mine to hunt, not yours. Didn't your father teach you where the boundary between us lies?"

"Yessir," Billy said quietly. "But ain't them things everyone's? On account of they're wild?"

"Sounds just like a nigger," Locke said. He twisted around to look at the two distant captives and the trooper holding their chains, and spat.

"No, son," Sullivan said. "No, they're not."

In the silence that followed, Tommy glanced at the tall man, sitting at the back of the group. He was smoking his pipe and gazing disinterestedly into the scrubs, smoke dribbling from under his mustache and drifting over his face like a caul. His skin was stretched tightly over his cheekbones, and his eyes were soft and milky, no color in them at all, fogged like a lantern whose wick has burned out.

Sullivan said, "You're wondering about my associates here . . . well, the man at the back there is Inspector Edmund Noone of the Native Mounted Police. These are his troopers. As I'm sure you know, their business is the dispersal of those who don't belong. Chiefly that means myalls, but Mr. Noone's talents aren't particular to the color of a man's skin: boys, he knew you were hiding in those bushes probably before you even got there yourselves."

Noone turned his gaze on them. Tommy looked immediately at the ground.

"Now usually," Sullivan continued, "Mr. Noone will punish trespassers to the fullest extent of the law. To *disperse* them, as it were, as you have just seen. But since he's here on my account, and since this is my land, I suppose I have a say. So, here are the terms: first, that I never catch you past them trees again . . ."

He paused and looked at Billy, who nodded eagerly in reply.

"And second, that you tell your father what happened here today, understand?"

"Yessir," Billy said. "Yessir, we will."

"And you?"

Billy elbowed Tommy in his side. He nodded.

"He don't speak for himself? To my thinking a deal should be agreed out loud."

"Say it," Billy hissed.

"Yessir."

"Good," Sullivan said, taking up his reins. "Then on your way."

The boys backtracked hesitantly, as one by one the group turned their horses and rode toward the trooper holding the two chained men. Only Noone remained. Still smoking his pipe, watching the boys like he hadn't noticed the others leave. His gaze was steady and firm and his eyes were very white. Tommy felt that gaze run through him. It tiptoed down his spine. Billy tugged on his arm, pulled him away, and they set off scrambling for the distant trees.

The first time Tommy looked behind him, Noone was still there, watching. The second time he looked, he was gone.

2

When they rode into the yard Mother was on the verandah, sweeping, fighting her perpetual war against dust. A thin woman with a thin broom, pale in the shade of the porch, beating the wooden deck. Every day she swept, often many times, driving the dirt from inside their slab-walled house and around the small verandah, then expelling it down the steps. She swept, she cooked; privately, she prayed. She carried eggs from the fowl house in the folds of her apron; she taught all of her children to read. She had a hankering for the city. For city values, at least. She was a country girl now but not by birth—somehow she'd drifted out here. First to Roma, then Bewley, then this parcel of frontier land she'd wistfully named Glendale.

Other than the dead center, there was nowhere farther to drift.

As the two boys dismounted, she finished her round of sweeping, then stood on the front steps with the broom in her hands and watched them walk their horses past the house, toward the stables, across the yard. Tommy felt his throat tighten. Still an urge to run to her, to confess, to allow himself to be held, but Billy had made it clear they weren't to talk. Said Sullivan only wanted Father knowing because of the trouble it would cause. Mother smiled at them as they crossed in front of the house and Billy said it again: "Not a word, Tommy," but quietly, through lips pulled tight in a smile of his own.

"Well?" she called. "What have you brought me?"

"Scrubs are empty," Billy replied. "There ain't nothing left."

She raised her eyebrows. "I'm sure Arthur would have managed fine."

"So send him out next time."

"Tommy—what's your excuse?"

"Sorry, Ma."

She flapped a hand dismissively. "Ah, away with you. Useless boys. Me and Mary would fare better. Or maybe you just prefer my potato stew?"

"Best this side of Bewley!" Billy shouted. Mother laughed and shook her head and went back up the steps and inside.

They walked on. Past the long bunkhouse that had once held a dozen men and was now home to only two: Arthur plus the new boy, Joseph, Father's native stockmen. The double doors were open but there was no one inside, and when they got to the stables the other stalls were empty, meaning the men were still out working, seeing to the mob. There wasn't long before the saleyards: their year, their futures, tallied and sold.

In silence they unsaddled the horses, brushed them, fed them, tipped water on their backs, hung the damp blankets on the outside rail to dry. They walked down through the yard together, toward the well and the rusted windmill squeaking with each turn. Tommy fell back to let Billy have the first wash; he hauled up the bucket, watching Tommy as he pulled.

"There ain't no sense worrying about it. They never meant us any harm."

"You were scared the same as me."

"Only because of them natives. Bloody hell, Tommy—black police!"

Billy laughed nervously as he said it, dragging the bucket over the rim of the well and sloshing water onto the ground. He knelt and began drinking, washing himself down; Tommy stole fitful glances across the empty yard. Just the mention of them made him nervous, blurred memories of rifle muzzles and cartridge belts and the uniforms they wore. He hadn't looked at their faces, hadn't dared. Tommy knew nothing about the Native Police—Father didn't like talking about trouble with the blacks. Over the years he'd heard stories about fighting in the district—the whole colony, in fact—from stockmen and drovers and the odd traveler passing through. But Father wouldn't discuss it. Not their business, he said. They had plenty of their own problems without getting involved in someone else's war.

Billy finished washing and stood. Tommy came to take his turn. He tipped out the bucket and threw it into the well, heard it clattering against the walls, then splash into the water far below. He waited while it filled.

"They probably deserved it," Billy said. "Might have done anything."

"Trespassing, Sullivan reckoned."

"All I'm saying is there ain't no sense worrying about what we don't know."

Tommy didn't answer. He held Billy's stare. Billy shook his head and walked around the front of the verandah, toward the steps, and Tommy began pulling on the rope. He paused to listen to his brother's boots on the verandah boards, the door slapping closed in the frame, then lifted the bucket clear of the well. He knelt on the ground and drank, the water dusty but cool, set about washing his face and neck, and at one point sank in his whole head. He stayed under as long as he was able, eyes closed, listening to the tick of the wood and the beating of his own heart, a strange kind of peace in the confines of the pail, muffling the outside world. But then came a crack of gunfire and he saw the body twitch, the trooper standing over it, performing his little bow, and in the silence of the water he heard the horses advancing upon them, the rumble of their hooves in the ground.

Tommy lurched out of the bucket, gasping, jerking his head around. The yard behind him was empty. There was laughter from inside the house. Mary's voice, light and playful, some jibe at Billy's expense. Tommy pushed himself to standing and collected his hat. Water ran from his hairline, dribbled off his chin. He kicked over the bucket, the dirty puddle seeping into the soil, then he walked around the side of the house scuffing the wetness from his hair. He paused. In the north, beyond the cattle yards, three horses were coming in from the scrubs, lit by the fading sunlight in a rich and golden hue. Father, Joseph, and Arthur, the dogs trotting with them, a thin dust trail behind. Tommy took a deep breath and let it out slowly through his nose. He walked up the steps and went inside.

·   ·   ·

They sat around the table, mopping potato stew with freshly baked bread, Mary bemoaning her brothers and the lack of meat in the meal. She was eleven years old but thought herself eighteen; round-faced, with her mother's fair coloring, and little time for a woman's lot. She'd been pestering Father to let her work the scrubs ever since she was able to ride. Now all she wanted was to go hunting, instead of staying home with her chores.

"And who would help me?" Mother asked her. "Or do I grow another hand?"

"These two galoots. Let them clean and sew and see to the chooks. We'd be eating a nice fat possum if you let me go out. Or a kangaroo."

"There ain't no roos," Billy said. "Anyway, how would you get one back?"

"Drag it if I had to, but I wouldn't have rode so far."

"That was his idea," Tommy told them. "I never wanted to go north."

"Only to keep clear of the mob," Billy protested. "No other reason than that."

Father sat back in his chair, chewing, a faint smile on his lips. He moved with a cattleman's stiffness, and like all cattlemen his eyes were narrowed in a near-permanent squint. He wore his beard short, his dark hair too, and the lines in his face looked chiseled from birth. Only a few years past forty, he had the weariness of a much older man. Like every day was a struggle. Which in truth it was.

Father folded his arms and looked between his children. He was sitting at the head of the table, framed by the last of the sunset in the open window behind. Enough daylight still that a candle could be saved, and no need for a fire just yet. There would be, soon enough, once the sun was fully down. The walls of the house were made of ill-fitting timber slabs and the roof was shingled in bark, and both let in draft and dust and rain, if ever rain fell. Only the original building had a floor: the main room and a bedroom off it, separated by a blue curtain door. Annexed out back was another bedroom, where all three children slept, and an open-air scullery had been tacked onto the northern side. The whole dwelling leaned like a drunk on his horse, steadfastly refusing to fall.

"Your sister has a point," Father said finally. "You had any sense you wouldn't have been up that way at all. You're as likely to find something in the yard."

"We did, though," Billy said. "Maybe a dingo or emu, we wasn't sure."

"Well, they do look about the same," Father said. Mother and Mary laughed.

"We couldn't see it properly for the trees."

"Oh, aye? And which trees were those, then?"

Billy fell quiet. Tommy lowered his eyes too. Father wiped his bread around his plate, leaned his elbow on the table, and tore off a corner with his teeth. He chewed lazily, waiting. Mary's head jerked between her brothers like a bird hunting grubs.

"What's the matter?" she said. "Where'd you go?"

"Nowhere," Billy snapped. "Just . . . trees."

"The blue gums up Sullivan's way?" Father asked, but Billy only shrugged. Father turned to Tommy. "You'll have to answer for him. Your brother doesn't seem to know where he's been."

Tommy felt Billy staring. "We thought there might be rabbits in the shade."

Father leaned both elbows on the table, hunched over his bowl. "Might be a golden bloody goose for all I care, you stay away from Sullivan's place, understand? You've the whole country to hunt in—why in hell d'you go up there?"

"'Cause they're galoots, I already told you."

"Enough, Mary," Mother said.

"What's your problem with him anyway?" Billy asked. "What's he ever done to us?"

Father sniffed and sat upright. He popped the last of his bread in his mouth and said, chewing, "There is no problem. Just do as you're bloody told. Bloke like that could shoot you if he caught you hunting on his land."

"We weren't on his land," Billy said quickly.

"Close enough. Don't hunt in them trees again."

"They weren't hunting, neither," Mary said. "They were taking a nice long walk."

She laughed and Billy pushed her. Mary squealed and ducked away. Mother grabbed both of their arms and told them to settle and eventually they went back to their meal. Tommy paid no attention. He was staring into his bowl, watching the stew creep through the crumb of his bread, grain by grain by grain. He lifted the bread to his mouth but it collapsed into mush in his bowl. He glanced up and found Father watching him; Father rolled his tongue, shook his head, looked away.

.   .   .

He was woken by Billy kicking, fighting in his sleep. Tommy shoved him, rolled onto his back, and lay listening to the tick and yawl of the scrubs outside, and the catch in Billy's throat when he breathed. The bed wasn't wide enough to lie like this—his shoulder dug into Billy's spine—but Tommy liked watching the stars through the gaps in the shingle roof. Sometimes there'd be a faller, and he would make a wish, but he never got to see one fall the whole way. The width of a crack and that was all. Like a match being struck in the sky.

He shivered, reached for the blankets, felt his nightshirt clinging damp against his skin. Though the night was cool, he'd been sweating; might have been dreaming himself, maybe. When they'd first come to bed, Billy had accused him of dobbing to Father about them having been up in those trees. But Mary had been listening from her cot across the room, so they lay in sullen silence in the dark, until both fell asleep and they were at it again, arguing in their dreams.

Tommy swung out his feet and stood, crossed the room to Mary's cot. She was huddled in her blankets, her mouth hanging open, spittle running from the corner of her lips. He smiled and turned away, paced up and down, rubbing himself briskly, trying to get warm. He paused by the doorway curtain. A faint light framed its edge: the fire was burning still. He pulled back the curtain, went into the other room, and stopped just past the threshold. Though the fire was glowing, it was candlelight he had seen. Father was at the table, a bottle at his elbow, a glass in his hand, his pocket notebook open before him, the little red pencil resting in the fold.

Father looked up slowly. The light from the tallow candle flickered on his face. One half in darkness, the other in flame. He peered at Tommy a long time.

"What is it, son?"

"Billy's kicking about."

"So kick him back."

"I did." Tommy's eyes went to the hearth and again he shivered. "Thought I might use the fire awhile."

"You sick or anything?"

"I don't think so."

Father gestured grandly toward the fireplace. Tommy came around the table and stood with his back to the embers, waiting for the warmth, avoiding Father's stare. Father poured himself a drink and sipped it, offered the glass to Tommy; Tommy shook his head.

"Help if you've a fever."

"I'm not sick, I said."

Father nodded slowly, lips pursed, head rocking up and down. The fire spat and hissed. "You know," he said, "it felt earlier there was something you and Billy might be keeping to yourselves."

"Only that we were up in them trees. We knew it wasn't allowed."

"Nothing else happened?"

"Like what?"

"Anything. You two have been off all night."

Tommy shook his head. A quick little burst side to side. Father sniffed and drank again, hesitated, then drained the glass. "Ah, it's not your fault. This ain't no place to live, raise a family. I shouldn't have to warn my own children off the bloody neighbor's land."

"Weren't you friends once? You and Sullivan?"

Father drew himself tall, scraped his palms over the tabletop.

"Working for a bloke doesn't make him your mate, Tommy. The opposite, in fact. That was a long time ago anyway, lots of things have changed."

Tommy was about to respond when Father leaned on his elbow and pointed at him, continued, "A man shouldn't answer to anyone. He makes his own way in the world. You understand what I'm telling you? Being a wage slave ain't much better than being a blackfella, you're both some other bugger's boy. What you want is your freedom. Don't give it away, Tommy. Not for any price."

He wagged his finger, then dropped it, rapped his

knuckles twice on the wood. He closed the little note-book, laying one hand on top while the other poured a drink. Thoughtfully he sipped it. Staring into the candle flame.

"How bad is it?" Tommy asked quietly.

"There's a drought. The cattle's starving. How bad d'you reckon it is?"

"Will we be alright, though?"

Father looked up then. His eyes softened and his mouth pulled tight in a grimace, and he breathed out heavily through his nose. "Aye, we'll be alright."

"But they're starving, you just said."

Father reached for Tommy's arm, pulled him close, then cupped the back of his neck and dragged him down until the two of them were butting heads. Tommy could smell the rum. He squatted awkwardly in the embrace, as Father brought his other hand around and slapped him on the cheek.

"You know I love you, Tommy. That I'll look after you, all of you, keep you safe. You make a decision you think is for the best and it's too late when you realize it's not. I'm bloody trying, though, eh. Doing the best I can. All I need from you and your brother is to help with the work and do what you're told, and we'll get ourselves out of this mess. Reckon you can do that for me? Can you do that, son?"

"Yes."

"Good lad," Father said, patting his cheek again. "Proud of you. Good lad."

He released him. Tommy retreated to the fire. Father saw off his drink and pushed himself to his feet. The chair scraped on the boards. He picked up his notebook and wedged it into his shirt-breast pocket, then moved unsteadily around the table, holding the chair backs as he went. The candle flame wavered in the disturbed air. The wick was almost drowned. Father lunged across the open space to his bedroom, paused at the curtain, and said, "Busy day tomorrow. Don't be late turning in."

"I'll just wait till I'm dry."

He looked at Tommy queerly. "Dry?"

"It's sweat," he said, smiling. "It's only sweat, that's all."

Father returned the smile, pulled open the curtain, and went into the bedroom. Tommy heard him staggering about, taking off his clothes, then the creak of the bed and low voices exchanging a few words. After a moment there was silence, nothing but the crackle of the bush outside, that constant rustling, and the faraway howls of dingos hunting in the night. Father began snoring and the silence in the house was broken, and Tommy was grateful that it was. Grateful for the distraction, for his family, for the warmth of the fire on his back.

3

After breakfast Tommy and Billy pulled on their boots and came out onto the verandah and found Arthur standing alone with the horses and dogs in the yard. The sun was not long up, the morning still cool, the sky fresh and clean and new. Tommy raised a hand against the glare as he came down the steps, and the old blackfella laughed his rattling laugh and called:

"Ah, look at 'em! Like two baby possums just crawled out the nest!"

Tommy had known Arthur all his life. He'd come with Father from Broken Ridge when Father first took on the selection, and these days was part of the family just about: other stockmen came and went but Arthur had always been there. When Tommy was a boy he'd seemed truly ancient, but after all these years he'd hardly aged. He wouldn't say how old he was, claimed not to know himself. Other times he'd twirl a hand in the air like he was conjuring, then make some outlandish claim. He was a hundred, a thousand, as old as the trees; or he was still only seventeen, or twenty-one, immune to the passage of time.

The dogs ran toward them as the boys crossed the yard. Red and Blue were heelers, a kelpie-dingo cross bred for the scrubs, and excited to be working despite working every day. Tommy scratched Blue's ear and patted his flank. Red circled Billy impatiently, hoping for the same.

"Where's the others at?" Billy asked Arthur.

"Sheds," he replied, nodding in that direction, flicking tangles of gray hair. The gray had crept into his beard too, but hadn't taken it yet, the beard a thick black slab reaching down to his chest. He was still smiling, his laughter slow to fade, the skin creased in heavy folds around his nose and eyes. One of his front teeth was missing: Arthur had grown up the old way.

"Heard you youngfellas got lost yesterday. Best stay close out there, I reckon. Big old place them scrubs. Dangerous country for two lost boys."

Tommy smirked, but Billy snapped, "We was hunting, not lost."

"Well," Arthur said, sorting through the various

sets of reins and offering one to Billy, "your old man wants you on Jess anyhow, stop you wandering off."

Billy scowled at the packhorse, heavily laden with supplies. Feed bags, water bags, lifting ropes, dog muzzles, even the billycan for their tea. Jess had a put-upon expression well suited to her trade, and for all the world seemed to return Billy's scowl; the horse looked just as unenthusiastic about their pairing as he.

"Joseph can take her. I'll ride Annie."

"Boss says Joseph's on Annie today."

"Beau, then."

Arthur began chuckling. He shook his head. "Your brother's on Beau. It's Jess or nothing for you, except maybe a bloody long walk."

Tommy mounted up quickly, before Arthur changed his mind. Beau was a dun-gray gelding he preferred over all the rest. Other than Buck, the brumby Father broke and would let no one else ride, the horses were generally shared. But everyone had their favorite, and being the new boy Joseph was usually given Jess. Billy was still complaining as he took hold of her reins, the packhorse standing sullen as a mule. He mounted her roughly. Jess stepped and flicked her head but Billy brought her round hard and she settled soon enough. She wasn't the type that needed romancing; small mercies at least.

Arthur mounted up too, and together they sat waiting, until Father and Joseph came out from the store shed, Joseph carrying the last of the supplies. As he secured them onto the pack saddle, Father stood between Tommy and Billy and held up the flask of strychnine powder for both of them to see.

"Don't touch this," he said, more to Tommy than Billy, it seemed.

"I know that," Tommy said.

"Well, I'm telling you again: don't touch it."

"Alright, but I know."

Father wedged the flask into his saddlebag, buckled the strap, mounted up, and they waited for Joseph to finish loading, all of them watching him, this new man in their little crew. He had short hair, no beard, and looked barely out of his teens. Tommy didn't fully trust him yet, had hardly ever heard him speak. Three months he'd been at Glendale and he'd barely said a word, not to the family at least. Mother thought him surly, she'd said so more than once, and Father didn't disagree—he'd only taken him on because Reg Guthrie quit for the diggings and he couldn't afford another white man's wage in a drought. Arthur's opinion had swung it; he'd decided Joseph was alright. That was enough for Father. For all of them, in truth.

Joseph finished packing and mounted up. Father

whistled for the dogs and they rode out, heading north and then west, empty country to the horizon, and for many miles beyond.

·   ·   ·

Midmorning they found their first carcass. The dogs stopped their weaving through the spinifex and pointed themselves stiffly at the scrub. Steadily the five horses approached, no faster than walking pace in this heat. There was no shade, no respite from the sun, the wind only made it worse. All of them were sweating. Dark stains on their shirt backs, faces glistening beneath the brim of each hat. Joseph had his shirt open, and the sweat stood in beads on the scars that climbed ladder-like up his chest. Tommy couldn't stop staring at them, couldn't help but guess what those scars meant. They looked like notches: a tally carved into the skin. The thought chilled him. He counted four scars—did that mean four men? And what about those troopers yesterday? How many must they have had? Were their torsos, their entire bodies, riddled with marks?

Tommy was pulled out of himself by Father swinging down from his horse, handing off his reins to Arthur, and walking toward the dogs. Flies hung over the clutch of scrub in a rolling dark cloud, diving and lifting and diving again. The dogs yapped, then fell still. The others waited. Wafts of spoiled meat carried on the air. Tommy took off his hat, wiped himself down, swatted the flies. He glanced at Billy, looking miserable on Jess—Tommy knew how her gait would be hurting his backside; there was no pleasure in riding that horse. He offered what was meant as a conciliatory smile. Billy snorted and looked away.

With his sleeve covering his mouth, Father leaned over the carcass like a man over a ledge, then came back shaking his head.

"No good. Maggots are already in there. Must be three days old at least."

Arthur handed back his reins. "Dingos get into her yet?"

"Aye," Father said. He mounted up and took the notebook from his shirt pocket, licked the tip of the pencil and made a mark.

"Not blackfellas, though?" Arthur asked him.

"Nope. Drought. Which is something, I suppose."

They moved on. Tommy looked at the cow as they passed. She was sprawled on her side in the dirt, hide hacked open, innards dragged out. There were pockmarks in her skin from the eagles and crows, and both eyes were gone. Flies lay upon her like a newly grown pelt; as one they rose when the horses went by, a shadowlike swarm hanging, then descending again as soon as the party was clear.

The next carcass was more recent, not yet a day old. Father inspected it, then came back and unbuckled the strychnine flask from his saddlebag.

"You two muzzle the dogs. Joseph, open her up."

The young stockman frowned at the instruction. Arthur explained, mimicking a blade with his hand, pointing at the cow and the flask Father held. Joseph shook his head. He turned and stared off into the scrub and Arthur reached out and slapped him on the arm, but Joseph didn't respond.

"Problem?" Father asked.

"Might be," Arthur said, glaring at Joseph as he fidgeted on his horse. This wasn't the first time he'd been like this. Tommy remembered him refusing to shift grain sacks, not long after he was first set on, claimed they were too heavy to lift. There'd been days he'd missed the sunup, gone off wandering and come back hours late, then whenever Father got into him, Joseph would just stand there and take it, not a word in return, like it was nothing to him, like he didn't care. He had a long and empty stare that slid right off you, but there was always something brooding in him. Mostly against Father. The two of them had been at odds from the start.

"Bloody hell, Arthur, will you just tell him."

Arthur drew his bowie knife and offered it hilt first. Joseph glanced at the knife, then away. Arthur said, "Well, I ain't bloody doing it, and he's not gonna ask the boys. So it's either you or the cow, mate—which'll it be?"

Joseph chewed on his tongue, then reached out and took the knife. They all dismounted. Joseph threw Father a look as he went by. Father shook his head and went after him, directed where to make the cut. Joseph lifted the hind legs, sawed the carcass sternum to tail; the innards came sluicing out. Joseph stood aside, holding the knife, blood coating his forearms, and Tommy found himself counting the scars on his chest again.

"Tommy! Wake up, son!"

Father was unscrewing the strychnine. Tommy took a muzzle from Billy, caught hold of Red and pinned him between his knees, wrestled the muzzle on. Red didn't like it but knew what to expect: both dogs had been with the family since they were pups. Tommy tied the buckle and held Red back, Billy did the same with Blue, all of them upwind of the cow. Father motioned for Joseph to lift the hide, and when he did so, Father tipped in the powder, then quickly jumped away. Joseph let the belly flap closed, walked back to his horse. Already the flies were gathering—the dingos would soon catch the scent. But strychnine was totally odorless: before they knew what they'd eaten, they'd be dead.

They poisoned two other carcasses as they rode across that featureless scrubland broken only by lonely gum trees or thin pockets of brigalow, all of it drenched in a hard and endless sun. There was a gentle incline to the landscape, sloping down toward the distant creek, and from here they could just about glimpse the ranges in the west; a low, dark outline crouched upon the horizon like a storm cloud touching the earth. It was a week's ride to those ranges, across unsettled country where few men had ever been, no telling what lay beyond. Father had a surveyor's map showing their selection and the surrounding land, everything to the north, south, or east. The lines went only so far west, then faded into nothingness; the interior blank, like some vast uncharted sea.

The cattle they found wandering loose needed droving back down to the creek. Father and Arthur mustered them easily, one on each side, their horses positioned just so, walking them slowly forward, everything nice and calm. Tommy was always impressed by how simple it looked, when he knew it was anything but. Small details. Mostly reading the cattle, Father said. The last few years Tommy had been allowed to go out with the men on the main spring muster, but he'd done little more than make the tea and cook. That was how everyone started, Father had told him. That was how you learned.

Some of the cattle they found simply lying in the scrub, too weak and exhausted to stand. The dogs nipped around them, but even then they wouldn't move: gaunt, with their legs tucked beneath them and tongues lolling, moaning pitifully when the horses came into view, might as well have been waiting to die.

"She'll need lifting," Father said, when they came across the first. He nodded at Tommy and Billy. "On you go, then, get her up. Billy's got the sling."

They looked at each other. "Just us two?" Tommy asked.

"Aye, just you two. Or did you reckon I'd forgotten about yesterday?"

"She's only a littl'un," Arthur said. "Doubt she weighs much more than you."

Arthur was laughing as Tommy climbed down. He'd helped lift cattle before but never done it on his own. He walked around to join Billy, who was unstrapping the harness from his pack, a homemade sling of stained canvas with thin ropes through metal eyelets in each corner of the sheet.

"You know how to do this?" Tommy whispered.

"Course I do. So do you. Come on."

They spread the sling on the ground beside the cow, Billy at the hindquarters, Tommy at the head, and worked it under her body with the ropes. The cow watched them warily, grumbling and shifting as they dragged the sling through. Tommy stood back, panting, but Billy was already passing his end of the harness back over the cow and tying off the ropes to pull it snug. Tommy copied him, glancing up at Father, who stared impassively down.

"I didn't ask you to dress her, Tommy. Lift the bloody thing!"

They got a grip on the ropes and began pulling. The cow didn't so much as flinch. Tommy's hands slipped on the rope, his palms burned on the weave. Billy was struggling just the same; he wrapped the rope around his forearm, Tommy did likewise, both of them grunting and cursing, their boots sliding backward in the dirt. And still the cow didn't move.

Tommy turned his back on her, hooked the rope over his shoulder like a horse pulling a dray. He lost his hat. The sun stung his eyes, sweat soaked his face, his hands were burning, and somewhere the dogs were barking, then suddenly Arthur was shouting, "Yes, boys! Lift her! Yes!" and there was movement behind them, the cow inching sideways through the dirt.

Tommy glanced over his shoulder and saw her rock herself forward, then the hind legs straightened and she was tottering unsteadily to her feet. He dropped the rope and collapsed. Billy began cheering, Arthur too; even Father smiled. The boys untied the harness and the dogs got into the cow, making sure she kept her feet, and Tommy and Billy came together in a clumsy half embrace.

"Alright, that'll do," Father said. "Get it rolled and packed away. I doubt we're done with it yet."

They all took the ropes for the next one, and three more after that, and by the time they reached the creek they were driving two dozen head back into the main mob. If it could be called a mob: a smattering of moaning cattle strung out across the floodplain, desperately foraging for feed. The grain sacks piled on Jess were emptied in the troughs, but there was only so much grain to go around. Father watched the cattle bitterly. A kind of hatred in his eyes. Blaming them, almost. As if what had become of them was somehow their own fault.

The group took lunch by the creek, in the shade of the red gums that grew along its banks. Salted beef, bread and butter, but it was too hot for tea and there was no sense risking a fire. Bush this dry was like tinder. One spark and it went up.

After they'd eaten, they lay on the bank while the horses took a spell, and soon there were sounds of light snoring as one or another slept. Tommy lay looking up at the leaves, listening to the trickling creek and remembering the rains they used to get when he was young. When the flow became a torrent and the whole floodplain drowned—they'd have been six feet underwater, lying on this bank. Miles downstream, there was a waterhole called Wallabys, where the family went in the summertime to bathe. The river fed a waterfall spouting directly from the rock face, and the pool was often deep enough to dive. He wasn't much of a swimmer, but he'd loved it, the feeling of plunging into that pool, Mother clapping each dive from the side. How many years since they'd been there? When was the last time he swam?

Tommy rolled his head toward Father, sitting along the bank, his notebook open in his lap, staring across the creek. The land on the other side belonged to Sullivan: the creek marked the western boundary of Glendale. Father noticed Tommy watching, closed the notebook, put it away.

"I'll bet you're bushed after all that?" he asked him.

"I'm alright," Tommy said. "Hands are a bit sore."

"You did well. I didn't reckon you'd lift her."

"Showed you, then, didn't we?" Tommy said, smiling. Father smiled too. There was a pause, then Tommy asked him, "So how bad is it? How many we lost?"

"Ah, don't worry about it. Couple of dozen, that's all."

"Feels like more."

"Is that right now?"

"There's no grass. How long have they got?"

Father sighed and looked at the creek. "They've got long enough."

Billy was lying on Tommy's other side. He rose onto his elbow and called, "I'll bet John Sullivan's got plenty fodder. Grass to spare up there."

"I'll bet you're probably right," Father said.

"So why not ask if we can graze them? Only till the sales come round, and if he wants something for it we'll pay him out of the take."

Father snorted bitterly. "Like he doesn't get enough."

"Still, it's better for us than if the whole mob starves."

"The answer's no, Billy."

"Can't hurt at least to ask him."

"Yes it can. The answer's no."

Father rocked himself forward and groaned as he climbed to his feet. He nudged Arthur and Joseph awake with his boot cap, then went to where the horses were tied in the trees. The group rose wearily, gathered up their things, and followed. As they walked, Tommy leaned close to Billy and whispered, "How would you know about Sullivan's paddocks if we never went past them blue gums?"

Billy shrugged. "I'll say I was only guessing. You saw what he has, though. Imagine the take if we got them fattened up first."

"He won't ask him. You won't change his mind."

"I know. Man's more stubborn than that bloody packhorse. My arse is on fire, Tommy. I'll be lucky if I can sit down for a week!"

Tommy was still laughing as he walked Beau out of the trees. The group made its way upstream, north-west, into the far corner of the selection, the mob thinning out the farther north they rode, their painful moans of hunger replaced by the silence of the bush, only the whisper of the horses and dogs through the scrub and the rustle of leaves in the wind.

"Hey," Tommy said to his brother. "Remember Wallabys?"

"Wallabys—too right."

"Reckon we'll ever get back there?"

"Not anytime soon."

"Good, though."

"Yeah," Billy said, nodding. "Yeah, it was."

They'd been riding two miles upstream when the

dogs stopped gamboling and pointed themselves at the creek. Both let go a series of short warning barks, then fell silent as behind them the party bunched to a halt, warily studying the trees.

"What is it?" Tommy asked. "What they seen?"

"Quiet," Father snapped.

Arthur leaned toward him in the saddle. "Probably just smelled another dead bugger. Might be one drowned in the creek."

Tommy could smell nothing different. Heat, sweat, horse. He thought he could hear flies buzzing, but flies gathered everywhere out here. He glanced behind at the open grasslands and the scrub swaying gently in the breeze. His damp shirt rippled. He cleared his nose and spat. Father was hunched over in the saddle now, craning for a view through the trees. Very slowly he straightened. He reached out an arm, appealing for quiet, for calm, then his other hand went for his carbine: he shouldered the stock and took aim at the creek.

Tommy scrambled for his rifle. It was strapped across his back and he struggled to bring it round. Billy and Arthur trained their weapons blindly at the trees, while Joseph sat unarmed and motionless on his horse. Tommy got his rifle down and roved it along the tree line, his breathing quick and panicked, his eyes very wide, but there was nothing in the branches that he could see. Fragments of sunlight glinting on the water. The leaves fluttering in the breeze.

Father dismounted, his carbine raised. His boots hit the ground and he started walking. "Joseph, with me," he said quietly. "You lot stay here."

This time Joseph obeyed. He dismounted and Arthur handed him a pistol, an old open-frame, five-shot, percussion revolver that was missing half its grip. Joseph took it from him dumbly, held it flat in his palm. Father called from the trees and Joseph went after him, the revolver swinging in his hand. Together they ducked beneath the low branches and were gone, the dogs following them in, kicking through the deadfall and splashing through the creek.

"We should go with them," Billy said. "We should go too."

Arthur hushed him. They waited. Watching, listening, glimpsing their shadows rising up the far bank and passing into the clearing beyond, onto Sullivan's land. Dead silence. Not a sound. Tommy was holding his breath, waiting for a gunshot, an ambush, some indication of what they'd found, and yet the noise that broke the silence was somehow even worse: Father's voice, flat and wary, saying, "Boys, don't come over here. Don't come over, understand?"

Billy slid down from his horse. Tommy did the same. Arthur protested but he was also dismounting, following them into the trees. Rifles raised, they crossed the shallow creek, through columns of sunlight falling between the leaves. The dogs were on the far bank, waiting. They whimpered and sniffed the air. Tommy and Billy came up the slope and into the clearing, and Tommy caught a breath of the odor, rank and unwell. Father and Joseph were standing about twenty yards away, weapons lowered, arms limp at their sides. Neither was moving. They both had their heads bowed. Father looked up and saw his sons and his face sagged in sudden grief. They moved closer. Neither boy looking at him now. Their eyes were on the large red gum behind him, alone in the clearing, like a sentry in the scrub.

From its branches, ropes creaking, two bodies hung.

Both had been mutilated, both had been burned. Two knotty, dark medallions, dangling. Carrion birds hunched in the branches above their heads and flies crawled over their charred skin. Gently they swung in the wind. Ticking back and forth, back and forth again. Beside them on the trunk a word had been carved: NOONE read the engraving, in letters a foot tall.

4

Tommy stared at the bodies. Couldn't look away. Watching how they tilted, pirouetting slowly, the branches sagging, the feet only just clearing the ground, lumps of flesh that were once feet, legs that were once legs, men that were once men, turning, turning, the rope knots ticking, flies rippling on their skin, crawling in and out of cavities, a steady and hungry hum, the air alive with it, scent of char and rot, foul and sweet, drawing bird after bird into the canopy above, squatting there and waiting for the chance to feed on these men whom Tommy had no doubt he knew. He had seen them yesterday. He had seen them dragged in neck chains behind that trooper's horse. He had seen their friend shot. Then he and Billy had gone home and eaten supper, kept their silence, and slept.

Now Billy was beside him, no longer watching the

tree, gazing casually around the clearing and scuffing at the dirt with his boot. Arthur brushed between them and went to where Father and Joseph stood, Joseph agitated, wringing the revolver like a rag in his hands. Father had not moved since Tommy got there, his jaw working minutely up and down, clenching and unclenching, his eyes fixed on Joseph all the while.

"Best get that off him," Father said, and Arthur laid a hand on Joseph's shoulder and eased the revolver from his grip. He slipped it into his belt, then spoke with Joseph in a low murmur none of the whites could understand.

"He's asking what that word is. That one written there."

"Noone," Father said, his voice flat, resigned. "He's Black Police, new to the district, John'll have brought him in."

Arthur relayed the information. Joseph's eyes flared. He spun away and walked to the tree, turned, and came back again.

"He alright?" Father said warily. "He knows this wasn't us?"

"Is bad for him, Boss."

"It's bad for us too."

"They're Kurrong, his old mob."

Father waved his carbine toward the bodies. "How in hell can he know that?"

"The markings," Arthur said. He touched his chest. "Is same, see?"

Father closed his eyes, wiped a hand slowly over his face, then made a fist with the hand and tapped it against his lips.

"You never told me he was Kurrong when I agreed to set him on."

Arthur shrugged. Father stood a moment, then sniffed and snapped into motion like something had been decided; he walked a few paces, then paused.

"Look, there's nothing can be done about this now. We leave it alone. It ain't none of our business. Hell, this ain't even my land."

He set off walking again, past Tommy and Billy, toward the creek.

"Boss!" Arthur called. Father stopped and turned. Joseph had his eyes down, his arms locked tightly at his sides. "He wants to stay. Here. With them."

"What's that now?"

"To see to 'em," Arthur said. "Get 'em down, take 'em back, do it right."

"Take them back where?"

"Their people, their land. Send 'em on the proper way."

Father took off his hat, ran a hand through his hair, gazed up at the sky. "I know, alright. I understand. But this is John's business; I can't afford to get involved. The answer's no. We're going home."

"You won't do anything?" Tommy said.

"Look at them, Tommy. Look. What am I supposed to do about that?"

"He says he won't go, Boss," Arthur called. "Says he's staying here."

"Stay," Joseph echoed, nodding.

"Only take him a week," Arthur continued. "Maybe less, I don't know. Ride 'em out, ride straight back, be here in time for mustering, no problem."

Father sighed. "What if we just buried them?"

"That's not how they do it, Boss."

He threw up his arms. "So I'm meant to lose a stockman and risk a horse in a drought so two dead blacks can get their bloody funeral dance? Have you heard yourself, Arthur? Have you heard what you're asking from me here?"

"No ask," Joseph said. "Tell."

Father cocked his head and stepped toward him, hefting the carbine in his hand. "What did you just say to me, boy?"

Joseph squared his shoulders and returned Father's stare. Arthur stepped between them, his hand raised for calm.

"His words aren't so good," he said.

"Well, you can tell the cunt in whatever words he understands that if he doesn't cross this creek with us right now, I don't want him back. Not ever. He makes his choice. And he's not getting a bloody horse neither. He can drag them by their nooses if he's that bloody keen. You've five minutes, Arthur, then we're setting out for home."

Father spun and walked away, calling for Tommy and Billy to come. Billy hurried after him; they collected the dogs, and together went sliding into the creek bed and disappeared behind the trees, leaving Tommy alone with Joseph and Arthur and the two bodies hanging there, all of them watching him, men and bodies both, it seemed. He scoured the ground, trying to think of what to say. Arthur and Joseph waited. Father shouted Tommy's name across the creek and he went to leave but hesitated, half turned, forced himself to meet Joseph's eye.

"I'm sorry," he said shyly. "We didn't know they were your friends."

. . .

They had rounded up the horses and remounted by the time Arthur came trudging through the trees. Billy was riding Annie now, the packhorse already tethered to Arthur's saddle ring. They sat together watching him clear the tree line and cross the fringe of scrub, walking slowly, his shoulders stooped.

"He ain't coming, then?" Father called.

Arthur shook his head.

"Where's that revolver? The old five-shot—you got it still?"

Arthur squinted up at him. "I thought you might lend it."

"Lend means I'll get it back."

"Give it, then."

"Bloody hell, Arthur. Most blokes would have shot the bastard, not given him a bloody gun." He sighed and looked away. "Alright, suit yourself. That thing never fired straight anyway. Bring Jess. We're going home."

Father tapped his horse and set off at a trot, the dogs at his side, Billy following quickly behind. A thin cloud of dust kicked up from their hooves. Tommy handed Arthur his reins, and he took them solemnly, head lowered, eyes down. Tommy waited until Arthur had climbed into the saddle, and for a moment the two of them sat there together, Tommy watching Arthur's shadow in preference to watching the man, then he tapped Beau gently and walked him on, checking behind to see if Arthur would come. He didn't. Not yet. He was staring at the tree line, at the creek. As Tommy rode away he heard him shout something, a single word, and faintly in the distance heard Joseph echo the same word in reply.

5

Tommy rode alone through the empty scrub. Father and Billy were not slowing for him, two dark outlines flickering in the haze, and Arthur trailed even farther behind. The sun was low and glaring, slicing beneath his hat brim; pain bloomed inside his head. Tommy closed his eyes, rode blind for a while. The sun tormented him still. Painting shadows on his eyelids, oily figures morphing between branches and bodies and birds flocking in the trees . . . he snatched open his eyes. Emptiness all around him: empty sky, empty land, on and on. Father and Billy had disappeared now, swallowed by the horizon, gone. In three hours the sun would be down, fully dark within four, they would all be home, and Joseph would still be out here, cutting down those two bodies and dragging them through the bush, west presumably, toward the ranges, to where the lines ran out. Moonlit in the darkness, hauling on the ropes, the bodies scraping through the dirt and snagging on clutches of scrub. The idea sickened him. Tommy felt responsible, like he shared part of the blame. He had known about those men and done nothing . . . but then what could he have changed? Noone was police and police were the law—what's to say those natives weren't criminals, killers themselves? It happened all the time out here, Tommy had heard plenty of tales. Reg Guthrie once told him a story about a selector up near Emerald, got speared while squatting in the long grass for a shit. The spear had passed right through him, pinned him where he sat; he'd still been crouching like that, britches round his ankles, when the body was eventually found.

Tommy swallowed grimly. The saliva caught in his throat. He coughed and spat and cleared it, shortened Beau's reins, and rode him hard for home.

. . .

The yard was quiet when Tommy rode in, but by the time he'd stabled Beau and was crossing back toward the house, Billy and Mary were sitting together on the verandah steps. Mary was tiny beside her brother, hands cradled in her lap, picking at the folds of her housedress, and when she lifted her eyes fearfully Tommy knew what Billy had done.

"You mongrel," he said, standing over him. "You told her?"

"It's only two dead blacks—so what?"

"She's eleven, Billy."

He shrugged. "She wanted to know."

"Is it true they'd had their pizzles lopped?" Mary asked, at which Billy let out a braying laugh.

"He's only trying to scare you. There wasn't no way to tell."

"Yes there was. I saw them. All trunk, no branch."

Again Billy laughed, as from inside the house Father shouted, "Noone *is* the bloody police, Liza!" before his voice fell away again.

"We need to tell him," Tommy said. "About yesterday, what we saw."

Billy's smile slipped. "Why do we? What would that change?"

"I don't know. Neither do you. That's why we're telling him now."

"Telling him what?" Mary asked. "What happened yesterday?"

Tommy stepped past them, onto the verandah. Billy jumped to his feet and grabbed Tommy's arm, but

Tommy shook him off and opened the door. Father was sitting at the head of the table, leaning on his elbows, his forehead resting on his hands as if in prayer. Mother was pacing the room; she halted midstride when she saw him, and said, "Tommy? What is it? You're paler than whey."

Billy and Mary had followed him in. Father mumbled, "I told you two to stay outside. That meant your brother n'all."

"We saw them. Yesterday. When we were out hunting we went past the trees and saw Sullivan and Noone, them Black Police as well. They had three natives in chains. One they shot and the others they kept, same two that was in the tree. We were meant to tell you but didn't. We both gave our word."

Father lowered his hands and sucked his lips so tight the cheeks hollowed. "Your word about what?"

"Telling you. And that we wouldn't go up there again."

Silence save their breathing. Father's gaze slid to Billy and back again.

"Sit down, the both of you. Mary, get back outside."

"Me? What for? Billy already said what you lot found."

"Ned," Mother said gently. "She'll only hear it after."

He hesitated, then nodded at the chairs; they took

the same places as for a meal. Father folded his arms and glowered at the two boys, eyes ticking between them, until they came to rest on Tommy, and Father said, "Right, then, let's hear it. Everything that happened. Every word said."

Billy answered, "We was hunting like we told you, but—"

"Not you," Father said sharply. "Tommy, on you go."

He could feel the others staring. Billy huffed in his chair. Tommy traced a finger around the knots in the table, the lines of the grain, cleared his throat, and began: "It's like Billy said, we were hunting, chasing something through the trees, might have been a dingo or emu we thought but . . ."

He told them everything. The troopers, Noone, the warnings Sullivan gave. Hesitant and faltering in the telling, stumbling on the words, a struggle to tell it right somehow, to convey all they had seen, but nobody interrupted or tried to hurry him on. They sat in total silence, Father listening gravely, his chin resting on his chest, breathing through his nose. When Tommy told of how the captive had been put down, Mother clicked her tongue and shook her head; beside her, Mary leaned eagerly on the table, lost in the tale, her gaze distant, watching it all somewhere. Billy wasn't so attentive. He nibbled the skin on the side of his thumb and held himself tightly with the other arm, and hardly seemed to be listening at all.

Silence followed the confession. They all waited for Father to speak. He unfolded his arms and laid his hands on the table and stared at them a long time. He turned to Billy. "And you didn't think any of this was something I should know?"

"I figured Mr. Sullivan was only stirring the pot."

"So you're protecting me now, is that it? Sparing my feelings, Billy?"

"Spare you the trouble, is all."

Father jabbed his thick finger into the table like a gavel. "Let me make one thing clear. John Sullivan is mine to worry about. Not yours. Or yours. Any of you so much as hears that bastard sneeze, you tell me about it, understand? Same goes for this Noone or anyone else. They're rounding up natives yon side of our run and you stupid buggers don't tell me? The hell's wrong with you two?"

"What would you have done anyway?" Billy asked. "You always say to leave that sort of thing alone."

"Aye, but that's for me to decide, not you."

"I just thought since they was police there must have been a proper cause."

"Proper cause?" Mother said. "Come on now—have we raised you so dumb?"

"What kind of police has blacks in?" Tommy asked.

"No kind," Mother said. "They're killers, that's all they are. Using blacks to hunt other blacks, it's disgraceful. They should have been done with all that years ago. We've no need for them here."

"So they'd not even done anything? Them natives?" Tommy said.

"Must have," Billy answered. "Or why else was Noone there? Duffing or trespass, wasn't that what Mr. Sullivan said?"

"And then it's justified?" Mother asked him. "A man's life for a cow, Billy?"

"Might be. If it was ours they were duffing we'd feel the same."

"This ain't about the cattle," Father said. He slid his hands over the table and folded his arms again. "Fact is, John hunts blacks for sport. Hates them, the Kurrong especially—he's been chasing them off his station since before you were born. Sees them no different than a crop farmer does rats. This Noone, it's his job, it's what they do. John's been wanting more Native Police out this way for years. So fine, now he's got them, but the last thing we want is to get ourselves caught up in some bloody black war."

"Ned," Mother scolded. "You can't mean to let all this stand?"

"No, I'll talk to him. John. We can't be having bodies strung up by our creek."

"Or anywhere, surely."

"Black Police is still police, Liza. They aren't going to stop for me."

Billy said, "There wouldn't be any trouble if they stayed on their own land."

"The natives aren't to blame, Billy," Mother said.

"They were proper police, though," Tommy said. "Had on real uniforms, even. Must have had some cause to do what they did."

"Are you not listening?" Mother asked him. "What have we just told you?"

"Daddy?" Mary's voice was like a needle, puncturing the room. "Why wouldn't you let Joseph take them home? Why not lend him a horse?"

Father inclined his head and tried to smile. "Because then I'd be down a horse as well as a man, which would be even worse."

"Is he really not coming back?"

"No, he's not. Joseph's gone away."

"I never liked him anyway," Billy said. "We're better off rid."

Mother stiffened suddenly. "We should report them, tell Magistrate MacIntyre what they're doing out here.

If he sent word to Brisbane, they might make Noone stop."

"Make him stop?" Father said. "Who d'you reckon sent him out this way in the first place? Who buys their weapons, their tucker, pays their wage? Christ, Liza, where d'you think he sends his reports when he's done?"

She sat there chastened.

Tommy said, "Aren't they meant to be on our side too?"

"Supposed to be. Meaning we'd be the dogs that turned on our own."

"They hanged them others after Myall Creek," Mother said defensively.

"Which was forty bloody years ago, and this is Queensland now, don't forget—Billy Fraser shot six blacks on the steps of Juandah bloody *courthouse* and they let him walk away."

Mother crossed herself at the mention of the Fraser family and the events at Hornet Bank. "That was different. As you well know. But we can't just sit here . . ."

"I already said I'd talk to John."

"When will you?"

"After the sales. Same as always."

"For all the good it ever does."

"Meaning what?"

"Meaning nothing. Talk to him. Again. See how much things change."

Father was still glaring at her as the slow clap of hooves came into the yard, Arthur mumbling to his horses, encouraging them on. The family sat listening: Mother stiff-backed and formal, might have been in church; Father with his brows furrowed; the children's eyes darting between each other and the door. No one said anything. Waiting as he passed by the house. Arthur chatting amiably, the dog muzzles jangling, two sets of hooves plodding by. The noise receded and the room took a grateful breath. Mother smoothed her apron on her lap. Father pushed himself to his feet, crossed toward the door, and Mary asked him, "Daddy, will Joseph be alright out there on his own?"

"I don't know. It was his choice to go."

She frowned and looked ready to ask another question, but Father went out through the door. As his boots thudded down the steps he shouted, "Arthur! Hold up!" then his footsteps crunched away across the gravel in the yard.

"If he wasn't so soft on them in the first place," Billy said, sliding back his chair and standing, "Joseph would never have dared leave."

"You don't know anything about it, Billy," Mother told him. "You should learn to watch your mouth."

Billy shrugged, went to the bedroom, flapped open the curtain, and walked inside; they heard the bed joins creak. Mother came and stood between Tommy and Mary and draped an arm around each, drew them into her sides. Her hips were sharp through her housedress, the bony ladder of her ribs, but Tommy took comfort from her warmth all the same. He felt her hand move softly to his head and her fingers comb his hair. He needed a bath, she told him. They all did, after today. She noticed the rope burns on his hands, turned them over, inspected both palms, then ordered him to stay put while she went into the scullery to fetch her healing balm.

6

The bunkhouse door was ajar but there was no answer from inside. Tommy knocked again, called Arthur's name, still no reply. He transferred Mother's food parcel into his other hand and heaved open the door, stirring a flurry of dust into the air, and slid himself in through the gap. He stood at the threshold, waiting. It took a while for his eyes to adjust. Blinding sunshine outside, murky twilight within. The bunkhouse was long and empty, as big as any barn; a single window threw a column of sunlight across to the other wall. Dust motes hovered like flies. The air was thick and close, fusty, and strewn about the floor were the remnants of the last man to leave: Reg Guthrie's litter and the abandoned iron frame of his bed. It was turned on an angle and had drifted from the wall, like a boat come loose on the tide. Even alone, Arthur had kept to his end, behind the curtain two-thirds of the way down. Force of habit maybe. Father was unusual in allowing his black stockmen to sleep indoors: most were made to live apart, in camps. But the white workers had never liked them being there, so the curtain had gone up, and each color kept to its own end of the barn. Now only Arthur was left, and still the curtain was drawn.

Tommy walked through the building, scuffing the dusty floor, remembering the bunkhouse when it had been full. A dozen men once slept here, sometimes more, in the iron-frame cot beds that Father had since sold, or in swags rolled directly on the ground. Some preferred to be outside, beside the campfire they lit on the edge of the yard. Father would join them sometimes, sitting up late, drinking, laughing, and singing songs, and Tommy and Billy would lie awake, listening, trying to follow what they said, then fall asleep to the lullaby of some old bushman's lament. But that was many years ago. One by one the men had left or been let go, and Father did his drinking on his own these days. He didn't sing songs anymore.

Tommy felt along the folds of the curtain, searching for the divide, the material thick and plush as velvet in his hands. He found the parting and opened up a gap and peered through, into the quarters that Arthur and Joseph shared. Had shared. Here was another window, and the back door was open, light flooding into the room. Arthur's possessions were spread along one wall: his bed, a cabinet, a table and chair, a luggage trunk patterned in gold and silver leaf. Much of the furniture looked salvaged, repaired, and there were odd little trinkets on the shelves. Horseshoes, cigar boxes, ornaments gummed together with wax. On the floor by the bed a Bible lay open at the Gospel of John. The blankets were knotted, recently slept in, but Arthur wasn't there.

Tommy went to the open door, passing the few meager belongings Joseph had left behind: a blanket, a ball of dirty clothes, a necklace of braided leaves. Tommy shied from the sunlight. It was past midday, the sun high overhead; he shielded his eyes as he stepped outside and followed the wall to the back corner of the building. There was a dunny thirty yards away, in among the scrub, the door closed.

"Arthur?" Tommy called. "You in there? Ma sent over some food!"

"You don't have to bloody shout."

He was sitting in the shade against the back wall of the bunkhouse, shirtless, wearing only a pair of ragged shorts, his long, thin legs crossed beneath him, slumped in such a way that his beard covered most of his chest and his stomach was creased in deep folds. He squinted up at Tommy through straggles of gray hair, a faint smile in the corners of his eyes. He looked like a man at the grog but Tommy doubted it. He'd rarely ever seen Arthur drink.

"Howya, Tommy," the old man said. He patted the ground beside him. "Come and get yourself a seat."

"Ma sent some food," Tommy repeated. He held out the parcel, wrapped in a red-and-white-checked towel. Arthur took it from him, shuffled upright, and Tommy noticed on his bare chest and shoulders a series of scars similar to those Joseph had worn, so old and faded he must have missed them before, long-ago etchings worn smooth by the years.

Tommy slid down the wall and sat beside him in the dirt. Arthur carefully peeled back the folds of the parcel in his lap. Inside was buttered bread, meat, some cheese. He raised it to his nose, sniffed and sighed.

"Tell her thanks, won't you. You hungry?"

He offered the parcel. Tommy hesitated, took a strip of salted beef; Arthur began on the bread, still warm from the oven, the butter melted into the crumb.

"What you doing out here anyway?" Tommy asked.

"What d'you reckon: enjoying the view!" Arthur waved at the dunny and the barren scrub beyond, then broke into a rattling laugh. He backhanded Tommy on the leg and took another bite of the bread. "Too bloody hot inside, no air, gets that I can't hardly breathe."

"So you're just sitting here?"

"He doesn't want me working. Said to take a spell."

"He tell you we'll be mustering with you? Me and Billy, for real this time?"

"Well, he doesn't have much choice now, does he? We'd have a job with just two men." Arthur's smile sagged, then he brightened and said, "Who's gonna make my tucker, though? Who'll boil up the tea?"

"Still me, I reckon. I was hoping Joseph but . . ."

Tommy trailed off. Arthur waved a hand, dismissing it. Sat there chewing his bread. Tommy asked him, "You think he'll ever come back?"

"Nope."

"You don't seem too worried?"

"Brave for a youngfella, going off like that, no horse, all them police about, but he wasn't nothing to me. Moody little bugger, actually. Glad we wasn't kin."

"What about the scars, though? Joseph had the same ones."

Frowning, Arthur followed Tommy's gaze to his chest. "These? We've all got 'em, Tommy. Different ones for different mobs. Kurrong have their own ways, but I'm not Kurrong."

"Where are you . . . I mean, who are your people, then?"

He smiled at Tommy warmly. "Ah, my lot went bung a long time ago."

"How?"

"I never told you?"

"Don't think I ever asked before now."

Arthur considered him while he ate. There were bread crumbs in his beard. He shrugged and bit into a strip of beef and said, "Well, alright, then, since you're all grown these days. But don't go passing this on. Blokes don't like hearing blackfella talk."

"What blokes? Daddy?"

The food parcel slid from Arthur's lap. He caught it before it reached the ground.

"Nah, your daddy's a good man. What he said out there to Joseph . . . he was angry, didn't mean it, not all of it anyway."

Arthur offered the parcel again, but this time Tommy refused. Arthur put the cheese and bread together, took a bite, and stared into the scrubs as he chewed. Tommy waited. Finally Arthur swallowed and said, "It all started when I went to the Mission—"

"You were on a Mission Station?"

"Course I was. Where d'you reckon I learned to speak so good?"

"What about those other stories? The snakes and the birds and all that?"

Arthur moved his hands like he was weighing the two out. "I read that bloody Bible again this morning, first time in years. It's horseshit. You know what I reckon, Tommy: one's about as likely as the next, probably both a crock. This place . . . God might have made it, or some giant snake, or maybe it was just always here."

He sighed and leaned his head against the wall.

"Anyway, I was young like you back then, bit older maybe, but our mob was dying, getting sick, every time we saw a whitefella they'd chase us with their guns. Then one day this new fella came with no gun, talking about God and this station they'd built, plenty food, give us work—even had a bloody school. Them old buggers, they told him to piss off, but I was just a youngfella so I went to take a look. I liked it. Turned out they were mostly Germans but all whites seemed the same to me. I fell in with the blokes that looked after the cattle and sheep, learned how to ride and all that. All we had to do was follow whitefella ways and say prayers in their little church. I didn't mind. Told 'em I was Christian the first day I got there, never had no trouble since."

He paused to tear off another bite of bread and cheese, talking as he chewed.

"After a while I got married, had a couple of littl'uns,

then I heard about this other place offering blackfellas work. Real work, proper pay, none of the praying and rules. We wanted our own place, see, our own life. A cattleman he was, name of Cox—I rode down to find him, see if he'd put me on. Two weeks I was gone, then I came back for the missus and kids. Only . . . when I got there the Mission was empty, nobody about. The family, them German buggers, the cattle even, like they all just—"

He clicked his fingers, raised his eyes to the sky.

"There was marks on the ground showing what had gone on. No way of telling who was who. I reckoned a woman and kids might have got took, so I set out after 'em but it wasn't no good. In the end I went back to the old mob again, found there was only a few of 'em left. It was a bad time, Tommy. I moved or I died. So I rode back to Cox and he set me on, worked a couple other runs after that. The last was for a bloke up John Sullivan's way, north of there and east, they called it Denby Downs. Sullivan busted him. Took the run, the men, that's how I came to be his. Then your old man brought me with him when he got this place. Every day I'm happy he did."

Arthur went on eating. Tommy hadn't known he was once married, or had children, hadn't known any of the story other than he'd once worked with Father at Broken Ridge. He hadn't even noticed his scars. It shamed him. They had talked together many times, and Arthur knew him probably better than anyone who wasn't blood, but Tommy knew so little in return, hadn't even wondered, in truth. Other than a few attempts at learning his age, it had never occurred to him to ask.

"So what are the scars for?" he asked now. "What do they mean?"

Arthur looked at him playfully. "What do you reckon they mean?"

"Joseph's were different. Like notches, I thought. A tally, I don't know."

"They are," Arthur said. He pointed at his various markings, counted them up. "That's eleven men I've killed just here on my front."

Tommy stared at him, horrified, then Arthur's face broke into a grin. He laughed, slapped Tommy on the chest. "Stupid little bugger. They ain't all that different to the things you lot write down. Your papers and all that—we just wear ours on our skin."

Tommy was smiling shyly. He glanced at him and looked away.

Arthur said, "If you were a blackfella you'd be getting 'em soon. Means you can do things, get married, hunt, trade. Means you ain't a boy no more, that's all."

"I thought . . ."

"I know what you thought. You whitefellas are all the same."

They sat in silence awhile. Arthur finished his meal and folded the towel neatly into a square. "Ah, fuck it, eh, Tommy. Least we're sitting here together, I'm still living after all these years. Better a bloody coward than hanging in some tree."

"You're not a coward."

"You reckon? I seen them two blackfellas yesterday, same as Joseph did. Yes, they were his old mob but they could have been mine, and I still didn't know how to feel. He did. He bloody knew. He wasn't coming back here. Not me, though. Good old Arthur, follow what the boss says. And here I am, Tommy. Here I am still."

Tommy took the towel from him. Pressed it flat between his hands.

"Daddy's going to talk to him. Sullivan. Make him stop what's going on."

Arthur smiled knowingly, the smile between an adult and child. "Then you don't know John Sullivan. Or your daddy even. There's only one boss between 'em, and I'm sorry, Tommy, but it's never been your old man."

Tommy climbed to his feet and hesitated, like there was something still unsaid. He wanted to defend his father but couldn't; Arthur's words had been loaded with truth, not meant as some kind of slight. And Tommy knew so little. He was realizing that now. Three days ago the world had been one way, now it was twisted another way around. He couldn't get his bearings. Didn't know for certain where anyone stood. What he'd always taken as definite now felt flaky as the soil on the ground.

"Tell missus I said thanks."

He blinked and looked at Arthur. "When will we see you?"

"When I'm needed. I ain't going nowhere."

Tommy turned sharply and rounded the corner of the bunkhouse. He jogged across the yard, back to the house, found Mother sweeping dust through the doorway, onto the porch. He came up the steps and handed her the folded towel.

"He alright up there?" she asked.

"He said to tell you thanks."

"But he's alright? What did he say to you?"

Tommy paused before he answered. "He said to tell you thanks."

7

They ate their oats in the dark predawn, shivering by the fireside and squinting against sleep and the smoke belching into the room. Mother sat with them. Feeding up her men. She drank her tea slowly and watched them all eat, no one talking, a grim sense of ceremony in the air. Last meal. Last rites. Tommy went along with it, took his cues from the others, buried his excitement deep. Already Father seemed weary, Billy casual, though Tommy knew that was an act. Mustering wasn't boring. This wasn't a normal day. They wouldn't see Mother or Mary, wouldn't sleep in their own beds, wouldn't sit around this table again, for the best part of a week.

After breakfast Tommy and Billy went to the stables, where Arthur was saddling and loading the horses in flickering lantern light. Gruffly they exchanged their greetings, then went silently to work, too early for idle chat. When they were done they led the horses—all five of them, including Jess—by their reins down to the house, past the dogs roaming loose in the yard. Father was waiting on the verandah. He sipped the last of his tea. Mother came out behind him, wearing her nightgown still, and Father tossed the tea dregs over the rail and handed her the mug. She kissed him as she took it, set it on the bench. The food parcels were piled there; she came down the steps and handed them out, one for each man. There wasn't a week's worth. Only enough to start them off. She kissed Tommy and Billy and touched Arthur on the arm, then went back up the steps onto the porch. The four of them mounted up. She bid them good luck and they all said good-bye, then in the pale light of daybreak rode out of the yard.

"That's you there, Tommy! Get your bloody head out your arse! After him now, after him!"

It was nothing like he'd expected, nothing like the musters he remembered from his childhood, when he and Billy would climb high into the gum trees and watch for signs of the mob coming in. The swirling dust cloud, the bellows on the air, a trembling rumble of hooves. Then they would see them, a long train of cattle snaking through the scrub, stockmen casually patrolling its flanks, little signals between them, a raised hand, a flicked whip, and sometimes even laughter, piss-taking back and forth. As they neared, the two brothers would race to the cattle yards, open the gates and climb the railings, and balance there, breathless, hearts pounding, waiting for them to arrive. The press of their bodies coming in through the gates, the noise, the heat, the shit, the sweat, was like nothing else Tommy had known. Father directing it all, high on his horse, and when he saw them clinging to the rails he would smile and call a greeting, or even just tip his hat, and something in Tommy swelled. In those moments all he wanted in his life was to become that same man.

"Jesus Christ, Tommy, how many bloody times? Keep on their outside, don't let the buggers turn! Arthur, get over there and sort him out! The hell you doing, Billy—come around, come around!"

They were a sickly-looking lot. Not the cattle of musters past. Drawn across the haunches, bellies sagging, ribs poking through the skin, they moved in an agitated, jerking shamble and with drought-mad eyes watched for an opportunity to bolt. Which they did, often, and somehow it was always Tommy or Billy to blame. Father hounded them, all of them, including Arthur, the horses, the dogs. Just the manner of his riding set the cattle off, darting about the mob and heavy with the whip, the opposite of everything he'd taught his boys. He watched the scrubs constantly. Always the north and west. When Tommy asked what he was looking for he shook his head and told him to get back to work.

"Hold them, Tommy, fucking hold them! Do you want us to bloody starve?"

They camped in the scrubs every night that week, sleeping close by the mob. No holding yards out there, nothing but the natural arrangement of trees and scrub to pen the cattle in. They took turns watching them. A couple of hours each shift. Easy at first, but as the numbers swelled and tiredness bit, it became harder to keep things straight. Tommy sat with his rifle, flinching at every sound. Wild blacks and dingos Father thought the biggest threat. Maybe they were lucky. Though they heard plenty of dingos, none came, and at night the mob mostly behaved. Probably too hungry to stampede. The fodder became thinner the farther east they went, and water was scarce everywhere. The men had their bladder bags and Father had brought rum; every night after supper he would pass it around. They all took a nip, even Arthur and the boys, for warmth more than anything, plus it helped them sleep. Evenings they would sit around the campfire eating dry stores or whatever Arthur had managed to catch that day, rabbit or possum; there were no kangaroos. The four of them huddled in the firelight, the men maybe sharing a memory or singing a ballad, but there was little heart in those stories, not like Tommy had heard them told. Mostly there was silence. Long stretches of time in which they all stared into the campfire, the wood crackling, tossing sparks into the night, as the darkness loomed around them and distant creatures howled.

. . .

The cattle limped over the final paddocks and into the holding yards, Father droving from behind and the others corralling them into the pens. Familiar work for Tommy and Billy, but they were exhausted. Their bodies hung off their bones. Their clothes were stiff with sweat and the cycle of sun and cold. And still there was no respite. No shade in the yards. First glimpse of the house, Tommy had started dreaming of a bath, his mother's food, a lie-down in his own bed. No matter that Billy would be in it. He'd trade an hour with Billy's kicking for a whole night out there alone.

"Hands in the air, you dog fuckers! We're bailing you up!"

They all stopped and turned in the direction of the shout. Two men with horses were walking over from the house: Sullivan and his offsider, Locke. Tommy glanced across the yard at Billy, who only frowned and shrugged, but Arthur slunk toward the back of the pen. Father simply ignored them. He went on with the cattle until the last was in, Sullivan by now watching, his elbows on the rails, then Father handed off the horses to Arthur and sent him on his way. As Arthur passed by the squatter he kept his eyes on the ground and didn't look up. Locke mumbled something and both he and Sullivan laughed.

"You two as well," Father whispered, closing the final gate. "Wait at the house, see the girls are alright. I'll be over in a minute. Shouldn't take long."

"What's he want?" Billy asked.

"I don't know. Suppose I'm about to find out."

He walked toward them along the railing. Tommy and Billy peeled away.

"Not sure which looks worse, Ned," Sullivan called as Father neared. "You or these mangy cows."

"Been a tough year, John. Or have you not noticed the drought up your way?"

"Oh, we've had it, we've had it—hold up there, boys. Come and say hello."

Tommy and Billy hesitated. Father pursed his lips, gave a tiny flick of the head. They walked over. Sullivan was smiling broadly, the smile fixed and full of teeth. He was dressed in a town suit, green fabric, white shirt underneath. His thin hair was neatly combed, and owing to the smile his chin had sunk into his neck. He hooked one elbow on the wooden railing like he was the selector and Father the guest. They hadn't shaken hands. Father stood in front of him, taller by half a foot, and the boys drifted close to his side. Behind Sullivan, Locke stared at Father with hard, unblinking eyes. His sword hung against his thigh. He was hatless, and totally bald, his head lined with scars and discolored skin patches, like the shell of a no-good egg.

"Well," Sullivan said, "you've been busy. Just the four of you out there, Ned?"

"We lost one. Joseph. Had to let him go."

"Native, was he? I don't blame you. The good ones are bloody hard to find." Finally he stopped smiling. He looked at each of the boys. "Now, I'm hoping these two lads of yours are men of their word. They tell you we met the other week?"

Tommy's innards squirmed. He stared at the ground.

"Aye, they told me. Shouldn't have been up there. It won't happen again."

Sullivan was nodding. "They promised as much themselves. Did they mention Noone was with us? What went on? That I spared them from him?"

Father swallowed thickly. He set his jaw. "Noone

has no business with them and neither do you. There's a problem, you can talk to me."

Sullivan held up his hands. "Only you never come and visit anymore. I have to ride all the way down here just to check how things are."

"We're fine."

"Well, that remains to be seen." Sullivan glanced doubtfully at the cattle. "What'll you get for them, d'you think?"

"I don't know."

"Will it be enough?"

"It'll be what it'll be."

Sullivan laughed dryly. "What are you now, a bloody philosopher?" He turned to Locke, still laughing. "It'll be what it'll be!"

"There something you came for, John?" Father asked him. "Only we're tired and hungry and stinking, and I'd like to be getting on."

"Right . . . you know, I'd have given you men for the muster, you only had to ask. Or perhaps we can drove them for you? You selling in Rockhampton?"

"Lawton."

Sullivan's eyes opened. "Christ Almighty—Lawton?"

"Rocky's too far."

"So let us take them. You can ride along. I won't be there myself but . . ."

"Thank you, no."

"Why not?" Billy whispered, and Father shot him a glare. Tommy elbowed his brother's side. Billy looked pleadingly about.

"Now, there's a lad with some sense between his ears," Sullivan said, pointing. "Well, suit yourself, Ned, but there won't be any allowances made."

"I'm not asking for any."

"And we'll see you promptly after?"

"Aye, you will."

"Good. So tell me, how was it out there? Any trouble with the blacks?"

"Never had much ourselves."

"Well, lucky you. And why would that be, d'you reckon?"

Father shrugged tightly. "I leave them be, they do the same."

"Horseshit. If it wasn't for me this place would be overrun. Bloody Kurrong are back again, spearing the cattle, the sheep, then just last month we found a boundary rider with his face stoved, only way we knew him was his boots." He paused and glanced at Tommy and Billy, then looked at Father again. "But Noone—you met him yet, Ned? I tell you, effective as a fucking plague. We've not found a single myall out here since he came around."

"One," Locke corrected.

"Alright, one. The point I'm making, though, is the whole bloody reason you can take your boys into the scrubs, muster this miserable mob, and come home to your lovely wife, is because I look after the district, take care of my own. It wouldn't hurt you to acknowledge that. A bit of gratitude wouldn't go amiss."

"I don't want a war, John. There'll be reprisals. There always is."

"So what would you rather do? Put up a fucking sign? NO DARKIES ALLOWED—you reckon that would work? Listen, the only thing they understand is the gun. You kill enough, they'll get the message. You know all this anyway. You know how it's done."

Father turned his head slowly, peeling his eyes away, looking at his sons. "Go on now. Back to the house."

"Good to see you, boys!" Sullivan shouted, raising a pudgy hand. Locke didn't acknowledge them. Billy briefly waved. He and Tommy walked away, across the clearing, toward where Mother and Mary were waiting in front of the house. Mother held herself tightly. Mary was playing with the dogs. As they walked, Tommy looked back at Father and Sullivan still talking, Sullivan wagging his finger in front of Father's face. Father stood there rigidly, arms braced at his sides.

"What's he come for really?" Tommy wondered aloud.

"To help, was what it sounded like," Billy said. "Wasting his bloody time."

"Don't tell me you'll take his side."

"His side's our side, or would be, if Daddy wasn't so set against him."

When they reached the house Mother hugged them, looked them over, cradled their cheeks in her palm. As if they'd been away forever, not a week on their own land.

"Well? How was it? You have fun?"

"Yeah, fine," Billy answered. "Same as always. Drought's got 'em, though."

"Tommy? You okay?"

He nodded. "How long's he been here?"

She stepped back and fussed a little with her apron, her hair. "An hour. I wasn't expecting him. Don't think your father will have been either."

"That other one gives me the jips," Mary called, throwing up her hand to try and make Red jump.

"He do anything?" Tommy asked.

"No, no, nothing," Mother said. "John just talks and talks, and Raymond hardly ever speaks. Now, I've got a bath drawn. Which of you wants the first turn?"

Billy ran straight around the back of the house, to where the bath was kept. Mother tilted her head sympathetically at Tommy, but he shrugged and went over to the steps and sat down. He was used to going second. That had been the order all his life. Mother followed Billy, and Mary came and sat beside Tommy on the steps, as the dogs slouched away toward the kennels and the chance of water and food.

"You stink," Mary said, sniffing him. "I mean really, really stink."

"You should smell my bloody boots."

He made as if to remove them, but she squealed and grappled his arm. They settled and both watched Sullivan and Father still talking by the yards.

"Did he say much about anything? While they were waiting?"

"Not really. I kept out the way. Ma gave him lunch, the best of what we had."

"Nothing about Daddy, or the cattle, the sales?"

"Nope."

"Or what happened with me and Billy? Those blackfellas? Noone?"

"I was waiting for it but he never did. It was all proper kind of talk."

The conversation was winding up. Locke was already

mounted, and Sullivan was backing away, still talking, though too distant for Tommy to hear.

Tommy said, "I never knew his name was Raymond."

"I know. I'd have thought something harder. And dumber. Like Dirk, or Rock."

"Rock Locke," Tommy said, and they fell against each other laughing again. Mary recoiled at the smell, laughing all the harder, while in the distance Father stood alone beside the cattle yards, watching the dust trails of two horses peel into the scrub.

8

Father and Arthur would be gone a week, droving the cattle to the saleyards in Lawton, and behind them they left a lightness like the aftermath of a storm. Everyone was happier. The children shared chores without fuss or complaint, Mother hummed and sang songs while she worked. Before meals she gave thanks instead of prayers filled with want, and as they ate their potatoes and the last scrapings of beef they talked excitedly about life after the sales. They'd all seen the cattle but were each just as bad: planning and plotting like a make-believe game. The new stock they'd invest in, the repairs they could do, the men they'd put on and the luxuries they would be able to afford, if only for a little while. After three days of such talk Mother's mind was made up: she would take the dray to Bewley, she announced, fill the pantry before Father returned. Give him some reward for all his hard work.

"I'll come with you," Billy told her. "Help load it all, drive the dray."

She shook her head. "I need you here with Mary."

"But I'm the oldest."

"Which is why I need you to stay."

So Tommy squeezed himself into the suit he and Billy shared, once owned by a dead uncle neither of them had met, and waited with Jess and the dray in the yard by the steps, Billy and Mary waiting with him, chirping about Bewley and the favors they wanted bringing back. A new hat for Mary. Lollies from the store. A rubber band from Song's Hardware, so Billy could make a shanghai.

They quit when Mother came through the door. She was wearing her blue-and-white church dress, pinched at the waist with a ruffle of ankle-length skirts. She had pinned up her hair and powdered her cheeks, and none of them had seen her so pretty in a long time. A little gasp escaped Mary, and both boys stared, until Billy asked, "Is it proper, going out like that with Daddy away?"

"Oh, give over, Billy," she told him, coming down the steps. She kissed him and Mary, climbed into the dray, Tommy followed her up. They shuffled into position on the wooden bench, Tommy took up the reins, clicked Jess on, and the dust-clogged wheels turned. The dray juddered forward. The axle creaked. Mother gave a jaunty wave, and Billy and Mary stood watching as they rode toward the sunrise and the long dirt road heading east.

· · ·

It was midday when the few low buildings that made up the township first appeared on the plain. All alone in that amber scrubland, trembling in the haze. The dray rattled along toward them, Mother holding her hat against the wind, Tommy squinting into the glare, both of them grimacing at the ride. There was no give in the axle. Every rock and divot jarred through the bench. Before them the road stretched straight and narrow, little more than a horse track beaten through the bush, but the only road Bewley had. It ran through the center of town and continued east for hundreds of miles, supposedly to the mountains, then the coast and an ocean so big it covered half the earth. Tommy could hardly imagine it. But then the same could be said of the interior, which no man had ever crossed; must have been the size of an ocean at least. The thought made him woozy: the scale of it all, what lay out there, the world. One day, maybe. One day he might see some of it, leave these scrubs behind. It didn't seem possible. In his fourteen years, Bewley was the farthest from their boundary that Tommy had ever been.

A mile out from town they passed the first of the native camps, a shanty of humped bark gunyahs built among the scrub, home to the displaced and the desperate, those caught between the old world and the new, and now stranded here, squatting on Bewley's fringes, nowhere else to go. They carried out their chores, stood talking in groups, rested in the shade. All were naked. At most a woven necklace or adornment of some kind. Tommy watched them warily. They watched him in return. But they were doing the same things anyone did: a woman beat the dust from the front of her hut, a man crouched to skin the hide from his kill.

"Poor devils, look at them," Mother said. "There never used to be so many."

Occasionally there was shouting. A couple of words, nothing too hostile, some laughter, maybe piss-taking at their expense. Mother laid a hand on Tommy's thigh, told him to ignore it; his rifle was behind him in the bed of the dray. A clutch of grinning children ran alongside them on the road. Tommy held tight to the reins and resisted the urge to wave. In a clearing he saw a pair of girls, his age or thereabouts, near-naked, whispering to each other, smiling, looking at him; he felt himself beginning to stir. Quickly he fixed his eyes on Jess's bridle, brushed Mother's hand from his thigh. She removed it to her lap, and Tommy hunched awkwardly on the bench, shielding his crotch and hoping to God she didn't ask him what was wrong.

They reached the fringe of the town. A single street of low buildings ringed by a smattering of humpies and white canvas workers' tents, and the frames of part-built houses standing gallows-like in the sunshine, as if a mass hanging were planned.

Mother drew herself taller on the bench, instructed Tommy to do the same. She straightened her hat and dress and fixed a smile on her face. He glanced at her proudly. Easy to forget she had once lived here, working as a housemaid for the magistrate's wife. She'd been in Bewley only two years before she and Father wed, but as they rode in, she met the stares of traders and townsfolk and spoke by name to those she knew.

They drew up in front of the general store and climbed down from the dray; Tommy hitched Jess to the rail. As he tied off the rope he watched the crowd and scanned the buildings that lined the busy street, a mismatch of storefronts standing alone or grouped in narrow blocks linked by covered verandahs, their proprietors in the doorways or reclining outside on chairs, calling to each other and to passersby, multiple conversations taking place at once. A few stenciled windowpanes denoted the offices of solicitors, moneylenders, Dr. Shanklin's surgery, while in the center of town the Bewley Hotel stood apart from all else, a grand double-story mansion house painted yellow and red, its upstairs drapes twitching and its front railing lined with men from the downstairs bar. One staggered down the steps into the road and wandered along the side alley, a bottle swinging loose in his hand. He unbuttoned himself and pissed against the wall.

Opposite the hotel was the whitewashed courthouse, the only stone building in town. It was set back from the street and fronted by a dried-up lawn and small yard containing wooden stocks, where the Union Flag fluttered on a pole. At the far end of the strip a crude barn announced itself as a church by the cross above its door. A smell of shit tinged the air, from the deposits of horses and cattle and sheep, the slops thrown from windows, the open latrines. Gaunt dogs prowled, sniffing at the ground. In front of the butcher's stall a boy herded chickens, and the metallic clang of the farrier's hammer strike tolled throughout the town.

"Tommy! Come on!"

Mother was waiting outside the general store. Tommy ducked under the railing and ran up the stairs, and as she opened the door a little bell tinkled overhead.

Tommy followed her inside, closed the door once he was through, and behind the counter the shopkeeper looked up from his newspaper and smiled a narrow smile.

"Mrs. McBride, welcome. It has been many months, I think."

"Hello, Mr. Spruhl," she said briskly. "How are you?"

"Fine, fine, dying in this heat."

Spruhl fanned himself theatrically with a pudgy little hand. He was a squat man, pink-cheeked, with round-rimmed glasses that mirrored the shape of his face, and greasy hair parted precisely to one side. Trussed up in his collared shirt and green suit with red cross-hatching, he resembled a netted ham.

They walked toward the counter, their boots loud on the wooden boards. The store was empty. It smelled of rotten food. Three rows of dusty shelving were stocked sporadically with bagged and canned goods; and grain, flour, and sugar sacks were heaped about the floor, thin lines of ants harvesting the spill. Beside the counter was a glass cabinet containing meat and cheese, the glass sweating with condensation, the meat pooled in watery blood.

"So," Spruhl said, folding and setting the paper aside, "how can I be of service?"

Mother pulled a crumpled note from her pocket,

smoothed it between her fingers, and slid it across the countertop.

"We're in need of a few supplies, if you'd be so kind."

"Of course! Of course!" He adjusted his glasses and studied the list, nodding as he read. When he was done he smiled at Mother and put the list down, then reached beneath the counter and slapped a large ledger onto the wooden benchtop.

Mother turned away from the dust.

"My apologies," Spruhl said, opening the cover and thumbing through the pages, until he settled on one and traced his finger down the column of numbers written there. His lips drew tight, he shook his head. He tapped his finger slowly on the paper, then looked at Mother again.

"I am sorry. Is no good."

She was holding herself stiffly, elbows bent, one hand cradled in the other, and when she dipped her head and spoke to him, her mouth barely seemed to move.

"Is there a problem, Mr. Spruhl?"

"No, no, no problem. But I must take payment now."

"Excuse me?"

"Is too much—you see?" He spun the ledger around and pointed at the bottom of the column, all the while looking at her over his spectacle rims.

"Ned hasn't paid?"

Spruhl only blinked. He closed the ledger and turned it back around.

"A debt must be cleared, Mrs. McBride, or else is charity, you understand?"

She shook herself, a little shiver, stood tall.

"Well, Ned's in Lawton right now with the stock. It's been a very good year. Next week he'll be back and he'll come into town and clear this whole amount."

"Excellent. I see you then."

They stared at each other. Mother said meekly, "But . . . I need these things now."

"Without money to pay?"

"We've always bought on credit."

"I am afraid no longer. Besides, I hear is a bad time for you, maybe."

"What's that now?" Tommy said.

Spruhl frowned like he'd forgotten Tommy was there.

"Is just what I hear."

"Who from?"

The shopkeeper waved a hand. "Everybody is talking in Bewley, always people talk. I hear of many things out your way, about blacks, about drought, about debts not being paid."

"The hell's that supposed to mean?" Tommy said, stepping forward.

Mother shooed him back again, smiled warmly at Spruhl.

"You know what it's like in this town, Mr. Spruhl. Gossip's the only entertainment most people have. But you also know us. I bought from your father when he was alive. So let's forget the list, and I'll just take some flour and sugar and perhaps a few beans for now. How does that sound to you?"

"I am sorry. Is not possible. I have been told."

"Told what exactly?"

"Is business, Mrs. McBride. You understand, I am sure."

"She's only wanting a bag of flour," Tommy said.

"And I only ask to be paid."

Tommy saw Mother's eyes fall. He saw the fight drain from her and her thin body sag. He searched the sacks by the window, found one marked as flour, hoisted it into his arms, and stared at Spruhl.

"Add it to your list there. You'll get paid next week."

"Boy, is theft if you don't pay now."

"You miserable bastard. You'd see us bloody starve."

He took a step toward the door. Mother hadn't moved. Spruhl sighed wearily, reached beneath the counter, and placed a pistol on top of the ledger. He spread his hands on the counter edge and leaned his weight onto his arms.

"I shoot thief no problem. Mr. MacIntyre tell me, is the law."

"Tommy," Mother said gently. "Put it down."

He hugged the sack against him, glaring at Spruhl, then tossed it hard on the floor. The neck burst open and a cloud of flour came billowing out.

"Now he makes mess," Spruhl said, throwing up his hands.

Tommy yanked open the door. The little bell tinkled overhead.

"Good day to you, Mr. Spruhl," Mother told him. "My regards to Julie-Anne."

The slack on Spruhl's face tightened and a flush rose into his cheeks. Tommy stood back as Mother left the store. They came down the steps side by side.

"Who's Julie-Anne?" he asked her.

"His wife. Or used to be, before she ran off with his brother, Gus."

Tommy looked at her admiringly. She smirked at him in reply. They reached the street and both stared off into the distance, at this town that wasn't theirs.

"Who's been running their mouth about us, then?"

"Who d'you think, Tommy?"

"Sullivan? What for?"

"He does whatever he pleases. Or it might have been

one of his men. We'll survive anyway. Your daddy'll set things right."

"You reckon so?"

She turned toward him. "Meaning what?"

"You saw the cattle. There was nothing on them."

She winced, then took a breath and forced a smile.

"Come on. It's not so bad. There's more than one store in this town."

But the others were no different: word had got around. Every trader gave them the same response, and with each new rejection Mother shrank a little more; eventually she gave up altogether and said she was going to church. Didn't even make Tommy come with her. Said he could please himself. So Tommy sat down at the curbside and watched her walk away, her skirts whipping the dust, her arms folded across her narrow chest, until she was lost among the crowd. He leaned his elbows on his knees and let his head hang, dribbled a long string of saliva into the dirt. The town bustling around him: women with their baskets, moving briskly about; the butcher in his open-air stall chopping the heads off still-live chooks; the drunks on the hotel verandah heckling passersby.

Directly across the street was Song's Hardware Store. Song was asleep on the porch, arms folded on his belly, his chin slumped to his chest. Tommy rose and walked cautiously across the road, watching the China-man all the while. He was snoring. Each breath came thick and loud. Tommy went up the steps and prodded him, pressed a finger into his fleshy arm. Song didn't stir. Tommy checked the street behind him, then slipped into the empty store.

The rubber tubing was hanging in a coil on the wall behind the counter. Tommy crept around the bench and measured an arm's length from the roll. He found a folding knife in the drawer, cut the tubing, then de-cided to take the knife as well, sliding it into the breast pocket of his undersized suit. He went back around the counter and was making for the door when a voice called behind him, "Help you with something?" and he jerked to a halt and turned.

She was wearing a dirty gray apron and holding a broom. Fine features, finely boned, slender fingers gripping the wooden shaft. Young, with a long neck and black hair cut bluntly to her jawline, glistening where it caught a bar of sun.

Tommy stood there dumbly. She noticed the length of rubber dangling in his hand.

"You buying that? Or running off with it, were you?"

"No," he said quickly. "There was no one here, that's all."

"I was in the back. You could have called."

"I didn't know you were there."

She rolled her lips thoughtfully. Her free hand went to her hip.

"Who are you?" she said.

"Tommy McBride. Who are you?"

"Mia Song."

He glanced at Song, still slumped in his chair. "As in . . . ?"

"What d'you think?"

"I don't know," Tommy said, frowning, his gaze flicking between the floor and the girl's pretty face, watching him so intently, her bright hazel eyes.

"McBride," she repeated. "From out Mr. Sullivan's way."

"South of there. Glendale's our selection."

She nodded. "I know your father. How come I don't know you?"

"Same reason I don't know you."

"You never been in town before?"

"Course I have. Just . . . not often. And not when you're around."

"I'm always around."

"Good for you, then."

She relaxed her pose, leaned the broom against the counter. "Why don't you come to school?"

He shrugged. "I'm too old for school."

"I'm fourteen and I still go."

"I'll be fifteen soon."

"You've never come once, though. Can you read?"

"Ma taught us. All of us. There's Billy and Mary too. I'm the middle one."

"I've got two brothers, both gone."

"Gone where?"

"Diggings. Daddy sent them. Thinks they'll come back rich."

"Will they?"

"I doubt it. It's been a year nearly. Nothing yet."

"What about this school anyway? How many of you go?"

"About twenty. I'm the oldest there."

"You like it?"

"Mr. Drummond's a drinker but it's alright. I've learned all the lessons, but if I don't go, I have to work, which is worse."

"What you doing here, then?"

"Mornings is all we do."

"My sister would like it. Mary. She's eleven and sharper than a skinning knife."

"She should come, then."

"It's three hours' ride."

"Some ride farther."

Tommy shrugged. "We couldn't spare the horse."

They stood in silence a moment, Song's snoring carrying through the door.

"So, what d'you want that rubber for anyway?"

"It's for my brother. For a shanghai. To fire stones with, you know?"

"Sounds like fun," she said.

"Only, I've got no money to pay for it, so here . . ." He stepped forward, offered her the tubing, but her hands stayed at her sides.

"I'll write it in the book."

Tommy hesitated. "Alright."

"You want it, don't you?"

"I just didn't think you'd sell on credit is all."

"Of course we sell on credit. Unless you're not a real McBride?"

She was smiling, her eyes narrowed. Shyly Tommy returned the smile.

"There anything else you needed?"

"Thank you, no."

"Well, then. Maybe I'll see you next time. Or at school one day."

Tommy laughed. "I don't think so."

"Next time, then."

"Alright."

Mia began sweeping, delicate little brushstrokes

across the dusty boards. Her hair swung with the movement of the broom. Dust plumed with each stroke. She
smiled once at Tommy, then lowered her eyes again;
he forced himself out of the door. As he walked up the
street he looked back and saw that she'd come out to
watch him, her father still sleeping at her side.

Mother wasn't in the church when he got there. The
door was already open and he stepped into the shaded
porch, then scanned the rows of bare-wood benches
that served as pews. They were all empty. Not even a
priest about. Sunlight fell in broad columns through the
windows, and hanging above the altar was a carving of
Christ on the cross. A crown of thorns, blood trickling,
a scrap of cloth to cover his groin. As Tommy stared
at the carving, memories of the hanging tree pulsed in
his mind, the bodies dark and disfigured, flies feast-
ing, crows hunched in the branches above, and now he
saw all three before him, strung up in this church, two
bodies burned and blackened, the other lily-white.

Out he came, reeling through the porch and into the
dizzying sun, glancing over his shoulder as he hurried
along the street, bundling into people and searching for
Mother in the windows of each store. She wasn't in any
of them. He walked the length of the street and came
back again, then found her hurrying along the courthouse path, head down, arms folded, hair unraveled

from its pin. He went to meet her; she only noticed him waiting when they were almost face-to-face.

"Tommy? What is it? What's wrong?"

"Nothing—where you been?"

"Church, like I told you."

"I went to the church . . ." Tommy said, his voice trailing off. He looked beyond her to the courthouse, its thick black doors in a clean white wall, the little yard in front, the grooves of the wooden stocks rubbed so smooth they shone. He focused on Mother again. "What were you doing in there?"

"Nothing," she said, touching her cheek.

"Why'd you go in, then?"

"For goodness' sake, Tommy. I was just saying hello to an old friend."

"What friend?"

"It's none of your business. Come on, we're going home."

As they walked past the Bewley Hotel, the men at the railing leered. Filthy and ale-faced, Tommy saw how they stared at Mother. He read their whispers, the little comments they made. A voice called after them, "I've got a shilling you can make, love. Won't take long. Put a smile on that pretty face."

Thick laughter went up. Mother took hold of Tommy's arm and pulled him close, dragging him along the street. When they reached Spruhl's store, Tommy unhitched Jess and walked her clear of the rail, maneuvered the empty dray, and both of them climbed onto the bench. Tommy glanced back at the hotel. A couple of men had drifted down from the verandah and were idling along the road. One began humping the air. "Just ignore them, Tommy," Mother whispered. He flicked the reins and they moved on. A glass bottle smashed behind them. Again Tommy turned. One of the men was waving, and on the verandah of Song's Hardware Store, a slender figure withdrew from the railing and went inside through the door.

9

Billy made his shanghai with the rubber tubing, tying it between the fork of a broken blue-gum branch, and every day after chores the three of them practiced firing pebbles against the bunkhouse wall, taking aim at a target chalked with stone and tallying up their scores. Billy drew two start lines—one for him and Tommy, the other six feet closer to the wall—but theirs was the only mark Mary would use. She'd rather miss from a distance, she told them, than hit a bull's-eye from close in.

Tommy was taking aim when Mary saw the horses: the rubber stretched full-length in his hand, quivering as he held it, one eye closed and the other sighting the target on the wall. She let out a yelp and started jumping up and down, shouting, "They're coming, they're coming, Arthur and Daddy's home!"

"Quit it. I let you have your shot."

"It's them, Tommy," Billy said. "Look here."

He relaxed the rubber and turned. Two riders came slowly over the plain. Tommy handed Billy the catapult and they crossed to the far edge of the yard, calling for Mother as they went. She was hanging laundry on the line beside the house, poked her head around the corner to see, then finished hanging the last of it and came to join them only when the horses were nearly in.

"Well," she said dryly, "let's see, shall we. See what's to become of us now."

Father began waving. He bobbled about on his horse. Arthur followed behind him, and the difference between their riding could not have been more pronounced: Father swayed loose in the saddle, his shirt flapping open, his chest bare, the look of a man being carried, the horse leading the rider, not the other way around.

Mary returned his wave excitedly. Mother sighed and folded her arms.

It took Father two attempts to dismount, heaving himself upward, then an ungainly slide from saddle to ground. Arthur's face was set tight, his beard barely concealing a scowl. He also dismounted, then stood beside his horse, the reins in his hand, as Father took off his hat and spread his arms.

"Hello, family! Daddy's home!"

Mother muttered darkly under her breath. Mary ran to him and they embraced, Father spinning her, then stumbling, laughing, before setting her back on her feet.

"Well? Is this the only bloody welcome I get?"

Tommy glanced at the others. Billy stared blankly at Father. Mother sucked on her teeth. Father smoothed down his hair and Tommy saw yellow bruising around his left eye. And his shirt wasn't just open; it was ripped at the armpit, flapping at the seam.

"So?" Billy asked. "What happened?"

"It's obvious what happened," Mother said. "He's been on the grog."

Father was grinning. He pulled Mary into his side and shrugged.

"Well?" Mother said.

"Well what?"

She flicked her hand up and down, meaning the state of him.

"A man's allowed a bloody drink, Liza. After all we've been through."

"But did you sell them?" Billy asked, and Father whirled in mock surprise.

"Shit, Arthur! The mob! We forgot the bloody mob!"
He started laughing. Arthur managed a smile. Father
said, "Of course I bloody sold them. But you might as
well know, the state those buggers were in, all I could
get was for boiling down."

Billy cursed and kicked the ground. "Meaning what?"
Mother asked.

"Meaning just that."

"So we're short?"

"Short would be the least of it."

"Spruhl wouldn't sell to me. Said we owed too
much."

"I'll straighten that bastard out."

"The whole of Bewley was against us," Tommy said.
"Like we'd been marked."

Father pointed at him, squinting. "Exactly, Tommy.
Fucking marked."

"Call it what you like," Mother said. "We still have
to eat."

"I already told you, I'll straighten it out. Anyway,
look what I brought ye."

He gestured toward Arthur, who began untying
something from the back of his saddle. A thick woolen
bundle, which Tommy first took for a sheepskin blanket or rug, but when Arthur carried it forward and he

saw the hooves and dark head hanging, he realized was a whole sheep.

Father directed Arthur to give the sheep to Billy; he took the weight with a grunt and recoiled from the smell. "Thing's gone," he said.

"Like hell it's gone. Get it cleaned up, both of you. We'll have it tonight."

"You find that thing or kill it?" Mother asked him. "You'd best not have paid for it, Ned."

Father didn't answer her. He winked and tapped his nose, then set off with a stumble in the direction of the house. He leaned in to give Mother a kiss, but she pushed him away on the chest. "You'll be needing a bath before there's any of that," she told him. "Two baths, three!" Which at least raised a trickle of a laugh.

As Arthur gathered Buck's reins and led him away, Tommy tried to catch the old man's eye. Arthur looked at him only briefly, smiled and shook his head, then set off for the stables with both horses in tow. Tommy turned to watch him, but Billy was at his side, ordering him to take his share of the sheep's weight. Together they carried the carcass down to the old slab of red gum that served as a butchering block, and set about gutting it, cleaning it, and removing what was edible of its meat.

. . .

The following day, Father took the dray to Bewley and settled up with Spruhl, came back long after nightfall with a minimum of rations and a rum crate whose rattling could be heard from inside the house. They all sat listening. Mother looked up from her needlework, the children paused their game of cards, as Father slurred out a ballad, singing his soul to the stars. Mary started giggling, which set Tommy off too, but Mother stared bitterly in the direction of his voice, then drew a long breath and went back to her darning without a word.

It was a strange time between them. Tommy didn't fully understand. Father stopped working, claimed there was nothing to be done, spent his days drinking on the verandah or loafing about the sheds. He would carry out odd bits of carpentry, fixing things that didn't need to be fixed; he spent hours whittling Mary the kind of animal figurine he used to make when she was young. He and Mother spoke in snatched exchanges and twice Tommy found her in tears. Once in the scullery, then again in their bedroom: she stood in the corner, facing the wall, a handkerchief clutched in her hand. When he drew back the curtain she flinched and yelled, "Can I not just have a minute on my own!" and Tommy let the curtain fall closed again.

They saw little of Arthur that week. He looked after the horses, the dogs, kept out of everyone's way. The few times Tommy caught him skulking between the buildings they'd exchange a greeting, then he'd move on again. Avoiding the family, not wanting to be seen. None of the others seemed to notice, or if they did they didn't care. No one visited him, Mother sent no food parcels, as if he weren't there.

One morning after breakfast Tommy crossed the yard to the bunkhouse and walked along the outside wall to the back door. Whites weren't supposed to use that door but he didn't want Arthur to slip away. He looked in the window as he passed. Arthur lifted his head. He was standing by the bed, an open sack in his hand, and was in that same pose when Tommy came into the room.

"You're leaving?" Tommy said.

"Nah, just heading off for a spell."

"Where you going?"

"Dunno. Walkabout, I reckon. See some of the old bush."

"What for? What's happened?"

Arthur smiled warmly. "Nothing, mate. It's just got that it's time."

"Are you coming back? Does Daddy know?"

"Yeah, we talked about it. You'll have seen your old

man's not going so well—best I take off for a bit. We all could use it. Don't worry, be back soon enough."

"When?"

"Couple of weeks. I've not exactly got it planned."

Tommy stood there looking at him. Arthur scratched his beard.

"What happened in Lawton?" Tommy said.

"How d'you mean?"

"You've been off ever since."

Arthur waved a hand, dismissed it.

"Did you two fight?" Tommy asked. "Is that how his eye got busted up?"

"That wasn't me. Could have been, but it wasn't me."

"Who was it, then?"

"Some whitefella. Blokes drink then they fight, specially in a drought. Does things to a fella's mind, the drought. Sends him madder than the cows." He smiled quickly, went on, "Me and the boss—I've known him a long time, we'll be right, but it's for the best I leave awhile. This last month . . . look, when I come back the rum'll be gone and we can get on with the new mob. You never know, Tommy; this smell in the air, it might even bloody rain."

They didn't see him off. Tommy went on with his chores, then caught sight of Arthur riding past the cattle yards, a solitary figure heading out into the scrub.

He didn't look back. Tommy watched until he was no more than a speck on the sun-drenched plain, then swung the ax and splintered the next log and set the two halves on the pile.

By suppertime they all knew, sitting around the table, eating the last of the mutton and questioning Father in much the same way as Tommy had Arthur: Where was he going? How long for? Would he be back? Had he gone to find Joseph, maybe?

"I'm not his bloody keeper," Father said, waving his fork around. "Arthur's a free man. Anyhow, I'm sick of his bloody whining. Bloke's had a face on him like a chook's arse. Do him good to get away."

"Why?" Tommy asked. "What went on at the yards?"

Father shrugged and picked the mutton off his fork, sat chewing it around and around. "Same as always happens at the yards. Blokes get talking. He didn't like what was said. I can't blame him, neither. Not so soon after them two buggers in that tree. It was all blacks this and blacks that, who's done what to them, what they plan to do. And there's Arthur, listening to it all, no one minding their tongue, like he's not a real black-fella, least not from how he acts. You can see why they'd think it. He can't have it both ways."

"Will he be safe?" Mother said quietly. "All on his own out there?"

"Ah, don't worry about Arthur. The bush is in his blood. I don't know what you're all being such sooks about, anyway—him going saves us another wage!"

He broke into a hoarse laugh, took a drink, then laughed again. He reached over and slapped Billy on the chest, and they all sat in silence, watching him, as he speared another chunk of mutton and chewed it openmouthed.

. . .

When the dogs started barking and Tommy saw a horse coming down through the northern paddocks, he thought it might be Arthur returned. He'd been gone over a week, though it felt much longer, but as Tommy drifted to join the others gathering in the yard, he saw that the rider was white and scrawny, a boy, no resemblance to Arthur at all.

"You lot stay behind me," Father said, pushing between them. "And if I say to get inside, I mean bloody get inside."

Father had his carbine with him. He kept it pointed at the ground. The boy rode in cautiously, slowing his horse past the cattle yards, then walking it to where the family stood. The horse jittered as it came. The boy steadied it with his hand. He was wearing a dirty shirt and trousers that would have fit a man twice his size. The hems were double-rolled, the waist pinched tight by a rope belt. He took off his hat and scuffed his blond hair; his eyes found the carbine and darted between the assembled faces and the weapon Father held.

"A message from Mr. Sullivan," the boy announced.

Father jutted his chin. "What message?"

"It's wrote down—here."

He shoved his hand into his pocket, pulled out a crumpled sheet of paper, offered it to Father, but Father didn't move. The boy jabbed the paper in his direction and Father took the note without unfolding it. "Did you read it?" he asked.

The boy shook his head. "I just brung it."

"But you didn't read it?"

"I can't. I don't know how."

Father weighed the boy carefully. The boy squirmed under his gaze. Father still held the note unopened; without taking his eyes from the boy, he scrunched it into a ball and tossed it on the ground.

"You ain't going to read it neither?" the boy said.

"I don't have to. I already know what it says."

"But how can you, when you ain't read it?"

"Go on now. You did your job."

"You ain't got no message for the boss in reply?"

"No," Father told him. "On your way."

The boy sat there puzzling the exchange, staring at the note for which he'd ridden all that distance. Father waved the carbine and the boy flinched, turned his horse around. Nobody moved until he was clear of the yard, then without saying anything Father walked past his family and on toward the sheds.

Mary was nearest the paper. She snatched it up, unraveled it, and they all crowded round to see. The ink was smudged, the letters bleeding, but it was legible enough to read. There were only three words written: *I'm waiting Ned*, they said.

10

It began in a sudden skittering across the shingle roof. The noise woke Tommy with a start. He lay there listening. An irregular thudding sound, maybe insects, or the claws of flying foxes scrabbling to find grip. He could see nothing. Still fully dark outside. No moon, no stars, no movement in the shingle cracks. Tommy tried placing the sound. A faint hissing now, settling into a regular and steady din. Locusts, he figured, or a plague of some other kind . . . until something landed on his forehead and dribbled down his cheek and he bolted upright in bed and shouted the other two awake, and both Mary and Billy came grumbling from their dreams.

"You hear that? The noise?"

"What's happening?" Mary asked groggily. "What's wrong?"

"Nothing's wrong. Listen. It's raining. It's bloody raining outside!"

They leaped from their beds and were still hugging and jumping around the floor when Mother called from the other room. Through the curtain they stumbled, jostling and chattering, to where she stood by the open front door. She ran to embrace them, touching them fleetingly as if to prove to herself this wasn't some dream, then together they bundled out into the downpour and found Father standing half-naked in the yard. He was wearing only his white long johns and with his pale body and sunburned arms looked spectral in the rain-washed darkness. He wasn't moving. The water had flattened his hair and his trousers and he was gazing off toward the paddocks in the north.

The others ran down the front steps. They tilted back their heads, opened their mouths, stuck out their tongues; Mother raised her nightgown and danced a little jig. Already the ground was churning under their feet and squelching between their toes, the rain fat and thick, proper wet rain, the kind of droplets that promised a million more. Tommy could feel them bursting on his skin. He fell still and closed his eyes and stretched out his hands and tried to count them as they hit. It was impossible. Like counting seeds. Around him the others were still laughing and shouting and jumping like fools, but when Tommy opened his eyes he saw that Father wasn't with them anymore. He was walking slowly across the yard, as if drawn to something far away in the scrubs. The rain nearly swallowed him. It enveloped him until only the white of his long johns could be seen. Then they too were gone, as on the edge of the clearing, Father fell to the ground on his knees.

. . .

It rained for three full days, then in the sunshine of the fourth the earth steamed like it burned. Blankets of smoke rising and drifting across the ground, the air moist and close and fresh. The buildings creaked and ticked. The bush crackled as it dried and teemed with life, insects and animals awakening to a new world and curious to discover what had changed.

Even Father seemed restored. The rain had energized him. He was still drinking—in celebration now, he claimed—but he spent his days jotting numbers in his pocket book, drawing sketches, making plans. He talked about digging a series of irrigation ditches, running them off the creek, and about the crops they could try if the rains kept up, once the soil was fertile and damp. They would take up dairying again, he thought; he would clean the old separator, get it working, make their prospects less reliant on beef. Easily done, so long as they all pitched in, though it was clear Mother and Mary would get the bulk of that work. Tommy teased Mary about her elevation to milkmaid; she countered that if she was a milkmaid, what did that make him? Milkman? Milk boy? Milk master, maybe? And just like that, they were all laughing and hoping together again.

Before the rum ran out and Father got his plans straight and put them properly to work, Tommy and Billy set off for Wallabys one day before noon. The waterhole wouldn't be full, but there was a chance it might be deep enough for paddling, which was no bad thing since neither of them could really swim. Mother and Father were little better, so it had fallen to Arthur to give them the scant instruction they'd received. Tommy still remembered the first time he saw him swimming. As the two boys floundered, Arthur had slid through the water as smooth and graceful as an eel.

It was a two-hour ride, southwest through a country reborn by the rain. Gone was the sepia dust haze, replaced by a rich palette of green and gold and brown. The cicadas were out, screaming with joy; cockatoos chorused in the trees. Across the plains they spied emus standing motionless in the scrub, their fat feathered bodies blending with the fat tussock grass, noticeable only by the rubbery contortion of their necks, dipping up and down. Roos loped along, pausing to forage, or reclined in little mobs in the shade. The boys didn't try hunting them—they were too far away, the meat would only spoil—and instead rode happily together side by side in the sunshine, talking and joking and arguing over the best route to take.

Wallabys was a waterhole you had to know about, invisible from the flat: at a gallop you'd be airborne before you realized you'd left the ground. A deep horseshoe crater, sheer-walled, like a sinkhole in the earth, the walls layered in orange and ochre and red, chalky-white stains lining the rock face like scars. Birds nested in the crevices and shat onto the ledges below; trees grew improbably from the escarpment, twisting and reaching into the void. Water dribbled from an opening in the northern wall, falling weakly into a pool sparkling in the sunlight and nestled in a basin of rocks and trees and resurgent regrowth.

They rode around the crater's edge, peering over the drop, then followed the slope down to where a copse of trees hid a short canyon passable only on foot. They tied the horses and went through, clambering over boulders until they emerged onto a smooth, wide slab, where they stood looking out over the glittering pool,

the waterfall drumming softly, the sun painting a rain-
bow in its spray.

"Well?" Billy said. "What d'you reckon?"

"Well nothing. Let's go."

They set down their bags and rifles, stripped, and
waded into the water, cool at first but good once they
were in. At its deepest it reached only to their chests;
they ducked beneath the surface and came up gasping,
splashed and spat arcs into the air, took turns beneath
the waterfall, which even at a dribble pummeled their
heads and shoulders sore. Afterward they pulled on
their trousers and lay baking on the rocks, each to his
own slab, then sat together on a ledge, their feet dangling, sharing the tucker-bag Mother had made.

"Should bring Mary next time," Tommy said,
chewing.

"Mary? What for?"

"She'd love this. Hardly remembers the last proper
rain."

Billy laughed. "Be too busy milking, the way Daddy
talks."

"She's not so happy about it. Neither's Ma."

"They needn't worry. It won't come off."

Tommy looked at him. "We're starting after Christmas, he says."

"That's the rum talking. Don't get hooked in."

"You don't think he'll do it? What about them water troughs?"

Billy swiveled sideways on the rock, finished his mouthful, and swallowed. "If you've not worked it out yet, let me tell you: Daddy's full of shit. He's had years to dig them ditches. He gave up on dairying because he thought it was too hard. He's lost both his stockmen, sold his mob for boiling down, now he's acting like everything's different because a bit of rain fell."

"The drought's not his fault."

"No, but what's he done about it? Look at John Sullivan. Same drought, same soil, and I'll bet he's sitting just fine up there."

"We ain't nothing like Sullivan. The two can't be compared."

"We're something like him. Could be, anyway. Bloke even comes down and offers his help and Daddy's too proud to take it. Or stupid, it's all the same. Imagine some blackboy speaking to Sullivan like Joseph did, or people treating his missus the way they did you and Ma in town."

Tommy stared out over the waterhole. "I wouldn't trade places for nothing."

"Horseshit, you wouldn't. All that cattle. That land."

"It ain't worth it. You've seen how he is. What he does."

"That wasn't him, it was Noone."

"Same thing," Tommy said.

"How is it?"

"Daddy said Sullivan's the one that called Noone in."

"Christ, you sound as soft as him. When I get my own run—"

"Daddy ain't soft. Neither am I. And you need money to buy a run, you know."

"I'll find it."

"Oh, you reckon? Where at?"

"I'll go shearing, down south. Or to the diggings if I have to."

"The Song brothers did that and never came back."

"Song brothers? From town?"

"Mia told me. When I got your rubber band."

"Stole it, you mean. And that knife."

"She put it in the book."

"Not the knife she didn't."

Tommy sat there brooding. He felt bad about the knife but couldn't figure how to make things right with Song. He had no money to pay for it, too long had passed to pretend he'd taken it by mistake, and he didn't want Mia thinking of him as a thief.

"I'll set that straight one day," he said. "Or you can, when you're rich."

Billy was watching him carefully. "You've not shut up

about that girl since you got back from Bewley—you're sweet on her, aren't you?"

"Am not. She was kind to us, that's all. Gave credit when no one else would."

"Sweet on a chink, Tommy!"

Billy nudged him playfully; Tommy nudged him back, then ate in silence, ignoring the smirks and glances his brother gave.

"You ever wish we'd gone to school, Billy?" he said finally.

"School? What for?"

"She said she liked it. You learn more than just reading."

"You only want to go because she does. What's her name again?"

"Mia—but that's not it. There's about twenty of them there."

"They're welcome to it," Billy said, flicking at the flies. He fell quiet a moment. "So this girl, d'you reckon she was sweet on you too?"

"I don't know. I don't think so. She didn't even know who I was."

"What did you talk about, then?"

"Just that. And school. She said me and Mary should go."

"What about me?"

"You just said you didn't want to."

Billy shrugged. Tommy picked up a stone and tossed it into the pool, watched the ripples spread. A crescent of shadow fringed the water, peeling left to right. Insects danced across the surface, rose, and fell again.

"What was so special about her anyway? Why d'you like her so much?"

"No reason. I just liked watching her. Had hair as black as tar."

"What was she doing, then?"

He hesitated before he answered: "Sweeping."

"Sweeping? Sweeping what?"

"The floor."

"Sweeping the floor!" Billy shouted, and his laughter echoed around the walls. Tommy shoved him but he wouldn't stop laughing, so he shoved him harder and Billy slipped off the ledge and down into the shallows. "Sweeping!" he howled again, then ran away laughing as Tommy slid down and chased after him, splashing into the pool. When he caught him they briefly wrestled, throwing and holding each other under, before they came to a stalemate and drifted apart in a hesitant truce.

"Make you a good wife, anyhow," Billy said, "if she's skilled with a broom."

Tommy's scowl cracked. He smirked and Billy saw

it, and both were laughing now. Together they came trudging back out of the water and each went to the same rock he'd used before; they lay down to dry off, and both were soon asleep.

. . .

Tommy was first to wake. He lifted his head into a swarm of mosquitoes and leaped to his feet, flapping at the air. The waterhole was in near-darkness. Shadow covered the pool. Outside the crater the sun still shone, but little light made it this far down. A deep shiver ran through him. Like standing in the bottom of a well. The crater rim was fringed with brightness, and between the pillowy clouds the sky was a brilliant blue, but the walls were so sheer and tall, and down here was so dark, that Tommy felt a shock of abandonment, as if they had fallen from that world without knowing how or when they might return.

He went over to Billy and kicked him awake. "Time to go," he said.

They pulled on their shirts quickly, collected their things, and went back to where the horses were tied. Tommy walked Beau out into the sunshine, and even when the warmth hit his back it took a long time to reach his bones. Billy was already mounted. He sat waiting at the bottom of the rise; when finally Tommy joined him he frowned and asked what was wrong.

"Nothing. Just got a chill from that rock."

They moved on. Back onto the flat, then northeast toward home. The first strains of dusk falling over the plains, shadows lengthening on the ground. A soft sunset tonight. Fiery wisps of crimson in a cotton-ball sky. The colors swirled and deepened the farther they rode, and by the time they glimpsed the house and its outbuildings the sun had begun to pool and spread in the west. Glendale glowed warm on the vast horizon, that lonely shipwreck of little slab huts the boys called their home. Both smiled when they saw it. Tommy glanced at Billy and caught a strong look of Father in him just then. Steady brown eyes, stubble on his jaw, that same crooked grin.

"Beat you to the stables!" Billy shouted, and took off at a sprint.

Tommy was caught dreaming. He couldn't close the gap. He ran Beau as hard as he could but Annie was just as eager, and he was beaten by a couple of lengths, Billy whooping and shouting as he drew up to the stables; he dismounted and pulled Annie around, pointing and laughing as Tommy rode in.

"It wasn't even," Tommy told him, sliding down. "You got a start."

"It wasn't even to begin with—yours is the bigger horse."

They led them around the back of the stables to the doors. The horses whinnied and shied, their blood up from racing, reluctant to go in. Billy went to open the doors. Tommy stood by with the reins. The yard sloping away from him, down toward the house, its long shadow tapering up the hill. Peaceful, but still the horses wouldn't calm; Beau reared when Billy opened the first stable door and a waft of warm air escaped.

"Christ," Billy said. "Hot as hell in here. Stinks like it as well."

The horses inside began neighing. Sounds of stomping, of hoof striking wall. Billy dragged open the second door and came back for Annie, and they led them inside. The air was choking. It reeked of piss, shit, and sweat. Tommy began with Beau's saddle strap but watched the other stalls. Buck pacing. Jess cowering against the wall.

"They've not been out," he told Billy. "Look at them—they're heat mad."

"Daddy'll have forgot. Too worried about ditches, or milking, or rum."

They stabled their own horses, a struggle to get them into the stalls, then came gasping into the outside air, snorting and spitting dryly on the ground. They left both doors open, cool the place down—no doubt they'd be back up here after supper, cleaning and feeding and filling the water troughs. Tommy wondered if Father might have even left them like that on purpose. With Arthur gone, the horses were his and Billy's responsibility. A lesson in neglecting their chores.

Tommy spread the saddle blankets on the railing and collected up his bags, and when he came to Billy's side, Billy said, "Quiet, ain't it," staring across the yard.

"They'll be sat down for supper. Better have left us some."

He took a step forward. Billy gripped his arm.

"Where's the dogs at even? They never barked when we came in."

They stood listening to the silence. Little swirls of dust played across the yard. Down at the house the front door was open but there was no movement and no sound from inside. Clothes still hung on the drying line. An uncut log balanced on the chopping block, the ax beside it in the dirt.

"Something ain't right," Billy said.

"It'll be nothing."

Billy unslung his rifle. Tommy brought his own around. It was so quiet. Not a sound save the horses and the windmill creaking in the breeze. Tommy's breathing quickened, surged through his nose, quivering as his body began to shake. His gaze was fixed entirely on the house, a thing of total blackness haloed by the sunset, and in the middle of the dark verandah the faintest sliver of daylight through the open door.

Billy started walking. Tommy followed at his side. Edging into the long shadow that swallowed most of the yard, rifles braced, boots scuffing the dirt.

The silence. The silence. The silence.

They found the dogs first, in the clearing between the house and the well. Both had been run through. Lying together, one beside the other, tongues lolling, paws crossed; like they only slept. Around them a churn of bloody dirt, imprints of the scuffle, of boot marks and paw marks: a slow, unclean death. The brothers stood over them, incomprehension in their young eyes, then Billy walked around the bodies, toward the well, bent and collected something from the ground. He rose again. His back to Tommy, his head bowed, examining whatever he had found. He turned. Something metallic in his hands. He came forward. Tommy stared. He saw but did not see, not until Billy was right beside him, the thing in his outstretched hand like an offering, which Tommy would not take.

Joseph's old five-shot revolver, open-framed, missing half its grip.

Billy bundled past him, running for the house.

Tommy watched his brother vault the steps, onto the porch; heard his anguished groan. Tommy went after him, moving very slowly along the front of the house. Through the verandah railings he could see Billy on his knees and the tread of a pair of boots sticking out. Tommy turned the corner. He took each step slower than the last. Billy looked back at him, over his shoulder. His face was red and twisted and his narrow eyes brimmed.

"That fucking nigger cunt."

Tommy looked beyond him. Father lay slumped against the wall. He was wedged between the door-frame and the bench, and his eyes were open but they did not blink. He had three holes in him. Shoulder, stomach, chest. Blood soaked his shirtfront and pooled in his groin and spread over the boards below. His mouth hung slackly. His empty eyes stared. A fly crawled onto one of the eyeballs and sat in the corner of the lid, drinking. Drinking his final tears. Billy lunged to his feet and went into the house but Tommy stood watching the fly. He leaned and flicked it away, then propped his rifle against the frame of the door. Father's carbine lay in his lap. Tommy propped it beside his own, then crouched and looked Father up and down. It was him but not him: no longer the same man. He went to touch him, then withdrew his hand as, inside the house, Billy cried out again.

Tommy rose and went inside. The shutters were closed. Thin spindles of sunlight broke through the gaps and crossed the darkened room, and when Billy burst through the bedroom curtain the dust swirled wildly within each one. Billy was raging. A crazed and faraway stare. For a moment he seemed not to notice Tommy, then traced him from the boots up. When their eyes met, Billy's lips parted, strings of saliva peeling between them, and a noise sounded deep in his throat. He shook his head. Eyes pleading. Tommy's gaze slid from his face to the blue curtain swaying back and forth. He stepped forward. "Don't," Billy said, but Tommy reached out and parted the curtain and held it open with his arm. Mother was in there. She lay twisted on the floor. Her face was turned away from him, her hand reaching for the bed and the pistol they kept underneath. A hunk of her head was missing. A mush of flesh, hair, bone. Her skirts were ruffled around her ankles and from their folds her feet were poking out, dirty and rough-skinned, the little buds of her toes.

Tommy let the curtain fall. His stomach lurched and he vomited on the floor. He looked up for Billy but Billy was no longer there. Tommy spat, straightened, surveyed the room. Nothing was amiss. Nothing any different, the same as when they'd left. Tommy's eyes filled suddenly. He squeezed them closed and tears

ran. He could feel it coming now, the force of it breaking over him. He opened his eyes and his face began to
crumble, and at that moment Billy threw back the other
curtain, panting, "She's alive. I found her. Mary's still
alive!"

She lay on the floor in their bedroom, her hands
folded, covering a bloodied hole in her gut. Blood
stained her little fingers, stained her housedress, stained
the floor. But she was breathing. Shallow snatches of air
passing quickly in and out. She had her eyes closed. Her
hair in bunches still. Her freckles looked to be fading,
Tommy noticed. He hadn't seen that before. She'd have
been beautiful fully grown.

"She was under the bed, hiding," Billy said, crouching and raising her up. He tried to lift her but unbal-
anced and fell into a squat. "Will you fucking wake up
and help me! Tommy! Get her ankles—come on!"

Together they carried her out through the house.
Her skin was soft and cold. Her hands slid from her
belly and Tommy got a look at the wound. It had gone
in messy. You'd do an animal a kindness after a shot like
that. Not Joseph. And that bastard would have known.
He'd plugged her and left her to die slowly, and alone.

As they passed by the curtain, Tommy asked, "What
about Ma?"

"Leave her."

"No, Billy."

"She's gone. Mary's not. We'll come back later, do it right."

"Where are we taking her?"

"For help, Tommy. Where d'you bloody think?"

They paused in the front doorway, came cautiously onto the verandah, beside where Father lay. Billy didn't look at him. Tommy reached for Father's carbine but picked up his own rifle instead. Father was precious about that gun. Tommy nudged it so it fell back onto his lap, not neatly but it was with him anyway. He would have fought, Tommy knew. Would have fought as long as he could. As they came down the steps he saw bloody drag marks leading from the yard, meaning Father had crawled onto the verandah after he'd been shot, must have gone out to confront Joseph head-on. He imagined them arguing, Joseph pulling the revolver, Father too slow with the carbine, three balls already in him . . . *bang, bang, bang.* The noise would have brought Mother onto the verandah and Joseph would have chased her back into the house, got her before she reached the pistol under the bed, Father crawling after them but it was too late, too late. Mary hiding, petrified, but Joseph knew where she would be; the dogs must have tried to get him coming out. No balls left in the revolver so he had to use his spear, or maybe there was another one, an accomplice, some other Kurrong bastard come with him for revenge.

Tommy could almost see it, their ghosts all around, as he and Billy lumbered across the yard with Mary in their arms, then lowered her gently outside the stable door.

"I'll get the dray," Tommy said.

"Too slow. The track's not clear. Get the saddles on."

"Me and Ma managed."

"The saddles, Tommy."

He stood there numb. Billy fetched the blankets from the rail and shoved one into Tommy's arms. The blanket still warm and sweat-damp, the horses still unsettled in their stalls.

"If we hadn't slept at Wallabys, if we'd come back after lunch . . ."

"That's enough."

"We might have stopped him, though."

"Or we might be dead. Get your bloody saddle on."

When it was done, Billy hoisted Mary onto the front of Tommy's saddle, her legs skewed together at one side. Billy tied a rope into a harness that Tommy looped under her armpits then wore like a cartridge belt across his own shoulders and chest. He had his arms around her also, and he gripped tight on the reins. Her hair brushed his face, through it the soft shell of her ear.

He put his lips there and told her she'd be alright, they would make it, they'd be in Bewley in a couple of hours.

"We're not going to Bewley," Billy said, mounting up, both of them walking their horses clear of the barn.

"Shanklin's in Bewley—who else is there?"

In the leeching twilight Tommy saw his brother's head turn.

"Sullivan's got a medic up at Broken Ridge."

Billy didn't wait for an answer. He set out across the yard, yelling for Tommy to follow; Tommy pulled Mary against him and did so, leaving the house behind, everything within, riding for the northern scrublands, into the darkness they held.

11

Through the trees, across the border, onto Sullivan's land, past the bushes from where they'd once watched a man killed. A low moon rising, the light slippery and faint, objects rearing from the shadows and making the horses flinch. Already they were wary, of the scree underfoot, of how the boys rode, of this strange nighttime mission, of the darkness, of the cold.

In the valley the terrain plateaued and they found a trail leading northeast, through swaying grass meadows, undulating like the sea; beneath trees whose tall branches spread spidery against the gloom. Neither brother speaking. Sounds only of hoof fall, occasionally a rustle in the treetops, the downbeat of wings, the pained catlike screech of flying foxes overhead.

And all the while Tommy cradled Mary against him, held her body tight to his. She wasn't waking. Was hardly even breathing, so far as he could tell. Her head lolled forward and hung there; her body was cool and limp. He felt for a pulse but couldn't find one, clumsily fingering her neck. Difficult enough to keep her upright, to keep Beau steady on the track, to follow Billy's outline, the shape of him, pale shirt flapping in the moonlight, the glint of their two rifles strapped across his back.

The track opened into a clearing ringed by trees. Billy slowed, and when Tommy drew alongside him he saw the reason why: a candle flame quivering in the darkness, hovering across the clearing as if magically conjured there.

"Alright, far enough. You the McBride boys?"

They stood the horses and peered into the gloom. The outline of the watchman was only just visible behind his lantern flame. Thin body, ragged clothes; a sickly, hoary face. He held the lantern above his head and in the other hand, braced against his hip, was a twin-barreled shotgun, pointed their way.

"We need help," Billy said. "Blacks got us."

The watchman tilted his head. "Got you how?"

"How d'you think—please, she's hurt bad."

"Her sleeping there?"

"She's not sleeping," Tommy said. "She's shot."

The watchman sniffed and looked about. "I wasn't told about no girl."

Billy said, "I heard there was a medic?"

"Aye, there's a medic."

"Come on, then. We need to bloody go."

"Touchy bugger, ain't ya? Alright. Toss down them guns."

"We're not here for any trouble," Tommy said. "We're asking for help."

"I heard you. But the boss says get their guns, so I got to get your guns."

Billy unstrapped the rifles and threw them on the ground. The man juggled the lantern and the shotgun and stooped to pick them up, his eyes upturned, the pale oval of his crown as he bent, then he was backing away again, fumbling the rifles in his arms.

"Yous lot stay put while I get my horse out."

The lantern mapped the clearing as he retreated: a smoldering fire, kicked over in haste, outside a windowless hut. The hut was walled with thin slats, no door, barely wide enough to lie down. The watchman went around the back, into the trees, and emerged with a scraggy-looking mare. He slung the two rifles onto his shoulder, then climbed into the saddle and brought the mare to where Tommy and Billy waited. He held the lantern to his face, grinned a toothless grin, and blew out the candle flame.

"On you go, then," he told them, his shotgun wagging. "And don't get no funny ideas—there's a fistful of shot for both of yous in here."

Single file, they followed the trail out of the clearing and on toward the station compound. Billy leading, then Tommy, the watchman close behind. He wouldn't let them gallop. A steady trot the most he'd allow. As they rode, he started whistling an old Irish ditty Tommy had heard his mother sing, something about a girl left behind. The song filled his eyes immediately and though tears dribbled down his cheeks, he did not wipe them and did not sob. The watchman finished his tune and moved on to the next, and Tommy held tight to his sister and blinked his eyes dry.

. . .

They came upon the workers' camp before they reached the homestead. A village of rough-built barns and slab huts lit by the glow of scattered campfires. Smoke hung over the rooftops. Voices rose in laughter or quarrel, then quickly fell away. A smell of burned wood and meat char and the heavy stink of men. Dogs began barking as the three horses neared, and some of the stockmen drifted out between the buildings and stood at the trackside watching the party pass. Arms folded, picking at their teeth, swigging on their grog, cradling their pipes or pinching hand-rolled durries to their lips, as the watchman like some crier announced:

"Got the McBride boys here, fellas! Bloody blacks have done 'em in!"

There wasn't any sympathy. A muted grumbling, some shifted or shook their heads—if anything, Tommy felt a kind of contempt. He caught a few of the men eyeing Mary and hitched down her dress, turning her into him until they were clear of the camp and onto a long broad track leading straight uphill to the homestead, perched high on the hillside, ablaze with candlelight. A grand two-story mansion, painted brilliant white and cobwebbed in ornate metalwork. Lanterns burned along the verandah and down the wide staircase, yet the hollow beneath the stilts was so dark and indistinct from the shadowy hillside that the house appeared to float there, unanchored, ten feet above the ground.

Billy dismounted short of the stairs, ran to Tommy's side.

"Hold up!" the watchman shouted. "I ain't said to get down!"

He was brandishing his shotgun but they ignored him. Tommy lowered Mary into Billy's arms, then dismounted himself, and together they carried her to the stairs, her arms draped behind their necks, her head hanging forward and her feet scraping through the dirt, then thudding against each step as they began to climb.

"I said wait, you bastards, before I—"

"Alright, Jessop, that'll do. You can put that thing away."

Tommy and Billy halted. Sullivan stood framed in light at the top of the stairs. He paused a moment, then came down very slowly, step by step, rolling back his shirtsleeves, fold by careful fold. The shirt was white and freshly pressed, and he wore slack green trousers tucked into high leather boots whose polish glinted in the lantern light. Braces dangled loose at his sides. Cheeks smooth and slightly flushed, damp hair neatly combed. Total calm in his face, like they'd just popped by for tea.

"Get their weapons, did you?"

"Yessir," the watchman said.

"So, then, boys," Sullivan called, "what kind of trouble have you come to make for me now?"

"She's hurt, blacks got her," Billy blurted. "They killed our daddy and ma."

Sullivan paused. Midfold, midstep. He tilted his head to one side, narrowed his eyes. "Blacks, you say?"

Billy nodded furiously. "We was gone swimming when they came."

"And the girl?"

"Shot," Tommy said. "She's not woken up."

"Has she spoke?"

"No."

"But she's alive? You're sure?"

"I don't know," Tommy said. "Maybe only just."

Sullivan considered all three of them for what seemed a very long time, then he snapped into life and called over their heads: "Fetch Weeks! Now, man! Go!"

The watchman turned his horse and galloped away along the track. Sullivan hobbled quickly down the stairs. He hoisted Mary into his arms and carried her up to the house, her hands and feet swinging, the little bunches in her hair, Sullivan talking over his shoulder as he climbed:

"Don't worry now, boys, you've done all you can. You were right to bring her here. Weeks'll take care of her, see she's alright. Let's get the two of you warm, cleaned up, some food in you, must have been a hell of a ride . . ."

The air inside the house was close and scented with flowers, and the boys followed Sullivan along a wide hallway with a maroon carpet runner and green gold-leaf wallpaper as thick as a pelt to the touch, the walls themselves decorated with gold sconces and gold-framed paintings of sun-blushed English hills. The sconces flickered as they hurried past, marching toward a vast white atrium with a broad, sweeping staircase rising high above, until Sullivan stopped abruptly, just short of the atrium, beside a white wood-paneled door.

"Wait in there, the pair of you. I'll have some food brought."

"Where you taking her?" Tommy asked.

"Upstairs, lie her down. Somewhere quiet so Weeks can work."

"No, we're staying with her."

Sullivan's jaw clenched. "Look, you asked for my help and I'm giving it. Nearest other doctor is Bewley. What d'you want to do?"

"He didn't mean nothing," Billy said, and Tommy looked down at the floor. Sullivan nodded. He hefted Mary's weight and carried her across the atrium to the stairs. A housemaid came running to speak with him. Sullivan glanced back at the boys, dismissed her, then mounted the stairs and disappeared from view.

"You trust him?" Tommy asked.

"Why not?"

"Daddy didn't."

"Daddy's dead."

Billy's words shocked both of them. He turned away ashamedly; it took Tommy a long while before he followed his brother into the room, a drawing room, roughly equal in size to their entire house. Separately they explored it like a museum. Rich wooden furniture, finished in a waxy sheen and adorned with trinkets of silver and gold. A sofa, the cushions thick and plump; ornate wooden chairs upholstered to match the papered walls. A fire burned in the cavernous hearth, its flames reflected in real window glass, and beside the fireplace was a tree unlike any Tommy had ever seen. It had a million little needles and was decorated with baubles, candles, and gifts. An angel sat askew on the topmost branch, twisted like she was ready to fall.

The housemaid brought a bowl of washing water, two towels, and a bar of soap, then returned with a platter of food and a pot of English tea. She was young and white, their age or thereabouts, could have been Mary in a few years, Tommy thought. "Thank you," he said, but the girl hurried out of the room.

They washed their hands in the bowl, dried them on the towels, a trace of blood staining the water when they were done. Mary's blood. Blood that should have been inside her, not swirling in some bowl. Tommy couldn't look at it. He turned away and went to the other table, inspected the platter the maid had brought.

Meat, bread, cheeses, a few grapes. He picked up a grape and sniffed it.

"Don't touch that," Billy warned.

"Why not?"

"It ain't right to be eating."

"But I'm hungry."

"I don't care. I'm telling you, it ain't right."

They stared at each other. On the far wall, an upright pendulum clock chimed the quarter hour. Tommy wilted and broke the stare.

"What'll we do, Billy? What now?"

"I don't know." He shook his head very slowly. "I don't know."

Running footsteps sounded on the outside stairs, then thudded mutely along the hall. A man burst into the drawing room. Bedraggled and panting, he carried a black medical bag in his hand, yet more resembled a bushranger than any doctor Tommy knew.

"Where's she at?" the man asked. "I was told a girl's been shot?"

"Our sister," Billy said. "She's upstairs."

"Right you are."

He went to leave but Billy called him back: "You're the doctor?"

"In a way."

"What's that mean?"

"I'm actually a veterinarian, but—"

"A what?"

"Oh, don't worry, I know what I'm doing, we're all roughly the same underneath, you know . . ." He hurried away, his footsteps crossing the atrium, then padding up the stairs.

Billy glared after him, at the open door. His cheeks were flushed and his jaw offset and his head bobbed minutely up and down. "A vet?" he mumbled. He looked at Tommy. "A bloody vet?"

"A medic, you said."

"That's what I was told."

Billy went over to the fire, lost himself in the flames. Tommy laid some cheese on a slice of bread, took a bite, and retched. The taste of the cheese curdled in his mouth, the bread became a thick and claggy wad. He fished it out again and placed the puttylike ball on the edge of the tray, then looked up to find Billy coming at him across the room, shoving him backward, shouting, "The hell's wrong with you? Where you at? Where's my brother gone, eh? You did nothing in the house, didn't cry, didn't scream, like it was any other fucking day, now you're standing here eating while Mary's getting fixed up by some vet and the others are still down there—"

"Boys, boys, boys. This isn't doing anyone any good."

Sullivan strode into the room. He stood directly between them, laid a hand on each of their shoulders, and squeezed. He was Tommy's height, shorter than Billy, his eyes dark and faintly bloodshot, and up close the skin on his cheeks and nose was as pitted as rind.

"Now listen to me," he said, still squeezing. "There's no use fighting each other, understand? It's not your fault what's happened. It's not your fault."

Billy relented.

"Good," Sullivan said, reaching between them for a slice of beef, which he folded into his mouth and chewed. "You eaten anything yet?"

"We're not hungry," Billy said.

"You should eat. Can't do nothing without a feed. What about a drink? You want something stronger than tea?"

"Thank you, no."

"Suit yourself," Sullivan said, shrugging. He snatched a slice of bread from the platter and steered the boys around to the sofa, motioned for them to sit. Tommy sank awkwardly into the cushions, then shuffled forward to perch on the edge, as Sullivan positioned one of the wooden chairs in front of them, so close that when he sat down their knees almost touched.

He smiled and ate his bread. Watching them back and forth.

"What about Mary?" Billy asked him. "What's that vet say?"

Sullivan answered between mouthfuls: "No news. Too soon."

"He even know what he's doing up there?"

Sullivan flapped a hand dismissively, went on eating, watching them all the while. The boys waited. Finally he popped the last of the bread into his mouth, brushed the crumbs from his hands, and leaned forward on the chair.

"Let's get this done with, shall we? Which of you wants to tell me what went on down there?"

His gaze slid past them as Locke came into the room. Both Tommy and Billy turned. The overseer skulked toward the sofa and leaned against the wall, working a lump of tobacco around his mouth. He nodded awkwardly at the two of them and scuffed his bare scalp with a white-bandaged hand.

"They were just starting," Sullivan said. "On you go, boys."

Tommy pressed his hands flat between his thighs and listened as Billy spoke. Telling them about the mustering and the time they'd all had of it these past few weeks, how glad Father had been for the rain. Then Wallabys, the chance to get away, the long ride home and the silence in the yard, not even a sound from the dogs.

One beside the other, tongues lolling, paws crossed; like they only slept.

And Tommy was right back there, standing in the clearing as Billy found Joseph's revolver and offered it to him like a prize. Walking past the front railings, the tread of Father's boots, Billy crouched before him; coming up the steps.

His mouth hung slackly. His empty eyes stared. A fly crawled onto one of the eyeballs and sat in the corner of the lid, drinking.

Into the house. Bars of sunset streaking through the shuttered window, dust motes dancing; lifting back the curtain, Mother facedown on the bedroom floor.

Her feet were poking out, dirty and rough-skinned, the little buds of her toes.

Tommy was shaking. Rocking back and forth. Sullivan reached out and cupped his knee and Billy wasn't talking anymore. Then Sullivan's voice, coming in gradually, as if from very far away, or carried on a shifting wind, asking, "You alright, son? What's his name again? Tommy? You alright?"

Tommy looked pleadingly at his brother; Billy only frowned. Sullivan stood and went to the drinks table, poured a measure into a crystal tumbler, held it for Tommy to take. He sipped at the drink, coughed, took another sip.

"Best Scotch outside Sydney," Sullivan said, sitting. "That'll see you right."

Tommy drank the whiskey. Gradually the trembling eased. Sullivan turned his attention to Billy again.

"How are you sure it was this Joseph?"

"We found his old five-shot, here . . ."

Billy pulled the revolver from his waistband; Locke levered himself from the wall and reached immediately for his ankle piece, but Sullivan gestured for calm. He took the revolver from Billy, turning it over in his hands.

"It's empty," Billy said. "I think the dogs was speared. Both was run through."

Sullivan glanced at Locke, now resettled against the wall.

"And this was his weapon? You're sure about that?"

"Yessir. We were there when Arthur gave it. Joseph had it with him when he left."

Sullivan was still inspecting the revolver. "He's the one Ned let go?"

"We found those two natives hanging in that tree. Joseph didn't like it, wanted to cut them down, take them back to his people—he's Kurrong, see, same as them."

Sullivan looked knowingly at Locke, took a long breath, shook his head.

"Fucking Kurrong," he said. "So, him and Ned argued, the boy took off, might have got together with a few more of them, then came back for revenge. Doesn't sound like the kind of thing he could have done on his own."

Billy nodded. Sullivan leaned and handed the revolver to Locke.

"And what about the other one?" Sullivan said. "The old boy—where was he?"

"Gone too. Daddy gave him a spell. You think he was involved?"

"Probably, son. Blacks side with each other. Always have."

"Arthur didn't do it," Tommy said. They all looked at him.

"You don't know that," Billy said.

"I do. He never would. He's not even Kurrong."

"The tribe doesn't really matter," Sullivan said. "Like I say, blacks side with other blacks. Sorry, boys, but it all seems pretty clear to me." He slid his hands over his thighs and drew himself tall in the chair. "A fucking outrage, that's what this is, same as Cullin-la-Ringo, Hornet Bank. And right here in my own bloody yard."

Locke spat discreetly into a handkerchief, balled it, put it away.

"Arthur didn't do it," Tommy repeated.

"We need to get out after them," Billy said. "Now. Tonight."

"Well now, let's sleep on it," Sullivan said. "There's plenty time for all that, but we're not riding anywhere tonight. Tomorrow we'll get 'em buried, we've an ex-priest who can say a few words, do it right. I always respected your father. Might not have seen eye to eye, but I respected him. And your mother, of course."

"Tomorrow's too late," Billy protested. "They'll be too far gone."

"Don't worry, son. Noone's boys track natives like hounds after blood."

"Noone?" Tommy echoed. "Billy, please . . ."

Locke grunted distastefully. "Aye, anyone but that cunt."

"He has the district now," Sullivan told him. "We don't get to choose."

"Rather just do it ourselves, like we used to."

"This isn't the old days, Raymond. I don't intend on getting hanged."

Billy jumped to his feet. "You killed three of the bastards for duffing, now our whole family's been done and you won't even—"

Sullivan rose also. He held out both hands. "Easy now, son, easy. I'm not saying I won't help, but there are other considerations, we have to be careful with these things. Tomorrow we'll talk it all through."

"I don't need to talk it through. I'll ride out myself if I have to."

"You wouldn't last two days," Sullivan said. He picked up a handbell from the mantelpiece and rang it. "I'm not going to stop you, but if you want my help you'll sleep on it. Jenny'll show you to your room."

The housemaid appeared in the doorway. Sullivan gestured for them to leave. Billy shook his head and stomped to the door; Tommy was slower in following him out. As he left the room Tommy glanced back at Sullivan and Locke, whispering together close-in. Sullivan caught his eye and smiled at him, nodding enthusiastically, the smile supposed to be reassuring, Tommy guessed. He didn't return it, hurrying after the others as they went along the hall.

The atrium was square and entirely open, vaulted into the roof space and encircled by a balcony landing that covered three sides of the first floor. Its walls were decorated with ornaments and display cases and, on one side, a row of animal heads mounted on wooden boards. There were doors everywhere—Tommy had never seen so many doors. All of them identical, white-paneled; all of them closed. As he walked up the stairs he looked over the rail and the height made his stomach dip. He gripped the polished banister. The wood felt oddly cool. He followed Billy and the girl around the landing and onto a corridor lit by golden sconces and lined with more doors, until Billy stopped suddenly and asked, "Which one's Mary's room? Our sister, which one's she in?"

The housemaid looked around nervously, then pointed to the door nearest Tommy. "That one there. Only, I'm not meant to say."

The room glowed in candlelight. Weeks was hunched over the bed. As they entered he glanced over his shoulder, then continued with his work. Mary lay beneath him, only her face visible, the blanket pulled to her chin. She had her eyes closed and her bunches spilled across the pillow. Her skin was pale and bloodless, but she looked peaceful, asleep.

They weren't alone in the room. A woman sat on a chair by the window at the end of Mary's bed, fingering rosary beads in her lap. She wore a cream housedress and heavy ringlets of dark brown hair fell onto her chest. She stood when she saw them, her skirts ruffling as she crossed the little room.

"I'm so sorry to hear what happened. They're monsters, all of them. A terrible, terrible thing. I'm Mrs. Sullivan. Katherine. Kate. So sorry for your loss."

She offered her hand. Tommy took it awkwardly, more of a hold than a shake. She smiled and he saw her age for what it was: she resembled a girl playing dress-up in her mother's clothes. Could not have been out of her teenage years.

"How is she?" Billy asked, and Weeks straightened, wiping his hands on a rag.

"I took the ball out. It had gone in deep, tore her up on the way through. She's all but bled out, unfortunately. I doubt she can feel anything, but I gave her a drop of laudanum all the same. There ain't nothing for it but to wait."

Tommy edged forward to look at her, lying there so peaceful and small. The stain of her wound showed on the blankets, a faded crimson spot. Up close her face looked yellow and tired, her lips like cracked earth.

"You boys look wrung inside out," Mrs. Sullivan said. "Why not get off to bed? There's some clean clothes for both of you, and a basin for a wash. If you leave your things outside your door we'll get them scrubbed and dried."

"Thank you," Billy mumbled.

"Shouldn't we stay?" Tommy asked.

Mrs. Sullivan smiled at him warmly. "If she changes, we'll wake you. You have my word. But the best you can do for her is to get some rest yourselves. I promise, someone will fetch you. Go on now. Get yourselves to bed."

That night they lay in separate iron-framed beds, in a room whose walls were floral-papered, the drapes blanket thick. Tommy couldn't sleep. The mattress was too soft, the feather bedding too heavy and warm. The total silence was unnerving: the glass windows masked all outside noise, and there were no gaps in the walls, no uneven shingle roof. Sometimes a sound would travel through the house, echoing footsteps, a door closing, someone coughing or clearing their throat, and Tommy would try to trace it, mapping the rooms in his mind, wondering if it was Mrs. Sullivan or Jenny or Weeks bringing news. It never was. There wasn't any news. The light around the door never darkened, until Tommy woke to find that he'd been sleeping and all the candles had been snuffed. He lay listening. He was sweating, his stomach churned, the dawning recognition that this was all real. He couldn't help but picture them. How they'd both been lying, all else he had seen. Or maybe he was still sleeping, he couldn't quite tell; a night filled with delirious, lucid dreams. At some point he felt Billy crawl into bed beside him, his back against Tommy's back, the way it had always been. But the next time he woke it was morning, and Billy was gone again.

12

Two pairs of stockmen carried them from the house, bundled in white bedsheets, gleaming in the sun. A slow processional across the clearing and out into the nearby scrub, to the bald patch of earth where the little group was gathered and two graves had been dug, mounds of red soil piled alongside.

Tommy watched them come. He was standing with his brother, both of them smeared in dirt and sweat from the digging; Sullivan had offered his men but the boys had refused, it felt like their task to do. Father would have wanted it, certainly. Would not have liked Sullivan's men preparing a McBride grave. Bad enough Sullivan was even here, squinting solemnly at the bodies as they advanced. He had brought his ex-priest with him. He waited at the head of the graves. A grizzled old bushman, gray beard and flaking skin, sun-narrowed eyes and a body of bones, clutching a ragged and loose-leafed Bible in his hands. Tommy didn't even know his name, this man who would be sending their parents off, but he knew what Father would have made of it, all this, them standing here with Sullivan, using his priest, his tools, wearing his clothes. Nothing felt right about it. Shame on top of grief.

On the stockmen came, behind them the house and a thin column of smoke still rising from the yard. Both dogs had been burned. They'd done it while Tommy and Billy were digging, hadn't thought to ask, they were only dogs after all. Tommy had smelled the tinge on the smoke and guessed what it was, swung his spade all the harder, mumbled his own good-byes to Red and then to Blue.

The men set the bodies at the gravesides, then re-treated a few yards. Drinking from their flasks, lighting smokes, whispering between themselves. Didn't even take off their hats. The ex-priest opened his Bible and the pages rustled in a wind that trickled dust into the graves and pulled the bedsheets taut. Tommy stared at the outline of his parents: their faces, their bodies, such as he could make out. Mother looked so much smaller, nearly half Father's size. She had not seemed it alive. She was beside the hole that Tommy had dug and he worried that he'd made it too big, that she'd somehow be uncomfortable down there. He imagined her scolding him, a smile in her voice: *Look here now, Tommy, look what you've gone and done,* and a hundred petty crimes skipped through his mind. Trailing mud onto the verandah, waking baby Mary as she slept, letting the hens out of the fowl house, spilling the last of the flour . . .

"Sorry, Ma," he muttered, and Billy looked across at him and frowned.

"Come on, man, get on with it," Sullivan ordered.

The ex-priest glanced up from his flimsy Bible, settled on a page, cleared his throat, and began: "The Lord is my shepherd. Uh . . . I shall not want . . ."

Tommy knew the passage. Mother had read it to them many times—she could have probably delivered it backward without need of the text. Father had no time for the Bible. Nothing but made-up stories, he said. Many times Tommy had listened to him railing against God: "That bastard don't care nothing for us, whatever your mother says. We're on our own, Tommy. There ain't no God out here."

"Thou prep-preparest a table for me . . . before me, in the presence of mine enemies. Thou, uh, an-an-anointest my head with oil. My cup runneth over. Surely goodness and mercy shall follow me all the days of my life and I will . . . dwell in the house of the Lord for ever. Amen."

"Amen," Sullivan echoed irritably. He looked at Billy and Tommy. "Either of you want to say anything?"

"No," Billy said.

"No."

Sullivan whistled to his men. "Right, get 'em in."

"We'll do it," Billy said, nodding for Tommy to come. Hesitantly he followed, watching the flies crawling between the folds of Father's bedsheet. The smell was sickly and strong. Billy took hold of the shoulders; Tommy couldn't move. He stared at Father's feet, wondering if it was proper they hadn't taken off his boots.

"Tommy. We need to do this. Pretend like we're lifting cattle. Come on."

He gripped Father's ankles and his eyes filled. He let go, turned and spat, wiped his mouth on his sleeve, then went back into a crouch and held the ankles again. Billy counted three and they grunted with the heave, crabbing the short distance to the grave, Father sagging between them, scraping along the ground, the others all watching; dead silence save the boys' breathing and the scuff of their boots, until the grave was upon them and Tommy's grip failed: before Billy was ready, he let go of the ankles, and the body tumbled and rolled and the bedsheet unraveled, and Father lay exposed in the earth, bloated and white, riddled with a veiny fungus, ravaged by the flies.

Tommy recoiled from the graveside. Billy stared at him, aghast.

"Hellfire," Sullivan said. "Don't neither of you think about getting in there. Do the other one and we'll cover them both up. Quicker you do it, quicker we can start."

Billy went to Mother's body and waited. Tommy trembled and seethed. He looked from his brother to Sullivan, to the bearded ex-priest, to the house and the fire in the yard. He screamed. The scream drifted on the wind. No one else moved, no one else spoke. Sullivan's gaze passed from Tommy to Billy, and away.

Tommy lunged for Mother's ankles. Slender in his hands, warm from the sun. Billy took hold also, and they carried her easily to the hole, lowered her, then dropped her, and she landed with a soft puff of dirt. Tommy stepped away. The ex-priest was making eyes at the mounds of earth and Tommy grabbed a handful and tossed it down. It pattered on Mother's bedsheet. Billy did the same. Tommy took another handful for Father, threw it in blind, then stomped through the fringe of scrub toward the house, as Billy returned to stand at Sullivan's side. The squatter cupped his shoulder, acting like he knew, like he understood how it felt, when he didn't understand a bloody thing. Tommy walked to the house and sat down in the shade, leaned his back against the scullery wall. He drew up his legs and rested his chin on his knees, watching the stockmen shovel the earth and listening to the ex-priest recite the passage about ashes and dust.

. . .

The curtains were drawn against the sun, the room warm, the air stale. Tommy closed the door behind him, cracked the window ajar, and flicked the curtains along the rail. Light spilled onto the floor space and the bottom of Mary's bed; he adjusted the curtains so she was shaded, then knelt on the rug and began fidgeting with sheets that were already pristine. Her arms were exposed, the hands flat, palms-down, little blond hairs raised on her skin. She looked to be wearing a clean nightdress and the stains were gone from the sheet. Beneath the bed was a bowl of water and a still-damp flannel draped over the rim.

"We buried them today," he told her. "In that clearing behind the house. Even put in little markers, Sullivan gave them, two white crosses, which would keep Ma happy, though I know what Daddy would have said. It looked nice anyhow. Two proper graves. Me and Billy dug them—Daddy would have liked that—but it was hard getting them in. We dropped him. The sheet came loose. It doesn't really matter but you want these things done right. Ma went in fine, anyway. She got her prayers and all that; a good death, she'd have said. You remember that? Her good deaths and bad deaths, like there were two different kinds? That woman from Bewley who fell off her horse and when they found her she'd been half et, Ma went on about it for weeks. Like it was the woman's own fault the state she'd be in when she went up to meet God."

His laughter was as fragile as glass, and broke as quickly as it came. He slumped backward, onto his heels, covered his face with his hands, and sobbed into the darkness and the warmth of his own breath: shoulders heaving, rocking back and forth; a desperate, helpless wail.

Then just as abruptly, it was over. Men did not cry, not even in grief. Tommy caught himself and straightened and scrubbed his face dry. Sniffing and blinking and wiping his eyes, Mary blurred before him—could she hear all this, he wondered, how much did she know? He imagined her waking and teasing him for it, telling him he was more of a girl than she was, and he couldn't help but laugh again. He took a long breath; it washed out of him in trembling waves. He shuffled back to the bedside, sat tall on his knees, studied Mary's face but nothing had changed.

"I'll pretend you never heard that. Don't tell Billy if you did. He's not blubbed once, not that I've seen anyway. Seems angry more than anything, just wants to get out after Joseph, but even if we find him, arrest him, kill him, what good is that going to do? Won't bring them back, won't heal you up, though the way Billy acts you'd think it will. Really it's so he can impress Sullivan—he follows him round like a bloody lost dog. I suppose he's been good about all this, taking us in, but there's something about him I don't trust. Maybe it's just because Daddy didn't, yet here you'd think we were family the way he carries on. Daddy said a bloke like Sullivan won't do anything unless it's for his own gain. So how does he benefit? What does he want in return?"

Air gurgled in Mary's throat. Tommy wet the flannel and squeezed water on her lips; her breathing slowed and calmed. He dabbed her forehead, her cheeks, rinsed out the flannel, and folded it over the rim of the bowl to dry.

"Maybe I'm being ungrateful. I don't know where we'd be without his help. And maybe the best thing is to go after him, Joseph, not that I've got any say. Billy won't listen to me. Reckons himself the big man. If they go I suppose I could stay here instead, but then I'd be known as a coward my whole life. I don't know. Sullivan might not be in favor anyway; needed to sleep on it, he said. Billy thinks he'll help us, maybe give us work after, but I can't get a read on him, Mary. The whole thing makes no sense: he's got a vet for a doctor, and here's his wife watching over you, rubbing them wooden beads, she can't be much older than Billy just about, which is half Sullivan's own age. Dressing up like a lady when she's not but a girl . . . and I know what Ma would have thought about that, beads or no bloody beads."

He snorted a short laugh, levered himself up to his feet, and stood over the bed, watching her. Little twitches in her face. The rise and fall of her chest. They said Weeks had given her more laudanum, but he didn't know what good those drops were doing. She didn't look any better. In fact, she looked worse than yesterday: a grayness had crept into her skin. Tommy bit his lip and touched her on the arm, then turned and left the room, closing the door softly, like he was afraid his sister might wake.

13

But see the market's not just Australia, it's the whole bloody world. We've the East Indies on our doorstep, a million chinks wanting leather and beef, and more grazing land than we can fill—if only it'd bloody rain. Not even America's got our potential, and there's none of their politics here either, thank God. This country could be the greatest on earth, boys, if them bastards on the coast weren't so keen on buggering it up. The colonies can't be run from London, or Sydney, or Brisbane even, and certainly not by a bunch of fucking wig wearers—pardon my French, dear—who don't have a clue how things work out here."

Mrs. Sullivan acknowledged her husband's apology with a slight tilt of her head, then went back to her meal. They were sitting at either end of a long maple-wood table, lit by claw-footed candelabras and an enormous chandelier. Tommy and Billy were in the middle, opposite each other, directly beneath the chandelier, dressed like church boys in their borrowed suits, their hair neatly combed and parted to one side.

"Problem is," Sullivan continued, pointing down the table with a polished silver fork, "those city blokes won't come out here, get their hands dirty, see what it's all about. Bastards stick to the coast like fleas on a dog, passing their selection laws, giving it all away, as if any bugger could start a run. But what happens when those runs fail? I'll tell you—you've a bankrupt country broke beyond repair, and all because they're scared of a few old boys like me."

Sullivan took a long drink of wine. It stained his lips dark red. He looked intently at Billy, who had not eaten in a long time, nodding and listening to him speak. Tommy kept his eyes on his plate. Strips of tenderloin beef with baby potatoes and green beans, served on a flowery china plate. Tommy couldn't eat it. The meat was soft and spongy and had little taste, and its blood had seeped into everything else. He sliced a pink potato. The knife scraped the china as he cut. He put the potato into his mouth and winced as he bit down.

"There now, darling," Mrs. Sullivan said. "The boys are probably tired."

Sullivan looked at her along the table, took another sip of wine, raised a hand, and said, "Aye, I know. I just get carried away. Those Macquarie Street bastards aren't fit to shine my shoes."

"No, it's interesting," Billy said. "I never heard it put like this before."

"See?" Sullivan said, gesturing to his wife. She flicked her eyes to Tommy, smiled faintly, sliced her beef. Straight-backed and formal, the cutlery inverted in her hands, a delicate kind of grip that Tommy had tried to mimic but could not.

"It's all about control, Billy. First time they landed here they stuck a flag in a beach and claimed the whole lot, but what does a fella on the coast know about us out here? Crown Land, they call it. Crown Land. This isn't Crown Land any more than I'm the bloody queen—can you imagine good old Vic clearing a paddock or roping a bull?"

Billy laughed at that. He took a sip of wine.

"See, they let the pioneers have it first-off. Anyone who made it this far out and survived could take whatever land they bloody liked. Blokes like my grandfather—it was the only way. But now the hard work's been done, they try and tell you none of this is ours, or we're borrowing it, or we're only allowed so much . . . it's *Crown Land*, Billy, whatever the hell that means."

Tommy said, "Daddy thought everyone should be allowed his share."

Sullivan's gaze slid across the table. "But you see not everyone's cut out for it. Running livestock's harder than it looks." He stabbed his fork into a piece of meat, put it in his mouth, and sat there chewing, waiting for Tommy's reply.

"Drought can't be helped, though. Or disease, or anything like that."

Sullivan smiled at him. "Them that know how can still do alright."

Tommy ate another potato. He felt Sullivan's stare. Their cutlery tinkled the plates. The candles flickered and smoked. Mrs. Sullivan cleared her throat and said to the table, "The fillet's nice, don't you think? And the wine matches very well."

No one responded. Tommy was aware of Sullivan mouthing something to Billy, then Billy leaned forward, into the light of the chandelier, and said, "John's going to help us. Leaving tomorrow, he thinks."

Tommy looked up sharply. "Leaving? Where?"

"To find Joseph. He's sent word to Noone."

Sullivan smiled as he drank. Mrs. Sullivan lowered her head.

"We never decided," Tommy whispered to Billy. "Sleep on it, he said."

"We did sleep on it."

"You and me never spoke."

"Billy and I discussed it," Sullivan said. "Came up with a suitable plan. The telegram's already gone to Inspector Noone, telling him what's happened; he'll get here when he can. Of course they might not be at their barracks, in which case it'll be a couple of days, but all being well tomorrow, assuming the inspector comes."

Tommy looked between the two of them. "But . . . what about Mary? She needs a proper doctor—that vet's not doing her any good. She's getting worse up there."

"I'll send for Dr. Shanklin. He can see to her while we're gone."

"And you could stay here with her," Billy said. "You don't even have to come."

"It's not about me coming or not."

"So what's it about, then?"

"I don't know. You and me should have decided."

"He killed them, Tommy. What's there to decide?"

"I do think it's for the best, son," Sullivan said.

"What happens when we find him? What'll we do then?"

Sullivan shrugged. "That's police business. I leave it to Noone."

Tommy glanced at Mrs. Sullivan. She was sitting with her eyes down and her hands folded in her lap, like she had simply drifted out of the conversation, or was lost in her own thoughts.

"This is horseshit," Tommy said. He pointed at Billy. "This ain't for you to choose."

"Actually, it's not just about the two of you either," Sullivan told him. "What happened concerns the whole district, of which I am patron, which carries a weight of its own. These Kurrong bastards, they've been coming at us for years, won't learn their bloody place. The other blacks round here have either left or joined the Missions or gone to the camps: they've accepted the situation, moved on. But the Kurrong are stubborn, don't know when they're beat. I've got plenty of the buggers already and still they keep coming back, going after my cattle, my water, even caught them doing dances on my own bloody land. And now this, killing whites in their own home—it's an act of war, boys, we can't let it stand. If we don't retaliate, if we don't impose the law, well, we might as well pack up and run back to the coast tomorrow at first light."

Tommy looked from Sullivan to Billy, who held his steady stare.

"Your brother agrees with me," Sullivan said. "The least we can do for your family is find those responsible for this outrage and see to it that they hang."

Tommy lowered his eyes to the plate, now awash in

watery blood. He tried to go on eating but found that he could not, so he set his cutlery together and waited for the others to finish their meal. Sullivan began talking about the colonies again, Billy following his every word, while at the other end of the table Mrs. Sullivan said nothing at all. She caught Tommy staring and briefly smiled, then dabbed her napkin to her lips, her jewelry sparkling in the candlelight, folded the napkin on the table, and sat listening to her husband talk.

When all were finished, Sullivan rang a handbell and a native houseboy came into the room. "You can clear now, Benjamin," Sullivan said.

The houseboy was dressed in a shabby livery of white shirt and red waistcoat and must have been well into his middle age. He moved stiffly around the place settings, gathering up the plates, stacking them in one hand and laying the cutlery on top. The table waited silently. Sullivan poured himself more wine and drank, watching the houseboy as he worked.

"You shouldn't ever talk business or politics in front of them, Billy. They understand more than they let on—isn't that right, Benjamin?"

At the sound of his name the houseboy hesitated, gave a small nod, went on.

"I make them wait down the hall so they can't listen in. It pays to be wary, I don't care who they are. Benjamin here's been with us for years, and I still don't trust the bastard an inch."

He spluttered a short laugh, took another sip of wine. The houseboy had now reached Tommy's place and was collecting his cutlery and plate.

"Some like to keep their boys in the room while they eat. Can you imagine? Who wants to look at that over dinner, or smell him—can you smell him, Tommy? The bastards have a stink that's all their own."

"John, please," Mrs. Sullivan said.

Sullivan ignored her. As if she hadn't spoken. He waved a hand and went on laughing, and when his plate had been cleared and Tommy lifted his eyes, he saw that Billy was laughing too.

. . .

He lost them after dinner. Returned from the outhouse to find the dining room empty, the chairs askew, napkins on the table, and a seam of wax dribbling down the candelabra and pooling on the tablecloth. Tommy backed into the atrium and stood listening. Faint kitchen clatter but otherwise the house was silent, every door closed. He went to the drawing room, the only other room he knew, and put his ear against the paneled wood. Nothing. He opened the door anyway.

Mrs. Sullivan was standing alone by the decorated tree, one hand toying with the baubles, the other holding a thimble glass of liquor. She smiled when she saw him, waved him into the room.

"Come in, Tommy. Come in. Don't be shy now. I won't bite."

"I was looking for Billy."

"John has him. I thought he had you too . . . but come in, close the door."

He shuffled forward. Unsure where to put himself, unsure where to look. She was still in her dinner dress, cream-colored and very tight, corseted, and her hair had unraveled from its nest of curls and tumbled around her face. Her cheeks were freshly rouged, or perhaps she was flushed from the fire behind her, or whatever was in the little glass.

"Have you seen this yet?" she asked him, meaning the tree. "They're all doing it in England these days. Even the queen has one. Isn't it just marvelous?"

"What's it for?" Tommy asked.

"Sorry? What do you mean?"

"Why've you got it? A tree in your house?"

There was pity in her smile, warmth too. "Oh, Tommy, it's a Christmas tree—have you never heard of a Christmas tree before?"

Timidly he shook his head.

"The idea is that you decorate it, hang balls and presents and all sorts of things. Here—would you like to try one of these?"

She picked off a parcel and held it out for him to take. Oval-shaped, wrapped in a purple paper twist. Tommy opened it and found a yellow boiled sweet, hesitated, then popped it into his mouth and sucked.

The lemon flavor burst on his tongue. Sour and sweet all at once. Lemon had always been Mary's favorite; Tommy usually preferred butterscotch, but he wouldn't have swapped the lolly for the world.

"You like it? Is it good?"

"Really good."

"Well, help yourself. There are plenty, and that's what they're for. It's silly of me really, doing all this when there's no children around, but we had one at home, so . . ."

"What kind of tree is it?"

"Spruce. You don't get them here. I had it brought up especially. Where I'm from, down in Victoria, there are whole mountains covered with these kinds of trees. They like the cold, see, and in winter we'd even get snow high up in the hills. Daddy would take us tobogganing; it really was the most wonderful thing." She sipped at her drink. "I don't suppose you've ever seen snow?"

"In a picture book once. Like feathers in the sky."

She smiled and touched her cheek. "Well, yes, I suppose it almost is."

Tommy sucked on the lolly, Mrs. Sullivan watching him, the upright clock ticking with each pendulum swing and the fire spitting its embers onto the hearth. A new log was struggling to take, the wood mostly ashen in the grate.

"Have you always lived here, Tommy? Around here, I mean?"

"Yeah," he said, shrugging.

"You're lucky. I mean, I know this is a terrible time for you, but at least you're where you're supposed to be. I've gone from snow in winter to seasons of dust and heat; city trams to no roads at all. You have to be born to it, I think. I don't know how you all stand it here, but somehow you do."

"You don't like it, then?"

"No, I don't." She leaned close and lowered her voice to a whisper. "But don't tell John I said that. He thinks this place is paradise."

"So why'd you come? Why not leave?"

She inclined her head ruefully. "You mean it, don't you—you really are that naive. It's adorable, actually. But you must have wondered about us, or your parents must have talked? Everyone in the district knows. Besides, it's obvious—I'm closer to you in age than I am to John."

"Daddy didn't like us talking about Mr. Sullivan at home."

"Well, that's very polite of him. And I've not been here so long, I suppose: we only married last year, the same day I turned eighteen. John wants a son, you see, is desperate for one, in fact, and his first wife, Jacqueline, well, she wasn't up to the job. His freemartin, he calls her—can you imagine! So he moved her on quietly and came down to Melbourne looking for a new wife . . . and, lo and behold, found me!"

She spread her arms when she said this. Her neck had reddened, her cheeks too, and her voice had become harsh. Tommy went to speak but she waved her hand to silence him.

"Oh, don't worry, there's nothing to be done, it's just the way of the world. Think yourself lucky you're a man, that's all I can say. John bought me off my father no different than a cow. I'm his prize breeder now, Tommy, that's what I am. A breeder meant to give him a son."

She drained her drink and went to the table, laughing as she poured. When she turned around again she was damp-eyed and her lips ticked from grin to grimace and back again.

"And so," she said shakily, sipping, "here I am, waiting to breed, stuck where I don't belong. Which is bad enough but now . . . now there's a war coming, these blacks killing families right here in their homes." She crossed herself. "In Melbourne they wouldn't have dared—I don't mean to sound callous, talking like this when you've suffered so much, but this problem with the natives: it's all of ours, Tommy, John's right about that. If this is what they're capable of, none of us is truly safe."

She pulled a handkerchief from her sleeve and dabbed carefully at her eyes. Tommy crunched the lolly and ground it between his teeth, glancing at the door and the chance to leave.

"I know this must seem overwhelming, but John'll take care of you, and your brother and sister. He's not such a bad man. Do you go to church, Tommy?"

"Not really. Ma did sometimes."

"No, John doesn't either. He's quite scornful about it, actually. But he has his principles, which is something. He'll see that you're alright."

"Him and Daddy didn't exactly get along."

"Well, John doesn't have what you'd call friends. But you're our neighbors, and didn't your father used to work here, I believe?"

"Once. A long time ago."

"Still . . ."

"They didn't see things the same. About the blacks, Noone."

She shook her head. "Which only makes this all the more tragic."

There was a silence. Tommy took a breath and said, "What he was saying at dinner, though, about going out after Joseph and them Kurrong . . . maybe if you spoke to him he might change his mind about that, see if we couldn't—"

Tommy stalled. Her eyes had hardened and her lips were drawn tight.

"I think perhaps you misunderstand me, Tommy. I might not approve of how John speaks to the house-boy, but he's my husband, I stand at his side. These natives, from what I've seen, they've been given every opportunity and still they refuse to change. Work, education, we've tried to civilize them but the savagery is in their blood. I've even heard they eat their own young, for heaven's sake. And yet they're all around us, we have them in our house! There's knives in the kitchen, fire-arms . . . most of them are as familiar with a rifle as they are with a spear. Honestly, it's terrifying. In fact, I wish there were a hundred Mr. Noones out there, Tommy, making sure that we're safe." She shook her head de-terminedly. "No, justice must be done, then perhaps the wretches might think twice about attacking a white family again. Surely you of all people cannot disagree?"

"No," Tommy mumbled.

"Well, good. I'm glad to hear it." She stepped a pace closer and delicately lifted his chin with her fingertip. "Look at you, you're exhausted, poor thing. It's no wonder you're not thinking straight. Why not go up to bed, get a good night's rest?"

"Alright."

"God bless you, then."

He nodded faintly, backtracked, hurried across the room, then paused in the doorway and turned.

"Thanks for the lolly. It was really good."

"My pleasure. Help yourself. Anytime."

"We should save some for Mary. For when she wakes up."

"We've a jar in the pantry big enough she could sleep a whole year."

"A year?"

"I didn't mean—" Again she smiled at him. "Good night, Tommy."

"Good night."

He was asleep when Billy came into their bedroom, but was woken by the door latch and the noise of his brother stumbling about, trying to get himself undressed. Tommy lay still, facing the wall, blinking into the darkness, then closing his eyes when he felt Billy at the bedside, standing over him, a smell of smoke and grog.

"Tommy? You awake?"

He didn't answer. Billy nudged his shoulder, Tommy let himself be nudged. Billy grumbled something, then went to his own bed; Tommy listened to him thrashing before he fell still and his breathing slowed and began its familiar ticking sound. Both stayed in their own beds that night, the first time they'd slept apart in their lives.

14

He rode up the track in a fury of hooves and dust, longcoat flaring, a winged and dark silhouette against the sun-bleached soil.

Noone.

Tommy watched from Mary's bedroom, cowering beneath the sill, wide eyes peering through the bottom windowpane. He watched him ride full gallop almost to the steps, bringing the horse up so hard it reared its head and bared its teeth; he watched him dismount and hand off the reins to the waiting stableboy, then climb emu-like up the stairs, long legs reaching out before him, two or three steps at a time, the body upright and static, a long body, the proportions all wrong, nothing on the bones. Fluid and agile, no stiffness in him, not a stockman's gait. As he reached the top of the stairs Tommy rose with the angle, but soon lost him beneath the verandah roof, the tread of his boots sounding on the boards, then voices, Sullivan greeting him at the door.

Tommy hurried around the bed, Mary lying there just the same as yesterday, and the day before that. Out into the hall and along to the balcony landing, where he crouched behind the balustrades and saw Billy standing stiffly in the atrium below, his hands crossed behind his back and his eyes fixed on the front door.

Tommy whistled to him. Billy found him among the rails.

"What you doing?" Tommy whispered.

"Meeting him. Noone. John said to wait here."

"What for?"

"Give our account of what happened."

Tommy stood, leaned on the railing, lost the whisper from his voice.

"What about me, then?"

"What about you?"

"I should give mine too."

Billy glanced anxiously between Tommy and the approaching voices. "Just . . . wait in the room. I'll come up when we're done."

"Like hell you will," Tommy muttered, rounding the balcony. Billy glared up at him, then dropped his gaze again, as Noone and Sullivan emerged directly beneath where Tommy now stood: the blade-thin parting in Noone's black hair; Sullivan's threadbare scalp. The tail of Noone's longcoat floated around him as he moved. His boots echoed heavily from the walls. He walked directly to Billy, Sullivan introduced them, Noone didn't take Billy's hand. He stood appraising him and, as Tommy continued around the balcony, the inspector's face peeled into view. His thick mustache, the cheeks sunken to the bone, those pale and glaucous eyes. Noone looked up and Tommy stalled at the top of the stairs. His hand gripped tight on the rail. It was the same sensation as when they'd first met: the feel of him tiptoeing down Tommy's spine.

"You won't be needed, Tommy," Sullivan called. "Go on back to your room."

"Ah, the little brother," Noone said. "I suppose you saw all this too?"

Tommy nodded uncertainly. The accent was strange, inflected, from elsewhere. Noone motioned grandly down the stairs. "Well, then, down you come."

"He's only a child," Sullivan protested. "It was Billy that found them first."

Noone ignored him. All watched Tommy descend, slowly, like a lag to gallows, it felt. He stood beside his brother and Noone weighed the two of them, expressionless, nothing whatsoever in his face, until Sullivan led him beneath the stairs to a door in the corner of the wall, and as they followed the two men Billy leaned close to Tommy and whispered, "Agree with what I tell him."

"About what?"

"Just do it, alright?"

The room was a cramped wood-paneled parlor with a broad writing desk, orderly bookcase, and various weaponry displayed on the walls. Two stud-leather wingback chairs were angled in front of the desk. The sun streamed through the window and fell directly between them, an imprint of the cross frame shadowed on the rug. Sullivan poured two drinks and handed one to Noone, then inched around the desk and sat down in his chair. Noone eased himself into one of the wingbacks; Billy took the other, leaving Tommy to stand in the shadow on the rug. Noone crossed his legs and sipped his drink.

"Right then," Sullivan began, "Billy, d'you want to—"

Noone raised a hand for silence. They waited while he swallowed and positioned his glass on the corner of the desk. "Let's begin with the wife—she was in the bedroom, I assume?"

All three frowned at him. Hesitantly Billy said, "Yessir."

"Was she raped?"

Tommy reeled like he'd been hit. Billy stared horrified at Noone.

Sullivan said, "Christ, Edmund, that's their mother. Both were dead when they got there—how in hell would they know that?"

"Well, how was she lying? What did they see?"

He alternated between Billy and Tommy like he'd just inquired as to the time.

"She was on the floor," Billy said finally. "Her skirts were down."

"A pity. What about the young girl?"

Sullivan threw up his hands. "Hellfire!"

"It would help if she had been. One or preferably both. They usually are. Adds to the public outrage, you see. Assists with your cause."

"No," Billy said firmly. "Neither."

Noone took another drink. "Well, that might need to change. In the final account, you understand. And what about the father? How was he found?"

"Sitting on the verandah," Billy said. "Had his carbine with him."

"Meaning he fought them. Must have hit at least one, I assume?"

Billy glanced doubtfully at Sullivan. Sullivan said, "Ambushed, I reckon."

"Strange for a man to be ambushed when he was already armed."

"He was shot in the yard," Tommy blurted. "There were drag marks going up."

Noone arched an eyebrow. "Well, well. The boy has a good eye."

"It doesn't matter who was where or how any of them was found," Sullivan said. "What matters is who killed them. Billy—tell him about Joseph and them others you saw."

"Joseph was our blackboy. He took off a few weeks back. Him and Daddy argued over those two others you put in that red gum by the creek."

"He was Kurrong," Sullivan added. "From the same mob."

"He had a revolver with him, same one we found by the well, empty, all five shots used. The dogs was run through with spears, I reckon, and Ma and Daddy had their heads stoved after, clubs it looked like, them tomahawks they have, the wooden thing with the blade."

Billy fell silent. It had left him in a burst. He waited stiffly in his chair.

"But not the girl?" Noone asked. "She's still living, John said?"

"They must have got spooked by the boys coming back," Sullivan suggested. "A big group ran out the house, didn't they, Billy? Took off into the bush?"

Billy nodded furiously. Tommy could only stare.

"How many?" Noone asked. "How many blacks in all?"

"Maybe a dozen," Billy told him. "More than we could have fired on anyway. We only had our muzzle-loaders. We'd have been overrun."

Noone turned his head slowly toward Tommy. "All this sound right to you?"

He could feel the others glaring. It was all he could do to nod.

"Strange, then, that I found no tracks," Noone said. "Since there were so many."

"You've been down the house?" Sullivan asked him.

"Of course. Saw the bloodstains and plenty boot marks, but no native tracks."

"Well, we buried the pair of them yesterday," Sullivan said. He took a long drink and winced. "Had men with us for digging and carrying, we'll have trampled over the tracks, I reckon. Plus, don't forget this Joseph boy was shod. Them with him might have been the boot-wearing kind n'all."

"Of course," Noone said equably. "Anything amiss inside the house?"

"Amiss?" Sullivan said. "Apart from them all being shot up?"

Noone looked at Billy. "Anything taken? Disturbed?"

"No. Just them three."

"And this Joseph—you're sure it was him? You saw him?"

"Yessir. Plus there was the revolver, like I said."

"Way I see it," Sullivan interrupted, "is Joseph took offense to them two in the tree, went back and told his mob, they set about the McBrides instead of coming here, since he knows the family and how little they were armed. Snuck up on them quietly. Ned stood no chance, the poor bastard. Just him and the missus and the girl."

Noone considered him steadily. Raised his glass, sipped his drink.

"Surely now this'll persuade you?" Sullivan asked him. "On top of everything I've already told you, here these Kurrong have murdered a whole family just about—what more evidence do you need?"

"I saw no evidence, John. I'd be relying on the word of two boys."

"They'll swear to it—won't you?"

Billy nodded eagerly. Tommy kept his head down.

"And remember you'll be rewarded," Sullivan

added. "Handsomely, since I'd consider it a personal favor, and you already know what those are worth. We ride out, come up with them, you make yourself a rich man. Likely get a promotion after—they'll think you a hero when word gets around."

"The terms can be discussed privately. Now is not the time."

"But you'll do it? We're asking for protection here. Isn't that what the Native Police is bloody for? I can't do this on my own."

Noone took a long breath, exhaled.

"I will need both testimonies. I cannot be seen to act without proof."

"They'll give it, whatever you need. When can we leave?"

Noone hesitated, angled his head. "We being?"

"Me, Locke, the two boys here. They deserve to see it done."

"You and your monkey man are bad enough, John. Really I shouldn't even allow that. But I certainly can't be taking two children along."

"We ain't children," Billy said. "I'm sixteen and a half and he's fifteen almost."

Noone stared at him. Billy shrank back into his chair.

"I already promised him," Sullivan explained. "I'll

double the fee if that'll persuade you. Make it more than worth your while."

Noone snorted a brief laugh. "Fourfold, I should think. One for each man."

"Call it three—young Tommy can stay behind."

"I'm coming," Tommy said. "I've as much right as Billy does."

A smile flickered on Noone's lips, a twitch beneath the mustache. He drained his drink, replaced the glass precisely on the corner of the desk, adjusting the base against the angle like he was measuring its fit.

"In fact, I insist," he said. "It's both boys or none at all. If you want to save yourself money, John, you can leave the ape at home." He turned to Tommy and Billy. "You can shoot, I take it? You have weapons, horses?"

"Yessir," Billy said.

"Horses are in the stables," Sullivan said. "Got all four of 'em here."

"Four horses were left behind?"

"Two," Billy said. "We had ours with us."

Sullivan added, "And the others are a broken-down packhorse and a brumby with eyes madder than yours. There's no bugger would want either of those things."

"I see," Noone said. There was a long silence. "Well, we'd best get on with it. We're not going anywhere until I have both testimonies written and signed."

. . .

After it was done, their false confessions sworn, Tommy dragged Billy along the back corridor and out into the rear yard. Heat hit them like a wall. Servants hanging clothes and washing crockery paused to watch them pass, as Tommy cajoled his brother through the yard and into a grassy clearing up the hill. To the east were the stables and other storage sheds and, in the foreground, a little fenced-off area with a struggling lawn and two short rows of evenly spaced headstones.

"Well?" Tommy said.

"Alright. I know. But John said we had to, or Noone might not have agreed."

"Why wouldn't he?"

"Joseph on his own, even Arthur, John didn't think—"

"A dozen blacks, you said! Their heads stoved, Billy!"

"John thought—"

"John, John, John . . . have you heard yourself these days?"

"I'm only trying to do what's right."

"Which is what?"

"See to it there's a dispersal, or whatever they call it. See the bastards hang. I was aiming to keep you out of it, Tommy."

"Horseshit. You want it just you and him. Crawling after him like a whelp."

Billy threw out his arms. "All I'm doing is seeing us through this, Mary too if she pulls round. There's expectations on us to put right what's been done. And then afterward—you ever think about that? What'll happen to us then? We're minors, you and me, can't take on Daddy's run, can't do nothing on our own. They'd make us wards if they found us, put us in some lockup or Mission house, no better than the fucking blacks. But if John agrees to help us, gives us work, lets us stay on . . . he's the best bloody chance we've got."

"I don't want to stay here."

"Where else would we go? Where would Mary get well?"

Tommy looked out across the scrub. "I don't know."

"Because there is nowhere else. This is it. But if you keep bleating on and causing trouble, he'll turn all three of us loose."

"I don't trust him. How do you even know he wasn't involved?"

Billy fell very still. He narrowed his eyes. "Involved in what?"

"There was something else between him and Daddy that we didn't know."

"We found Joseph's bloody gun."

Tommy frowned into the dirt. "What about Noone, then? You trust him?"

"No," Billy said. "But we need him, John says. Let me worry about Noone."

"I signed his testimony same as you."

"I know you did."

"There wasn't a true word in it."

"You were offered to stay here and you wouldn't. I said to wait in the room."

"I ain't staying behind."

"Well, then."

"Well."

They stared at each other in silence. The pair of them had never been great talkers but Tommy had always felt that most of what lay between them didn't need to be said. He'd known Billy as well as he knew himself; could guess what he was thinking, read his moods. It didn't feel like that now. He looked at him, at his dark heavy eyes, the eyes of their father if he thought on it too hard, and couldn't be sure what was in his brother's mind. He was presuming the worst these days, and felt himself justified.

Billy nodded like they'd resolved something, walked away down the hill.

15

Nobody came to see them off. Nobody stood waving on the verandah; there were no faces in the windowpanes. As he rode away down the track, Tommy looked back at Mary's bedroom but all he saw was the outline of the drapes. As if she might have been standing there, ghostly in her nightgown, her little hand raised. Dr. Shanklin was coming to care for her, was expected later that day; she'd be recovered by the time they returned, so everyone said. Billy believed every word of it. He saw things as simply as that. Mary would get better, Sullivan would take them in, their grief would soon pass, and justice would be done. Like knocking down tins on a stall.

Sullivan and Locke, Tommy and Billy, four horses passing by the workers' camp and then out along the same trail the boys and the watchman had taken coming in. The horses were laden with supplies: bags bulging, bedrolls bouncing, weapons and accoutrements hanging from their saddle rings. Pistols, Snider carbines, ammunition belts, bayonets; the silver blade of Locke's sword slapping against his thigh. Tommy had only his rifle and the folding knife he'd stolen from Song's, but Sullivan had given Billy his own revolver, a six-shot Colt Navy he wore like a trophy on his belt. He hadn't told Tommy about it. But then neither had he attempted to hide it from his brother's view.

They rode through the scrub and between the scattered trees, and when the track forked they followed it northwest. The sun warm and gentle, early morning still, the bush filled with chirruping and chatter and indifferent to the passage of these horses and men. Tommy closed his eyes and listened. Sounds of his country, sounds of his home. A sickness in his stomach at what lay ahead, though in truth he didn't fully understand. Vague notions of justice, of revenge, and with them a vague and hopeless dread, the fear a lonely child feels after dark, knowing the bunyip is out there, that it's coming for him, that it cannot be outrun.

Noone was waiting in open ground another half mile to the west. He sat his horse ahead of his troopers and watched them come, small clouds of his pipe smoke drifting on the breeze. His horse flicked its tail and shook away the flies, and behind him the troopers were mounted in a crooked line, four indistinct shapes on horseback, three slouching forward in the saddle and one sitting tall and very straight. Tommy scanned the figures but couldn't properly make them out. Little details only: two were bigger, one was young, the one sitting upright looked withered to his bones.

"Don't talk to the niggers," Sullivan warned. "Treat 'em like you would dogs."

"Worse than dogs," Locke added. "Vermin. Fucking snakes."

They walked their horses over the final stretch and came to a halt in front of Noone, the inspector smoking like he hadn't noticed them arrive. How much did he see? Tommy wondered. How did the world look to him? Once in Bewley there'd been a beggar with eyes no different to Noone's—children bared themselves in front of his face and he hadn't ever known. But Noone wasn't blind. Far from it: he'd picked them out of those Moses bushes from half a mile away.

Tommy watched the troopers furtively under the low brim of his hat, snatching quick little fragments and assembling them into a whole. Four natives, dressed in scruffy, ill-fitting uniforms: white trousers, blue tunics, white hats, the clothing tight or hanging off them, meant for other men. Cartridge belts slung across their chests, the leather faded and worn, every loop full. Martini-Henry rifles stowed in saddle holsters or carried on their shoulders, wooden war clubs dangling from their belts, the smooth-polished blades marked and bloodstained, the stains faded and very old. Scant supplies on their packs: water bags, weaponry, little else besides. A range of ages between them: the one sitting upright was ancient, skeletally thin, his hair receding from his forehead and half-moon cheeks hollowed and drawn; the youngest too was slightly built, sinew and bone, his face bat-like in the protrusion of the jaw, the high and heavy brow. He was smiling. A fixed and absent grin. As if instructed to make sure he bared his teeth full.

The other two troopers were similar in both age and build. Big men, twenties, thirties maybe, broad in the shoulders and full in the chest. A lazy kind of violence in the way they leaned: one was bearded and dead-eyed, a stone-still stare at the ground; the other was smoking a rolled paper cigarette pinched between thick fingers, nostrils flaring as he exhaled. Tommy had never seen a durry-smoking native before, but he did it as expertly as any white, with one eye half-closed in a squint against the smoke, Tommy assumed, until he noticed the knot of scar tissue webbing the brow and eyelid, gumming the eye like drippings of candle wax.

And supposedly they were policemen. Supposedly they were safe.

"Well?" Sullivan asked. "What's the holdup? What we waiting for still?"

Noone withdrew the pipestem from his mouth and exhaled.

"We're waiting for you, John. Been waiting a long time. This is not dawn."

"Aye, well, there was a lot to get done before we left."

"So already you're slowing us down, with your monkey man here and these two orphans you're now intent on dragging around."

"I've told you not to call me that," Locke said. "Bloody mean it n'all."

Noone cocked his head and studied him. "You've injured your hand, Raymond. What happened? A little overzealous with yourself last night?"

"Fuck off. Got snakebit." He spat tobacco juice on the ground.

"How careless of you. Hope it wasn't poisonous. Hate to lose you so soon."

"Well, I've bloody warned you. So there it is."

"So there it is," Noone repeated. "Consider me suitably warned."

Noone was smiling at him. The troopers hadn't moved. Locke nodding and nodding at the others as if convincing them of something, convincing himself.

"Alright," Sullivan said. "We've a bloody long ride ahead, don't the pair of you start. I suppose you've already got the track on them, Inspector?"

"I told you: the only tracks I found at the house were yours."

Sullivan looked about anxiously. "So, what are we going to do, then?"

Noone beat the dead tobacco from the bowl of his pipe, stowed the pipe in his longcoat, and reached for a wide-brimmed slouch hat balanced behind him on his pack. He squared the hat on his head and began turning his horse around.

"We already know where the Kurrong are," he said. "The best thing about natives is they stick to their own lands. We ride west beyond the ranges and we'll come up with them soon enough. One way or another, John, we'll find your man."

The troopers parted to let him pass, then circled

into a column and followed on behind. Sullivan glanced at Locke, at the brothers, the slightest hesitation in his eyes. Almost immediately it was gone. He clicked his horse forward, the others did the same, and one by one each of them joined the back of the line.

16

They were a whole day crossing Sullivan's station; Noone and the troopers fell back in the line and allowed the squatter to take the lead. A thin column of horses snaking through undulating yellow scrubland, through pasture, through brigalow, through sparse stands of gum trees and the shadows they threw. There was no other shade. Their backs burned all morning, then their faces all afternoon, and their pace was slow and measured in the unrelenting sun.

Tommy rode in the middle of the group, Billy in front of him, the first of the troopers directly behind, the young one with the bat-like face and grin that never seemed to fade. Tommy tried to keep a gap between them, rode tight to Billy's heels, but the trooper was always there, the sound of his hoof fall, the other noises he made. Spitting or laughing or chattering, to whom it wasn't clear. Tommy risked a glance backward, pretended he was studying the terrain. The trooper was watching him. Wide-eyed under that low slabbed brow, smiling and nodding and keen. Beyond him the others were in reverse order: Noone at the very back, the old man in front of him, as easy and nonchalant as if taking a Sunday ride.

Tommy turned forward, stared at Billy's back, tried imagining the troopers were not there. He thought of Mary, back in her bedroom, Mrs. Sullivan on the chair, Shanklin might even have been there by now. He knew what he was doing. Better than some bloody vet. With his medicines and his doctoring, he'd see she was back on her feet to meet them by the time they came home.

Tommy shook his head. The reasoning didn't hold. Weeks had taken the ball out, patched the wound, made her comfortable, and still she wouldn't wake. What more could Shanklin do? How could he fix her if she was already bled out? Tommy looked about nervously. As if searching for an answer, a sign; the bush gave only silence in reply. He wasn't the only one twitchy: Billy rode like he was expecting a sudden war. Reins pulled short, back rigid, hand resting on the revolver Sullivan had loaned, ready for an ambush or the chance to set one himself. Not worrying about Mary, anyway—Billy was already seeking their sister's revenge.

For a while they followed the line of the ridge, then angled away south through a thick band of scrub, keeping clear of grazing sheep and new cow-and-calf pairs. The ridge fading into the distance until all that remained was the jagged imprint of its spine against the sky, tapering down low in the west. The old people believed the ridge was a crocodile, or made by a crocodile, or something like that. Arthur had told Tommy the story, but he couldn't recall it now. He could see the resemblance: the downslopes contoured like limbs, head, and jaw; the swell of a belly where they met the land; the spine and the tail and outcrops like scales on the sides. So what was to say Arthur had been wrong? Why couldn't a crocodile have made the ridge? Tommy doubted Arthur even believed those stories himself anymore, pictured him sitting against the bunkhouse wall weighing his beliefs in his hands, each as insubstantial as air. He'd looked utterly lost that day. A man without faith or a place in the world. Was that why he'd left them, to find wherever else he thought he belonged? Where else was there? Way out in this nothingness, his family and people dead . . . the others were still saying Arthur was involved, that he'd joined up with Joseph, been part of what was done.

Tommy didn't believe it. In just a few weeks Arthur would be coming back, oblivious to everything. Stay gone, Arthur, he thought to himself. Stay gone.

Strange how the land plays its tricks on the mind: Tommy was used to heat haze and mirage, but now beyond the dots of cattle grazing the faraway plains he thought he saw waterbirds swooping to the ground. Long-legged things, egrets maybe, looked to be feeding but surely not. He tipped back his hat and watched them. The ground up there shimmering, different to heat haze, glistening in the glare of the sun. If Tommy didn't know better he'd have said it was a floodplain, but how could there be a floodplain when it had rained only three days in the year?

He moved his horse forward. Billy flinched when he drew alongside.

"You seen that?" Tommy said, pointing. "That look like a floodplain to you?"

Billy followed his finger, eyes narrowed, straining to make it out.

"Might be. What of it?"

"It's not hardly rained, Billy."

He shrugged. "So maybe it's a lake."

"Exactly. And how's he got a lake in the middle of a bloody drought?"

"You don't get a lake. Either there is one or there's not."

"It should be all dried up, though. Must be full for us to see it from here."

Billy looked at him irritably. Tommy went to argue again but there was a whistle from behind, two-toned, an up-and-down *cooee*. Both of them turned. Noone was now directly behind them, alongside the young trooper; he nodded toward the water, tutted, and shook his head. The boys jerked back around, and Noone went on whistling a jaunty little tune.

"Can't you just leave it?" Billy whispered. "Quit your questions all the time?"

"You don't think it's off he's got a lake?"

"No, I don't. And neither should you. How many more warnings d'you need?"

Tommy eased back into line. He kept his head down. Noone was now humming and sometimes singing and his voice was deep and full. They rode on. A long sweep through dry bush until they reached a struggling creek, by the look of it the same creek that flowed south onto McBride land. The group watered here, let the horses drink, and Tommy found himself squatting at the waterside a little way along from the young trooper who had been following him all day.

Tommy tried to not look at him. Filled his flask,

watched the water trickling by, dappled in shade. Billy was with Sullivan and the others at the top of the bank, acting like one of the men. Tommy could hear them talking: "Not until the ranges," Noone said. Tommy raised his flask dripping from the creek, stoppered the neck, and caught a glimpse of the young trooper filling one of the bladder bags. It was made of stitched kangaroo hide and bulged with trapped air as the trooper forced it down. His waddy dangled at his side. His arms were long and thin. He had both sleeves rolled, and with each surge underwater it looked more and more like he was drowning something there. An animal, a small child—hadn't Mrs. Sullivan told him they liked eating their young?

Tommy fumbled his water bottle and dropped it in the creek. He plunged down after it, paddling into the water on his hands and knees, just reaching the flask before it was lost. He backed out of the water. He'd soaked his trousers and shirtsleeves. As he rose he saw the trooper coming for him, his mad eyes bulging, the drowned hide dripping in one hand and the other outstretched.

Tommy lurched clear and scrambled up the bank to join the other whites, wet and panting and scared. They frowned at him. Looks of confusion, distaste. Then Sullivan said, "Poor lad looks like he's pissed himself," and all of them, including Billy, laughed. Tommy walked to where Beau waited in the shade of the trees, stowed his flask in the saddle pack. While he was fastening the buckle the trooper emerged from the creek bed. He saw Tommy staring, and waved.

· · ·

At sundown they scattered their tracks and made camp in a clutch of weeping myall trees, the low branches giving shelter from the cold and shielding their fire from view. A small fire at first: the troopers built it up and stacked wood into a pile; they cleared the ground around it, saw to the horses, then retired to make their own camp outside the cover of the trees. They did not light a fire. Faint sounds of them moving out there, scrabbling around, whispering, and sometimes a burst of hushed laughter, the whites listening in silence as Sullivan parceled out dry stores in the makings of a meal. Sausage and biscuits. A quart of rum. Quietly they ate their food. Dusk drawing in around them, darkness coming quick, and as Tommy nibbled his biscuit he watched the others in the firelight. Billy alongside him, Sullivan, then Locke sitting cross-legged with a revolver in his lap, gnawing on the sausage like it was boned. On the far side of the fire, Noone sat alone, reclining against the trunk of the myall tree. He had his bowie knife out, picking at the sausage with the tip, dissecting it, piece by little piece. The gristle he would flick into the fire, and when he found a morsel that interested him, he would skewer it on the point of the knife tip and place it delicately between his teeth, before sucking it sharply into his mouth.

"They ever fucking shut up?" Locke grumbled, tearing off another bite.

Noone watched him through the flames. "They being?"

"Your niggers. Couldn't you muzzle them or something, let us eat in peace?"

"Funny, I was just having that same thought about you."

Locke spat into the fire. Tommy saw Sullivan smirk. Noone held Locke's stare, then smiled and went back to his meal and there was silence between them again. Embers crackled in the darkness. A sweet smell of violet from the trees. The branches were draped like curtains around the little camp and the shadows of the men played upon the leaves.

"I knew a bloke once," Sullivan said. He paused to take a swig of rum, then leaned and passed the bottle to

Locke. "Heard about him anyway, this fella down near Bathurst, somewhere round there, kept his blackboys chained to a stake in the yard. Might have even muzzled them, I'm not sure, but the point is he wouldn't leave them loose after dark. Didn't trust 'em. Chained 'em to a fucking pole. Long chains, mind you, let 'em wander a bit. Fed 'em from a trough, gave 'em a bucket to shit in, they slept right there on the ground. Course, people didn't like it, church and city types, but you wonder if he didn't have the right idea." He looked meaningfully at Tommy and Billy. "Fella works for you for years, next thing you know, he's killed your whole family just about."

"Wouldn't trust 'em any farther than I can spit," Locke mumbled.

"That's because you don't understand them," Noone said. "You don't have the capacity for it. Hence, you're afraid of them. It's only natural, I expect."

"I ain't fucking afraid."

Noone picked thoughtfully at his sausage meat. "Men fear that which is alien, that which they cannot control. Hence most are afraid of certain animals, predators, those they cannot tame. In this country that would be snakes, dingos to an extent, but mostly the wild native. It is remarkable really, to see how afraid you all are. They have become like the Devil in the minds of white men."

"And what?" Sullivan asked him. "You think they're alright?"

"I think they are unnecessary. Mankind has moved on. I don't suppose any of you have read Darwin, but he makes the case very well. As a race the negro has fallen so far behind the rate of human evolution that for the most part they are unsuited to the civilized world. We have seen it everywhere, the Americas, Africa, the Indies, tribes who left to their own devices have advanced little further than the apes. Your native Australian is no different. Darwin saw it for himself, visited these very shores. They are a doomed species, gentlemen. Those who won't adapt or be trained will be gone by the century's end."

Sullivan was nodding admiringly. Locke scoffed and said, "You can't train a black, not really. Deep down they'll always be wild."

"No?" Noone said. He sucked another morsel of sausage meat from the tip of his knife, rolled it around his mouth with his tongue. "Then consider our present situation. Here we are, in the middle of the bush, soon to be asleep, four armed natives not fifty yards away. And not just any natives: these are Murray blacks, have you heard of them? The finest fighters and trackers this bitch of a country ever birthed. We are entirely at their mercy, and yet I doubt you would be any safer lying at home in your beds."

"They're wary of your rifle," Locke said. "That's all it is."

"You have a rifle, Raymond, but I doubt they're very wary of you."

Locke glowered into the flames. Sullivan said, "Well, if they do what they're here for, I don't have a problem with 'em. Wild enough when their blood's up. That'll do for me."

"Precisely," Noone said. "It is not about taming them, but about making them obey. Your half-civilized native, a Mission black, let's say, he's no good for anything. Can't hunt, track, or fight; no obedience in him, might as well be culled."

"Arthur was on a Mission and he can do all that."

Tommy shriveled in the silence. He'd spoken without thinking. All of them watched him; he buried his gaze in his lap.

"Arthur being . . . ?" Noone asked.

"The other one," Sullivan said. "Their old boy. I let Ned have him when he left. We reckon he was a part of it. Did I not say about him?"

"Must have slipped your mind, John. You left that part out."

"Arthur never did it," Tommy said. "I already told you that."

"Either he was there or he wasn't," Noone said. "Did you see him or not?"

"No," Tommy said.

They all looked at Billy. He was cradling the rum. He took a slug, winced, then handed the bottle to Tommy. Warily, Tommy drank.

"I ain't sure," Billy said. "But he took off beforehand, a few weeks back, must have known what Joseph had planned."

"Horseshit," Tommy said. "He only took off because Daddy was drinking and there was no work to be done. Told me so himself."

"Was he Kurrong?" Noone asked.

"I reckon so," Billy said, but Tommy was shaking his head.

"He wasn't nothing. His lot died out years ago. Arthur was the last one left."

"There's always an exception," Noone said. Tommy crawled around to hand him the rum; he nodded, took a swig, passed it back. "My boys over there are similar—not all blacks are suited to this kind of work.

Many sign up, then desert. A weakness of the system, unfortunately. You don't always know the bad ones until you've got them out here, and by then it's too late."

Locke mumbled, "Just so long as they know their fucking place."

"Or what? What will you do if they don't?"

Locke only stared at him. Noone continued, "You know, Raymond, above all else I consider myself a scientist, a chronicler of humankind. Over the years I have met many men like you and have come to the conclusion that beneath your bluster you are fundamentally all the same. You are cowards. That is what you are. Keen for any fight you think you can win, scared of those you cannot. I would wager you beat your animals. Horses, dogs, pets. And your women, probably—"

"I've fucking had enough of this."

"He's only pulling your pizzle," Sullivan said. "Calm down."

"I mean it," Locke growled. He pointed across the fire at Noone. "You'll get what's coming one day, you keep going as you are. I ain't scared of you."

"How truly prophetic. Do you know that word, monkey man?"

"Fuck off with you."

"Alright, that's enough. Both of you pack it in."

"You know," Noone said, ignoring Sullivan, "by

Darwin's logic you are bottom of our particular evolutionary pile, a throwback even amongst whites. In fact, there must be some overlap between the very lowest of our caste and the most evolved blacks. I should make a study of you, before your kind becomes extinct."

Locke raised his revolver and pointed it at Noone. Noone did not even flinch. He leaned against the tree and picked at his meal as if Locke and his weapon were not there. When his eyes flicked up to look through the flames, the stare was steady and cold. Already Sullivan was crawling to Locke's side, telling him to stop, grabbing his pistol arm and pressing the rum bottle into his hands instead. Locke shook his head and relented. He swigged a long mouthful of rum, wiped his mouth with the back of his hand, then flapped out his bedroll and lay down, his back to the group, his head cradled in the crook of his arm.

"Night-night, Raymond," Noone whispered. "Sweet dreams."

Sullivan spluttered a laugh, tried to muffle it in his hand. Locke gave no sign of having heard. Tommy smiled nervously but kept his head down, unsure what was expected of him, whose side he was supposed to be on. This kind of banter was new to him. Father had not been a bantering man. Now here were two strangers teetering on the edge of violence as casually as if they were shaking hands.

Sullivan took another drink, belched, then he too turned in. Billy unrolled his swag, Tommy did the same, then he staggered to the tree line to piss. Facing the low branches, his piss drumming into the soil, he searched the darkness for signs of the troopers out there. He couldn't see them. Probably facing the wrong way. Or else they were so expert at staying hidden in the bush that one could have been right in front of him and he wouldn't have known. He squinted drunkenly. The rum had taken hold. Imagined that young one with his madman's eyes staring back from the night. Or the oldfella with his hollowed-out face, or that one with the melted brow . . .

Hurriedly Tommy buckled himself and came back into camp. All of them save Noone was asleep. He was still leaning against the tree trunk but now had a stump of firewood in his hands. He was whittling it with his bowie knife, picking off the shoots one by one. He watched Tommy climbing into his roll; Tommy turned his back on the fire. He lay there listening to the knife blade scraping the bark, then closed his eyes and tried to sleep. It didn't seem real that he was here, in this camp, with these men, all that had gone before. Not four nights ago he was lying in his own bed, Billy alongside him, dreaming about Wallabys in the wet. They'd never go back there, he realized. So much had been lost. He would never think of that waterhole without remembering: every memory, not just Wallabys, every memory was tainted now. One way or another they all led to that day, to the house at sunset, to what was inside. There wasn't anything else. Nowhere he could go to forget.

·   ·   ·

His own name woke him, a whisper in the night. He opened his eyes and lay listening. *"Tommy, Tommy . . ."* Noone called across the clearing, repeating his name like a chant. Tommy rolled over to face him. The fire now low and smoldering, little more than a dying glow, and beyond it the dark figure of Noone still leaning against the tree, whittling another branch, longer than the first, stroke after careful stroke.

"Ask me about the lake," he said.

Tommy sat up slowly, clutched his bedroll to his chest. "What?"

"The lake you saw today. Ask what it's doing there."

Noone's voice was slow and heavy, changed somehow, slurred like he'd been drinking all this time Tommy slept.

"*How's he got a lake in the middle of a drought—* wasn't that what you said?"

"It's not my business. I didn't mean nothing by it."

"To which your brother replied . . . ?"

Tommy hesitated before he answered: "That you don't get a lake. You either have one or you don't."

"Precisely. Do you agree with him?"

"I don't know. It looked strange, that's all."

"So it should. Drought's crippling the district, most of the colony, in fact, and yet here's John Sullivan with an abundance of water and cows fatter than a whorehouse madam. Am I right?"

"I shouldn't have said nothing. Sorry."

"It was very astute of you."

They sat awhile in silence. The knife blade whispered against the wood. Smoke from the fire wound its way through the branches and into the night.

"Are you able to keep a secret, Tommy?"

"I think so."

"Come on now. Either I can trust you or I can't."

"Alright, then."

Noone paused. He held up the branch and studied it. He had whittled it into a neatly tapered stake, roughly two feet long, with a hollowed-out section partway down. He set the stake and knife aside, then leaned into the fire glow. A redness crept over his chest and face, and the tip of his tongue wet his lips before he spoke.

"He dams it. The river. He dams it, then drains it into reservoirs that feed only his land. Your family gets his runoff. You and everyone else downstream."

"But how can he . . . ?"

"There's a word for it. Peacocking. Have you heard of this phrase?"

Scowling, Tommy shook his head.

"It's actually quite common. Scuttling surrounding land for the benefit of one's own. Probably illegal, not that anybody cares."

"We did. Daddy cared. We were getting by on bran mash by the end."

"If I were a betting man, Tommy, I'd say your father was well aware."

"He would never have allowed it."

"You assume he had a say. He used to be John's man, I believe. Quite a rise in fortunes over the years. There are always compromises to be made."

"But . . . everything hangs on that river. Everything."

"We never actually met, your father and I. Didn't seem necessary when I was already working Broken Ridge, the two are one and the same. A spirited fellow, though, John says. Are you much like him, I wonder? How old did you say you are now?"

"Fifteen soon. I'm not sure what today is."

"Twentieth."

"Two days, then. Two days I'm fifteen."

Noone spread his arms. "We shall celebrate. At fifteen you're almost a man."

"Why did you just tell me that? About the lake?"

"Seems to me you deserved to know. You noticed, at least, which is more than your brother did. And I rather like you. I think perhaps we can be friends."

Tommy looked away, blinking. Clutched tight his bedroll.

"I see Rabbit's also taken with you. The young trooper over there. A strange boy, very lonely, I think he might be retarded in some way. Apparently we killed his family and most of his tribe—we being whites, not me personally, you understand. Now it seems he craves our approval, which is a very fine trait in a recruit. Makes him obedient, loyal, but he's a dangerous young man. I wouldn't suggest you choose him for a friend out here."

"I ain't looking to make friends," Tommy said.

"Good. That's good. You were born with a suspicious mind. But no man is an island: you are never entirely alone. You still have your brother, but who else? John? I don't think so, Tommy. John is not your friend. Taking your family's water like that, not very neighborly of him, wouldn't you say?" He wagged his finger back and forth, tutting in time with each pass. "The Bible tells us to love thy neighbor—do you read the Bible, Tommy? Do you follow the word of the Lord?"

"No. I don't reckon he even exists."

Noone's gray eyes flared. "A boy of many talents. Bravo, Tommy. Bravo."

Tommy felt himself flushing, tried to hide a rising smile.

"You don't read the Bible neither?" he asked.

"On the contrary," Noone said, reaching into his coat pocket and pulling out a tattered old book bound in a soft leather cover. He rifled the pages so Tommy could see. Half of them were missing, a stub of ragged paper torn along the spine.

"In fact, I read a page of this nonsense daily, gives me a bloody good laugh while I take my morning shit, then it does a fine job of wiping clean my hole." Laughing, he raised his arms skyward. "Halle-bloody-lujah! Praise be to the Lord!"

His laughter died out and he lowered his arms and Tommy waited but Noone didn't speak again. Tommy lay down slowly, pulled his bedroll to his chin. He was facing the fire this time, facing Noone. Through the quiver of the charcoal he saw him reach for the two pieces of wood he had trimmed, and fit one against the other to make a cross, which he then began binding with string.

Tommy soon fell asleep. Dreams of Father and of a lake—the first time he had dreamed of Father since. He was standing by the lake, looking out over its surface while from a distance Tommy called his name. Father didn't turn. Tommy shouted louder but still he didn't respond, unreachable at the water's edge, lost, and Tommy shouting, shouting . . . until he woke panicked into daylight to find that the shouting belonged to Locke. He was raising hell in the camp, cursing and fighting with his bedroll. The cross that Noone had made last night was embedded in the ground, just above Locke's head. His name had been carved upon it. His death foretold.

17

Midmorning they cleared the station boundary. There were no markings, no fence posts, but as they passed between a pair of bulbous bottle trees Sullivan drew a line with his finger across the ground.

"Here's about where it ends, so the title says. I ain't finished with it yet, though. You see them ranges yonder? Up to there's my claim."

He spoke for Billy's benefit. All morning the two of them had ridden side by side, Tommy trailing just behind. He could hardly stand to listen to them talk, but there was nowhere else for him to be. Noone and the troopers were leading them now, the old man at the front of the line, while Locke skulked alone at the rear. He hadn't said a word since waking that morning, when he'd tossed Noone's crucifix onto the newly kindled fire and sat shivering with his tin cup cradled in his hands, moodily sipping bush tea.

The frontier crossing turned Tommy's gut, their passing from settled land to wild. All his life he'd feared it, the uncharted west, looming like a shadow on the edge of their world. The center was filled with legends such as men like Burke and Wills, who had tried to cross the country and died along the way, or the everyday tales of vanished drovers and mysterious lost cattle mobs many thousand strong, swagmen blinded by sandy blight or sent mad by the bush. Sometimes they came to the house, asking for food or work, muttering darkly about the places they'd been, and Mother would take pity on them and allow them a meal and a night in the bunkhouse, then Father would chase them off come the dawn. Even in Bewley they weren't welcome; Tommy had seen them raving in the street, staggering about like drunks. And yet always they went back there, into the nothingness that broke them, bewitched by it, entranced. That very same nothingness into which Tommy now rode. The empty swath of country on the surveyor's map. The place where the lines ran out.

And there really was nothing. The landscape stretched endlessly before them, a flat and uniform tundra of sunburned grasslands, broken scrub, the tufted tops of trees or the skeletal outlines of their remains, blackened by bushfire, withered by drought. The ranges squatting low on the horizon, shapeless and obscure: a day and a half riding and still they were no nearer. It would be days more before they got there, and nothing in between. No towns, no settlements: nothing between here and Perth, thousands of miles away on the western coast; nothing except wild bushland and the lonely wooden shack that served as a telegraph station in a place called Alice Springs. And pity the poor bastard who found himself posted there.

They rode on. Nine liquid shadows slipping over the rubbled ground. The soil different out here, desert soil, pebbled and sandy and corrugated by the wind, firebrand red. The heat incessant, engulfing them, choking them—sweat streamed down Tommy's face and neck and suckered his clothing and boots to his skin. He took a long drink, rattled his flask, and guessed at only an inch or so left. He tightened the stopper and stowed the flask in his saddlebag, pushed it low, hoping to keep the water cool, and as he did so felt the rustle of paper down there. A packet of some kind—he fished it out and opened it and found a handful of Mrs. Sullivan's lemon lollies inside. He ached just to look at them. A little moan escaped. She must have smuggled the packet into his bag herself. Tommy swelled at the thought of her doing that. He wasn't far from tears.

He checked along the line in front of him, then over his shoulder at Locke. No one was paying him any mind. He pried a lolly from the clump, popped it in his mouth. Sticky and dry at first, but as he worked it the sweet lemon flavor began dribbling into his parched throat and he closed his eyes in bliss. He hid the packet in his saddlebag, and for the briefest moment he was not in that desert convoy anymore, his world reduced to tongue and tooth and lolly and throat, feeling every movement, savoring every taste, mourning the speed with which it shrank and then evaporated and somehow left him even thirstier still.

When Billy and Sullivan finally parted, Sullivan riding on ahead to talk to Noone, passing the troopers without acknowledgment, oblivious to their glares, Billy fell back to join Tommy and said casually, not looking across, "Hot, ain't it?"

"Uh-huh."

"Wind's picking up n'all."

"Yup," Tommy said.

Now Billy looked at him. "What's got into you?"

"You need me to tell you?"

"I asked, didn't I?"

"Alright," Tommy said. "What was all that about?"

"All what?"

"You and him. You'd think you two were the ones that's kin."

Billy blew out dismissively. "We was only talking. Don't be such a girl."

"Talking about what?"

"This—what else?"

"What about it exactly?"

"Nothing exactly."

"He tell you about that lake of his, did he?"

"Not you and that bloody lake again."

"He dams it, you know. Keeps most of the water for himself. That's how come our creek gets so low in the dry. Peacocking, they call it. Even got its own word."

Billy scowled at him. "Where'd you get all this from?"

"Noone. Last night. Reckoned Daddy would have known about it too."

"Well, there you go. There ain't no way."

"He seemed sure enough."

"That bloke's crazier than a bag of snakes, Tommy. You seen him last night with Locke. Lucky he didn't get his head shot off."

"Locke would never have dared."

"Well, you can't trust him anyway. John's already said. He likes causing trouble, that's all. Does it for fun."

"Says Sullivan."

"Yeah, says him." Both were quiet a moment, then Billy said, "Tell you what, though, wouldn't mind them finding us a lake out here sometime soon."

Tommy snorted a quick laugh. "Bloody oath."

"You got much left?"

"Hardly any. You?"

"Same. I've not seen them blacks take theirs out once."

"They don't eat neither, it's not normal."

"Nothing about them's normal, Tommy. They give me the jips, every one."

"Noone said that young one had his family killed by whites."

Billy looked at him doubtfully, then sniffed and said, "Probably deserved it."

"You reckon so?"

"Aye, I do. No one gets killed without a reason. Even blacks."

They both fell silent. Tommy said, "Camels don't need much water."

"Camels? What you talking about camels for?"

"It's true. A camel goes weeks without drinking.

They're made for all this. Maybe some natives are built the same."

Billy broke into a laugh. He shook his head. "A black and a camel ain't nothing alike."

"I'm not saying they're alike, just that there might be a reason why—"

"They don't even have bloody humps!"

Billy was laughing fully now. The bearded trooper looked at them, and Billy bit his tongue until he'd turned back around, then muffled his laughter with a hand. "Camels, Tommy!" he whispered, and Tommy briefly smiled. Smiling more at the fact that they were laughing together than anything either had said.

That night they camped in open scrub, beneath a pair of coolibahs, the troopers alternating watch while the others ate and slept. Another low fire, another meal of dry stores, everyone wary, watching the open plains, not much talking and no trouble this time between Locke and Noone. Tommy didn't like looking out there. He could see only so far and then nothing, total darkness, a shadowland filled with his fears. He imagined wild blacks circling, dogs prowling, snakes sliding into camp. When he lay down to sleep he kept hearing them, their footsteps and low moans, and though he knew it was only the troopers patrolling, that knowledge did not make him feel any more safe.

. . .

In the afternoon of the following day they came across a dwelling house, sitting lonely and incongruous on the empty plain. Noone halted the group a half mile clear. They gathered in a line and watched the house, tiny at that distance, quiet and still. The posse waited. Hot wind ruffled their clothing and whipped dust across the ground; the horses shook off the flies. Noone extended a brass spyglass and studied the little house, and Tommy watched him while he did. The idea seemed faintly magical. Bringing the distance closer, moving yourself near.

Noone lowered the scope and contracted it again. They walked the horses on, toward the house, the line fragmenting as they went, Noone and the troopers in front, the other four whites behind. The young trooper grinned at Tommy excitedly, nodding and pointing and bouncing in his saddle.

"Look at him," Sullivan muttered. "Little bastard's keener than a bitch in heat."

They halted again a hundred yards short. All eyes on the ruined house. Its walls were still standing but the roof was part-caved, a hole in the shingles on the right side. There was one uncovered window and the door was open, no front yard to speak of, uncleared scrub right up to the walls.

Noone raised his chin. "Jarrah," he said. "Take a look."

The trooper with the eye scar dismounted. He handed off his reins, checked his rifle, set out walking through the scrub. No hesitation, no pause. He carried the rifle by its forestock and walked casually to the house, as if he already knew it was safe. Tommy didn't trust it. Didn't trust the silence, the darkness inside. He watched Jarrah breathlessly, followed his every step, like he too was approaching that open door . . . and Father lying slumped beside it, three holes in him, and Mother behind the curtain, missing half her head.

Tommy turned away, couldn't watch. He took out his flask and drank, kept his eyes on Noone instead. He looked almost bored. Hands folded in his lap, fingers drumming; he took a long breath and sighed. Tommy glanced back at Jarrah. He was creeping along the front wall. He ducked his head through the window, then went to the door, and Noone ordered him inside with another jut of his chin. Jarrah slipped in through the gap. Tommy stared at the darkened doorway, expecting a gunshot, a cry, lost in the trauma of what might be in there, and didn't see the trooper emerge from around the back of the house.

"Empty!" Jarrah shouted; Tommy flinched and dropped his flask and the last of his water glugged onto the ground. He jumped down to retrieve it, peered into the mouth, but there was barely anything left. The others set off for the house and Tommy looked forlornly at Billy, who only shrugged.

"Might be a well," Billy said, before turning and following the group in.

There was no well. They rode around the house, into the rear yard, and found a three-walled barn and rusted wire coop, and by way of a scullery an open stone fireplace and the rubble of a collapsed chimney stack. Crumbling wooden palings lay about in piles and there was a spool of old fencing wire, but not even the yard had been properly cleared let alone the surrounding land. Maybe someone once intended grazing here, but there were no signs of cattle having ever been run.

Noone dismounted, went to the back door, leaned his head inside, then poked about the scullery with his boot. He wasn't wearing his longcoat, and his collar was open and bare, nothing official about his appearance anymore. He picked through the rubble and turned up a shelf and a fire grate and a rusted iron skillet, lifting them one by one from the dirt, then tossing each aside. He crouched and inspected the leavings in the open fireplace.

"Anything?" Sullivan called.

Noone took a long time to answer. "You know whose place this is?"

"Never knew anyone was out here. Crazy bastard's doomed."

"Well, someone built it. And there's a fire inside not a couple of days old."

"Was it them?" Billy asked. "Joseph and that lot?"

Noone ignored him. He and Jarrah walked back to the group. Billy went to ask again but Sullivan told him quietly, "Don't push it, son. Leave all that to me."

They moved on. Mile after mile and still the ranges seemed no closer, lying on the horizon like something buried there. Easy to question whether they were even real, wavering like a mirage—many times out here Tommy had blinked and some landmark had shifted or disappeared. The shimmer of a waterhole. A flurry of wild dogs. A native warrior, ochre-painted, standing with his spear at his side; on second glance a termite mound or tangle of bare tree limbs. The heat working its spell, the sun directly ahead of them, blasting in their faces, swollen by a wind that seemed to build with every gust. Tommy was parched. Lips cracked, throat burning; his eyes so dusty it stung when he blinked.

Gamely he tried sucking another lemon lolly but it hurt just to swallow and he spat it on the ground.

Billy noticed and waited for him.

"What was that?"

"You got any water?" Tommy croaked.

"They said to save it till camp. You've none left at all?"

Tommy shook his head. "Please, Billy."

He reached for his flask. "If you weren't so bloody jumpy you'd still have your own." He pulled out the stopper with his teeth, handed it across. "Just a sip."

Tommy guzzled the water, it dribbled down his chin.

"Fucking . . . give it here!"

Billy snatched back the flask. Tommy reached for his saddlebag, intending to repay him with one of the lollies, and didn't notice the young trooper falling back along the line, until he slid into place at Tommy's side. He was holding out his own water flask, offering it for Tommy to take.

"Get you good drink now, youngfella."

Tommy watched him warily. The trooper nodded and offered the flask again. His face was glistening with sweat but he didn't look so crazy, Tommy thought. No mad eyes or inane grin. He could hear the water sloshing in the flask. His left hand dropped the reins but Billy warned him, "Don't you fucking take that."

"I'm thirsty, Billy."

"It's black water. It ain't clean."

"Water's water," Tommy said. He took the trooper's flask and drank. Billy began shouting at him, and Sullivan called for the trooper to leave the two brothers alone. At the head of the column, Noone twisted in his saddle to see.

Tommy handed back the flask, nodded in thanks.

"Rabbit," the trooper whispered, tapping his chest. "Bye-bye."

He moved on ahead, retook his place in the line.

"The hell's he saying about rabbits?" Billy said. "I've not seen a bloody one."

"Not rabbits—Rabbit. That's his name."

"What sort of a name's Rabbit?"

"Ask him. I doubt he even knows himself."

Billy put away his flask. "Well, you ain't drinking no more of my water now your lips have been on his."

Tommy left the lollies in the saddlebag, buckled up the strap.

The troopers saw the signs before any of the whites: a flurry of birds overhead, flocking for the east; a darkness creeping over the ranges, though there were hours until dusk. The party bunched to a standstill. They sat watching the land in the west. The horses twitched irritably, neighing and stepping about. Tommy stared at the horizon the same as the rest but saw no trouble at first. And yet. The ranges were dim and hazy, the air thickening, becoming opaque, a shadow slipping over the foothills like an early sunset fell.

The dust cloud swept over the ranges in an immense orange flood, engulfing them in a roiling, tumbling wall of dirt and sand and earth stretching a mile into the sky and many more wide, pluming upward and outward as it moved. And it was moving, quickly. To the naked eye it seemed almost motionless, like some terrible mono-lith newly raised from the ground, but anytime Tommy picked out a landmark it was consumed almost immedi-ately, and lost.

"We have an hour," Noone announced. "Pope—what do you say?"

The old man nodded. "Hour, Boss, that big bugger come."

"Might only have dust in it," Locke said. "We could ride right through."

"Or it might not," Noone replied. "Might be a sand-storm, blind the horses, strip the skin from your bones. You're welcome to stay, Raymond. Please do. But the rest of you, back to that shit-pile of a house we found this afternoon."

Locke began protesting but Noone didn't wait. He turned his horse sharply, gave it both spurs; the horse bared its teeth and took off like it had been shot. Noone didn't check who was following, though all of them did. Pushing their horses desperately, frantic backward glances as they rode. Tiny little figures on the darkening plain, the wall of earth behind them, its shadow lengthening, swallowing all before it, and gaining. Like the advance of the end of the world.

18

They huddled all together in the filthy little room, mouths and noses covered, eyes closed against the dust that gathered steadily upon them, coating their shoulders, their hats. Outside, the wind growled and swirled and strafed the building with stones, spattering like hail through the open window and collapsed section of roof, a cacophonous drumming overhead. Dust seeped through the walls. Grit shrapneled between the mismatched slabs and the men flinched and grunted when they were hit. Otherwise no one moved. They sat on the bare earth floor, heads bowed, cross-legged or with knees drawn, all facing the same way, their backs to the west and the brunt of the wind. Dark as night inside the house. A world of black and gray. No telling who was who. Tommy was beside his brother, he knew that much. They had entered the house together, then sat down side by side, their knees and shoulders touching—how long ago was that? How many minutes, hours, had passed? The storm seemed to come in cycles, and for a while Tommy expected each cycle to be the last, then he gave up expecting and simply sat. He worried about the horses, about Beau and Annie, tethered in their three-walled barn. Open to the east, mercifully, but with every lull in the wind he heard their petrified screaming and doubted whether the barn would hold. The house too: the roof was being stripped piece by piece, the shingles peeling and flipping away, the hole widening all the time. Tommy could see nothing through it, a strange and murky darkness, no hint of breaking light. He closed his eyes again, held himself tightly with both arms, leaned against his brother. After a moment, Billy leaned back.

Slowly, imperceptibly, the worst of it passed. Less anger in the wind, the patter of grit becoming more like rainfall, a hesitant half-light creeping into the room and giving the swirling dust a warm and pinkish hue. The air was choked with it, all but unbreathable, and the men fell about in racking coughing fits as they stirred. Rising ghostly from the silt, dirt tumbling from their shoulders, they blew out their nostrils, wiped their eyes, spat on the ground, and for a while simply stood there, looking about in a kind of wonderment, like the survivors of some great collapse.

Billy dug out his water flask, rinsed his mouth, spat. He handed the flask to Tommy and he did the same. The group slowly reassembling, each man brushing himself down, little bursts of chatter breaking out here and there. Noone struck a match and lit his pipe, then wandered to the open window and considered the view. Tommy dabbed water on his cuff, wiped his eyes, but the cuff was so dirty it only stung more. He winced and pressed the heels of his hands into his eye sockets and from across the room heard Sullivan laughing, "And there was you wanted to ride right through the fucking thing," to which Locke grumbled a reply that Tommy didn't catch.

He followed the others outside, through the back door, and stood in the ruined scullery, surveying the yard. The soil lay in contoured mounds and was piled in thick drifts against the rear of the fireplace and the west-facing side of every structure or wall. The barn was still intact. Beau and Annie were in there, skittish but seemingly well. One of the other horses had broken free. She'd cleared the yard but gone no farther than the nearby scrubs, where she pranced about madly like the earth was on fire. Two troopers went to bring her in: the old man, Pope, and the bearded one they called Mallee. They walked slowly, casually, like they'd seen all this before, extending their hands to the storm-crazed horse and talking the animal down; the horse moving slowly also, lifting and stretching out its hooves, a dreamlike fluidity in all Tommy saw. He wandered into the yard and looked east, trying to make out the storm but he could not. There was no tail to it, no wall of dirt like there had been at the front; a lingering darkness and that was all. He turned and saw Billy in the barn with Beau and Annie, stroking both horses—might have been anywhere, at home in the stables even, a lifetime from this place—and then he noticed, as his gaze slid across the yard, a nearby dirt drift and buried within it, camouflaged by the soil, a wounded but still-living kangaroo.

Tommy squatted down beside her, looked into her eye. The pupil was black and very wide, around it a damp brown film and a gathering of blood. The eye rolled side to side. Her mouth hung open and her breathing came rapidly in short little pants. Her tail twitched. Thudding into the soil. Little arms hanging limp and wizened like the arms of an old man, dirt and dust piled over her like a blanket had been pulled. Tommy hushed her. Told her it would be alright. He didn't know what he was saying. He wiped his hand over his filthy, sweat-stained face and glanced again at the scene: Rabbit and Jarrah milling about the yard; Sullivan and Locke laughing together by the door; Billy petting the horses and Noone pacing thoughtfully with his pipe; the mare prancing in circles through the scrub and Pope and Mallee waiting for her to calm; the crumbling house and barn and the desolate nothingness all around; and then at the roo blown in by the storm and dying here before him in the dirt . . . all of this he saw in a strange tableau, like a painting on a wall, and his eyes filled at the hopelessness of this world in which they found themselves, a world he wanted no part of and yet here he was, orphaned and alone, a brother slipping away from him and a sister dying in her bed, and he—

The waddy flattened the kangaroo's head without Tommy having realized anyone else was there. The club whipped past his face, sucking the air behind it in a fierce *whooshing* sound, and he only just recoiled fast enough to avoid the worst of the blood and cranial tissue thrown out by the blow. The club withdrew. Rabbit was standing over him, eyes shining, face painted in dust. He rested the waddy on his shoulder and smiled, then something caught the trooper's eye and he glanced down the length of the kangaroo, to the belly, where first the ears, then the face of a joey came wriggling from its pouch.

Rabbit swung the waddy blade first and near-decapitated the baby roo. He wiped the blood on the mother's hide, then collected up her tail and said, "Good tucker these buggers," before adding, as if sensing Tommy hadn't fully understood, "Yum yum!"

Rabbit dragged the animals to the house, the joey's head bobbling, a bloodstain lengthening in the soil behind the roo. Jarrah greeted him excitedly. The other two troopers bringing in the mare clapped in brief applause. Rabbit dumped the roo by the scullery, and he and Jarrah set to work with their knives. The joey was freed from its pouch and hung for bleeding by its tail. The mother's belly was slit, the innards removed and set aside. Locke began gathering palings and breaking them for firewood, and through all of this Tommy hadn't moved. Still on his haunches in the middle of the yard, trembling faintly, his eyes very wide, a trace of blood spatter on his dust-streaked face.

· · ·

The roos were skinned and butchered and cooked on the scullery fire, smoky from the dust, hissing with each drip from the joints and cuts piled on the rusted grate. Another fire was lit inside the house, beneath the open section of roof, flames reaching high into the cavity and shadows flickering across the room while the group ate. The whites took the joints and prime cuts; the blacks favored the organs and tail, the latter cooked in an ember pit dug in the ground. Before serving themselves, the troopers offered the organs to Noone, Pope bringing them forward on a pair of roof-shingle platters and presenting them so he could make his choice, and Tommy watched Noone take out his bowie knife and slice small pieces of liver, kidney, and heart, leaving the tail and intestines intact for his men. Something almost ceremonial in the act. The other troopers watching him too, patiently waiting in a huddle at the open end of the room, all of them shirtless now, and barefoot. No such courtesy among the whites: having each helped themselves, they sat apart along the wall, scoffing at their supper, tearing at the meat.

Noone nodded to Pope and the old man withdrew. He sat down cross-legged in the circle near the fire, placed the platters in the center of the group. Tommy waited for the scramble, the fight for each piece, but there was none. One by one the troopers took their allotted share. Conversation rippled between them, now and then a muffled laugh, picking at their offal and eating with a cordiality so at odds with all Tommy had expected and heard. He'd imagined them ripping raw meat straight from the bone, no different from scavengers or carrion birds. Yet here they were fine dining. Might as well have been in some restaurant in town.

"You should eat," Billy said quietly, leaning in close.

"I ain't hungry."

"You must be." He noticed Tommy watching the troopers across the room. "Don't watch them if it puts you off. Here, try this."

Billy reached for the platter, fetched Tommy a boned joint that looked to have been part of the ribs. The meat steamed and dripped its juices on the floor; Tommy dropped it into his lap, shook his hand against the burn. Sullivan laughed at him. He sent the rum down the line. Locke, then Billy, then it was Tommy's turn. He waved the bottle away. Billy pressed it on him but Tommy refused.

"What's wrong with you?" Billy whispered. "It looks bad if you don't."

"I don't care how it looks."

"You sick or something?"

"You know I ain't sick."

"Best not be."

"Or what? You'd leave me behind?"

Billy frowned at him. "What's that mean?"

"You never wanted me here, so fine, leave me. Pick me up on your way back through."

Billy stared at him a long time, clicked his tongue,

said, "Don't be so fucking soft." He took another swig of rum, handed it back to Locke. Sullivan was making eyes at the overseer to offer the bottle to Noone. Locke wouldn't do it. Sullenly he shook his head. From his seat by the front doorway, Noone took bites of each organ from the end of his knife and watched the brief exchange. He was smiling. Nibbling the joey's heart. Firelight and shadow dividing his face. Sullivan sighed and reached for the bottle, passed it across to him, and Noone took a very long drink, his eyes resting on Locke the whole time.

"We shouldn't even be here," Tommy whispered. "All we told him was lies."

"Shh," Billy hissed. "Shut up about that."

"What if he finds out?"

"He won't. Eat your fucking food."

"Look at us, Billy. We don't belong here."

"Aye? And where would you rather be? Home? Where's that now, hmm?"

"Don't be like that."

"I mean it. At least we're doing something. And here's not so bad."

Tommy looked around the room. "Oh, you reckon?"

"We've shelter, fire, food . . ."

"Quit acting what you're not."

Billy shook his head and gnawed on his bone, then an

idea struck him and he looked up again. "Hey, when's your birthday anyway? What's the date?"

Tommy whispered it sadly: "Today."

"It's Tommy's birthday!" Billy announced. "My little brother's fifteen!"

A small cheer went up. Billy slapped him on the back. Sullivan crawled over the dusty floor and pressed the bottle of rum into Tommy's hand and told him he had no choice but to drink. He did so, then sat there shyly while Sullivan began slurring "For He's a Jolly Good Fellow," and the others steadily joined him, even Noone, even the troopers, a mangled attempt at the words. A chorus of voices echoing around the walls and spilling out of the little house. Aglow in the darkness. Alone on the plains.

19

They were most of the next morning recrossing that same stretch of terrain over which they'd fled yesterday, now littered with debris from the storm. Trees bent and broken, tumbleweed strewn about, a flotsam of deadwood and plants uprooted by the wind. No wind this morning, though. The day hot and clear and still. Their tracks had been covered by a fresh dusting of topsoil and they rode into virgin land. Untouched plains before them, the ranges inching closer, and in the wake of the horses a single trail of overlapping hoofprints, stretching mile after mile back to the house lying empty and abandoned once more.

Around midday Pope halted and the column bunched behind his horse. The old man spoke briefly with Noone, then dismounted and wandered out into the scrub, unhurriedly weaving his way through. The group sat watching him. Tommy heard Locke curse and spit violently on the ground.

Pope stopped to examine a particular clutch of bush. Nothing untoward about it. Nothing that Tommy could see. Pope bent, then squatted to sit on his heels. He was still shirtless, they all were; that morning none of the troopers had bothered to re-dress. Pope's skin pulled tight against his ribs. His concave stomach creased. "He taking a fucking shit?" Locke scoffed. Nobody answered him. Pope reached into the bush and tugged something free from the branches, then carried it back to the group, a square of fabric flapping in his hand. The same measured walk he'd taken out there. Face as placid as stone.

What he'd found was a handmade dilly bag, woven from grass, feathers, and bark; an expert, intricate weave. Pope dipped his hand inside and removed it in a fist, letting a stream of dirt dribble out before opening his palm to reveal berries, seeds, and other pickings, which he fingered carefully like runes. Pope passed up the bag and the findings for Noone to inspect, and while he did so, Pope scanned the country to the west.

"Still ripe," Noone said, sniffing them. "Yesterday, you think?"

Pope nodded. "Wind carry 'em. Been hiding last night them too."

"In the ranges?"

"Nah, them buggers too long way still. Blackfella got no horse."

He said the word like *hoss*, watching the ranges as he spoke. Noone looked toward those same hills, then turned to Sullivan and smiled. Pope remounted. Noone clicked his horse forward and dropped the dilly bag on the ground and each hoof trampled it deeper into the dirt.

There wasn't a trail to follow, the earth blown clean by yesterday's storm, yet still Pope knew the direction they would have taken: the pickers of the berries, the carriers of the bag. He led the group into increasingly rocky terrain, undulating in hummocks and dips, the scrub thinner on open ground now, concentrated instead around the base of giant boulders or in the clefts of sandstone mounds that rose like totems all over the land. Bizarre rock formations, improbable to the naked eye: house-sized boulders, as smooth and round as red marbles, balanced on the tip of a slab; others piled together as unstable as eggs; longer stones stacked in triangular amber cairns, dark caves at their heart, as if laid according to design. They couldn't have been. To move just one of those rocks would have taken twenty horses and just as many men. Yet there was no explanation for them: they couldn't have rolled from the ranges, no other source around. Tommy wondered what story the old people must have had for this place; to him it looked like the kind of thing children would have built, giant children playing giant games a long time ago. But then it didn't feel much like a playground. Nothing joyful here. It reminded him more of a graveyard, each cairn a marker, each rock a protruding bone. That seemed more fitting. Dozens of buried giants, hundreds, too many for Tommy to count.

A cluster of gum trees gave away the waterhole: Pope pointed and led them in. A leafy stand shielding a chain of little pools, fed by an underground spring, miraculous in this barren wasteland. Since crossing Sullivan's boundary they had only refilled their flasks from the bladder-bag reserves, and by now all that was left was tepid and dirty and stale. They dismounted and lunged for the water, men and horses both, even the troopers this time, even Noone. They drank and refilled their flasks and bladder bags and washed off the dust from the storm. Tommy sank his head into the pool and let the water cocoon him awhile. He could hear the others through it. Sounds of them drinking, talking, splashing with their hands. He came up breathless and shivered as the water dripped inside his shirt. A rare thing to shiver—he smiled and twisted as it wriggled down his spine.

He and Billy found a spot in the leaf-dappled sun and sat leaning their backs against a rock. Eyes closed, hair damp, faces dripping: Tommy had memories of having done this many times, and inevitably of Wallabys, that day only a week ago, when they had lain drying in the sunshine while at the house, at the house . . .

He opened his eyes again. Billy was watching Noone and Pope circling the waterhole, stepping between the pools, talking and studying the ground. Everyone else was resting: Sullivan smoked a cigarette, Locke lay by the water, the troopers idled in the sun.

"You reckon he's some sort of witch?" Billy said, nodding.

"Who? Pope?"

"Since when did you know their bloody names?"

"They do have them, Billy."

"Well, yeah, that old one, I meant. He knows just about everything, it seems."

"He knew the waterhole on account of the trees. It ain't that hard."

Billy frowned at him. "What about the bag, then? How'd he read the storm? And how does he know where they're headed when there's not even any tracks?"

Tommy shrugged. He didn't care.

"Exactly. Blackfella magic. I'm telling you, he's some sort of bloody witch."

"It's not magic to read the land. Or spot a bag in a bush."

Billy spat on his hand. "I'll wager you."

"And what? You'll ask him? *Hey, Pope! You a witch or not?*"

"No, we'll just . . . there'll be proof come along one way or the other."

Tommy scoffed. He didn't take Billy's bet. They sat watching the men until Tommy said, "You ever think about Mary? Reckon she's on the mend?"

"Should be. Shanklin'll be there."

"What if she's not? You think about that?"

"Why would I? What's the use?"

"She's on her own, is all I mean."

"I just said, Shanklin's with her. Better be anyway. It's been long enough."

Tommy reckoned it up. "It's only been four days."

Billy looked at him. "Horseshit, four days."

"Means she's been lying in that bed a week."

Billy was shaking his head. "Feels more like a bloody month."

They lapsed into silence. Tommy pushed himself to his feet and went to his saddlebag and returned with the packet of lemon sweets.

"What you got there?"

Tommy dropped a lolly into Billy's hand. His eyes

widened; he popped it into his mouth and, as he sucked, his eyes squeezed tight and a smile came to his lips.

"Where in hell did you get these?"

Tommy took one for himself and hid the bag behind his back. "Mrs. Sullivan gave them. Don't tell anyone else."

"How many you got?"

He fished out the bag again and showed him.

"Bloody hell, Tommy!"

"Shut up, will you. Keep your voice down."

"Here, give us some for my pocket."

Billy reached for the bag but Tommy snatched it away. He counted two of the lollies into Billy's lap. Billy started to argue but didn't, pocketed the lollies instead. He rested his head against the rock; Tommy watched him a moment, then did the same. Smiling and sucking their sweets, faces upturned to the sun.

Tommy felt the shadow sliding over him, opened his eyes, and found Noone standing there, smoking his pipe, gazing across the waterhole. Tommy elbowed Billy gently and he jerked upright, then fell still when he saw they weren't alone.

"Lovely day for it," Noone said, smiling. "Having fun, boys?"

"Just resting," Billy said. "Same as them."

Noone nodded and drew hard on the mouthpiece, his

hollow cheeks hollowing farther still, then he blew out the smoke and lowered himself down next to Tommy, the brothers shuffling to make room. Noone leaned against the rock and sighed. He was close enough that Tommy could feel the heat of the man, could smell his smoke and sweat. He had his shirt unbuttoned to the middle of his chest—the dark hairs damp and matted— and his sleeves rolled elbow-high. He sat there smoking. The smoke drifted over both of them, sitting awkwardly alongside.

"I'd ask for one of those lollies but I think the to- bacco would spoil the taste."

Tommy scrambled for the packet behind his back. "You're welcome to—"

"Put them away, lad, or Locke will take the lot. They're from that garish tree John has at his place, I assume, all whored up in tinsel and balls?"

"Yessir. A Christmas tree, she said."

"Quite. Even more ridiculous. Still, if it keeps Mrs. Sullivan happy . . . she can't have too much to smile about." He exhaled heavily through his nose. "So, how are the pair of you enjoying your little adventure so far?"

Tommy glanced at his brother. Billy said, "We're . . . it's fine."

"You're both keeping well? Food, water, supplies?"

Hesitantly Tommy nodded. Trick questions, it seemed.

"Good, good, it's not to everyone's taste, of course, traveling in this manner, being out here, but there are moments of enjoyment, I believe, moments of peace."

Tommy was still nodding. Wondering what the hell Noone was about. Sullivan and Locke were watching them curiously from the water's edge.

"Sadly, they are all too brief, these periods of respite. A sweet or a smoke in the sunshine, then we must move on again. Always moving, always moving. Of course, it is tempting to stay here, to camp here tonight, but there are hours yet until sunset and it would be a shame to waste the light. Not to mention the risk that the trail will be dead come dawn."

Billy leaned forward. "You found something?"

"Indeed. Natives were here just this morning. Seems they camped after the storm, probably sheltered in those rock caves we passed back there. We might have only missed them by a couple of hours."

"Was it Joseph? Him and the rest?"

Noone inclined his head and looked at Billy indulgently, eyebrows raised, a knowing half smile. "No, I don't believe so. Barefoot, it appears, plus a couple of gins and some dogs . . . hardly your murderous mob. Tommy—what do you say?"

He looked up, startled. "What about?"

"Well, how should we proceed?"

He could feel himself flushing. He shrugged. "Leave them, if they're not him."

"Really? You're not keen to get out after them? Find out who they are?"

"Be a waste of the horses. Might be in the ranges by now anyway."

"Doubtful. Even on horseback we'd only just make the ranges ourselves. But remember, they'll be Kurrong, they would know where Joseph is. Still not keen?"

"There's women with them, you said."

"And?"

"Well, there weren't no women involved."

"True. But that didn't spare your mother. Or your little sister."

Billy was stirring, rising to his feet. "We should leave," he said. "Catch 'em before dark."

"Tommy," Noone said, pouting, "I'm disappointed. I thought you were with us. After all, we are here on your behalf. On your word, no less."

"I am with you, it's just—"

"You see, we can't have any dissenters. Even my blacks are fully committed to the cause. And yet I worry about you, Tommy. I worry you see too much. There is a little dissent in you, I think. I do not like dissent. It is a wound that festers and slowly eats away at a man, then next thing you know he has turned. That is not good for me. Or for him, in fact. Best thing with a wound that looks like it will turn is to cut off the limb before it takes. If that is not possible, kill the man altogether. It is kinder all round, more effective, saves everyone a lot of trouble and pain." He pushed himself to his feet, groaning as he rose, then stood over Tommy, staring down. "I do hope I'm wrong about that, Tommy. I think maybe I am. More likely you're upset about your family still, perhaps a little afraid?"

"He is," Billy said quickly. "Has been since we left."

Noone looked at him coldly. "Better afraid than a fool, Billy. At least your brother has some sense. Oh, don't worry, I have the measure of you too. Had it the moment I saw you crawling out of that bush."

Noone clapped his hands as he walked away, gathering the others around him. The troopers drifted in from where they'd been sitting, and Sullivan and Locke came close, Sullivan watching the brothers as they joined the back of the group, Tommy the last to arrive.

"Good news!" Noone announced. He was a head taller than all of them, even Locke, Jarrah, Mallee. "It seems that our native friends who dropped their little bag camped at this waterhole last night. They'll be headed for the ranges, no doubt, but depending on the time of their leaving we might still catch them before sundown. They are on foot, women with them, won't be in a rush. They don't know we're coming, so we have the added advantage of surprise."

Locke rubbed his hands greedily. Nodding up and down.

"How many?" Sullivan asked.

"We think five. Three men, two gins, a small pack of dogs."

"Always fucking dogs," Locke said.

"The horses are well rested, so we ride hard until we lose the sun. And for God's sake, don't shoot them. These ones need questioning first. Don't anyone fire without my say-so. John, Raymond—that includes the pair of you."

"Aye, aye," Sullivan said, and the group parted. They each went to their horses and began checking their weapons and tightening their straps. Tommy dropped the packet of lollies into his saddlebag, Billy spun the barrel of his revolver and snapped it into place, opened it up, snapped it again.

"About as useful as your pizzle, that thing," Locke said, walking his horse by.

"I can shoot."

Locke dropped his reins and came to stand between them, close to Tommy's side. He peered down over his shoulder. "What about you? What you ever killed?"

Tommy kept his head lowered. Fiddling with his strap.

Billy said, "We've both shot plenty. Rabbit, possum, roo."

"What about a nigger?"

"Not yet," Billy said.

Locke smiled at that. A smile stained brown with chew. He cupped Tommy's chin and turned him around, tilted back his head, his face in Tommy's face, the foul tang of his breath, the rough grip of his fingers squeezing Tommy's jaw.

"How come you never speak, boy? You missing a fucking tongue?"

Tommy's teeth were clenched. "I don't have nothing to say."

Locke dug his finger into Tommy's mouth. It wriggled thick and wormlike between his teeth and gum, prying the teeth apart. Tommy gagged. The finger tasted of shit. Same taste as the smell. Now Locke's thumb was in there too, groping for Tommy's tongue; he writhed and shook his head but Locke's grip on his jaw was too strong. "Hey!" Billy was saying. "Let him go!" Locke pinched the tongue with his nails and the pain made Tommy's eyes fill. He stopped fighting and let him have it. "There you go now," Locke said, his eyebrows rising on the bald mound of his head as he pulled out the tongue. "There you go—ah, look at the size of it, no wonder you never speak. Smaller than a baby leech, that thing. Christ help you, boy. Your pizzle that small n'all?"

He brushed his hands and walked off laughing. Tommy retched and spat, and when he straightened Locke had picked up his reins, ready to lead his horse away.

"Keep the hammers down on them rifles, and that bloody revolver, else you'll get yourselves all excited and fire off too soon. I don't want one of you little cunts shooting me in the back."

Don't tempt me, Tommy thought, rinsing his mouth clean.

20

They led the horses around the waterhole and out through the last of the trees, then mounted up and rode west through the same terrain of stone-riddled soil, those uncanny rock mounds, a sparse smattering of bushes and scrub. Pope leading them, reading the trail, but even Tommy could make out the markings in the soil. Only faint, but there was no question: a series of human footprints, heel, arch, and toe; a scattering of paw tracks from the dogs. Tommy couldn't look at them, kept his eyes on the back of Billy's shirt. Someone had made those footprints. Someone with feet, legs, arms, heart. One looked as small as Mary's, just about. He exhaled shakily. He hadn't been expecting it, this sudden call to arms. And now there were footprints. These people they chased were real. Somehow being out here, surviving each day, had become an end in itself. Easy to forget it had only ever been the means.

Out of the trees meant out of the shade, into the blazing sun. It seared the ground before them and raised a haze upon the empty plains, no sign of the natives out there, they were beyond the horizon at least. In the distance the ranges loomed more clearly than Tommy had ever seen them, within reach by nightfall maybe. Not quite mountains, more substantial than hills, with rounded peaks and smooth hollows like something molded from a vast putty of dirty red clay. The base was fringed with trees and brush and the downslopes were scarred by a network of what looked to be canyons and caves. Plenty of places to hide in, plenty of routes to take. A slim hope sprang in him: if the natives reached the ranges, they might yet manage to escape.

It could never have been so simple: within two hours they had run them down, tiny ant-like shadows appearing on the trembling plain. Noone gave a cry and all spurred their horses and drove them mercilessly across that broken ground, riding high in the saddle and keen with the whip, Billy waving his revolver above his head while Tommy struggled to keep pace with the stampede, clinging to the reins and to Beau's body with his knees, eyes blurring, gasping at the air, a confusion of wind and glare and dust. He dipped his head against it and saw Billy's face peeled open in a joyful howl. Billy shouted something, whooped, pumped his revolver in the air, as all the while the figures grew closer on the plain. Their arms flailing, heads twisting, glancing behind them as they fled: five desperate natives and a scattered pack of dogs. The posse roared in unison and sent their calling on the wind. A calling of hatred and of bloodlust, and of thirty-six hooves pounding the red earth, which shook like the skin of a drum.

They overtook the natives and corralled them by circling the horses head to tail. Three men, two women, one of them very young, cowering together in a melee of wild dogs. All of them were naked, the women holding each other tightly by the arms, as if preparing to dance, and the men crouching with their spears raised ready to throw. They turned as the horses turned, bare feet shuffling in the dirt, eyes flashing around the circle as it closed and closed and closed.

Tommy scanned the men's faces: Joseph wasn't there.

The corral stopped revolving and the posse faced them front on. Everything was still. The horses panted from the chase, frothing at their mouths, bodies heaving with each breath, and the riders panted also, recovering themselves, rifles lowered or propped in the crook of an arm. The natives moved only their heads, twitching man to man. Tommy felt their eyes pass over him, felt their terror just the same, and realized that to them he was no different from Noone or anyone. He had drawn his rifle obediently; now he let it hang.

Some of the dogs began growling and barking. Maybe ten dogs in all, mangy and piebald, ribs jutting beneath their scarred coats. Not full dingo, not full anything, just dogs. A brown-haired thing, its yellow teeth bared, snapped at the shins of Locke's horse. The horse drew back, startled, nearly threw its mount. Locke righted him and leveled his carbine at the dog, then thought better of it and drew his sword instead. The blade was slightly curved and it glinted in the sun. Locke taunted the dog, waited for it to lunge again, and when it did so he leaned and ran the sword through its neck. A quick thrust, in and out: the dog keeled onto its side, bright blood spurting, and sniggering rippled briefly around the corral.

Locke examined his bloodstained blade, ceremoniously turning it this way and that, then he stared at the natives and settled on the nearest man. The man still had his spear raised. It was aimed directly at Locke. Locke pointed the bloodied sword at him and roared, held it until his breath gave, the only sound out there, echoing all around. His face turning red, his chest swollen, purple veins bulging on his skull. When finally the roar left him, he took a long breath, glanced at Sullivan beside him, and laughed.

The native threw his spear.

He launched it without warning, without back lift, the shaft quivering softly as it flew, followed by a hushed tearing sound as it pierced Locke's skin. Barely a sound at all. Like a knife through an unripe pear. Locke reeled from the blow and for a second sat there looking at the spear. It was embedded in his shoulder, a few inches above his heart. He tried to cry out but hadn't the breath; the cry gargled in his throat. He looked at the native. The man was crouched as if ready to run. Locke dropped his sword. It landed beside the dead dog. He reached for his carbine but struggled to free it from the strap. The spear wagged as he moved. He took hold of the shaft with both hands, as if to pull it out, then in one quick jolt he snapped it and seethed with pain. Spittle foamed between his teeth. His face was damp and pale. Only the surge of his breathing in the silence of the tight corral. The others watching on, their rifles aimed at the spear carriers, whose spears sagged slightly in their hands.

Locke unstrapped his carbine, wheeled it around, and took aim. His face and head glistened. Sweat streamed into his eyes. The carbine trembled in his hand and he tried to steady it with his left forearm but the arm wouldn't fully raise.

"Well?" he shouted, wiping his brow with his sleeve. He stared at the native and the native returned the stare.

Noone rolled his eyes and nodded.

"Aye, get on with it," Sullivan said.

Locke leveled the carbine again. The barrel wavered horribly. Still the man didn't move. Facing his assassin down. Locke drew the air hard and fast through his nose, breath after surging breath, then suddenly the breathing stalled. His trigger finger clenched. An almighty noise spewed from the rifle's maw and the recoil threw Locke's arm high above his head. There was screaming. A flurry of canine howls. Locke straightened and peered at the native but the native crouched before him, unhurt. Another dog collapsed to the ground, half its side blown out.

"Christ in hell," Sullivan said. "Can't you just shoot the bloody thing?"

Locke cursed and tried to reload, fumbling a cartridge from his belt, pinning the carbine in his armpit and pawing at the chamber bolt. Blood seeped from his shoulder and spread on his shirt. His hands trembled. Grunting darkly as he worked. The woman began talking, high-pitched and desperate, pleading for mercy, maybe. She spoke to the troopers, the whites; all ignored her. Everyone waiting for Locke. But he fumbled the new cartridge and dropped it on the ground, and as he fished out another Sullivan groaned and lit a cigarette, and on the far side of the corral Noone swung over a leg and jumped down from his horse.

"Alright," he said. "That's enough from you."

"I ain't done with that bastard yet. Look what he did to my fucking arm."

"It won't kill you," Noone said. He waded through the dogs, then stood towering over the natives, who gawped up at him in awe. He looked feral. His shirt was ragged and his hair was wild, his face dark with stubble and his empty eyes very wide. In his hand he carried an ornate silver revolver; it dangled casually at his side. He stood regarding the natives awhile. Two of the men still brandished their spears, the tips only yards from Noone's face. Could have been through his skull before he'd even had time to blink, Tommy thought. Yet Noone stood there perfectly calm, a slight frown, as if reckoning something about the scene, while around him the others waited, Sullivan smoking his cigarette, Locke fiddling with the spear stub embedded in his shoulder. He glared at the man who'd thrown it.

"You'll get yours," he said.

Now Noone raised his left hand in greeting, fingers

straight, palm flat. The natives watched the hand fearfully. The woman pulled the girl close. And she was a girl: while the woman was full in the hips, belly, and chest, the girl's body was straight up and down, barely adolescent, little different than a boy.

"Please," Noone said kindly, lowering his hand. "Drop the spears. Go on now. This isn't a fight you are going to win."

Their eyes wandered. To each other, the troopers, perhaps hoping they would translate but they did not. Noone waited. The young girl peeked out from the woman's side and he smiled at her, the smile fading the longer the two men took to comply.

Noone tilted his head slightly, and in a low voice told them, "I won't ask again. Drop the fucking spears."

Neither man did so. Noone turned his eyes skyward and shook his head, let out a heavy breath. Then he raised his pistol and shot the nearest spear carrier square in his face.

The head burst in a spatter of tissue and bone, spraying Noone and the natives and some of the dogs. The body collapsed in stages—waist, knees, legs—then slumped awkwardly face-first on the ground. The spear seesawed before coming to rest in the dirt. The girl was screaming, a chaos of dogs leaped and howled, a cheer rippled through the group, and Sullivan shouted, "Now that's how you bloody do it!" while Tommy leaned and retched at the side of his horse.

"Don't," Billy said. "Stop it. Sit up."

Tommy felt hands on his shirt, Billy dragging him upright; he brushed him away and did it on his own, sat there coughing and gasping and finding nothing but irritation in his brother's face, no upset, no concern. Tommy wiped his mouth and spat. Billy tapped his shoulder and gestured for him to watch.

Neither Noone nor the natives had moved. They stood dripping in the dead man's gore. The girl cried into the woman's side, the woman's hand clamped over her mouth. All were trembling. The last remaining spear carrier placed his spear carefully on the ground and stepped back, and Noone nodded like a courtesy had been observed. He picked at his chest and shirtfront, flicking away deposits of bloodied flesh and bone.

"There there," he said idly. "There there."

When he'd finished his preening, Noone stepped over the body, parted the men, and stood before the woman and girl. Neither would look at him. Noone reached between them and tried peeling them apart, but they squealed like they'd been burned and only clung to each other all the more. Noone frowned, stuffed his revolver into his waistband, and held them each by the jaw, cheeks bunching, lips puckering; both had their eyes clamped shut, sobbing quietly as he turned their faces back and forth in the low sunlight.

"Look at me."

They would not.

"Look at me."

He let go of the girl, pulled his revolver again, and leveled it at one of the men. The muzzle butted against his temple: he flinched but otherwise didn't move. Noone corkscrewed the barrel into the side of his head and the native grimaced and moaned. Now the women were looking. Watching Noone toy with their man.

"Thank you," he said. He put away the revolver and took hold of the woman's hand. She watched him raise it daintily above her head. Noone tried leading her but the girl had the other wrist and would not let go. Noone looked at her. The muscles on his jawline clenched. The older woman spoke and the girl hesitated, then released her wrist. Noone brought the woman out into the open and like some bloodied whoremaster began a ceremonial lap of the corral, to the grunts and calls and whistles of the watching men.

"She'll do," Sullivan mumbled, flicking away his cigarette. "Yep, she'll do."

Tommy tried not to watch. He turned away but saw Billy eyeing the woman up and down, and heard across the circle Jarrah and Mallee clapping and howling, telling the woman what they planned to do to her, what they planned for her to do.

"We don't got time for all this," Locke grumbled. He leaned in the saddle and with his rifle muzzle hooked his sword through its guard and lifted it from the ground. He sheathed it and poked idly at the spear. A fresh gout of blood bubbled from the wound. "I need this thing out my shoulder, get the hole properly packed."

"You'd be at it worse than them if you'd not got yourself hurt," Sullivan said.

"Good of you to bloody notice, I'm sure."

"Ah, stop whining. You should have shot the bugger when you had the chance."

"I ain't done with that cunt yet."

"So you keep saying," Sullivan said, chuckling. "But you'll have to find a way to reload your carbine first."

Noone finished his presentation, released the woman back into the group, and steered the girl forward by the waist. He did not offer her to the other men. Instead he led her to his own horse, where he took a handkerchief from his pack and began dabbing at her tenderly, swabbing the mess away. The girl stood rigidly before him. Noone cleaned her cheeks, her neck, her chest, and her eyes never once left his face. While he worked, Noone called for Jarrah and Rabbit to see to the others: they dismounted and unraveled the neck chains, kicking aside the dogs. Rabbit brought the two men into line and Jarrah positioned the woman behind them, and like bewildered children they stood meekly as the chain was hung and the neck cuffs clamped shut. Jarrah groped the woman. Between her legs, her buttocks, her breasts. He grinned at her. She spat in his face. Jarrah slapped her and laughed and went back to his horse, and Tommy heard Sullivan mutter, "He can wait his fucking turn."

Noone put the girl on his saddle, climbed up behind. He gave her his longcoat, draped it over her shoulders, she pulled the collar tight to her neck. Noone reached around for the reins, then left his hands there, clasped around her middle, the fingers of one hand splayed on the bare skin of her belly where the folds of the coat did not meet. He checked the group behind him and they rode on, making for the ranges again, each taking his place in line, Tommy behind his brother, same as it had always been. He could not see the captives without turning around and could not see the girl in front: he pinned his eyes on Billy's back and tried to forget what had just occurred over the past quarter hour. He shook his head. Only a quarter hour they'd been waylaid. No longer than if they'd stopped to piss or fill their flasks. But now they rode to a percussion of neck chains and left a dead man in their wake, a pack of wild dogs picking at his body and the two of their own Locke had killed. A quarter hour, and all was changed.

21

In the last of the twilight they tied the horses in the trees and shambled with their packs up the rubbled hillside, dragging their captives high into the ranges and the smooth-walled canyon in which they made camp. A long and bell-shaped runnel hollowed out by the wind, broad in the belly and narrow at the neck, twisting like a wormhole through the rock. Dark in there too, little moonlight through the slim gap, only the fire to see by once they'd got one lit: the wood burned quick and hot and the curved walls cradled the warmth.

The group laid out their things. Bedrolls, weapons, packs, the whites taking up positions nearest the fire, the troopers staying close to the prisoners they held. They'd been separated: the women seated with their wrists bound on a ledge formed by the rock face; the men chained together on the other side of the canyon, back-to-back on the floor. Rabbit guarded the men; the others watched the woman and girl. Perched on their ledge, they sat with their heads down and their hands between their legs, the woman entirely naked still, the girl wearing Noone's longcoat. All eyes on them. Sly and lustful stares. The occasional catcall. They didn't ever respond. Leaning their shoulders and sometimes their heads together and closing their eyes as if asleep.

Supper was damper bread and the last of the roo meat—sweaty now, and tough, but it hadn't yet turned—and afterward the group lazed about, smoking and taking their rest. Locke claimed a bottle of rum and wouldn't give it up on any account, argued it helped soothe the pain of his wound. Pope was to see to it after supper: despite Locke's protests, Noone had refused it done sooner. It could wait until they'd eaten, he said.

So Locke staggered around camp with the bottle in his hand, babbling like a barroom prophet and ignored by the rest of the group. He talked to the troopers, to the captives, to the moon and the stars in the sky. Like a fool ranting wildly in the streets. When he passed by the man who had stuck him, he sank down before him in a crouch. Peering into his face, but the man wouldn't meet his eye. Locke took hold of his hair. It was short and knotted, and he gripped it like a fleece. He hoisted the man's face level with his own, then let go of the hair and slid a finger up the man's torso: crotch, belly, neck.

"I'm gonna gut you, nigger."

"Leave him," Noone warned, talking directly to the fire. "We've questions that need answering first."

"So long as I get what's owed after."

"Being what exactly?"

"This darkie's head on a stick."

Noone turned his gaze on Tommy and Billy and regarded the brothers gravely. "I'd say these two boys have a better claim on him than you."

Locke rose and lumbered to the fireside, stood over the gathered whites. "It wasn't them two that did their lot. Fucker speared me, though."

"And how are you so sure it wasn't them?"

"Their two blackboys done it—ain't that what you said?"

"What I was told," Noone corrected. A lengthy silence hung. "Either way, they're due a killing. Two of theirs for two of ours. You'll remember that you were afforded the same courtesy, and with it you shot a dog."

Locke stood there dumbly. He took a pull of rum. The liquid sloshed in the bottle and he gulped it down his throat, eyeing Tommy as he drank. Tommy looked away. Locke finished and wiped his mouth and shifted his weight from foot to foot, then he turned and moved on again. Reeling toward the troopers, calling, "Priest, I'm sick of waiting. Come and fix me fucking arm."

"Think on it," Noone told the boys softly. "Perhaps in the morning, if you'd prefer."

Billy frowned like he was still catching up with what had been proposed.

"You mean for us to shoot them?" Tommy said.

"Yes."

"Just like that? For no reason?"

"For every reason. The reason we are all here. Wait and hear their confession, see if that won't change your mind."

At which Sullivan snorted in laughter like a joke had just been told.

Through the smoke and flames Tommy watched the two chained men. They didn't look much like killers. Naked and filthy and bloodstained, caked in their own piss and mess, they looked miserable and hungry and scared. Their faces were gaunt, ribs visible under the skin. They were still only young, Tommy thought. Be lucky if they were out of their teens. Yes, one had put his spear into Locke, but in his position Tommy would probably have done the same. As would Billy, Sullivan, and no doubt Locke himself. As would any man.

There was a squeal, and Tommy turned. Locke had begun molesting the woman with his one good hand.

She wriggled and squirmed on the ledge. Locke cooed at her and mimicked a mouth with his hand, like it was a puppet, a bird. In a childish high-pitched voice he made the creature talk, telling her where it would nibble next, then he plunged the hand downward, grabbing for her breasts, between her legs. The troopers scowled at his performance and spoke between themselves.

"Best control him, John," Noone said. "The men are not amused."

"They can please themselves. It ain't none of their business what he does."

"He's insulting them. They covet her, consider her theirs."

"Horseshit, theirs. They should learn their fucking place."

"Well, I won't discipline them. Not for him. The man's a buffoon."

"They've no bloody respect. You're too soft on 'em, that's what you are."

"You haven't the faintest idea what I am."

Locke was now grabbing his crotch and humping his own hand. "Raymond," Sullivan called. "Leave the gin alone."

"Oh, but she's a shy one. I'm only warming her up."

Behind him Jarrah rose slowly to his feet, stepped

over Pope's outstretched legs, and walked toward Locke, squinting at him, his lazy, half-closed eye. He was unarmed but his hands hung heavy at his sides, the fingers curled almost to fists.

Locke caught sight of him and chuckled. "Wait your turn, darkie. Whites before blacks is how it goes."

Jarrah didn't answer him. Advancing carefully, one step at a time. Locke turned to face him front on, only six feet between them now.

"Oh, aye? And what's this?"

"Call back your boy," Sullivan told Noone. "The hell's he think he is?"

Noone was tamping tobacco into the bowl of his pipe. His eyebrows lifted and he smiled at Sullivan. But he didn't call Jarrah off.

They fronted each other. Shadowy figures in the firelight, Locke's pale head glistening. Physically they were even, similar height and build. Locke placed the bottle of rum carefully on the ground, then stood with his chin tucked and his good fist raised in an uncertain boxing pose. Jarrah waited. Locke rocked on his heels and ducked his head from side to side, weighing up his move, but comically, as if putting on a show. He paused, began laughing, then pulled back his fist and swung.

The punch looped wildly toward the trooper's face; Jarrah parried it and coiled Locke's arm inside his own, pinning it behind his back. He stepped forward, tightened his grip, and Locke arched his back and cried out, his injured arm twitching lamely at his side. Jarrah held him there awhile. Their faces were very close. Jarrah said something, but quietly, his voice a low rumble in the white man's ear. He raised his free hand and held it above Locke's face, the fingers clawed. Locke watched the hand fearfully. Jarrah lowered it toward the spear. He took hold of the broken shaft and rotated it slowly around. Locke's eyes widened. He groaned in muted pain. Jarrah began inching out the spear, teasing it from the wound.

"Fucking—" Locke slurred, but no other words came.

As the spear left his body his mouth gaped, his legs buckled, his eyes rolled. Jarrah laid him on the ground. He tossed the spear stub aside. It tinkled on the stone and the sound echoed around the walls. The woman slid from the ledge and began begging him, her bound hands raised. Jarrah shoved her backward. She shuffled back onto the ledge. Jarrah returned to his place and sat down, took a turn on the pipe the troopers shared. They were struggling to hide their amusement, like some great mischief had just been performed.

Sullivan shook his head. "And you'll stand for that, will you?"

"I'm not obliged to him, John. He hasn't the temperament for this kind of work. Treats it like a sport, which it is not. It is not. I warned you both the last time. You should have left him on the farm."

Noone pulled contemplatively on his pipe. Tommy watched Locke's prone body and in the firelight could just make out the rise and fall of his chest, and a small pool of fresh blood collecting beneath him on the ground.

"You rub him up wrong," Sullivan mumbled. "That's all it is. But you let them treat a whitefella like that and there'll be a mutiny next. Mark my words there will."

"Their problem's not with me."

"All I'm saying is they'd better know their place. I shouldn't have to watch my back against my own bloody men."

"My men."

"Last time I checked I was the one paying for all this."

"Actually, Her Majesty's government is footing the bill."

"So what the hell am I buying, then?"

"You are paying me, not them. Buying my cooperation in your little charade, plus passage for yourself and your boys. You are buying my attention, John. The frontier is a big place. There are plenty other errands I could run."

"Still. A bit of fucking respect wouldn't hurt."

"You'd be a fool not to be wary of them," Noone said, smoking, staring into the fire. "All that money of yours, all that cattle, that land, even the color of your skin carries little weight out here. What do you think they care for all that? For your wealth, your authority back home? Don't equate them to your houseboys; the two are not remotely alike. Truth is, my men only tolerate you in deference to me, your monkey man even less so. They are not civilized, they are not tame. If we did that to them, they'd be about as useful a gelded bull. The point is, John, the problem doesn't lie with them but with you and Raymond and maybe even these two boys."

He withdrew his pipe and gestured to the canyon, the sky, the country beyond.

"Look where we are. This isn't your station anymore, isn't even part of the colony, whatever the map says. You need to recognize that fact. Your so-called laws and principles, they do not apply here. White men come this far out and think they're still in Queensland, but they're not. This is blackfella country. We're in their territory now."

When the meal was over, Pope came and knelt at

Locke's side, peeled back his shirt collar, and cleaned his injured shoulder with rum. On a flat boulder top, he emptied a handful of leaves and berries and other bush pickings from a pigskin pouch, and began tearing and grinding them into a mixture that he moistened with saliva until it became a coarse yellow paste. He cupped the paste in his hands, warming it, kneading it, tossing it gently back and forth like a baker working dough, then knelt again and packed the putty into Locke's wound. He pressed with his thumbs and then his palm, building the plug piece by piece, and through all of this Locke did not so much as flinch. A full half hour now he'd been out. Pope unraveled the bandage Locke wore on his hand and used it to dress the shoulder wound. He examined the injured hand, held it up to the firelight, and turned it around. The flesh was raw and mottled and not yet healed. Two well-spaced bite marks had punctured deep into the skin. He called over to Noone and asked what had bit him.

"Snake, so he said."

"Bloody big snake with dog tooth that bugger," Pope replied, letting the hand fall. He pushed himself to his feet and stood looking down on Locke. In the firelight Pope's face was haggard and very old, and there was no emotion in his eyes. As indifferent to the creature beneath him as if it were a lame mule.

Wearily Noone rose too. He tapped his pipe into the fire and the dead tobacco hissed. "Bring the men," he said. "Rabbit, watch the girl. And don't let that fire go out, though I doubt this will take very long."

He looked pointedly at Sullivan, who nodded and said, "Right you are," rubbing his hands together like a feast had been proposed.

And with that Noone was gone, striding past the troopers and disappearing along the dark ravine. Jarrah and Mallee fetched the two men and dragged them up to their feet. They could hardly stand. Their chains were unlocked and unwound and they fell to the ground with a clang. Rabbit stooped and gathered the chains in his hands, and the captives were led into the ravine. Pope followed them out of camp. One by one they vanished into the cleft of the rocks, until all that remained was the sound of footsteps on bare stone and the whimpering pleas of the men.

Sullivan clapped his hands. He stumbled to his feet. He went to where the woman and girl were sitting and took hold of the woman by her wrists. Briefly she fought him, then complied, sliding off the ledge. Sullivan slapped her anyway. Backhanded across the face. Her head twisted and she stared at the girl, then she turned toward Sullivan again. Dead-eyed. Resigned. Sullivan smiled. He led her past the fire, pausing to collect his revolver, which he showed to the woman, then pushed inside his belt. He looked down at Tommy and Billy, asked them, "Don't suppose either of you two wants a go on her when I'm done?"

Tommy felt himself flushing. A rush of panic and blood. Billy sat there blinking like he hadn't even heard. Tommy couldn't look at the woman, or at the girl. By now Rabbit had finished coiling the chains; he dumped them on the ground and nodded at Tommy. Tommy lurched to his feet and, for want of anything else to do, fetched fresh firewood from the pile.

"You've never done it before, have you?" Sullivan asked Billy.

"It ain't that."

"What then? Don't be scared, son. They're all the same down below."

Tommy threw the wood on the fire and sat down. A shower of sparks rose.

"I ain't scared. It's just—"

"Look, I'm not going to force you," Sullivan told him. "But you do this and shoot that other black like he said and you'll be a man by morning, simple as that. It's up to you. But think on it too long and Locke'll have killed both them cunts and Noone's boys'll have had their way with the gin, and she won't be no good to you then."

He shoved her out of camp, the opposite direction from that which Noone had taken the men, back toward where the horses were tethered and a shallow cave they'd passed coming in. The woman struggled briefly but soon relented, and the last Tommy saw of them was the revolver pinned to her spine and Sullivan's hand clamped on her bare backside, the fingers pressed hard into the skin.

They were alone. Tommy and Billy, Rabbit and the girl, not one of them yet adult. Locke snored as he slept. The fresh wood crackled on the fire. Lightning flashed silently: no rain, no thunder, a white pulse in the darkness and that was all. Tommy watched it fading, the sky seeping to black, and noticed the girl watching it too. She was shivering. Rabbit sat beside her now, cross-legged beneath the ledge, studying his fingernails. Again the lightning flashed. A volley of laughter carried faintly along the canyon and all of them looked up.

"Them buggers get it now," Rabbit said absently.

"Look at her shivering," Tommy whispered, but his brother was elsewhere, scowling hard into the fire, cheeks drawn, chewing on his lip. "Billy—the girl. We should bring her over here."

"What for?"

"She's not got any clothes on. Be warmer by the fire."

He looked at her. "She's got a coat, hasn't she? Why d'you even care?"

"You're thinking on it, aren't you? Doing what he said?"

Billy's hind teeth clenched. He wouldn't meet Tommy's eye.

"Have you not got a mind of your own? There's him with a wife at home and look how he carries on—that's how you want to be?"

"You don't know nothing about it."

"What would Daddy say? Or Ma? Bad enough we're even out here but—"

"Daddy wouldn't say a bloody thing," Billy snapped. "He was weak, Tommy; it's time you saw him for what he was. He spent his whole life with his back turned and his head down, and look what he became. Poor and half-starved and dead on his own front porch. I don't aim to end up the same."

"You're a fucking mongrel. Here," Tommy called to the girl, "come and get warm."

"I said no."

"I ain't asking."

Tommy waved the girl forward. Her big eyes watched him but she stayed where she was. First Tommy stood, then Billy, blocking his path.

"Reckon you're the boss now?" Tommy said.

"I'd say so. My little brother plus two blacks puts me in charge of camp."

"You ain't the boss of me. Or him even." Tommy pointed at Rabbit, still sitting on the ground with his long legs crossed. "She's not but Mary's age, Billy. Look at her shivering. What harm would it do?"

Billy glanced between them, then threw up his hands. "Ah, fuck it. Do what you want and answer for it. I'm not stopping around."

He went to leave but Tommy grabbed him. "Don't. Not that."

"Not what? I'm checking on the horses, if that's alright by you."

"You're checking on the horses?"

"Aye, the horses." He shook off Tommy's grip but wouldn't look at him.

"You're not going to find them? Sullivan?"

"I just told you, didn't I?"

"It ain't right. Being with a woman like that."

"What would you know about being with a woman?"

"I know it ain't right that way. I know that much."

"Well, what I know is I can't stand listening to you whining like a bloody pup anymore. It's time you grew up, Tommy. See things for what they are. Glendale's gone. Ma, Daddy, Mary—all of them are gone. So now we have to choose. Either we roll over like he did or face the world front on, bollocks first, like men."

There was a silence. Tommy said quietly, "That Sullivan's speech or yours?"

Billy didn't answer. He shrugged past his brother and marched along the ravine, and for a while Tommy stood watching helplessly, then hung his head and looked at the others again. Rabbit on his feet now, guarding the girl.

"Just . . . come over here. Both of you."

"Watch girl, Marmy says."

The word was lost on him. He had never heard the troopers call Noone by that name before. "You can still sit with her," Tommy said. "But he already gave her his coat—he won't be happy if she's cold."

Rabbit stood thinking, then pulled the girl roughly from the ledge. The coat slid from her shoulders and her nakedness was all the more shocking to Tommy for having been so long concealed.

"Cover her," he said, averting his eyes. "Bring the bloody coat."

They seated themselves self-consciously around the fire—Tommy opposite the girl, Rabbit between them—and for a while said nothing at all. Rabbit held his hands to the flames and the girl let go three great shivers as the warmth worked its way to her bones. Tommy watched her furtively. Watched the flames cast their shadows on her cheeks. He had not been so close to her before and wondered if he'd misjudged her age. There was a sadness in her face that made her seem much older than eleven. Older than himself, even. Or maybe she was only scared.

"Tell her . . ." Tommy said, then faltered. "Tell her that she's safe, that we won't do what they're doing to her friend."

Rabbit smiled at him conspiratorially, like this was some kind of ruse.

"I mean it. Can you tell her that? Please."

As the trooper spoke, the girl stared blankly into the flames.

"Did she hear you? Did you say what I said?"

"Is different words. Not all blackfella talk same."

"So she doesn't understand you?"

Rabbit shrugged. They sat in silence again. Another lightning flash.

"They said you were from New South Wales?" Tommy asked.

Rabbit nodded, said a word Tommy didn't catch. Sounded like *a jury*.

"What is that? A town?"

"Is people. Not much that mob left no more. Them all gone bung."

Tommy looked down at his hands. He could hear raised voices and a distant slapping sound, no telling from which direction it came.

"They killed my family too. What happened to yours?"

"Was long time ago. Small Rabbit then." His face was set, the expression severe, talking into the flames. "Plenty blackfella before Rabbit born, now is small mob blackfella, big mob whitefella. We is running, running, hiding, hiding. Then one whitefella come looking, says good job here Queensland, join up whitefella mob. Is better in big mob, I reckon. I says yes."

"You . . . chose to be here? Why?"

"Here tucker, shillings, woman, grog. Learn white-fella ways. Show them other black buggers who boss here now."

"By hunting your own people?"

Rabbit shrugged. "Them not own people. And is law, Marmy says."

"Don't you . . . I mean, don't you want to go home?"

He said it sadly, quietly: "Is no more home."

Tommy stared into the fire. He had assumed the troopers must have been press-ganged into service, not here of their own free will. If it could be called free will. Your family all dead and nowhere to turn, so you side with the enemy to get by. He could understand how that felt. Maybe not wholly, but he had an idea.

The girl had been watching them talk. Listening, it seemed. Tommy nodded at her. "What's her name?" he asked Rabbit. Then to the girl: "What's your name?"

She looked uncertainly at each of them. Tommy pointed to himself and gave his name, then to Rabbit and gave his, then extended his finger toward her.

"Kala," she said in a low voice. She tapped her chest and repeated it: "Kala."

"Kala," Tommy echoed. "Are you thirsty? You want water?"

He mimicked drinking, the girl nodded. Tommy sprang to his feet and hunted out his flask. Not full or fresh still, but he gave her what he had. She sniffed the open neck, tested it, then gulped the contents down.

"There's not much to eat, neither," Tommy was saying, casting about the camp for food. He found only a piece of damper crust and a stale hunk of roo; the girl refused the roo but held the bread in her bound hands and nibbled at its end.

"I know—just a minute, wait here."

He went to where his bedroll and saddlebag were piled against the canyon wall, and from the bag retrieved the packet of lemon sweets. There were roughly half a dozen left. He took out three, replaced the packet in the bag, then squatted between Rabbit and the girl—Kala, he reminded himself, Kala is her name.

"Here, take one. You suck them. They're good."

Rabbit snatched a lolly and tossed it into his mouth. His eyes flared and he grinned. Tommy waited with his hand outstretched. Kala reached out hesitantly and twisted one hand over the other, pivoting her wrists. She picked up the lolly and examined it, sniffed it, touched it with her tongue. Tommy nodded her on. She watched him very carefully, her eyes searching his, and when she slid the little lolly into her mouth and faintly smiled, the intimacy sent a tingle right through him. He crawled back to his place at the fireside and in the warmth and the silence the three of them sat together, contentedly sucking on their sweets, as the lightning crackled above them and the echoes of grunting and whip cracks came whispering through the ravine.

· · ·

In the night he heard her crying. Kala. A soft and high-pitched whimpering beyond the coughs and snores. Tommy lifted his head and searched the shapes and shadows, the dark lumps of bodies curled on the bare ground. The fire was down. A deep charcoal glow but little light to see. He waited for his vision to come. Listening to Kala's muffled sobs. He made out Billy and Sullivan, Locke and Rabbit, Jarrah, Mallee, and maybe Pope. And then there she was, lying near the wall, on her back with her bound hands covering her face and the longcoat spread open at her sides. Noone lay beside her. He was raised on his elbow, cradling his head in his hand. Talking to her. Whispering. A dreadful low hum. He lifted his eyes—chalk-white in the darkness—to look directly at Tommy but did not stop talking to the girl. There was movement. Noone's other hand. It crawled pale and spiderlike over her skin. Tommy lowered himself back down. He rolled onto his side and closed his eyes. Noone hushed the girl but she would not stop crying.

22

The gunshot woke him into a mad scramble of men fighting off their bedrolls and lunging for their weapons, as the booming pistol report caromed around the chamber walls. Tommy went for his rifle but it wasn't there. He hadn't slept with it to hand. On his knees he crawled through a chaos of shouting to where it lay beneath his pack, and had only just reached the stock when he felt the tension in camp subside. He glanced over his shoulder and saw weapons slowly coming down.

"Christ in hell, Raymond," Sullivan said. "You nearly got yourself killed."

Locke was standing over the two male prisoners, his back to the group, pistol raised, and seemingly oblivious to the panic he had caused. Overnight the men had been rechained back-to-back and reseated by the wall. Now one was rocking and moaning, his face crumpled, his eyes clenched, while behind him the other slumped forward, a deadweight held in place by the chains. Locke had shot him through the head. The plum-sized hole steamed. A smell of burned powder in the air.

Locke turned and surveyed the group as if surprised to find them there. His face was sickly white, his eyes red, his skin lathered in sweat. He flexed his wounded shoulder and stretched out his neck until it clicked, then scratched his cheek bashfully with the pistol end.

"Well, I told you. Told that bastard too. Didn't mean to scare no one."

A grumble rippled through the group. Hesitantly Locke returned to his bedroll and began packing up his things. Noone was glaring at him. Locke kept his head down. "There any breakfast?" he asked. "I'm hungry as a horse without teeth."

The camp settled. No one paid the dead man any more attention than when he was alive. Tommy looked for the girl and found her huddled against the wall, knees to her chin, alone. Noone wasn't with her, and the woman wasn't there; Tommy waited for Kala to notice him but she did not. She stared only at the dead man; Tommy looked at him anew. He'd been someone to her, he reminded himself. A brother, a friend. Like he'd seen Billy executed just now. And yet around them the camp was rousing as if nothing out of the ordinary had occurred. Men rolling up their swags, pulling on their boots, shaking off the cold of the night. The fire was rekindled. Tea was boiled. Like any other morning on earth.

"Some cockcrow that," Billy said, appearing at Tommy's side. He was tying his own bedroll, fiddling with the knot, trying to appear casual but he did not look well. Eyes like mad cattle, his complexion watery and gray.

"It's like he ain't nothing," Tommy said. "No better than a dog."

Billy glanced to where the two men were chained. One holding up the other, fighting his deadweight pull. Billy spat on the ground.

"Worse than dogs, both of them. Murdering bastards, that's what they are."

"How's that now?"

"They confessed."

"Confessed to what?"

"What d'you reckon? Gave up Joseph and all them other cunts."

"There were no other cunts, Billy. You made the other cunts up."

"Keep your voice down."

"You've swallowed your own bloody lie!"

"There might have been others, we don't know there weren't. Anyway, they confessed, I just told you. Only a day or so's ride, Noone says."

Tommy watched his brother doubtfully. Billy went on fumbling with his pack.

"And when did he tell you all this?"

"Last night. After you turned in. I'd have woken you but . . ."

Billy waved his hand, indicating the nature of things between them after he'd returned to camp, more reticent and flush-faced than anyone checking on horses ought to have been. Seeing him, Rabbit had hauled up the girl and taken her back to the ledge, and if Billy had noticed the goodwill between the three of them, he was too preoccupied to care. He sat down by the fire and took a slug of rum and ignored Tommy's glaring.

"You did it," Tommy had said finally. "You did it, I know."

Billy wouldn't answer him. Wouldn't look anywhere but the flames. Soon Sullivan returned also, dragging the woman along. She was limp and walked unsteadily and held a hand to her face. She'd been crying.

"Sure I can't tempt you?" Sullivan had said with a grin.

He'd spoken to Tommy, and Tommy alone. Billy's

head hung. Tommy turned away from both of them and lay down on his bedroll. At one point he'd heard Noone returning with the men, then Jarrah and Mallee taking the woman away for themselves; at another he must have, mercifully, fallen asleep.

"Where's she at, anyway?" Tommy asked Billy now. "The woman, where's she gone?"

"I ain't seen her," Billy said.

"You seen her plenty last night."

"They never brought her back after. The blacks."

"Meaning you know exactly where she's at, what they've done."

"Just quit, will you. She's only a gin."

Tommy walked away, sat down by the fire, drank tea from a stained and flaking tin cup he cradled in his hands for warmth. Noone was giving a briefing. He stood beside the two chained men. Based on their information there was perhaps only one more day of hard riding, he said, gesturing at the men as if acknowledging the contribution they had made to the cause. The one still able did not look up. He slumped miserably with the body on his back. Noone finished talking, then came to sit with Tommy at the fireside. He called Billy over, then when both brothers were seated, offered them the chance to take the remaining man's life.

"What did they tell you?" Tommy asked. "Last night—what did they say?"

"The evidence will show that both of these men know Joseph. And that they were in the group which came to your property and killed Mr. and Mrs. McBride."

Tommy glanced at the man sniveling by the wall. "He said that?"

"It will be in the evidence. A matter of record. A proven fact."

"I don't—is that what he said, or what you're saying?"

"You doubt me, Tommy?"

"He just don't look like much, that's all."

"He ain't," Billy said. "I already told you that."

Noone leaned close, looking one to the other and back again. In his empty eyes Tommy saw the outline of a pupil, a deep, dark circle shrouded in fog.

"Listen," Noone said. "Listen to me now. I'm going to tell you what will happen if we were to let that man live. He will hate us. Not only you and I personally, but all white men. He will become like a tick on the back of a beautiful horse, biting and gnawing and burrowing into the very fabric of this country we are trying to build. He will hunt us, all of us, we will never be safe in our homes. Your families, should you have

them, will not be safe. Your children, your grandchil-
dren, will not be safe. Remember, he will breed also.
He will produce a dozen heirs, all with his hatred in
their blood. In the cities they talk of civilizing them, of
whites and blacks living side by side. It is a noble ideal.
It reads very well in a newspaper or book. But tell me,
boys—you have seen it, the reality out here—do either
of you think that can ever be done? Those people on
the coast, they expect the black man to throw down
his spear and integrate, like he realizes suddenly he's
been living all wrong. It is laughable, the ignorance of
the educated classes, sitting in their parlors and their
clubs. The blacks don't want to *integrate*. They want
for us to *leave*. So either we domesticate them, or we
kill them; there really can be no other way. The truth
is, it doesn't matter whether this man killed your family or not. He would have done so if given half a chance,
and he will do so again. We cannot release him, we
cannot take him with us, so we must shoot him. The
only question is whether you two will pull the trigger,
and take your share of responsibility for what must be
done?"

"I will," Billy said. "I'll kill the cunt."

"Good lad, Billy," Sullivan called. "Well said."

"And you?" Noone asked, as each of them stood.

Billy answered for his brother: "He doesn't have to. I already said I would."

"You should both do it. Fire at the same time. No dissenters, remember."

"Just give him to Billy," Sullivan said. "The other's as green as a tree frog. He's got his father's spine. Ned had no stomach for this kind of thing."

"As I recall," Noone said, "you once told me the opposite."

Sullivan laughed and shook his head. "Long time ago, that."

"You never were a good judge of a man, John. You underestimate this one. I don't expect that you'll listen to me, but you're courting the wrong son."

Something in Tommy quickened at the praise and he hated himself for it. Billy cast about for a weapon, found his rifle, strode over to the chained man, and took aim. The man cowered behind his hands. From across the camp Kala began shouting, begging, and the man spoke to her through his fingers. His voice was broken but firm. Kala quietened. She held herself, sobbing gently, rocking back and forth.

"Hold up, lad," Sullivan said, grabbing Billy's arm. "Not with the rifle, not in here." He motioned to Locke, who gave his pistol, the same percussion revolver he had used on the other man. Sullivan inspected the chamber. "Loaded? Capped?"

"I put two shots in," Locke said, shrugging. "Just in case."

Billy took the revolver and weighed it in his hand. All eyes on him now. Noone leaned and whispered to Tommy, "You should be part of this. It's more important than you think." He nudged him. Tommy looked down. Noone was offering his pistol. A gleaming silver Colt self-cocking revolver, ornately patterned on the barrel and grip. Tommy kept his hands at his sides, as Billy cranked back the hammer and pointed Locke's pistol at the native's head. He stood with his legs wide, arms straight, but couldn't halt the tremor in his hands. The native watched through his fingertips, damp lips moving, a faint plea or prayer, as all the while Noone whispered in Tommy's ear:

"I heard your father was more efficient. John once spoke highly of his skills. Of course, this was before you knew him, but then you can never truly know. The men on John's station used to hunt them for pay. Same as you would a dingo, a shilling per scalp, though perhaps it was more or less, I'm not sure. For some it proved very lucrative. Helped them get ahead."

He was still offering the revolver. Tommy only half understood. His eyes were fixed on Billy, though he couldn't see his brother's face. From behind it didn't even look like him. Everything was wrong. That wasn't Billy's shooting stance. He never shot square on.

Billy shook his head. A tiny birdlike movement, twitching side to side. A flush crept up his neck, and into his hairline. His arms slackened. The pistol sagged.

"They killed your family, son," Sullivan said.

Billy fell deathly still. His trembling stopped. He raised the pistol and fired and Tommy saw the gun smoke puff into the air. The native convulsed and smacked against the wall, only to rebound into place, righting himself like a bucket in a well, anchored by the body on his back. His eyes closed briefly, then opened in an unfocused stare. His head flopped sideways and wouldn't straighten. His mouth gaped, his bent arms rose, the hands floating in front of him until they very slowly found his body and felt their way up his chest. Like they weren't his hands at all. Like it was not his own chest. The fingers crawled over the scars and lumps and bones until they reached the base of his neck. There was a hole in it. Billy had blown out a chunk where the neck and shoulder met. Blood poured from the wound. The raw flesh pulsed. Frowning, the man fingered the hole and his eyes rolled toward Billy. A sound gargled in his throat. One of his legs began twitching. Billy cocked and pulled the trigger once, twice, but the hammer only clicked. He whirled around desperately, and Locke searched his pockets for powder and balls, impeded by his lame arm. Billy kept glancing at the man pawing meekly at the air. Finally Sullivan came up with some ammunition and handed it to Billy, but he spilled the powder, dropped the caps and balls. Sullivan knelt to help him. Kala began screaming and a sickening rattle sounded in the wounded man's throat. Rabbit muffled Kala's screams. She tried to fight the trooper off. Her eyes found Tommy and his found hers, and he saw rage in her stare, hatred, then a sudden softening as tears came. They welled in her eyes and dripped over Rabbit's fingers, over her cheeks. And still Billy fumbled to reload the gun.

"He'll thank you for it," Noone said. "As will your brother. As will the girl."

The revolver was still there in his outstretched hand. Tommy stared at the glinting metal for what felt a very long time. The injured man wheezed dully, his eyes searching the canyon and the sky like he knew not where he was. Again Kala screamed. Tommy snatched up the revolver, marched across camp, shoved his brother aside, and fired a single cartridge cleanly into the man's failing heart.

23

Silence followed the gunshot. Sounds of breathing and boots scuffing the dirt and Kala sniffing back her tears. Tommy lowered the revolver. His own breathing came quick and hard through his nose. His chest heaved. The man lay dead against the wall, steadily bleeding out. Nobody moving, all of them watching Tommy, as if waiting for something more. Billy weakly pushed him. Tommy slammed the revolver into Noone's hand, then grabbed his saddle pack and bedroll and walked out of camp, back along the ravine and down through the sloping tree cover to where the horses were tied. Beau was standing in the rocky glade, lips slopping as he chewed, his wise and kindly face, and at the sight of him Tommy sank to the ground and clutched his head in his hands, fingers gripping his hair so hard the tips were white, his eyes filling with tears. He had killed a man. He had taken a life. He didn't believe the native had killed his parents, and he didn't believe in Noone's notion of any black will do. How was that justice? Where would it ever end?

"Bloke was dying anyway," he mumbled, and this was surely true. If Tommy hadn't finished him, then Billy would have, or any of the others up there. Would have taken their time about it too, maybe toyed with him awhile first. It was a mercy he had performed and that was all, and to hell with bloody Noone. He'd been smiling when Tommy gave back the revolver, like he'd proved himself or some horseshit. Fuck him. Fuck Billy too. Fuck all of them and their—

Footsteps scraped through the scree and dry leaves above, coming down the hill. Tommy rose and wiped his eyes and face, spat, went to where Beau was tethered. The horse watched him. Tommy stroked his nose, let him nuzzle his hand.

"Don't suppose you saw our Billy down here last night?"

Beau sniffed his palm.

"No," Tommy said quietly. "I didn't think you had."

The group arrived and readied their horses in silence, the atmosphere oddly downcast, like something had been lost up there. Rabbit clapped Tommy warmly on the shoulder and as Noone helped her into the saddle Kala's eyes were on him too.

Billy sulked alone. He untied Annie and stood waiting at the edge of the trees, and when all were ready they walked their horses out of the cover and onto a narrow track leading across the hillside and around the ravine in which they'd camped. Bulging headland on their right, rubbled downslopes below. A little way above him, Tommy saw the cave Sullivan had likely used. A dark and shadowy slit in the rock, and the woman still up there, he assumed. But then as they walked he noticed two wedgetails circling high overhead and he examined the country to the east. A beautiful country, bathed in golden dawn. He read the wedgetails' position. They were over the foot of the same downslope the group now traversed, where boulders lay piled and mulga trees grew. And there, part-hidden among them, the woman lay broken on the rocks. Marks in the scree showed where she had rolled, must have been tossed from the cave. He looked to see if Kala had noticed, but she had not. She rode naked before him, prized and protected and favored by Noone, carried like a princess on his horse, and Tommy only feared for her all the more.

. . .

White clouds blew overhead as the party rode through the shadow of the ranges and into the sunshine of the western plains, the nothingness that lay there, as empty and unyielding as all they'd crossed before. The ranges hadn't changed anything, hadn't signaled a frontier or marked a shift in the terrain. They were their own anomaly. A knot in a vast sheet of lumbered wood. They were there, then they were not there, and the land went on and on.

Late morning the two riders hove into view and Noone brought the party to a halt. They sat watching the two small figures shimmering on the horizon and the dust rising from their hooves. The wind blew gently. The sun warmed their backs. The riders had been heading southeast; now they turned and rode directly to where the party stood. Noone clucked with displeasure. Glaring at the horses advancing across the open plain. He looked at his men with eyebrows raised, then shook his head and sighed. There was muffled laughter. Locke spat a string of brown saliva onto the ground, and though Noone addressed the group, he stared directly at him: "Don't anyone shoot these bastards unless I give the word."

On they came. Noone called for Jarrah to help Kala from his horse.

"Put her with the oldfella—Pope, keep your hands off." He caught Tommy's eye and corrected himself: "Actually, give her to the youngblood there. He's more than capable of taking care of her, I'm sure."

Jarrah lifted the girl onto Tommy's saddle and he inched himself forward to make space. Beau stepped uneasily at the extra weight but settled under Tommy's hand. He felt the warmth of Kala behind him, the heat coming off her skin. She didn't touch him that he could tell, but kept herself back on the horse. He glanced once over his shoulder, then quickly away, no clear look at her face, saw only the presence of her there. Her bare legs dangled behind his legs. Dark feet dusted in a fine red dirt.

Steadily the riders closed. Two men: one white, one black, both dressed neatly in trousers and shirts. The white man was waving, swinging his hand wildly in the air.

"Look at this fucking fruitcake," Sullivan muttered. "Who does he think he is?"

Noone motioned for quiet, walked his horse a few paces ahead. He leaned forward in his saddle and waited for the men trotting merrily on.

"Hello, neighbors! Hello there!"

He spoke with a plum English accent, no slippage, no slurs. He dismounted and led his horse by the reins; Noone remained in the saddle, peering down. The man was slight, auburn-haired, the hair combed primly to the side; his freckled face had burned until it peeled. He grinned stupidly at Noone, like the two of them were old friends. But the closer he came, the more his eyes roamed the assembled company of men, a wild and hellish mob, filthy and part-clothed, armed with all manner of things, an easy malevolence in their stares, and by the time he reached Noone he wasn't grinning anymore.

His accomplice followed closely behind, sense at least to stay on his horse.

"Good day to you, gentlemen," the white man said, shielding his eyes from the sun.

Noone nodded at him. "Good day."

"It's so unusual to encounter anyone out here . . . we thought perhaps you might be lost, or that we might be able to assist in some small way."

Noone glanced over his shoulder. "Do we look like we need your assistance?"

"Well, no, I don't suppose you do," the man said, chuckling. "But you can't blame me for trying. Better to be the Samaritan than the Levite or the Priest."

"Ah, a missionary," Noone said. "A man of God."

He nodded proudly. "Yes, sir, I am. Reverend Francis Bean, pleased to make your acquaintance." There was a silence. The reverend asked, "And your name, sir?"

"Noone."

"You are . . . explorers? Surveyors of some kind?"

"What brings you out this way, Reverend?"

He waved a hand dismissively. "Oh, we have been traveling a long, long time. Doing God's work. Spreading His word amongst the people of this land."

"And how goes it? Are they converted?"

The reverend laughed. "If only it were so simple. It will take many years."

"Long is the way, and hard, that out of Hell leads up to light."

"Yes, quite. Milton. Not that I'd call this Hell exactly but—"

"Oh, you'd be surprised," Noone interrupted. "Perhaps you just haven't been here long enough. But your boy there looks a convert. You've enchanted him, I see."

"This is Matthew, my loyal friend. Might I inquire as to your associates, sir?"

Noone stared at him for a very long time. "Tell me something, Reverend, when was the last congregation you held?"

"I wouldn't presume to call anything I've ministered a congregation, but—"

"Sermon, then. When was the last time you preached?"

"Recently, I suppose . . . but, why do you ask?"

"Well, you see, I'm wondering whether you've visited a native camp hereabouts. In the last day or two, let's say."

"Why would you be wondering that?"

"Because I too have work to attend to. You might even call it the work of God."

The reverend shook back his shoulders, bristled. "I can guess the kind of work you do, Mr. Noone, and it is certainly not the work of God."

"Allow me to enlighten you. Behind me here you'll see two white boys. They are orphans, their parents have been brutally killed. Murdered by the natives once in their employ, and aided by members of the Kurrong tribe. God's first law, broken. So now we are charged with bringing those responsible to justice, charged to do so by the Crown, by the authority of Queen Victoria herself, the head of the church in this land. If that is not God's work, Reverend, then I don't know what is."

The reverend stood stiff-backed and square, the fire of righteousness still in his eyes.

"I doubt His justice is the same as yours. You are

Native Police, then. What is your business with the girl?"

"Tragically lost and abandoned after the dust storm. We are caring for her, until we are able to return her to her people, assuming we can find them, that is. She is also Kurrong, and unfortunately they have a somewhat nomadic urge. Will you not help her, Reverend? Allow the poor girl to go home?"

"I'd be more than happy to take her myself. Lighten your load."

"But you're headed east, are you not?"

The reverend brushed back his hair with his hand. "It's true, we're in need of supplies, but we've enough to provide for the girl."

"As do we. And we are headed west."

"Yes, well . . ."

Noone squinted off into the scrubs. "The camp, please, Reverend Bean."

"It's not that I doubt you personally, you understand, but the reputation of the Native Police rather precedes you. The stories I've heard . . ."

"Are probably all true. I have asked nicely. There are other ways I could ask."

The reverend's accomplice slid his hand toward his saddle pack. Jarrah raised his rifle and pointed it at the man. The hand slid back onto his lap.

"We're expected in Mulumba two days from now. Questions will be asked."

"Of course they will. But what are the answers? Anything can happen out here, many a man has simply"—Noone twirled his fingers—"disappeared."

The reverend glanced back at Matthew, worried his reins with his thumb.

"You know, I have my own copy of the Bible," Noone said. He pulled the slim and ragged book from his pack and flapped it in the air. "I make a point of reading it every single day. Truly. All the stories and parables on how we should live—do you follow that advice, Reverend? Do you listen to what it says?"

"I . . . I do my best, yes."

"The people in those stories, they always seem to be traveling. As you are. As are we. Then they come to a crossroads, a juncture, perhaps an unexpected meeting such as this, which will prove to be a defining moment in their lives. I believe that every man has these moments, whether he wishes for them or not. Do you believe in such things, Reverend Bean?"

"I believe that we are tested, and that we must—"

"So now I'm going to tell you a story. You might not have heard this particular story before, so I'd suggest you listen well. It concerns a holy man, much like yourself, who traveled all around the world telling people to follow God, telling them how good and benevolent God was, and how when they met Him, provided they had lived a noble and Christian life, He would bestow His virtue upon them.

"The holy man had no evidence for this. He had faith and that was all. Enough, he thought. God would protect and guide him. So he preached this same message to others: faith will see you through. One day the holy man found himself in the desert, in a cruel and dangerous land, only his boy with him; they were very much alone. They believed themselves shielded by God since they were doing God's good work, but then lo! a stranger appeared before them on the plain. They talked, and as they talked the holy man judged the stranger and found him lacking in the eyes of the Lord. He held that he was dishonest, that he was evil, that Satan guided his hand. He was correct in this judgment, but also foolish. He underestimated the stranger. He disrespected him. With God at his side he believed himself immune to Satan's reach. He was not immune. The stranger cut out his tongue. He removed his eyes and ears and stripped his clothing and sent him wandering naked across the land.

"Oh, and he killed the boy, also. Left his body for the dogs.

"So now the holy man wandered blindly through the desert, and as he wandered he prayed and prayed but

God did not come. God did not listen. God did not help. After many days and nights the man was in such torment that he abandoned his faith and begged Satan for mercy, but Satan has no mercy; he should have known better than to ask. Eventually, the holy man reached a town where the people gave him shelter but Satan visited him in that town and every other place he went. He hunted him for eternity, wouldn't let him rest, while God . . . God was never there. The stranger learned of the man's family, whether in this land or over the seas, and he visited them also. His wife, his children, his parents who were very old.

"When finally the man died he hoped for salvation but he found that there was none. There was only the agony of death. He looked back on that meeting with the stranger and wished that he had understood. When the truth of it was, he had understood. He had understood all too well. But he'd believed himself higher than the stranger. He'd been arrogant enough to think that the words of a parchment best suited to wiping one's hole could protect him on this earth, an arrogance which led him to question the stranger, to preach to him, to imply certain things about his character, leading the stranger to consider the holy man untrustworthy, to consider that perhaps he might speak ill of the stranger, to talk of their meeting with others; to conclude that the two of them were not friends.

"And although it was bad luck for the holy man that the stranger stood at Satan's side, that is surely the chance you take, Reverend, is it not, when you decide to make an enemy of anyone you meet upon the empty Queensland plain?"

A long silence followed. Beneath his sunburn, the reverend had turned pale. He looked ready to vomit. His thumb stroked the leather rein, back and forth, back and forth again. The light wind ruffled his yellow hair and the shadows of the clouds slipped and swirled around him on the rutted ground.

"Quite a story, isn't it?" Noone said.

The reverend answered breathlessly: "Yes, it is."

"Might just be the most important story you've ever heard in your life."

The reverend nodded.

"I like stories like that. Where the message is nice and clear."

"Very clear."

"Will you heed it, I wonder?"

"Yes, sir. Yes, I will. But, in all good conscience, I cannot tell you the location of the Kurrong if you mean to treat them ill."

Noone smiled. "That's alright, Reverend, you just have. On your way now."

The reverend stood there blinking, his mouth hanging open. Noone motioned for him to remount his horse and he did so, though it took him three attempts to climb on. He looked from Noone to the others, surveyed the gathered men.

Noone inclined his head. "Safe journey. Godspeed."

The reverend gave a mumbled reply, they walked their horses on, and all heads turned as they went by, the two groups watching each other like deckhands on ships that unexpectedly cross. Then the missionaries kicked their horses and were gone, and the party sat watching the dust trail floating on the breeze.

"You don't think we should have done them?" Sullivan asked.

"It would have brought us no benefit if we had."

"Shut the buggers up at least."

"They won't talk. I know a man when I see one and that was not a man."

"You seen his face?" Locke said, laughing. "Looked like he'd shat himself!"

"How do you figure he gave up the Kurrong, though?" Sullivan asked, and Noone pointed to where the reverend had been standing with his horse, then trailed his finger toward the horizon in the west.

"He'd had contact with them only recently, perhaps as recently as yesterday. We follow these tracks, we'll come up with them soon enough. The stupid bastard didn't know what he was saying." Noone grinned wickedly. "By God's good grace we'll be on them by nightfall."

24

The tracks led clear as a bridleway through the dusty scrub, and they followed at a canter until the horses tired. The heat was searing, the air stifling and close, though at least now there was some cloud cover, the first clouds Tommy had seen since they left. Smell of lightning still, he thought. The charge of it, the spark. Might have struck the earth nearby. Or was the smell his own, maybe? A trace from the gunshot he had fired? He sniffed at his shirt, his fingertips, smelled sweat and wood smoke and something burning; he wiped his hands clean on his thighs. Did those new cartridge revolvers even leave a stain? Did a killing? Would he be smelling that gunshot for the rest of his days?

Kala sat quietly behind him. Bouncing lightly with

each stride. With his head half-turned Tommy could glimpse her, and if he pretended to watch the ground he could see her feet. Sometimes she touched between his shoulder blades for balance, steadying herself with her still-bound hands, or even fell against him, her chest against his back, and he would brace himself in the saddle to support her flimsy weight, until she moved away again. He would have liked for her to stay there, to press herself into him, rest her head and sleep if she was tired. She never did. The briefest touch between them, and she was gone.

"I'm sorry about your . . . what was he anyway? Your brother? Friend?"

Of course she didn't answer. Might not have understood, or even heard. Tommy spoke quietly so the others couldn't listen, his voice vibrating inside him; he imagined she could feel it too.

"I didn't even want to come out here. This was all Billy, Sullivan, Noone. They say we're after Joseph, but I don't see how he could have made it all this way on foot. Daddy wouldn't lend him a horse. We found these two blacks—men—in this tree by our creek, and Joseph was Kurrong, same as you. He wanted to bring them back to your land, must have dragged them, I reckon, since he didn't have nothing else."

He felt her touch him. No more than a tap. He

turned. Kala eyed him warily, leaning away with her head angled to the side. She signaled for water. Tommy went scrambling for his flask. He pulled out the stopper, gave it to her, watched her put the bottle to her lips and her long neck contract. He faced forward again. Listening to her drinking, a faint gasp after the final sip. She handed back the flask and their fingers lightly brushed, and Tommy made a point of taking a drink of his own, deliberately placing his lips where hers had just been.

On they rode. Nothing more from Kala and nothing more he could think to say, his thoughts instead spiraling back through the hours and replaying the dull *thump* of the round slamming into her kinsman's chest, the way his body had twitched and then fallen still, the silence in camp, the smile on Noone's face, the whispered truth he'd offered about who Father had really been.

Efficient, he had called him. Claimed they used to hunt blacks for pay.

Father hadn't spoken much about his time at Broken Ridge. Hadn't spoken much about anything, in truth. He was a man of silences and of secrets: if he had something to tell you he would say it, but idle gossip and chatter only got in the way of work. He worked, he ate, he slept: there had been no more to him as far as Tommy was concerned. The broodiness, the impatience, the outbursts of emotion when he'd embrace one of them so hard they couldn't breathe . . . all these things he took at face value, hadn't ever questioned what was happening underneath. The same could be said for Mother, Tommy supposed. He had not considered either of his parents people in their own right; or rather, he had not thought it possible there could be anything more to them than what he already knew.

Certainly Father didn't like talking about the natives—said the violence against them was not his concern—but he wouldn't let his white stockmen mistreat black workers in the same way Sullivan did. Tommy had never seen Father beat them or whip them or call them nigger or such things, and though Billy reckoned him soft, Tommy had always put it down to Arthur, a closeness between them going back years. But what if Noone was right? What if he was actually trying to atone for what he'd done at Broken Ridge? And, worse still, how would Tommy ever know?

He was remembering things now. Arguments Father had had with his men, warnings he'd given them. He had warned his family too, warned the children not to listen to the stories they might hear, about fighting and cruelty on both sides, blacks being shot, whites being speared. At one time hadn't Father even allowed wild natives to cross over his land, to camp in his scrubs, and then . . . and then Sullivan had come down to the house one day and there'd been a big blowup, Sullivan telling Father to end it or he would, and Father trying to stand his ground but there'd seemed no ground on which he could stand. The men had all been watching, out in the yard, and when Sullivan was gone and Father had marched back into the house, Tommy had heard them mutter and scoff. He couldn't have been much older than eight. He'd not connected it before now, but that was the night Father had burned the toy wooden horse Sullivan had given him years before.

Tommy watched the column snaking on ahead, following the reverend's tracks. A feral band of men, and Billy as wild as any of them, his shirt flapping open and his hat tilted back and his hand resting on the revolver at his side. Tommy didn't know him, not after last night, not after what he'd done. And this morning, shooting that native . . . his mind wasn't his own anymore, he'd been twisted, twisted by Sullivan and Noone.

Noone—Tommy watched him at the front of the line, shoulders back, paling-straight in the saddle, not even so much as a twitch. While the others fidgeted and drank and spat and smoked, Noone simply rode, studying the horizon with those eyes Tommy had seen chalk-white in the darkness, as his hand crept over Kala's skin.

Tommy winced at the thought of it, set his jaw, nudged Beau forward along the line. As he passed, Billy asked him, "What you doing?" but Tommy didn't look across, then kept his head down as Sullivan shouted, "Watch out, fellas, here he comes! Tommy the nigger hunter and his pickaninny bride!"

He passed by the troopers. Felt them stare at him one by one. He glanced only at Rabbit, exchanged a brief nod, the beginnings of a smile on the young trooper's face before Tommy looked away. He was always bloody smiling. Couldn't be happier, it seemed. Like this was all good fun to him, one big bloody game.

Tommy drew alongside Noone. Sullivan yelled another catcall. Noone didn't look at Tommy but kept his eyes on the horizon as he spoke: "The rich have plenty money but very little class. Have you noticed that, young man?"

He nodded hesitantly. Behind him in the saddle he felt Kala squirm.

"You want to talk about this morning? About your father, maybe?"

"Kala," Tommy croaked. He cleared his throat. "The girl."

"I see. Well?"

"What'll happen to her? The same as the other one in them rocks?"

"You miss nothing, do you, boy? Did your brother notice, I wonder? Did John?"

"I don't know."

"Tell me something, do you smell that? The air is different today, no?"

"I thought lightning. Or gunpowder, I'm not sure."

"Very good. Look over there." He pointed north. Far beyond the curve of the horizon the sky was gray and full. "That's a bushfire, traveling north and east, and quickly, a mile a minute, I would say. You have a sense for these things, Tommy. It's a skill. You should use it to your own gain. Also, there is rain coming. Can you feel the change in the air? To a black it is intuitive, as obvious as night and day. It must become like that to you."

"For what?"

"For you to make something of yourself out here. You would become a fine officer one day, I'm sure enough of that."

Tommy scoffed a short laugh, but a redness crept into his cheeks and neck.

"Come now, Tommy. You are without prospects, without the makings of a life. On your little farm you'd be lucky to last a year, and though you could probably scratch a living as a station hand somewhere—"

"Billy says Mr. Sullivan'll set us on."

"John has his own reasons for making you his boy. But do you want to end up like your father? I'm curious—why aren't you asking about him?"

Tommy shrugged.

"Alright, then," Noone said, sighing. "What about this girl?"

"I already said—what'll happen to her when you're done?"

Noone swayed his head slightly, like scales tilting side to side.

"Sell her, I'd imagine. They fetch a fair price at her age."

"Sell her as what?"

"Housegirl, most likely, she's young enough to be taught. There's always the cane fields but they prefer island negroes up there. Cannibals, I've heard it said."

"Couldn't we just . . . let her go?"

Noone tutted disapprovingly. Clicked his tongue behind his teeth.

"Only once we're done, I mean. Once the timing's right."

"Were you not listening to me this morning? She's a

breeder, Tommy. The future of her race is right there between her legs. We must appropriate her, domesticate her, sever the bloodline. Remember Darwin: a species adapts or it dies. We must not allow them to adapt. If we take their land, their women, kill their men, sooner or later they will simply expire. It is science. A most fascinating field."

He said nothing more. His gaze rested on Tommy, then shifted to the horizon again. The land gently inclining now, rising to the north. Tommy rode at his side. So many things in his mind and he could say not one. But then to imagine Kala as a housegirl somewhere—pinafored and bonneted, with food and shelter and a bed—didn't seem so bad at all. Better than her lying discarded in a ditch, after a half dozen men had done with her whatever they pleased.

"Was there something else, Tommy? Your father maybe?"

"Alright—what of him?"

"You weren't surprised by what I said? By the kind of man he was?"

"What's to say I believe you?"

"Well, do you? Did he tell you about his past?"

"You didn't even know him. The two of you never met."

"True. Even so, it must be of concern, what you

came from—don't you worry you're cast in the same mold?"

Tommy sniffed and shrugged at him. "Might be that I am."

"I believe you may be right. Tell me, what would he have made of all this? Our mission here, our plan?"

"He was against it. Against Sullivan. Against you."

"Really? And if someone had killed you and Billy, and knowing now what you do about your father's temperament, you don't think he'd have done the same?"

Tommy didn't answer. He couldn't think what to say. Behind him, Kala was twisting her body away from Noone and knocking out Beau's stride. Tommy eased him back, allowed Noone to move on. The inspector watched him over his shoulder until he had slid past the troopers and was out of his eyeline. Locke and Sullivan stared wantonly at Kala as Tommy went by. Then came Billy, asking, "What was all that? You wanting your turn?" and the same roving stares as the men. Smirking while he did it. Ogling her top to toe to tail.

Tommy fell in at the back of the line and gave Kala one of the lemon sweets. It felt like a grubby offering but she didn't seem to mind; she snatched the lolly from him and he heard it clattering around her teeth. Would have usually raised a smile in him, but he was thinking about Father, about what Noone had said. Since Billy first voiced the idea of coming out here, doing this, Tommy had clung to the assumption that Father would have been against it, would have been turning in his grave to see them with these men, avenging him and Mother in this way. What if he was wrong about that? Between them this morning his two sons had put down one of those supposedly responsible, and were riding out here on Joseph's trail—what was to say that if he was watching them now, Father wouldn't actually have been proud?

25

As dusk fell, the crater fire burned on the horizon like a torch buried deep in the earth. A few miles away yet, a small and faltering glow, but all knew what they had found. They stood the horses in a line, watched the distant firelight, and caught the strains of chanting and the rhythmic clapping of wood on wood, and Tommy heard Kala moan in a way he had never heard a person moan before. A dull, heartfelt keening that echoed in her chest and seemed born of another world.

"You can muzzle her now, Tommy. There's a good lad."

Tommy looked at Noone wide-eyed.

"Either muzzle her yourself or one of this lot will."

"What with?"

"I've got something that'll gag her," Locke said. Sullivan and Billy laughed.

Tommy surveyed himself up and down. All he had was his greenhide belt. His fingers went to the knot. He glanced at Kala and she flinched.

"Sorry, but they're saying I have to—"

"Here," Billy called, digging around in his pack. He tossed something that Tommy caught and dangled one-handed by its strap. A horse's burlap feed bag, saliva-stained and crusted in dirt and dried grain.

"That'll do you," Sullivan chortled. "Get it on her snout."

Kala eyed the feed bag warily. Tommy said, "It'll be better if I do it. Please."

Billy swung down from his horse. He grabbed Kala's ankle and wrenched her from the saddle, caught her just before she hit the ground.

"Hey!" Tommy shouted, dismounting. "Get off her!"

"Quiet, the pair of you," Noone said. "Unless you want me to muzzle you too. Tommy—give your brother the bag."

Billy's arm was across Kala's chest, his other hand outstretched. Tommy passed him the feed bag and he stuffed it into Kala's mouth. She choked on the rough gunny cloth. Billy looped the strap over her head then tied it tight at the back. Her bound hands tugged at the loose sacking falling like a beard to her chest. She couldn't loosen the gag. The straps dug into her skin. Billy slapped her on the behind and shoved her, and she fell against Tommy, sniveling. All he wanted was to hold her. To loosen the straps and tell her she'd be fine. But the others were watching to see what he'd do next, so he pushed her away and stared into her eyes. Trying to say all that couldn't be said. She returned the stare coldly, breathing hard through her nose. Tommy swallowed and steered her back to their horse, stood there dumbly, no idea how to get her up. He hadn't the strength to lift her, wouldn't know where to put his hands. He looked along the line of men and Noone nodded for Jarrah to come. Jarrah dismounted and walked toward them and Noone told him, "Best keep her with you. The boy's smitten, I fear. Some dissent in him yet."

Jarrah dragged Kala back to his horse. She sat small and hunched between his legs, her face in her hands, the dirty burlap dangling from her chin. They moved on. Toward the burning west, the last lickings of the sunset and the halo of the fire melding like some holy sign, then north, to higher ground and a small range of hills, bubbling hummocks of red rock silhouetted against the dusk. Noone sent the troopers ahead to make camp, while the whites turned and rode in the direction of the crater fire, and the thump of the beat getting louder as they neared.

"What's happening?" Tommy asked. "Aren't we all going in?"

"In the morning," Noone said. "Patience. We'll hit them first light of dawn."

A quarter mile from the crater they dismounted and Noone told Locke to gather the reins and mind the horses until they were back.

"The hell for?" Locke snapped. "One of them boys can do it."

Noone only glared at him. Sullivan said, "We'll be down on our bellies anyhow—how'll you crawl with that arm?"

Sullenly, dutifully, the overseer obeyed.

In the last of the light they walked through the scrub, Tommy's stomach knotting with each step. The noise grew louder. The hollow clacking of the rhythm sticks and the high-pitched strains of a male voice singing. Beneath it all lay the drone of a didgeridoo, ringing around the crater like the earth itself spoke, and Tommy felt something acrid rise into his throat. He swallowed repeatedly, but the taste would not shift.

Twenty yards from the crater's edge, Noone raised a hand and signaled for them to drop. The four of them went onto their hands and knees, and crawled through the warm, sharp dirt. Biting their palms, scraping their skin, Tommy at the end of the line, the crater peeling before him, a vast circular basin carved into the earth, so uniform it looked deliberate, as if scooped by some tool. First came the far bank, then the slow reveal of the camp below, a handful of humpies scattered through the sparse scrub, around a central clearing in which a great bonfire burned. Flames licked the darkness, sparks spiraled and danced through the air. A fire so big its makers must have thought it hidden by the crater walls. Or else they'd simply not figured on there being anyone to see; they'd believed themselves alone out here.

The last of the Kurrong numbered fifty, sixty . . . at most a hundred in all. Men and women of all ages, children, infants, dogs; must have been a good few dozen dogs. Most of the group were sitting in a loose circle around the clearing, clapping time with the musicians and watching their kinfolk dance. Others ambled through camp, seeing to chores or laughing and talking and dancing themselves. Children played. It was a convivial affair. Not much ceremony to it, though the dancers were painted in stark white lines, like they each wore their bones on their skin. Skeletons jigging in the twilight, jerking to the beat of sticks and the stomping of feet and the ominous moan of the didgeridoo. Mothers fed their babies; children joined the dancing, to the laughter and catcalls of the crowd. The dancers paused, then regained their rhythm; the singers rotated and another voice took it on, straining to be heard above the din. It was a peculiar kind of chaos but seemed innocent enough, not the hellish debauchery of the rumors Tommy had heard. They looked to be greatly enjoying themselves, lost to it, immersed in their songs and their dance.

Happy and helpless as lambs.

26

The rainstorm Noone predicted came at nightfall, and the men opened their mouths gratefully to the sky, scrubbed themselves clean, collected water in their flasks; the horses drank from puddles in the hollows of the rocks. But then the rain continued and the long night set in, and there was no shelter to be found in camp, if what they had could be called a camp at all: men huddling among the boulders and all but invisible in the gloom. The rain pattered on their hats and dripped from the brims, their clothes clung to their bodies like skin. There was no fire. Noone had forbidden one lit. The rum was gone and even when pooled their rations fell well short of a meal. So they sat. Miserably watching the distant glow of the native bonfire and listening to their revelry and smelling the trace of meat on the air. Sullivan promised a feast when they were back at Broken Ridge, but the station was many days and many miles away, and talk of a feast was just talk.

Still the rain fell. The ground became boggy and thick. There was no more talking. The rain so loud only shouting could be heard, and since shouting was forbidden, no one did. There was little to be said anyway. Those who were able, slept. Others glared grimly into the darkness, alone with their thoughts. Thoughts of elsewhere, of afterward, and of the task that lay ahead. Locke massaged his wounded shoulder as if coaxing it back to life. Sullivan smoked with his hand cupped around the cigarette end, shielding it from the wet. Noone had unfurled his bedroll and draped it over himself to form a makeshift tent, and in the dry it afforded, wiped his many weapons down. Rodding each barrel; cleaning hammer, cylinder, chambers one by one. The others soon did likewise, bedrolls popping up like toadstools among the rocks. Waddies were polished and cleaned, bayonets affixed to the troopers' rifle ends. Noone filed the long blade of his bowie knife on the edge of a boulder stone, the sound of its scraping slicing at the air.

Tommy didn't tend to his rifle, didn't sharpen his folding knife. He lay upright in the valley between two sheets of rock, watching the others through the curtain of rain, watching Kala most of all. She looked near-drowned. Sitting naked and uncovered beside the sheltering troopers, dark hair lying flat on her head and her skin shimmering in the dull moonlight, slick as cooking oil. She was still muzzled. The feed bag dangled from her mouth. Total resignation in her stare. Tommy spent a long time wondering what she was thinking, then realized that he could not understand. Her thoughts were not his thoughts. Her words were not his words. He felt a fool for having tried. He turned away again. It ached him to see the state she was in. And the only thing he could do about it was not watch her anymore.

Billy was huddled against another of the rocks, smoking one of Sullivan's cigarettes. Even had it cupped in his hand just the same. Good for warmth, Tommy supposed, though it wouldn't have been so cold if not for the rain. Mother used to call this the wet kind of rain, like there was another kind of rain there could be. They had teased her for it but she was right: this was about the wettest there was. She was funny like that, his mother: a worrier, a thinker, she noticed the little things. Maybe that was where Tommy got it from, this second sense Noone spoke of. She liked to classify in all different ways, wouldn't accept a thing was just a thing. Wet rain, dry rain; hard heat, soft heat; good death, bad death—might have been she was more superstitious than Tommy realized. Truthfully, he hadn't known her, not in the way he would have liked. All he had now were memories, fractions of memories, incomplete scrapings from his past like the leavings of a fire.

He flicked the rain from his face and wiped his eyes and turned his attention back to the men, still cleaning their weapons, rodding their guns. They were not just passing the time. The dull fascination with which each of them worked wasn't born of idleness but intent. Those weapons were being readied for use, each man making preparations for what he knew was to come, and which only now Tommy fully understood. It had taken him this long. Days of riding across the colony, farther and farther from home—he had believed they were on one path but he realized he was wrong. Not them. These men knew what they were doing. They'd always known, because they'd done it many times before. Joseph might be out here, or he might not: it was irrelevant, this had never been about him, or Tommy's family, or whatever else he'd assumed. It was only about the Kurrong: a mass dispersal was planned.

Abrupt as a dead heartbeat, the distant music stopped.

The night drew on, hour after hour, and still the rain didn't ease. The men slept upright, the ground too bogged to lie down, hunched in their bedrolls and no different in outline to the boulders and rocks. Tommy waited. Wedged into his crevice like a bilby in its hole, sheets of water sliding down the wall at his back. No stars visible, the moon shadowed behind the clouds. Tommy watched each of the men in turn and every now and then would see one of them flinch. A portent from their dreaming. A shiver from the cold. Who were they, these troopers? Who was Noone? If a bushman had come wandering from the west and described them around the campfire back home, Tommy doubted he would have believed they were real. Paid by the government to hunt down wild blacks, recruited from the south and keen, Rabbit had told him, so fucking keen. He felt such a child in their presence, helpless, unprepared. Father should have warned them. Should have taught them about this world. Maybe he'd planned to. "When you're older," he used to say. Too late for that now, Daddy. We're as old as we'll ever be.

The rain drummed his hat and bounced from the rocks, and everywhere was rain, rain, rain. Was it raining at Glendale? Tommy wondered. Soaking the paddocks, the northern fields, swelling the creek until it broke its banks and flooded the surrounding plains?

He remembered the night they had danced in the yard, Mother lifting her nightdress and Father falling to his knees. It seemed impossible. Less a memory than a dream. Yet barely a month ago he'd been out in those fields, mustering the cattle like one of the men. He'd been miserable that week because of how Father behaved; now he'd give anything to hear him complain. He remembered waiting with the others, watching him ride home drunk from the saleyards, Mother slapping him on the chest as he puckered for a kiss. Firing Billy's shanghai against the bunkhouse wall, laughing with Mary about the smell from his boots and her telling him, in that voice that would never grow up, *You stink. I mean really, really stink!*

He peeled himself from his hovel and crept across the camp. Billy was slumped under the hood of his bedroll, his chin on his chest and his breathing thick and slow. Tommy gently shook him. Billy woke with a start. Tommy leaned close and told him to hush.

"What is it?" Billy whispered. "What's wrong?"

"Come with me."

"What? Where to?"

"I want to talk to you. Don't wake them. Come on."

He tugged on Billy's arm. Billy threw off the bedroll, climbed to his feet, and followed Tommy along the little passage that led out of the rocks, past the horses standing stoically in the rain, the same disgruntled air as when they were first tied. Tommy brushed his hand along Beau's flank and the horse briefly lifted his head. Then out into the clearing, their boots suckering the ground as they walked, until they stood in the darkness and downpour, barely the light to see each other's faces not a couple of feet away.

"Well?" Billy said over the hissing rain. "What's this about?"

"You know what this is, don't you? What they've got planned?"

His silence gave his answer. Tommy thought he saw his brother shrug. He pointed in the direction of the crater. "There's babies down there!"

"We ain't here for them," Billy said.

"We ain't here for any of them. Joseph's not there. He never was."

"You don't know that. Even so, them others might be, them that—"

"There were no others, Billy! You lied! Bloody Sullivan—it wasn't ever about us, or Daddy, or Ma, we just gave them the cause, don't you see?"

"Killing them's not cause enough for you?"

"But it wasn't *them*"—he jabbed his finger toward the crater again—"that fucking did it!"

"How do you know that?" Billy shouted. "Anyway, it doesn't matter. Them is what we've got. Hell, the law's with us and John's with us; even the bloody blacks agree it's right. The only one that doesn't is you. It's time you took a fucking side."

"Your side? Raping and killing like you're some kind of man?"

"You were against shooting him. I was trying to spare you, that's all."

"Horseshit, spare me. Was the woman for me too?"

Billy threw up his arms. "Christ! Everyone did it! She's only a fucking gin!"

"They killed her, you know that? Threw her on the rocks."

"And they killed Ma—what's the difference? When are you going to learn?"

Billy's face swam in the rain, pale and hollow-eyed and nothing like the brother Tommy knew. "We can't go in there," he said quietly. "Tomorrow—we can't be a part of what they've got planned."

"We don't have a choice, Tommy."

"Yes, we do. We could leave. Tonight. Now. Untie the horses, ride off."

Billy hesitated, said, "Don't be so fucking dumb."

"Why not? What's stopping us?"

"No water for one thing, no supplies, we don't even know where we're at."

"We ride east with the sun. Keep going till we find a town."

"They'd hunt us like dogs, Tommy. We'd be cowards if we leave, worse."

"I'd rather live with that than what'll happen if we don't."

"Son, you wouldn't live to see the dawn."

Noone's voice. Both brothers turned. He came sloshing through the mud and out of the darkness like some pale apparition of the night. He was naked. Entirely unclothed save his boots. His body was white and wizened and unwell as a corpse. A thick mat of hair covered his chest and crotch. He stood close enough that they could smell him, feel the heat of his skin. Rain streaming down the crags of his cheeks and dripping from his stubbled chin, his mustache drooping sadly like a painted-on frown.

"The last deserter I had, I tied to a tree and burned. Slowly. Took about an hour before he died. We tended the fire just-so. He watched his own skin peel."

"We're not deserting," Billy pleaded. "We were talking, that's all."

"I heard you talking. I heard exactly what you said."

He reached down and cupped Tommy's chin with his hand, twisted his head around. Tommy tried to pull away but couldn't, the grip as strong as a dog's jaw. He lifted his eyes to look at Noone, his face looming close in the rain, and those eyes reaching in through Tommy's eyes and rummaging about in his soul. Tommy whimpered. He clutched Noone's wrist with both hands but couldn't shift it, like gripping an ancient tree limb. Noone squeezed and lifted; lifted him onto his toes. Billy pulled at Noone's other arm but the arm was too slick for him to hold. Noone slapped him. Billy fell backward, slipped in the mud, rose but didn't try again. Noone pressed his nose against Tommy's nose, his brow on Tommy's brow, and Tommy tasted the foulness of his breath when he spoke.

"I do like you, Tommy. But talk like that again and I'll see that you burn."

He dumped him back on his feet and Tommy reeled away, breathless, through the mud. Noone stood before them and neither brother moved. Slowly his face broke into a smile; he raised his arms at his sides like he held the world aloft.

"Isn't this beautiful? Can you imagine a more perfect night?"

He tilted back his head and arched his spine, his cock wobbling, his hair lank and flat on his head. He closed his eyes and inhaled through his nose, then breathed out with a satisfied groan.

"Back to your bedrolls, boys. Get yourselves rested for dawn."

They walked either side of him, past his outstretched arms, and made their way into camp. Tommy weak-footed, weak-legged, slipping in the mud. When they reached the mouth of the passage he looked back at the clearing and could still make out Noone, the shape of him, crucified in the darkness, imprinted on the night.

27

The rain had stopped come daybreak. The rocks dripped and the ground oozed and the air was close and thick. The camp slowly stirring, the men wringing out their bedrolls and moving stiffly in their damp clothes. Noone was the only one dry. Freshly shaved and fully dressed, including his longcoat, like a man stepping out from home. In the oily half-light he watched the preparations and snapped orders at his men. They too were in uniform: Noone inspected them one by one. Fiddling with each collar, adjusting each hat brim.

Tommy stood numbly among the boulders, his rifle dangling in his hand and his sopping bedroll clutched under his arm, the others milling around him, making for their horses, bustling back and forth. He couldn't bring himself to leave camp. As if he alone could hold them back, when of course he could not. Death is inevitable. Regardless, it comes. A man walks to the gallows and never thinks to try to run, stands obediently while the bag is draped and the noose is hung, waits patiently for the trapdoor to fall . . .

"Tommy?" Noone said. Tommy's eyes flicked toward him. "There a problem? You're not thinking of running off again, I hope?"

Sullivan overheard, called out, "The hell he is. On your horse, boy."

"What happens to the girl?" Tommy asked.

"She stays here until we're done," Noone said. He hooked Rabbit by the arm as he passed. "Hobble her with one of the ropes, there's a good man."

Rabbit nodded. He went to where Kala sat bound and gagged in the rocks, and wrenched her to her feet.

"I'll watch her," Tommy offered. "Guard her till you're back."

Noone was smiling. "Of course you would, Tommy."

"Get him on that fucking horse!" Sullivan yelled.

Noone scragged Tommy by his collar and tossed him out of camp. He sprawled in the mud, spilling his rifle and bedroll, right beside Locke, who was seeing to his saddle pack. The overseer ran his tongue around his gums, leaned to offer Tommy a hand, then when

Tommy reached for it withdrew the hand again, and Tommy fell back into the muck.

"Yellow little bastard," Locke said, laughing. "You won't last the first pass."

Tommy clambered to his feet, gathered his things, and went to Beau, who watched him warily while he packed. A horse always knows. Tommy checked his rifle and slung it on his shoulder, then stood there waiting, idly rubbing Beau's neck. In the east the sky was a sloughy mix of gray and blue, a red sun threatening, the light barely touching the plains. The crater was out there. They were likely all still asleep. Women and children and old folk and infants. He had seen them. Seen them laughing, dancing, singing around the fire . . .

The men were mounting up. Tommy had barely the strength to make the saddle but he did. He saw Sullivan vomit a dribble of green puke, wipe his mouth on his sleeve, then climb up. Locke spoke to him. Sullivan laughed and spat. Tommy turned Beau around and stood him beside Annie; Billy looked him up and down. Billy was trembling. He gripped the reins in his fists but his whole body shook. He eyed Tommy's rifle, then reached into his waistband for the two revolvers he now had tucked there. He handed one across. Tommy took the pistol by its grip. Six shots, loaded and capped.

"John gave me another," Billy said, shrugging. "Don't want you going short."

Tommy cradled the revolver loosely in his lap. He didn't speak. He was way down inside himself, or many miles distant, watching all this from afar. Him holding the revolver and Billy trembling and the horses stepping uneasily and Jarrah's waddy blade humming as he tested it on the air. Locke grinding his tobacco; Pope sitting still as an owl, his sunken eyes scouring the land. The faraway sun inching into the sky and behind them the water still dripping from the rocks, Kala lying among them, her wrists and ankles roped.

"You got any of them lollies left?" Billy said. "For after, maybe?"

Tommy only looked at him. Billy was smiling but seemed on the edge of tears, the smile clinging uncertainly to his face as Noone brought his horse around to address the group front on.

"Stay together for the first pass," he told them. "Then unleash hell. Don't let me see none of you waste a single bloody shot."

And then they were riding, full gallop across the plain, Tommy jerking out of himself and stowing the revolver in his waistband and clinging to Beau as they rode, watching for the crater far ahead, watching,

watching . . . and for a long time it was not there, then suddenly it was, the crater's edge looming upon them like the earth had fissured, like the edge of the entire world. None of the horses slowed for it. They cleared the crest as one. Nine riders sweeping down the crater wall in a tumble of mud and dirt that set the dogs away barking below. Descending on the camp like a flood, the dogs yapping wildly, and here and there Kurrong heads turned. Those early risen or woken by the noise. Then came screaming. At first a single shout ringing in the dawn, then a chorus of shouting and Noone began shouting also, his voice deep and otherworldly, drawn from long ago. He roared and the others roared and despite himself Tommy roared too. The camp below now an ant nest of people fleeing and running madly back and forth, men assembling loosely in a line directly in the horses' path. The first desperate spear was thrown. It landed short of the riders and Jarrah plucked it quivering from the ground. Other spears fizzed past them but none found their mark, and soon the spears were spent. Only their waddies left: the gathered men raised their clubs while their bare feet inched backward through the dirt. A jittering, doubtful stance. Jarrah launched the spear. It carved through the air and skewered one of the men and he went down. A Kurrong boy beside him fled. The others dared to hold their ground. They readied their waddies anew. Noone called for rifles and all rifles except Tommy's were raised, and they were holding, holding, holding while they rode . . . at twenty yards Noone gave the order, and in a thunderclap of gunshot, they fired.

Every man before them fell.

The horses trampled their bodies and swept into the camp.

28

They slaughtered them. Save a few women kept as bounty, they slaughtered them all.

29

Daylight peeled open the crater. A slow-moving crescent of shadow drawn west to east by the sunrise. The sodden ground steamed. A churned and bloody stew. Crimson soil, crimson wet. The steam whispered through the scrub and over the bodies and parts of bodies sunken there. Some still moved: inching through the slurry, dragging themselves along, raising a supplicant hand. A chorus of low moans underpinned the irregular popping of waddy and rifle butt, as the posse roamed the crater, finishing off its task. *Pop, pop, pop.* Not unlike the sound of a wheat field, ripening in the sun.

Tommy lost amid the chaos, rifle held before him, turning circles on his horse. Aiming nowhere, at no one, while around him the bodies fell. To rifle shot and pistol shot and the swing of waddy blade: Jarrah lopped the head off a kneeling Kurrong like a flower from its stem; Rabbit cleaved a path through the crowd, whipping side to side with the ease of splitting wood.

When the last of them was finished, when the moaning had finally ceased, the bodies were collected and heaped into a pile. A heavy slog with heavy cargo through the turgid mud. The few Kurrong who had made it as far as the crater walls could be rolled or tossed to the floor, but then needed dragging like the rest. The pile grew. A bonfire of torsos and limbs. Some were missing ears or scalps or teeth, fingers, heads, breasts: trophies taken, then discarded, for the taking had been all. They littered the soupy ground, were kicked and trampled underfoot. The kind of relics which in years to come might be unearthed and thought queer. What's this finger buried here? This jaw, this piece of skull? Why a single forearm bone?

Down they went everywhere. Down, down, down. Shot and clubbed and stabbed and trampled and drowned in the mud. A din to echo in the bones. Screams of life, screams of death, of joy, hatred, terror, despair. Children crying. Little faces riven by tears. Mothers, their mouths gaping, clutching infants to their chests and running for their lives. Men fighting hopelessly, pawing at the passing horses, until they too were dispatched.

Tommy watched Noone dismount and stride through the bedlam like a gentleman out of doors, picking them off as he went; he saw Sullivan thrashing and firing at will, flailing like a rabid old cur. Locke in the midst of it all took a girl to the ground and rutted with her in the slop, her dead eyes rolling, head bouncing with each thrust, while around them carnage reigned. Billy also part of it, revolver in hand, taking purposeful aim at the natives as they fled, shooting them in the back, the chest, the head. And down they went everywhere. Down, down, down.

At first they worked in silence, collecting up the bodies, building up the pyre. But soon the sun was upon them and the task was near done and the elation of victory found its voice. Hesitant talking between the troopers, stories traded back and forth. Sullivan wrapped Billy in a sidelong embrace, one arm around his shoulders, slapping his chest, both of them mud-slicked and red, Sullivan laughing, telling Billy how proud he was, how well he had performed. Billy nodded shyly but a smile teased his lips, the same reluctant smile as when Father gave out praise. Billy acting like he didn't care, when of course he always did.

Now the pair of them stood watching the troopers dragging in the last of the dead, and Noone wandered about the camp, making notes in a little book, like a man tallying up his stock. He inspected the bodies, rummaged through their flattened humpies and personal effects. When he found a woman still living he cupped his hand to her face and knelt beside her in silent prayer. The woman spoke to him. Noone listened and nodded and gently replied. Then he took out his knife and slit open her rounded belly and she gave out a cry and died. He rolled up his sleeve and rummaged in the cavity, then pulled out something clotted and lifeless and studied it awhile, before cutting it loose and tossing it aside and wiping his hand clean. He stood, scribbled something in his notebook, moved on to the next, and Tommy sank to his haunches and vomited on the ground.

The man was upon him without warning: a performer from last night's dance, white paint still smeared on his face, eyes wide and full of fire. He came yelping from out of Tommy's eyeline and leaped saddle high to grab him by his arm and drag him to the ground. They landed together but the man scrambled quickly and straddled Tommy from above, pinning him and trying to wrestle the rifle from his grip, while Tommy on his back clung to the stock and fought the muzzle into line with the man's sunken and scarified chest. He fired. Pulled the trigger and heard the empty click. Both fell still for a second. As if watching the misfire for proof. Tommy tried cocking the hammer again, but in the pause the man twisted the rifle free and flattened the barrel against his throat. Tommy sank deeper into the reeking mud, felt his windpipe closing, darkness creeping; he hadn't the strength to throw the man. He pawed at his face while reaching for the revolver tucked into his belt, fingering eyes and nose and mouth, feeling the damp of each orifice, the mucus and the warmth of his breath, no purchase to dig his fingers in. Suddenly the man bit him. Tommy cried out and gave up on the revolver—his last two fingers were knuckle-deep in the man's mouth and he was clenching down hard with his teeth. Tommy pulled but they were clamped there. He was helpless against the bite. Blood drooled from the man's lips. Tommy began hitting him, but his breath was almost out and each blow fell weak as a kiss. There was a crunching sound, and tearing, and the knuckles gave way. Tommy screamed but the scream gurgled mute in his throat and the man jerked his head and Tommy got the two digits loose. The hand came out mangled and bloody and limp. No pain anymore. Like it wasn't even his hand. The man started shouting, blood and spittle spraying, as he weighed down on the rifle again. Tommy's arms fell to his side and he felt himself going out, then his good hand brushed his pocket and the knife he carried there. The fold-

ing knife he'd stolen from Song's Hardware Store. He teased it out, worked open the blade, and with all that was left in him, swung.

The bonfire was doctored with gunpowder and kindling from the crater floor, then left to dry out in the sun. The posse sat resting on a nearby grassy bank. A gruesome collection of men. Caked in gore, smoking and drinking and eating the few provisions they'd rustled from the sacked camp, leavings from last night's meal. Huddled beside them, unbound but tightly grouped, were five females they'd retained. Six at first, but one had run; they'd let her get so far before Jarrah brought her down, a two-hundred-yard shot with his carbine balanced on the pivot of his knee. Now those five remaining shivered together in the sun. None looked older than eighteen.

The knife embedded fully into the native's neck. Tommy drew it out and through the thick spew of blood swung again. The man toppled. Clutching his neck with both hands, his life bleeding out in between. Tommy scrambled to his knees, gasping for breath and watching him expire. He tossed the knife away. Wiped clean his face and spat and inspected his hand and cried out. The last two fingers were barely attached. They hung like wrung chicken necks. Tommy looked about despairingly. Utterly alone in the melee. The Kurrong were thinning but some still ran, and the horses ran loose, and berserk dogs howled. Lone survivors scrambled up the banks of the crater and were chased or picked off from afar. A baby screamed somewhere. Tommy looked down at the man convulsing in the mud before him, drowning in his own blood. His wide eyes stared. Tommy spat at him. He kicked him in the side. The convulsions slowed, deathly tremors and no more. Tommy kicked the man again. He drew his revolver and leveled it at the man's forehead, saw him faintly nodding, and fired. The head jerked with the shot, then rolled to one side. Blood dribbled from the hole. Tommy turned and began walking, feet sucking in the bog, stepping over bodies as he went.

He ate none of the food that was offered and sat apart from the rest of the group, cradling his wounded left hand. Both fingers hung by their tendons, a pulsing husk of blood and bone. He wasn't the only one hurt. Rabbit had a gash in the side of his head and Mallee had been skewered in his side. He wadded the hole nonchalantly, packing it with grass and leaves; Locke retied his wounded arm in its sling. Tommy couldn't look at them. He watched the sun rising round and golden in the east, distant birds flying across it, diving and climbing again. After the chill of the night, animals would be lazing in the warmth, and in towns and on stations were men and women who were not him and did not know him and gave no thought to him or his fingers or anything else he had done. Most likely greeting the day with a smile.

Tommy picked up a stone and threw it. "Fuck 'em," he said.

He tramped through the dead and the dying, revolver raised, taking aim but never firing, his face expressionless now, bereft. A woman wandered by, her head already stoved, stroking the air with her hands. An old man hid in a tangle of emu bushes, whimpering through his fingers. Another man. And another. Barely noticeable who they were. A blur of bodies and of people running, wailing, crawling, and Tommy turning with the revolver extended as if trying to divine something there. "Tommy!" someone shouted. "No dissenters now, you hear?" It was Noone. He had an infant with him, dangling it by the leg. Tommy watched him, horrified. Noone began laughing. He tossed the child high into the air. It cartwheeled limb over limb, crunched when it hit the ground, and lay still. Noone glared at Tommy. He motioned toward him with one hand. Your turn, the hand said. So Tommy spun and found the nearest Kurrong lying facedown on the ground and emptied his revolver into her back, then looked again at Noone. He had his head tilted and was frowning, reckoning whether she was enough, while from across the killing field Billy raised a fist and called "Yes, Tommy!" and gave a triumphant cheer.

Now Billy came to sit beside him on the grassy bank, lowered himself wearily down. He saw Tommy's injured hand and drew in air through his teeth.

"Fuck, look at that. Might be Pope can save them, but I don't know how."

Tommy hid the wounded hand in his lap, covered it with his good.

Billy said, "You get him? The cunt that did it?"

Tommy didn't answer, turned away.

"They were game buggers, though," Billy said breathlessly. "Put up more of a fight than I thought. Reckon I got about a dozen myself—saw you do that gin stone cold at the end. Proud of you, little brother. Knew you wouldn't let us down."

Tommy swung his good fist and connected flush with Billy's eye. His nose gave and shifted with the blow. Billy fell sideways, then touched his nose softly and lunged. He wrestled Tommy into the mud. Blows rained down. Tommy fought back but pain ripped from his hand and through him, and all he could do was turtle up and cry for Billy to stop. It was a while before he did. Before voices broke in and Sullivan was there, hauling Billy away. Tommy clambered to his feet, pressed his hand into his armpit, doubled over with the pain. He screamed. One of the fingers had come all the way loose and lay like a discarded trophy in the mud.

"You fucking bastard!" he shouted. "You fucking cunt!"

Billy had his nose pinched and head back. "The hell d'you hit me for, then?"

"Look at 'em," Sullivan announced, grinning. "Little buggers got such a taste for it they're fighting their-bloody-selves."

Tommy sat down on the bank beside Pope and the old man considered his wounded hand, then looked at Tommy gravely and shook his head. Tommy only stared. Silently, Pope met the stare. His face was sallow and filthy and scarred. A face that carried the sadness of all his years. How many massacres had the old man seen? How many had he taken part in? How many had he survived?

With a strip of fabric Pope tied the stub and injured finger together at the base, then he pointed north out of the crater and said, "Camp." He thumped his hand flat into the opposite palm, edge first, mimicking a blade. Tommy's eyes flared, but Pope shrugged and told him, "Two finger now or hand after—you choose."

The horses were gathered and the last of the dogs chased off and the five women forced into neck chains.

The pyre hummed with flies. The bodies were knotted and twisted so tightly together they seemed melted into one; only the infants were visible whole. Dozens of eyes staring out. Hands and feet poking through. Rabbit and Jarrah lit the bonfire and the gunpowder fizzled and cracked. The flames burned high and quick, then fell as they steadily took. Thick smoke rose. The two troopers rejoined the group, and Noone stood before them and congratulated them all on their work. He spoke of the service they had provided, to the colony, the Crown, the memory of Mr. and Mrs. McBride. In his search of the camp he'd found evidence of the outrage, he said, and heads nodded solemnly like this was true. Tommy cringed. Sickening to hear his name, the lie it now held, and would forever hold. The group disbanded. As they trudged up the slope with the horses, Rabbit paused and called down to the smoldering pyre: "One-two-three in name of Queen surrender," and thick laughter rang out from the men. They walked out of the crater and onto the plain, where they mounted their horses and made for their camp in the rocks, the women chained behind, shuffling through the dirt.

Kala was in the clearing, a hundred yards from camp. Her wrists were still bound to her ankles but she had managed to roll all that way. When she heard the horses coming she raised her head and turned another frantic few rolls. Noone himself went to fetch her. He slung her like a grain sack onto the saddle of his horse and walked her back to the rocks. The group dismounted and saw to their kit, then went into camp and sat down. Noone gave them an hour to rest. Locke and Sullivan slept. Billy smoked a cigarette and stared madly about, his leg jigging up and down and his eyes never still. There was a frisson of excitement in how the troopers talked, but their chatter soon faded and only the women could be heard. They were seated in a circle in the middle of camp, the chains still looped around their necks. Sobbing together quietly. A low and mournful wail. When the time came to leave, they were strung out behind the horses and led east toward the ranges and the settled colony beyond, while behind them in the distance a thick, dark column of smoke rose from the crater that had once been their home, visible for many miles around, if only there were eyes to see it.

30

The washroom was on the ground floor at the back of the house and had been painted all white. Floor, ceiling, walls. Two paintings hung in gold frames: a seascape, and a man catching fish. The copper bathtub was near the window, half-filled, the clean water shimmering with a golden tint, and beside it lay a rug with a swirling pattern and a pile that was meadow-thick. A trio of candles burned. They were grouped on an ornate wooden pedestal table and sent a flickering shadow light across the room. Dusk fell outside. Purple clouds dotted the sky. The sunset was jigsawed by a lace curtain, irregular fragments visible through the weave, and the window was misted on the inside. Steam rose from the bathwater, settled on the panes, dribbled, and collected on the sills.

Tommy stared into the water and shivered. The rug pile bristled between his toes. He was naked. His bloodied clothes lay like entrails by the door. His gaunt body bore bruises, grazes, and cuts, and was darkly sunburned on the arms and neck. The burned skin flaked; the remainder was apple white. On his left hand he wore a fresh white dressing that Weeks had just applied. The vet had peeled open the sodden rags and winced when he'd seen Tommy's wounds. Two stubs, the last and the ring fingers, blistered and swollen and raw—after the amputation, Pope had cauterized the ends with a heated bowie blade. While he worked, Tommy asked Weeks for more detail about Mary's passing; Weeks shook his head and spoke with his eyes down.

"Your sister's been in the ground ten days just about. There ain't nothing can change that and talking won't help. Best make your peace with it, I'd say."

Tommy reached a foot tentatively over the rim of the bath and felt the water scald his skin. He held it there a moment, the water rippling in concentric rings. His foot prickled and steadily numbed, then he climbed fully into the tub and stood in the water to his knees. It burned him. He fought the instinct to get out. His feet and ankles looked red beneath the surface, but that might have been the reflection of the tub. A scum formed on the water. It clouded and thickened and swirled, and floating in there were twigs and burrs and other nameless things. Tommy sat down. He gasped as the heat caught his midriff and groin. The water washed against the sides of the tub. Steam clouded his face. Sweat broke on his cheeks and brow. He scooped up the water one-handed, tipped it over his hair, splashed his face, then sat there very still. The water ebbed gently. He closed his eyes and breathed the steam.

Mrs. Sullivan had told them about Mary the very second they rode in, like she'd been waiting on the verandah all that time. She ran down the steps to meet the horses, her eyes fixed on Tommy and Billy, barely a glance for her husband or the other men. None of the blacks were with them, neither the troopers nor the women they held. On the way in they'd found a blue-gum clearing that was suitable for camp; Sullivan had promised grog and tucker would be brought, then the whites had gone on alone.

Tommy watched her coming. Thought at first it might have been good news. She had her skirts bunched in her hand and her hair flew as she ran, and the house behind her was so grand and majestic that Tommy struggled to keep his emotions down. Everything perfect here, everything clean: as if he'd wandered from a nightmare into a rich and vivid dream.

"What is it?" Sullivan shouted, dismounting. He walked out to meet her but she ran past him to Billy, standing beside his horse. She went to embrace him, saw the state he was in, and instead touched him lightly on the arm. She waved Tommy closer. Her eyes went to his hand. She slung Sullivan a hateful glare. He tried to speak again but she silenced him, then told the two brothers, tears in her eyes, "She was just too young to fight it. Weeks did what he could, but Shanklin never came . . . he never came."

Tommy looked up at the house, at the window of Mary's bedroom, the room where he'd pictured her lying ever since they left; the room where she'd died on her own. They should have been with her. They should have been at her side. He should have known when he left her what would happen while they were gone. He didn't even say a proper good-bye. If they'd been here they could have helped her, or tried to help her, or at least could have held her hand, instead of which . . . instead of which . . . what were they doing, he wondered, the day their sister died?

Tommy was pulled out of himself by Sullivan spitting on the ground.

"Ah, shit," the squatter said, wiping his lips. "Well, least we got the cunts."

There was soap and a flannel on a stool by the bath;

Tommy reached for them and tried to rub up a lather but couldn't manage it one-handed, so applied the soap directly to his skin. It glided soft and smooth and smelled of blossom in the spring. A foam settled on the water. It washed like surf against his body and over his knees. He took hold of the flannel and scrubbed himself down. Gently at first but then harder and harder, until he was tearing at his skin, pulling hairs, breaking scabs, making sure it hurt. He cried out and tossed the flannel into the bath and sat there heaving, the breath surging out of him, body shaking, fighting back tears.

Slowly he calmed. Wiped his face, exhaled, leaned back, and stared through the pattern of window lace. She was out there somewhere, Mary, buried in the little graveyard on the hill. It hadn't seemed right at first, but now Tommy quite liked the idea of his sister's body in a rich man's soil. In years to come folks would see her name and assume she was grander than she was: she'd be a princess forever up here. Plus, it had really pissed off Sullivan, a McBride lying in his private family plot.

"I didn't know what else to do, John. She was rotting in the heat."

They were whispering between themselves but standing close enough for Tommy to hear, his boot caps nudging the graveside, Billy beside him but apart.

The grave was a strip of loose earth still, a cross at the head and a sprig of wattle leaf on top of the mound, the bright yellow flowers browning in the sun.

"Should be at their place, any of the blokes could have taken her down."

"It didn't seem proper without her brothers. I did what I thought best—where's the harm?"

"You can see it from the bloody house!"

"She died here so she's buried here; I don't think it's so bad."

"She doesn't belong here, Katherine. She'll need digging up and that's the end of it."

Tommy spun and glared at him red-eyed. "Don't you fucking touch her."

"Ah, shut your trap, boy. I'll do what I bloody well want."

Now he pushed himself awkwardly to his feet, hand and elbow on the rim of the bath. Water surged off him, and he stood there naked and dripping, searching for a view of the burial site through the window but there was none. Wrong side of the house, maybe. Billy had been for moving her down to Glendale—anything Sullivan wanted, anything at all. Claimed he'd rather she was buried with her own. Tommy wouldn't allow it. Told them it would be a bad burial second time around, and did they want that on their consciences along with everything else? That had quietened them. The threat of being cursed. Mrs. Sullivan suggested they think on it more, no need for a decision yet, and tenderly she'd steered the boys from the graveside, her skirts whispering through the long grass as she led them down the hill.

"I've asked for hot bathwater," she said. "Wash all this trouble away. How about we let Billy have the first one, then we'll boil another fresh for you, Tommy. While you're waiting, Mr. Weeks can take a good look at that hand."

He stepped out of the bath onto the rug and rubbed himself dry with a towel. At home they used fabric off-cuts or air-dried in the sun, but the towel was soft and thick as down. He pissed into the chamber pot and the piss stung coming out, a yellow so deep it was verging on brown, same color as the wattle on Mary's grave just about. He finished and stood looking around the room. There was a robe hanging on the door, intended for him, he supposed. He blew out the candles, watched the smoke curl, then went back to the bathtub and leaned over the rim. It had a plug in the bottom, the first of that kind he'd ever seen, rigged to empty the water directly outside, no tipping the bathtub off the verandah here.

He reached into the murk, the water warm and thick, pushing his arm deeper, through whatever floated there, felt around for the stopper, and yanked it from the hole. The water rushed in the pipe. Sounds of down-pour, of flood; Tommy watched the walls anxiously as if expecting a breach. As the bath drained it left a shitty sluice of residue on the sides of the tub; Tommy grimaced and knelt and tried to wipe it off but he couldn't, not without fresh water to rinse. So he leaned on the rim and watched the level fall, until the hole belched the last of it and all that remained was a mess of dirt and blood and other unknowable things . . . and in the mess were people running, dark little shapes scurrying everywhere like ants, and falling, falling to the ground, as others moved among them, cutting them down, and right there in the bathtub, revolver in his hand, was a tiny ant-like Tommy, firing and firing and firing again.

He lurched upward and reeled across the room, smacking into the door and tangling himself in the robe. He snatched it off the hook and wrapped it around his body and flung open the door. Waiting in the hall-way was Jenny, the housemaid, a pile of folded clothes in her hands.

"I brought you these. For while yours are being washed."

Tommy took the clothes from her as he hurried past.

"Burn them," he called, running for the stairs.

31

In his borrowed shirt and trousers he stood outside the drawing room, listening through the door. Sullivan was talking, the end of some tale, and when he paused in the telling, laughter rang out. Tommy swallowed. He looked along the hall. The front door was right there. Beyond it the steps, the track, and he could be gone. Collect Beau from the stables, ride off into the night. The horse wouldn't thank him for it, but no one else would complain. Sullivan would be glad to be rid of him and Billy . . . well, the last time he and Billy had properly talked was the night Noone caught them arguing in the rain.

Footsteps crossed the atrium: the houseboy bringing a silver platter of food. He saw Tommy and slowed, motioning toward the drawing room door.

"Excuse please, mister."

Tommy stood rigidly. He flushed and touched his face and hid his bandaged hand. "We've met," he said. "Before—what was your name again?"

"Is Benjamin, mister."

"I'm Tommy."

The houseboy kept his eyes down. "Excuse please, Mister Tommy."

Tommy didn't move. Building himself up to ask. "Where are you . . . I mean, who are your people, Benjamin? Where are you from?"

He frowned, then a cautious smile broke on his face. "I from Big House, Mister Tommy. I been always living here."

Tommy stepped aside. Benjamin opened the door. Sudden silence in the room, then Sullivan sighed and said, "Thought you were the bloody missus. Come on in, son, come on in. Get yourself a drink."

They were all there. Sullivan, Billy, Locke, Noone. Standing by the fireplace with drinks in their hands, the Christmas tree sparkling alongside. All were washed and shaved and dressed for the meal: Sullivan in a black dinner suit, Noone a starched dress uniform, Billy in a suit also, his hair slick and back-combed, and Locke in clean trousers and white shirt, his arm cradled in a fresh white sling.

Tommy edged into the room. Benjamin was offering the platter, but Sullivan waved him away, and he placed it on the sideboard and left. Tommy watched for some acknowledgment as they crossed, but Benjamin kept his gaze resolutely down.

"Get yourself a brandy," Sullivan called. "That decanter there. After two weeks of that other shite it'll do you good to have a proper drink."

Two weeks. It had only been two weeks.

Sullivan chuckled to himself and all watched Tommy move toward the drinks table and do as he was told. He picked up the glass and joined them, standing between Billy and Noone.

"Look," Sullivan said, "I might as well say, no one blames you for going off a bit out there. It's done with, forgotten, you came through in the end. The bush can do strange things to any bloke. We all go a bit off sometimes."

"Speak for yourself, John," Noone said. "It was rather pleasant, I felt."

More laughter. Sullivan continued, "What matters is we won. The bloody Kurrong—we've never been able to shake 'em, been after 'em for years. We're all better off because of it. The cattle, the land . . . you two included, I mean. We'll get to all that later, but Glendale's yours if you want it, get the place going again.

It's exciting times, boys. The future's in our hands now!"

He raised his glass and the others did the same, and the crystal clinked softly as it touched. They held the pose, waiting; Tommy lifted his glass and gave a mumbled cheer. Billy was grinning wildly, his cheeks flushed and his eyes already glazed, and Noone arched his eyebrows and inclined his head at Tommy, like this was all just a grand old game to him, and he was much amused.

. . .

Christmas and New Year had passed while they were gone, and Mrs. Sullivan had saved the feast. Pheasant, turkey, ham from a boar, carved and the joints broken loose, three steaming platters along the length of the dining table. Sullivan was seated at one head and Noone was at the other, with Mrs. Sullivan on her husband's left, Locke to his right, and Tommy and Billy facing each other either side of Noone.

There was little conversation at first. The men gorged on the meat, rich and moist and thick, and though Tommy had doubted his appetite, the meal had him gorging too. He struggled with the cutlery. Couldn't grip with his left hand; the fork slipped when he used it, the silver tines screeching on the china plate, and Billy scowled across at him as if only just noticing his brother was two fingers short.

"Tommy, just use your hands," Mrs. Sullivan told him. "Put the cutlery down."

"I'm alright, thank you."

He glanced shyly at her along the table. Her eyes were soft but insistent. Tommy laid down his knife and transferred the fork to his right hand, stuck a lump of boar, and took a bite from the edge. Mrs. Sullivan smiled and went back to her meal, then as an afterthought added, "You too, Raymond, of course. If that shoulder's bothering you still."

Locke dropped his cutlery with a clatter and pounced on a pheasant leg. He tore into the meat, mumbling, "Much obliged, ta."

Mrs. Sullivan nodded primly and smoothed the napkin on her lap. "You know, I probably shouldn't ask, but what on earth happened out there? How did the two of you get so badly hurt?"

"Native speared him," Sullivan said, nodding at Locke, who lifted his eyes in acknowledgment, then went back to his bone. Sullivan shook his head, added, "Useless bastard had a free shot and only hit a dog."

"Got him in the end, though," Locke said, chewing. "Got him in the end."

She turned her head slowly. "And you, Tommy? Your hand?"

Noone lifted a finger to silence him. "I'm sorry, Mrs. Sullivan, but it's really quite a gruesome tale. Such is the nature of the task, unfortunately, and we are talking about savages, after all. Not the kind of conversation suitable for a lady, and certainly not at her own dinner table. But I must congratulate you on this supper, and at such short notice too. It really is a marvelous meal."

She held his eyes, a fixed but pleasant smile. "Thank you, Mr. Noone. The kitchen are responsible, but I'll accept on their behalf."

She sliced through a baby potato and popped a piece in her mouth. There was a silence. The silver tinkled the plates. Sullivan poured himself more wine and sent the bottle down the table, and when it came to him, Tommy filled his glass. He offered the bottle to Noone, who frowned and nodded for him to pour. Tommy did so. Billy slid his glass across the table but Tommy set the bottle on a mat. Billy glowered at him and poured his own wine.

"So are you married yourself, Mr. Noone? Any family of your own?"

All save Mrs. Sullivan paused. She went on eating in her delicate, precise way. Noone laid down his cutlery, dabbed his lips, took a sip of wine, then lowered the glass and affected a quick smile.

"It's kind of you to ask after them, Mrs. Sullivan. Thank you."

"How old are your children?"

Sullivan patted her wrist. "There now, Katherine. Leave the man in peace."

Noone raised his palm, took another drink of wine. "No, no, we must talk about something and it's preferable to the last line of inquiry at least. I have two daughters, Mrs. Sullivan. Ophelia and Bryony. They are, let me see, twelve and nine years old."

"Two daughters. Beautiful. If only we were so lucky."

Sullivan coughed and said quickly, "Problem with daughters is they grow into wives. Pity the poor bugger comes asking you for their hands."

Again Noone forced a smile. Mrs. Sullivan gestured to Tommy and Billy. "Two potential suitors sitting right here perhaps?"

Noone looked dead-eyed between them. "Perhaps."

"And how do they like living out here, Mr. Noone? All the dirt and heat and flies?"

"No, they're in Melbourne. A much more civilized place."

Sullivan pointed his fork at his wife. "That's where

I found this one. To hear her talk about the place you'd think the streets were paved with gold, not the shit of a thousand Jimmys come fresh off the boats. I've never liked cities. Living arse to cheek like that, it's not natural. A man needs space, land."

"You must miss them," Mrs. Sullivan said. "Being away for so long."

"The work is important. It's a small price to pay."

"Then perhaps the better question is that they must miss you?"

Noone stared at her. "They understand."

"As we all must, of course. It is an age of abandoned wives."

She said it evenly, unaffected, but Noone's eyes twitched.

"I provide them with a very fine life, Mrs. Sullivan. The best of the schools, house help, a substantial property in Kew."

She looked up sharply. "Didn't they build a lunatic asylum in Kew?"

Locke sniggered. Noone said flatly, "Cassandra has no cause to complain."

Mrs. Sullivan squared her cutlery on her plate, dabbed her lips, then folded her napkin and laid it aside. "Well, I have to say I had no idea policing paid so well. John, I fear you're in the wrong field."

Sullivan glared at her. She ignored him and sipped her wine. Locke said, "It ain't the policing that keeps him—" but Noone clicked his tongue and Locke fell silent and went back to his food. The others did likewise. Tommy glanced along the table at Mrs. Sullivan sitting straight-backed and formal with her hands in her lap, but there was an air of mischief about her, a smirk playing on her lips. Maybe the wine had done it, but in that one small exchange she'd said more to Noone than Tommy would ever have dared. Than any of them, in fact. And yet when he thought about it she'd not really said much of anything at all.

. . .

Shaken roughly awake, he came lunging out of the wallow of sofa cushions and grabbed Billy by his jacket lapels, pulling himself upright, their faces very close.

"Easy now. He wants to talk, said to wake you. Come on."

Tommy let go of Billy's collar and slumped back onto the sofa, peering around the empty drawing room. The fire was low, the candles too, the windows turned to mirrors by the darkness outside. There were crystal tumblers on the tables and ashtrays of burned-out cigars: the last Tommy remembered was accepting a drink but refusing a cigar, and the drone of their voices as he fell asleep.

He coughed and cleared his throat. "What time is it?"

"Late. He's waiting. Got a proposal for us, he says."

Billy stood over him, his body all atwitch. Tommy's eyes drooped and he let them close. "I don't want to hear it," he said.

"He says we both need to agree."

"Fuck him. You go. Crawl in on your knees."

"He's giving us Glendale, Tommy. We get to keep the run."

Tommy jerked awake and clambered to his feet, the two of them facing each other in front of the dying fire.

"Since when was Glendale his to give? What's he want in return?"

"I don't know. Got a plan, he says."

"I'll bet he fucking does."

Tommy glimpsed their reflections in the window. Like he was on the outside and two other boys were confronting each other through the glass.

"Look," Billy said. "You don't have to like the bloke, but let's at least hear him out. Everything's different now, Tommy. Everything's changed. You couldn't hardly eat tonight—how d'you think you'll go getting work somewhere else? Who'd take a cripple with eight fingers over a bloke with all ten?"

Tommy looked at his hand—that word, cripple—then back at Billy again. "Rather lose two fingers than my own bloody mind."

"What's that mean?"

"Means it's not just me that's changed. You're blind to it, to everything, to what's happened, to how things are between us now."

"Which is how exactly?"

"You'll make me say it?"

"Only way I'll understand you."

Tommy threw up his hands. "Fucking . . . me and you, I don't hardly know you anymore. Laying with natives, shooting them, anything Sullivan says."

"You weren't no different. I counted at least three."

"And I can't hardly stand myself for it. You act like we've been out mustering, not killing a hundred blacks."

"The law was with us. John said—"

"He's a fucking snake, Billy. You're going in with a fucking snake. The only reason he helped us was to get at the Kurrong; bastard's kept Daddy under his heel for years, then as soon as he's dead makes out like the two were best bloody mates."

"How did he? What did John ever do to us?"

"Damming that creek for one thing, and who knows what else besides."

"Well, might be he feels bad, or his wife might have put him up to it—I don't care, Tommy! The bloke wants to help us so why wouldn't we? Where else are we going to go? Me and you on the wallaby? You'd rather that than here?"

"Aye," Tommy said. "Or on my own. Either way."

Billy considered him carefully. "We're all the other's got left."

"If you say so."

"They fucking killed them! What else was I supposed to do!"

Tommy stepped a pace closer. "Joseph wasn't there."

Billy's face twisted in disgust. "So you're taking their side?"

"You see nothing, feel nothing . . . he's broke you and you don't even know it."

Billy rolled his tongue inside his lips. A hard and steady stare. He walked past Tommy, deliberately nudged his shoulder, then marched out of the room. Tommy heard him walking across the atrium to Sullivan's parlor. He looked at himself in the windows again. A stranger watched him back: a strange boy in a strange room wearing strange clothes.

"Tom-my!"

Sullivan's voice. Two distinct syllables. A rising, full-blooded scream.

"*Tom-my!*"

He swallowed. Fidgeting his jacket hem, blinking at the floor.

"*Tom-my!*"

His name tolled around the atrium and through the entire house. A savagery in how he said it, a threat. Tommy started moving and the boy in the window seemed to hesitate before following, until Tommy was in the atrium and alone. In the far corner the parlor door was open, light flickering inside. They weren't talking. Listening to his footsteps on the atrium floorboards.

Tommy presented himself in the doorway. Billy twisted in the wingback to watch him; Sullivan spread his arms over the desk.

"There he is. Thought you'd nodded off again, son. Come in now, take a seat."

Tommy inched forward. The sconces were lit and the room was full of shadows and there was a strong smell of liquor in the air. On the desk before him Sullivan had a decanter and a whiskey glass and he rotated the glass back and forth, watching Tommy all the while. The three of them were alone. Locke and Noone were gone. Tommy lowered himself into the other wingback and Billy straightened on his. All Tommy could see of his brother were his forearms and legs.

"There now," Sullivan said, smiling. "I know you're

a little reluctant but it's important you hear this. Drink before we start? No? Well, probably for the best—we've all had plenty tonight." He smiled, raised his glass, took a sip, and smacked his lips. "Anyway, I thought it best we got this done straight off. I don't like drawing things out, figured you two would want to know where you stand."

"Stand with what?" Tommy said, and Sullivan raised a pudgy hand.

"Boys, listen. I understand it's been a bad time, and you're not in the best of ways, but there's more bad news coming, I'm afraid. Your father, he didn't own Glendale. I don't know what he told you, but it's not a real selection in the legal sense of the word. He wasn't the one that cleared it, or settled it, or built the house and sheds. He took on the run from someone else. Leased, not bought. And unfortunately, now that he's gone, that lease becomes forfeit since you boys are still minors and too young to hold land. Are you following what I'm saying so far?"

He took a drink and looked at them, then nodded and went on.

"Good, because here's the thing: Ned had run up a fair debt over the years, and that debt still needs to be paid. The only ones left to pay it are you."

There was a silence. Hesitantly Billy asked, "What debt? To who?"

Sullivan spread his hands open then folded them on the desk.

"You see, the whole of this district, it's mine. You get on a horse, and just about anywhere you can ride in the space of two days, one way or another belongs to me. Name on a title means nothing. My grandfather was the only bloke who dared come out here and stake a bloody claim. He cleared the land, beat off the natives, got this whole valley ready to graze. They hailed him as a hero, now the wig wearers are trying to carve it all up with their bloody Land Acts. So what I do is, I dummy them. You know what dummying is? The land gets bought by my agent—he's just a name on a deed—then I put in a man of my choosing on a short lease. I set him up with all he needs, he pays me an amount in return. Not a share of profits, mind you: I get paid out first. Should be he can make a very fine life for himself, but sometimes they do fail and I have to find a new fella to take on the run . . . but the debt, the debt stays with the first bastard, minus whatever he leaves behind. You understand what I'm saying here, boys?"

He took a drink and waited. Billy said, "What's Daddy's debt to us, though?"

"Everything. You've been living in my pocket all your short lives."

"Meaning what?" Tommy asked him. "You want us gone? Fine, we're gone."

"No!" Sullivan said, laughing, slapping a hand on the desk. "I want you to bloody stay! There's potential in the pair of you. I'm going to give you a chance. I can't grant you a formal lease, but you'll be selectors in all but name, run the place as your own. Course, you'll need cattle and men, a few horses maybe, we'll get to all that once the rains have passed. You can pay back what's owed over time, same terms as your old man. Assuming you'd be interested, that is?"

"Yeah," Billy said quickly. "I mean, thanks."

"What do you get out of it?" Tommy asked.

"The debt gets paid, plus my own people on my own land. It's not hard, son."

"And how are we meant to feed our cattle when you've got the river dammed?"

Sullivan sniffed, took a drink. "That dam's been there for decades. Ned knew the conditions. Same as I'm offering you now."

"What if we don't accept?"

Billy leaned forward, looked across. "Will you shut your bloody mouth?"

"He ruined us," Tommy said, pointing over the desk. "That debt was a noose round Daddy's neck—you saw how he was. Even scuttled us in town when Daddy couldn't pay, starving us out by the end." He looked at Sullivan. "Tell me I'm wrong."

"I was his proprietor, Tommy: like it or not, your father worked for me. I gave him chance after chance . . . him and your mother had no right carrying on the way they did. Bloody well turned on me in the end. Lack of basic gratitude, of well-earned respect. And I'm sorry to say it, boys, but I'm starting to feel something similar from the pair of you."

"No, we're grateful," Billy told him. "For everything. Thank you."

Sullivan wagged his finger slowly at Tommy. "I'm not so sure about your brother here, Billy-boy. Makes me wonder if I'm not being a touch hasty, if I've judged the pair of you wrong. I take you in, care for your sister, petition Noone on your behalf, even pay his bloody fee. Hell, I just rode half the colony to get justice for your family and—"

"That was for you, not us," Tommy said. "Joseph wasn't even there. You're the one that wanted the Kurrong dead. That's what you paid Noone for."

Sullivan leaned back in his chair. The leather creaked. He drained his glass.

"Now we're getting to it. Alright, Tommy, let me make this crystal fucking clear. You two owe me. If you've any sense between you, you'll see your debt paid. You don't seem to recognize the position you're in. It's a good life I'm giving you, better than you could make on your own. But if you turn down this offer, there won't be another in its place. I fucking *own you*. I could have you arrested, locked up, hanged for false testimony and what you did to them blacks. I could put you to work slopping out the dunnies and shoveling horseshit, and no one would even wonder where you are. If you run I'll have you hunted down—you've seen what happens to them that cross me; don't make the same mistake yourselves."

"He didn't mean nothing," Billy blurted. "Tell him, Tommy."

"Yeah," Tommy mumbled. "It came out wrong."

Sullivan considered him a long time, sighed, and said, "Well, good. I'm pleased to hear it. We can't work together without trust. I think that's where it broke down with your old man. Trust. Too many things unsaid."

"We trust you. We're grateful. Honestly, we are."

"I know that, Billy. But it's him whose word I need to hear."

Tommy scratched at his dressing with his thumb. He nodded his head.

"You sure about that?"

"Yes."

"Then it seems we have a deal."

"Thank you," Billy said. "I mean it. We won't let you down, I swear."

Tommy looked up suddenly. "When's Noone leaving?"

"Noone? Tomorrow, I expect, day after maybe—why?"

"What if he left Kala, as a housemaid or whatever, help us around the place?"

"You mean that young gin?"

Tommy nodded. A smile spread on Sullivan's face. "Christ, if you wanted to fuck her you should have. You've missed your chance by now. Besides, you know the kind of state she'll be in, once those troopers are through?"

"He's selling her. You could buy her for us."

"We don't want her," Billy protested. "She ain't no good."

"But you could do that? Buy her? Talk to Noone?"

"Tommy, that's enough! I'm not buying some fucking gin!"

Sullivan was shaking his head. "Noone would never let you have that girl."

"He'd let you."

Sullivan seemed to be mulling on it. Hurriedly Tommy added, "I'll agree if you do it. Be your agent, or whatever you just said. Those are the terms. Or else no."

He held Sullivan's eye. The silence hung and hung.

"Well, well, at last the runt gets ahold of the tit." He let go a deep sigh. "Alright, young Tommy, I'll talk to the inspector, see what I can do."

Sullivan half rose in his chair and offered a hand across the desk. Billy jumped forward and grabbed it and they shook. Sullivan turned the hand to Tommy. When he gripped it the skin was plump and clammy and soft. He tried to pull away but Sullivan held him there, not even shaking anymore, staring at him until Tommy finally stumbled free. Sullivan flopped back into his chair. He waved them toward the door, reached for the decanter, and poured himself another drink.

32

I still see them, you know, be coming at me my whole
life is how it feels. Like we're back there, never
left—I'll be doing something and look up and I see it
all again. Smell the blood and the powder, hear them
scream. Earlier, in the washroom, they were in the bottom of the bloody tub. I fucking *saw* them, Billy, and
us too with our revolvers, shooting them one by one. I
thought after, that must have been how God saw it, and
maybe Mary if she was watching with him, though I'm
hoping Daddy was right about all that. I think he was.
We ain't worth shit to God.

"The dreams are the worst part. Reliving it bit by
bit. Most of the time it's as it happened and we're sitting out that dust storm, or hunting that first lot, or
waiting out the night in the rain, but then it jumbles

all together and I go from squatting by that roo Rabbit clubbed to drowning on my back in the mud. That native's on top of me and I can never get him off, my arms are weak as twigs. He's painted from his dancing and he's pressing me down, then either he bites me or I bite him, it changes dream to dream. I don't know how I do it but I get his fingers, his lips, his nose, and I can feel them crunching in my mouth. I don't stop, though. Tear into him like a dog. Then he pulls out a knife and slits my throat and I feel the blood run warm. It's happening backward, you see. Like I'm him and he's me, whatever that's supposed to mean.

"Only I don't know that I'm dreaming; it always feels so real. Noone's watching me shoot that woman in the back but she's moving. . . . I thought she was already dead but what if I was wrong? I had six shots in that revolver, could have used them on the troopers, on Noone, but I did nothing. The idea never even came to me before now. I went along with it all like the rest of you, killed three of my own, and that's the only truth that counts. You'd say that's one for Ma, Daddy, and Mary, but how can that be right? Three plus three makes six, Billy. It doesn't take it back to none.

"That's how you think these days, though, isn't it? Sullivan's twisted your head. I've seen you more chewed up about putting down a horse than you are about what we did. They're still people, Billy. If you talked to them you'd see that they're not that much different to us. Arthur started out the same as that lot . . . even Rabbit, Kala; you know Rabbit only joined up because his family was killed? Whites killed his family so he took our side, figured he was safer with us than them. It's like me and you joining a fucking Kurrong tribe.

"Throwing yourself at Sullivan makes no more sense—didn't I tell you he was a snake? Kept Daddy on a short leash all his life with this debt, what else was there between them you and me don't know?

"And we won't be no different. He'll treat us just the same. Daddy would be spitting if he saw the deal we made. We could have done all this differently, still could, but I know your mind won't be changed. Think about it. If we'd taken Mary to Shanklin instead of coming up here, told MacIntyre about the killings and let him bring in Noone. We'd have been free of Sullivan, could have done anything, me and you. Leave this place, work our way south on whatever stations would take both of us, keep a bit aside, then when we're old enough, put in for a selection of our own. Victoria, maybe, somewhere that gets the rain. Be nice, that. Later we could have put in for another run and had the two of them side by side. Sheep and cattle, maybe a few crops if the soil was right. Get married, have families, not answer to anyone but ourselves . . . I can't live like this, Billy. Stay if you want. I'll do it on my own.

"See, that's what I was thinking with Kala: I don't mean to set her on at the house like I said, I mean to turn her free. Soon as Noone brings her I'll ride her out Bewley way, to those camps they have out there. Figured she could take up with that lot instead. I saw girls there once, Kala's age, families and all that. Course, they might be a different kind of black—they don't all talk the same, Rabbit says—but she'll be better off there than wherever Noone has planned. Did I tell you that he fiddled with her? That night in the ranges, same night you . . . well, I just thought if I could help her before I left it was worth trying, that's all. I don't expect you'll agree with me, but I ain't asking, so don't start."

In the quiet darkness he lay on his back, listening to Billy sleep. The rhythm of his breathing, slow and steady, catching in his throat, that little ticking sound he made. Tommy rolled onto his side, hugged the blankets, and stared across at him, the shape of him. His family. Only a brother left. He slept so soundly, that was the thing. All this time Tommy had been talking, his brother had not so much as stirred. And yet here he lay awake, into the early hours, afraid to close his eyes.

33

He sat on the front steps, watching the west for signs of Kala coming in. Noone had agreed to sell her. Tommy didn't know the price.

He waited, idly stroking his bandaged hand, feeling the stubs of his fingers beneath. Tender to the touch, the skin as tight and stiff as unworked hide. It wasn't but half a hand. Still took him by surprise when the fingers weren't there. So many everyday tasks that would need to be relearned. Or done differently, anyway. He doubted he'd given a single thought to those fingers until they were gone. And isn't that the way of things. You only miss the missing, don't value what you have.

From here he had a view of the workers' camp, thin smoke trails rising from the scullery and the embers of last night's fires, all the way across to the cattle yards and sheds. Men wandered between the buildings and some rode out on horseback and their calls carried faintly up the hill. Too small for Tommy to make them out but there might have been one or two that he knew: Locke; the watchman, Jessop; and Weeks, not forgetting Weeks, who couldn't keep Mary alive long enough for Tommy to say good-bye.

He wished there'd been more between them. Wished he'd made more effort, given her more of a chance. When she was little she'd looked up to Tommy in the same way he did Billy; Tommy had been too distracted to care. She was always trying to prove herself, to join in, but Billy had never been able to see past the fact she was a girl, and Tommy was too young or too weak to decide for himself. He supposed he'd assumed she would always be there, that they'd have time. Now all he could do was miss her. There was plenty of time for that.

Tommy leaned against the balustrade and rested his head on the warm wood. The sun was high but clouds were gathering and threatening rain again. It went like this some years: a cycle of broken storms, then a downpour that lasted for weeks. He'd heard of families, up north mainly, who got it so bad they'd be cut off by floodwater for whole months at a time, needed a raft just to get across their yard. What cattle they'd not sold or put in the sheds, they'd find drowned the next time they rode out, floating in the creek or even stuck up a tree when the water went down. And yet they stayed there, year on year, everyone did out here. Clinging to whatever scraps of a life they were born into, no matter the cost. That's all Billy was doing, sticking with what he knew and to hell with everything else. Dumb as bloody cattle: a cow finds herself in a dried-up paddock and doesn't think to leave, next thing she's been hollowed by the dingos and finished by the birds.

Had Billy thought what it would be like, going back to Glendale and its ghosts? Nothing was living there now, no cattle, no horses, even the dogs were dead. Had he imagined them, sleeping in their bedroom, eating a meal at the table, looking out of the window and seeing two white crosses thinly coated in dust?

Footsteps sounded behind him, light footsteps, toe rather than heel. Tommy turned to find Mrs. Sullivan coming down the stairs, her skirts raised in her hand. She was dressed all in white. Her dark curls gleamed. She smiled at Tommy. He hunched forward again, his forearms on his knees, picking at his nails. She flicked out her skirts and sat down beside him with a sigh.

"These steps weren't made for women's shoes. They're too steep by half."

Tommy nodded vaguely, lifted his eyes to the view.

"How's your hand?"

"Fine."

"How's it really?"

"Sore."

She took his wrist, examined the hand, turned it back and forth. "So long as there's no rot, you'll survive. A couple of fingers can be compensated for—you'll have the measure of it soon enough."

"Billy says I won't can work."

"And what do you think?"

He sniffed and stared out. "I reckon I'll be right once I'm used to it."

"I think so too. And John'll see you're looked after."

"Yeah. I'm sure he will."

There was bitterness in his voice but she ignored it. "Well, I'm certainly glad we'll be neighbors. You're welcome to visit anytime. It would make a pleasant change to be on good terms."

Tommy's jaw clenched.

"I didn't mean anything, of course," she said hurriedly. "Other than I'd like it if we could be friends. You know, when I first came out here I was going to be at the heart of a whole community, until I found there wasn't one, and not even enough people for one to be formed. I had so many plans: you see down there, at the bottom of the steps, I thought I'd put a rose garden on either side, little hedgerows in boxes, with vines twisting up through these rails. Along the track I planted conifers, evergreens." She laughed and touched her lips. "Everything died. All of it. Not one thing survived. It's like the soil is poisoned. Only that awful scrub grass grows."

"Rain's coming," Tommy said flatly. "That might help."

"Oh, I'm past even trying now. Roses. Sounds ridiculous, doesn't it? John thought I was mad." He felt her watching him but kept his eyes on the view. "Have you been sleeping?"

"Not really."

"You should try. You look very tired."

In the silence, Tommy picked at the bandage on his hand. He said, "Do you know what went on out there? What we did?"

"I was against you going from the start. It's a terrible thing for a child."

"I'm not a child."

"No, I don't suppose you are." She sighed, glanced behind her, up the stairs. "Would you prefer to be alone? Only, I saw you and thought you might like some company, perhaps talk about Mary—you must be upset?"

He took a long time to answer: "How did it happen? How did she die?"

"I told you, she just—"

"No, I mean exactly. What did it look like? I should have been there."

"It was all very peaceful, Tommy. Mr. Weeks kept her comfortable with his drops. We were waiting for Shanklin the day you rode out. I sent the telegram that morning myself. He never came."

"And she died when?"

"Late the same night. I intended sending a boy into Bewley the very next day, fetch him out right away."

So they were camping, Tommy reasoned. That first night in the scrubs. Noone woke him. Leaning against the myall tree, whittling the cross for Locke.

"Did he come the day after? Shanklin?"

"No. Nothing. I don't know what happened."

They sat in silence a moment. Tommy said, "She always looked peaceful."

"Oh, she was. She was as comfortable as a person can be."

"Did you sit with her?"

She nodded. "For as long as I could."

"But . . . was she on her own?"

"Yes, Tommy, but listen—that's only natural, we're all alone at the end. She knew you and Billy cared for her and would have been there if you could."

"Least you were."

She reached out and cupped his knee. "Are you hungry? Shall I ask for an early lunch?"

"I'm waiting on Noone," he said.

"Noone? Whatever for?"

"He's fetching over Kala, one of them we found. For a housegirl."

"A housegirl? Goodness—is she trained?"

"What in?"

"Cooking, cleaning, laundry, and such. She won't be any good to you if not."

Tommy shrugged. "She'll be alright."

"No, that won't do. John should have told me. I'd rather lend you one of ours. You can't just take on anyone, Tommy. She's wild. Might not even be safe."

"Safe how?"

"Well, what if she means to harm you? No, you must have one of mine, while we train the new girl here. When she's capable we'll swap them. How does that sound?"

"Thank you, no. It's not really for that. I don't care if she's trained or not."

Mrs. Sullivan sat there scowling, then snatched a breath and said, "Even you, barely a man, I just don't understand it sometimes. It's really no better than fucking a dog. You know, John's been with so many his cock doesn't work. He's all dried up and limp as a leaf. Watch yourself, Tommy, or you'll end up the same, and bloody well deserve it too."

If she was shamed by her language she didn't show it. She stood and flicked her skirts and marched back up the steps. Tommy listened to her go. He wanted to call after her, to explain what he had planned, but he was learning. He'd asked for her help once and she'd scolded him, then given him a bag of boiled sugar sweets. The sweets had been a godsend, but she wouldn't have thought to give them to any of the men. Might as well have scrubbed his hair and pinched him on the cheek.

34

They brought Kala around the back of the house, meaning at first Tommy missed her coming in. He was still on the steps when he caught a burst of male laughter and what sounded like a muffled scream; he came down the stairs, followed the noise around the homestead to the rear yard. Rabbit had her. She was naked on his horse, bound, her head covered with a feed bag, but it was Mallee who was laughing and causing her to scream. He leaned from his saddle to poke and tickle her, putting on a show for the housemaids and kitchen hands who were gathered in the yard. They watched his performance vacantly, only their heads moving, slowly tracking the horses as they crossed from left to right.

"Hey!" Tommy shouted, running. "Hey, stop that!"

He met them in the clearing between the house and the sheds. Rabbit offered a muted wave. Tommy noticed scratches on Kala's body, marks on her legs.

"Where you taking her?"

Rabbit answered: "Tie her in stable, Marmy says. Big trouble this one."

"Leave her with me. I'll do it." He waved for them to bring her down.

Mallee was scowling at him. "Stable," he said.

Tommy looked from the trooper to Kala again, sitting upright and alert on the back of Rabbit's horse, listening from inside her hood. Tommy pulled back his shoulders and fixed Mallee in the eye.

"She's ours now," he said. "A gift from Noone—from Marmy. I'll tell him you wouldn't let me have her. He won't be pleased. I'll tell him it was you."

He pointed at Mallee. The trooper glanced worriedly at Rabbit, whose shrug said he didn't disagree. Mallee dismounted and dragged Kala kicking from the horse. She fought him all the way down. Tommy snatched the feed bag from her head and she fell still, stood there blinking and squinting against the sun. Air surged through her nose. Her face was swollen in places and her bottom lip was cut. She looked at Tommy and he smiled warmly but her gaze went right through him as if they'd never met. He took hold of her arm. She struggled and Tommy let go.

"Big trouble this one," Rabbit repeated, shaking his head. He smiled at Tommy and the smile was very familiar, like it meant something, like the two of them were friends. It wasn't impossible. In another life, maybe. Another place. Another world.

"Help me get her to the stables," Tommy said, then to Mallee: "You stay here."

To quieten her screaming, Tommy wrestled the feed bag back onto her head, then he and Rabbit each took an arm and dragged the writhing girl past the sheds to the stable barn. One of the doors was already open. They hauled her inside. The barn was empty, the air shaded and cool; Kala stopped fighting once they were in. The horses nickered in their stalls and watched the trio curiously—the smell of the feed bag, maybe. Tommy made for Beau's stall. His gray snout poked over the gate, sniffing at the air, then he lifted his whole head out. Tommy spoke to him. A hushed greeting and that was all. But Rabbit was reading his intentions and he pulled Kala to a halt, and he and Tommy stood facing each other in the aisle.

"Tie her in stable, Marmy says."

"No, she's mine now."

"Marmy says—"

"He's not even here."

Rabbit's eyes flared. He looked terrified. "Marmy *everywhere.*"

"Not where I'm taking her."

Rabbit's head inclined slightly. "Taking her?"

And Tommy was thinking: tell him Glendale, as their housemaid; or into the woods to fuck her; or somewhere she can be sold.

"The camps outside Bewley. I aim to turn her loose."

Rabbit stared at him a long time. Tommy fidgeted in his gaze. An urge to flee or lunge at him, neither of which felt sound. He'd lose Kala if he ran, and despite Rabbit's being unarmed, Tommy still had only one hand with which to fight. And then there was Mallee, waiting with the horses not a hundred yards away, out of sight behind the sheds. One shout from Rabbit and he would come.

Rabbit blinked and nodded, drew his lips tight. There was a sadness in him, a pain at the choice Tommy was forcing him to make. Whatever was between them was over now. One way or another, this was the end.

Rabbit reached for the bag on Kala's head, took it off slowly, and spoke to her. She looked at Tommy. Her eyes were wild and very wide. Tommy waited, unsure what to do. Rabbit offered him the feed bag.

"For she start screaming," he said.

Tommy took the bag. Rabbit turned to leave. Tommy called for him to wait but he didn't and it was to his back that Tommy said, "Thank you." Rabbit raised a hand. He didn't pause or turn. He walked out into the sunshine and over toward the sheds, and there was no telling what he might do next. Might have been genuine, might have been a ruse. Tommy hoped he knew. Hoped he'd read him right.

"Quickly," he said, grabbing Kala's wrist and dragging her into Beau's stall. She didn't fight him this time, stood by while he got the saddle on, difficult with his hand but he managed. She mounted up without him asking. Tommy found a folded blanket draped over the stable partition and offered it to her, thought she might cover herself with it, but she only held it to her chest. He didn't take the feed bag. Beau trampled over it as Tommy led him from the stall. They walked slowly down the center aisle, and at the door Tommy halted and stepped into the sunshine and scanned the clearing and the sheds. No one was out there. A man's voice was shouting: could have been Rabbit, the kitchens, the distant workers' camp. Tommy hesitated. Glanced up at Kala, who watched him dead-eyed. Nothing in how she looked at him. No warmth, no recognition, no thanks. Tommy led Beau by the bridle out of the stable door and doubled back around the side of the barn. He paused at the corner. In the distance two horses were crossing the yard behind the house, unhurried and casual: Rabbit and Mallee, calmly riding away.

Tommy mounted up clumsily, a struggle to get in front of her, to swing over his leg. She held on to him and the touch stirred a flurry in his gut. She had never done that before. One hand on his waist, a fistful of shirt fabric, the other holding the blanket, he assumed. They moved on. Down the side of the stables and into the scraggy bush that bordered the compound's edge. Some tree cover, plenty of loose scrub: his intention was to conceal their tracks until they were clear of the homestead, then pick up a trail heading southeast. He was assuming they'd be followed, but would they? Would anyone even notice they were gone? Tommy could have been taking Kala to Glendale for all they knew—in their eyes she was his property now. Billy certainly didn't want her and Sullivan wouldn't care: to the squatter's way of thinking, couldn't Tommy do with his property whatever he damn well pleased?

. . .

They picked their way along the tree line, then struck out over open ground, until eventually they came across a track. Tommy paused and traced its course through boulders and sparse bush, took a bearing off the sun, must have been a few hours after midday now. The track seemed a likely route. Roughly southeast in its heading, and where else but Bewley could it lead? He glanced back at Kala and caught her eyeing the country to the west. All through the ride he'd felt her twisting in the saddle, checking behind them, checking all around.

"It's alright," he told her, setting out on the track. "It's alright."

He had brought nothing with him. No weapon, no water, not even a hat. He wondered how close they were to Glendale, whether he should stop for provisions, use the well. No. It would cost them at least a couple of hours, maybe longer if he'd read their position wrong. They might have to camp there, which was not a good idea. Someone might come looking, Kala might be scared. Still, he imagined them bedding down in the house, maybe next to the open fire. He could show her the grave markers and perhaps her eyes would soften and she might see him differently then. Like he was forgiven, like she understood; like everything between them was changed.

She threw herself from the horse without warning and with only the blanket to break her fall. Tommy didn't even see her land. He felt movement behind him and thought she was checking the terrain again, then something in Beau's gait made him turn. Kala wasn't there. She was lying on the track a few strides back, dragging herself to her feet. Tommy reined up and brought the horse around, saying, "What happened? Are you hurt?"

She looked at him but didn't answer, hobbling to the trackside, the blanket in her arms. He swung down from Beau and let go of the reins. The horse dropped its head and sniffed the dirt. Kala shuffled into the fringe of scrub, watching Tommy over her shoulder as she went. He reached out toward her, calling, "Wait! There's a camp, I was taking you to a camp!" but she didn't stop, limping through the spinifex, until Tommy ran after her and she spun around to face him and screamed.

They stood watching each other, fifteen yards apart. Surrounded by wiry grass hummocks, flies buzzing, no wind. Silence save the noises they made. Their breathing. Beau snuffling at the ground. Kala jabbed her finger at the horse. Tommy didn't move. So she bent and picked up a rock and launched it at his head.

"Hey!" Tommy shouted, the rock flying by.

Kala picked up another and brandished it, ready to throw. Tommy held up his hands, then lowered them again, conscious of his bandage, of how he'd got his wounds. "Okay," he said. "Okay." He checked the ground behind him, took a step back. Kala did the same. They were many miles from Bewley and many more from Broken Ridge, the middle of the journey just about. Nothing else out here. Nothing around them but flatland and bush. Her direction was west, he realized; she was heading for the interior again. With only a blanket by way of provisions. And all on her own.

"I can help you," Tommy said. "Please—I want to help you."

Kala threw the rock. Tommy ducked out of the way. She yelled at him. Her voice trembling, her eyes wide. She waved the blanket, pointed to the sky, gestured at the surrounds. He didn't understand. They watched each other in silence.

"I'm sorry," he said weakly. He swallowed, raised his voice: "For everything. I'm so sorry. Please."

His eyes filled. Kala blurred. Blinking away tears, he thought he saw her nod. He wiped his eyes and she was moving, refolding the blanket and backtracking into the scrub. This time he didn't follow her. Fighting to keep it all in. He watched her turn and break into a weaving run. She looked back only once. When she was almost out of view Tommy returned to Beau and mounted up, and from the higher vantage was briefly able to pick her out again. A small, dark figure in the sunshine, moving swiftly through that land. And then nothing. He swept the terrain but she was nowhere, gone. He looked about hopelessly. She didn't reappear. The immense and total silence of all that empty bush. He drew a breath of hot air and let it out again, clicked Beau forward, and moved on, still watching for her as he rode, couldn't help himself, until the first speck of Bewley appeared in the distance, upon the sun-bleached plain.

35

He entered the town at walking pace, keeping to the center of the road. A man and boy loading a dray paused to watch him pass. Few other people about. The street mostly empty, the storefronts bare. Quiet. Lonely sounds of a dull hammering and the clang of the blacksmith's iron, which only amplified the silence more. He walked his horse in the direction of the general store, more out of habit than design. Dismounted. Tied Beau to the rail. The horse bent his head to the trough and drank the dusty green water it held. Tommy looked along the street. He shielded his eyes from the sun. Outside the Bewley Hotel two men were watching him, leaning on the rail, and he wondered if they were the same men who had called his mother a whore. He stared at them. They spoke to each other and one of them laughed. Tommy spat into the road and looked away. Across the street, the verandah of Song's Hardware was empty and the door was closed. Tommy glanced again at the men—still watching him—then turned and walked up the steps and into the general store.

The bell tinkled above the door. Spruhl looked up from his newspaper. He was red-faced and lightly sheened with sweat, and his shirt had stains on the chest and under the arms. He pushed his glasses up his nose, straightened, and attempted what Tommy supposed was intended as a smile.

"Master McBride. I am so very sorry to hear."

Tommy stalled, nodded grimly; he'd not counted on people knowing yet, when of course they all probably did. Word traveled quickly. Quicker than it ought.

"A terrible outrage," Spruhl was saying. "Those animals deserve the worst."

Tommy scanned behind the counter and along the dusty shelves.

"You got any water?"

"Of course," the shopkeeper said. He fetched a jug and a small glass and filled the glass to the brim. Tommy came to the counter and drank it in one.

"Thank you," he said, setting the glass down.

"Is my pleasure. Can I help with something else?"

"Sausage. Biscuits. Maybe a piece of cheese."

Spruhl glanced at the meat cabinet, but didn't move to serve. He worried his little hands. Tommy said, "How's our credit here these days?"

The shopkeeper's redness burned. His eyes fell to the desk. "Was different then, you understand. I didn't mean harm. But your father had not paid and I—"

"It was a bag of bloody flour."

"Is business. I am sorry."

"Sullivan told you, didn't he?"

"He is very important customer, very important man."

"So you pulled a pistol on a woman only trying to make some bread."

Spruhl held up a finger. "Ah, no. I pulled pistol on you."

"You planning on trying that again?"

"No, no, of course. Is okay, is okay . . ."

He bustled about, collecting the items, placed them into a paper bag. Folded the top, held the bag for Tommy to take.

"No charge," he said. "Is gift from me to you."

Tommy snatched the bag from him. The shopkeeper flinched. Tommy opened the door, then paused. "No

gifts," he said. "Put it on Sullivan's account; he's standing for us these days. Which I suppose makes me fucking royalty as far as the likes of you's concerned."

He opened the bag as he came down the steps, found
the sausage, took a bite. He stood in the street chewing.
The sausage was salty and fatty and good. Beau lifted
his head and watched him. Water dripped from the
horse's lips and matted the hairs on his chin. Tommy
rummaged in the bag and offered him one of the biscuits. Beau puckered his lips and drew it into his mouth,
then chomped the thing down whole. His tongue swept
the crumbs from his lips and he made a move for the
bag, but Tommy jerked it away.

"These are mine, you greedy bastard. Lucky I gave
you even one."

He wandered along the street, eating. The men were
gone from the hotel railing and only a couple of others
were about. Shuffling beneath their verandahs, smoking in the shade. The butcher stood glumly beside a
rack of bloody meat, cleaver in hand, watching Tommy
pass. Tommy nodded to him. The butcher simply
stared.

When he reached the doctor's surgery he paused in
the street and considered the stenciled window a long
time. A dog came sniffing past him but he paid it no

mind, munching idly on the stick of sausage meat. He could see Dr. Shanklin writing at his desk. Alone.

Tommy swallowed dryly. The lump slid down his throat. He went to the window and stood over Shanklin, just behind his shoulder, the other side of the glass. The doctor scratched entries into a notebook, dipped the nib, wrote again. Tommy could see only the top of his head. Thick black hair parted centrally and neatly combed. Tommy put the sausage back in the paper bag, made a fist with his hand, and banged on the window so hard the glass shook.

Shanklin jerked upright. Ink slashed across the page. He peered through the window as Tommy walked along the frontage, and was still half-risen in his chair when he came in through the door.

"Yes?" Shanklin said. He noticed Tommy's wounded hand. "Can I help you?"

"Know who I am?"

"You might need to remind me."

"You were meant to fix my sister only you didn't and now she's dead."

Shanklin exhaled. He sank back down and dropped the pen into its holder. "Billy McBride. I didn't recognize you. It's been a long time."

"Wrong brother. I'm Tommy."

"Oh, Tommy, right . . . you've grown."

Tommy was standing behind the chairs in front of the desk, the paper bag still clenched in the three fingers of his bandaged hand.

"Well?" he said. "What about it?"

"Will you sit?"

"Nope."

Shanklin shifted uncomfortably. He was dressed in a gray three-piece suit with a white pocket handkerchief and gold watch chain. Black mustache, weathered skin, tired eyes. "Look," he said, "I'm terribly sorry to hear about everything. What a rotten god-awful time you must have had."

Tommy said nothing. Breathing heavily through his nose.

"You know, when I first came out west I was more sympathetic to the native point of view, even wrote to *The Courier* about it once or twice. But you live here long enough, your opinion will change, and frankly I believe they deserve everything they get. They ever catch the culprits, I'll be there cheering when the trap-door swings." He paused and pointed. "Your hand, is it bad?"

"That's not why I came."

"The dressing looks fresh."

"Weeks did it. Sullivan's vet. Same one Mary had."

"Would you like me to take a look?"

"Why'd you never come? She died because of you."

Shanklin scowled. "No, she was already dead."

"On account of you never came. That vet's the only medic they've got."

The doctor reclined slightly, interlaced his fingers and laid them on his stomach, sat there frowning and tapping his thumbs.

"See now, I think there's some confusion here. Yes, I received a message saying a girl had been hurt, but before I could get up there I got another saying she'd died."

"You took long enough about it."

"On the contrary. There was barely even time to saddle my horse."

Tommy hesitated. The bag crinkled in his hand. He studied Shanklin doubtfully. "What d'you mean there wasn't time?"

"Well, I don't remember it exactly, but one message followed the other, an hour between them at most."

"She died that night."

"No, I'm certain. As soon as I heard, I began finishing up here, but the second telegram arrived before I could leave."

"Who sent it? The second one?"

"From Broken Ridge, that's all I know. There was no name."

Tommy tried to hold the stare but couldn't. His gaze wandered around the room. In the back was a wheeled curtain, a restraint table, a benchtop filled with bottles and implements of all kinds. Two human skulls on a shelf: adult and child.

"I never had a chance to get up there, Tommy."

"What you're saying, it can't be right."

"I can assure you it is."

"You got them two telegrams still?"

"No, but if you don't believe me you can ask at the courthouse. That's where they come. Honestly, I'd have helped her if I could; there just simply wasn't time."

Tommy stared out of the window, nodding minutely to himself, his jaw set and his eyes far away. He went slowly to the door and Shanklin rose, saying, "Hold up, now, hold up. You're clearly not well yourself. Feverish maybe. That hand might be infected. I should take a look."

"I'll see about them telegrams."

"Tommy, please. It won't take long at all."

He opened the door. Shanklin scrambled around the desk but Tommy was already outside. Their eyes met through the glass, then Tommy walked out into the blazing street and crossed to the other side, and from the direction of the hotel someone shouted: "Y'alright there, mate? Get a drink in ya, eh?"

He followed the narrow path between two squares of ruined lawn, grass as dry as kindling in a powdery red earth. The whitewashed courthouse looming ahead: sheer-walled, narrow-windowed, black-tarred doors riveted with metal plates; the stocks beside the entrance; a dusting of fresh sand beneath the splintered wooden cross.

Tommy reached the doors and halted. One was already open but the interior was pitch-dark against the sun. He set down the paper bag and waited; shapes emerged dully in the large hall. A guard asleep on a chair, behind him a short corridor lined with cells, where someone whistled an ebbing, haunting tune. To the left of the hall a young clerk sat at a desk, alongside doors to two further rooms: the courtroom itself and an office belonging to Magistrate MacIntyre.

Tommy stepped into the gloom.

The floor was flagstoned and dusty, no give underfoot. The clerk noticed him coming, looked up. There were no chairs inviting him to sit.

"Telegraph comes here, I heard?"

"Official use only. You'll have to wait for the mail."

"I'm not mailing nothing. John Sullivan sent me. From up Broken Ridge."

Now the clerk set down his pen and leaned back in his chair. The wooden joins creaked. The whistling from the cells rose and fell.

"You new? Got a name?"

"Tommy McBride."

The clerk's eyes pinched. "As in them that were done by the blacks?"

Tommy nodded. "We're working for Sullivan now, so can you—"

"Mr. MacIntyre'll be wanting a word," the clerk said. He angled his head toward the office and called, "Sir! Someone out here!"

There was a muffled response from inside the room. The clerk's shouting also roused the guard. He tipped back his hat and peered at Tommy, yelled over his shoulder for quiet from the cells. The whistling paused, then took up again, as Tommy leaned over the desk and said, "There were two telegrams sent a couple of weeks back, both for Dr. Shanklin, came the same day."

"About your sister," the clerk said, nodding. "And wasn't that a bloody shame."

"You remember them?"

"Course I do. Had me back and forth to Shanklin like I was on a spring."

"One followed the other, you're sure about that?"

The clerk was nodding, but the office door opened

before he could speak again. Magistrate MacIntyre stepped out. He was a big man, tall and broad, his buttoned suit jacket pulling at his gut, and ruddy in the cheeks, hair wild, like he'd just come through a sandstorm, or had been asleep.

"Sir, this is Tommy McBride," the clerk said, pointing. "One of them that—"

"I know a McBride when I see one, Walter," the magistrate said, barreling across to the desk. His accent was thick Scottish. He took hold of Tommy's hand and flung it up and down. "Good to see you, lad, good to see you. Circumstances aside."

Tommy had met Spencer MacIntyre no more than twice in his life. He'd once asked whether the name meant they were blood-tied, and while Mother had only laughed at him, Father had cursed and answered, "That snaky bastard's no kin of mine."

Now the magistrate took Tommy by the shoulder and steered him across the hall. The clerk and guard watched them go. There was a smell of drink on the man and a strong tang of sweat. He opened the office door, held it while Tommy walked through, then followed him inside.

"Best not to say too much out there, son. Walls are always listening in this place. Got eyes and mouths as well."

The office was cramped and airless. A desk, chairs, bookcase, faded paintings on the walls, a couple of official appointments bearing MacIntyre's name. The magistrate went around to his side of the desk, then thought better of it and came back again. He motioned for Tommy to sit, then did so himself, lowering his bulk into one of the flimsy wooden chairs, the two of them facing each other, knee to knee.

"Looks nasty," MacIntyre said, nodding at Tommy's hand. "What you done?"

"Ax slipped chopping wood."

The magistrate smiled knowingly. "Quite a trick to be holding and chopping at the same time."

"It was a hand ax. Splitting, I meant."

"Don't trouble yourself. You thirsty? Long ride down from Broken Ridge."

Tommy shrugged. "Water, if you've got it."

"Aye, son, aye."

He lumbered out of the chair. There was a drinks tray on the cabinet, a pitcher of water alongside. MacIntyre poured the water, then a measure of whiskey for himself, handed Tommy his drink, and offered his glass for a toast. They touched. MacIntyre saluted. Gulped a mouthful, sank back down with a sigh.

"I'd expected you earlier. Once I'd heard what had gone on."

He drank, watching Tommy over the rim of the glass, his eyebrows as thick and feathery as wings.

"Been busy," Tommy said.

"Heard that too. Terrible business, of course."

"Which bit?"

"All of it, boy, all of it." He took another sip. "John send you?"

"Not exactly."

"So you've come on your own account. I'd have thought your brother would be with you—you're the younger, isn't that right?"

"Billy doesn't know I came neither."

MacIntyre watched him severely. "Well, then, what's this about?"

"I was just asking about the telegraph."

"Oh yes, marvelous creation, a wonder of mankind. Soon there'll be lines between every town in the colonies. Imagine it, a letter arriving in, say, Swan River, right after I've written it here. Be months on a horse before it got there—months!"

Tommy sipped the water, shifted in his seat. MacIntyre drank too.

"So you've a letter to send, have you, son?"

"I was checking on something, is all."

MacIntyre slopped his tongue horselike around his mouth, leaned back, and folded his arms. "I'm on your side, you know, Tommy. Help you if I can. Consider me a friend of the family—I mourned both your parents when I heard what had gone on. We all did. Your mother used to work for me; she told you that, I assume. For Mrs. MacIntyre, I should say, over at the house there—till your father came along, that is. Now, there was a man liked to keep to his own, but I respected him, he had principles, however damn foolish they turned out to be."

Tommy looked at him sharply. MacIntyre held up a hand, drank, winced.

"Hold on now, hold on. Let me finish at least. What I mean to say is that what happened at your place could have been avoided, I believe. There's lessons to be learned. I said the same thing to your mother when she came in complaining about John and his patrols. I told her, 'Liza, what d'you think it is keeps you all safe out there? It sure as hell isn't blind luck that you've lasted this long.'"

"When was this?" Tommy asked him. MacIntyre waved a hand.

"Maybe a month or so back. Couple of weeks before . . . look, what I'm trying to tell you is that whatever misgivings you've got about me, or John even, or any other folks in this town, aren't worth shit against what you should feel about the blacks."

"You don't know what I feel."

"I've a good idea, son. Why else would you be in here asking about telegrams?"

Tommy traced his fingertip around the edge of his water glass. "How d'you know what went on after?"

"Well, I'm the police magistrate. It's only right that I'm informed."

"So you know what we did?"

MacIntyre shuffled himself upright in the chair. "What I know is that a terrible crime was committed and that the Native Police were dispatched to pursue the suspects in accordance with the law. I have since learned the expedition was something of a success, and that justice has been rightfully served. The precise details of what happened will be a matter for the report."

"You believe all that?"

"Every word. As should you. It's the truth."

"Horseshit, truth. Joseph did it and he wasn't even there. They wanted the Kurrong gone, so we rode out and killed them. We bloody killed them all."

The magistrate sat as calmly as if Tommy had reported a missing horse. He smiled wearily, then leaned close enough that Tommy could smell his liquored breath.

"Now, son, you're going to have to be more careful running your mouth like that. There's people on the coast would see you hanged for such talk."

"I wouldn't be the only one. There's seven others would go before me."

"You think so? Or would it just be you and your brother, on whose testimony the whole thing stands?"

Tommy looked down at his water. He raised the glass trembling to his lips.

MacIntyre said, "I had a reverend came to see me. Claimed to be, at least—fella can say he's anything and no one's any the wiser. But anyway, this man came in and sat in this very room, while Donnaghy out there removed his boy beyond our walls—the only natives allowed in my courthouse are them that are locked in the cells. The reverend sat where you're sitting and he ummed and aahed about what he wanted to say, mumbling about these Kurrong and a man he'd met in the bush. Named him, even: Inspector Noone. Right away I warned him that he might be about to make a very grave mistake, and all the color drained from his face like he already knew this was true. Said Noone had warned him the exact same thing, but God had other ideas. 'Well,' I asked him, 'who are you more afraid of?' and he thought about it, then got up and walked right out the door, and we never saw him again."

He paused, considered Tommy a moment, a faint smile.

"From the look of you, I'd say this story is ringing a few bells, so I really shouldn't have to spell it out. But consider the warning I gave to the reverend—and your own mother for that matter—just as applicable to you. Be very careful what you decide to do next, Tommy. Not just in here, I mean in your life. For both yours and your brother's sakes."

"So you ain't against any of what was done?"

"I'm against what was done to your family, that's what I'm against. Remember, the law was with you. Who are we to question the law?"

"It wasn't even the same blacks."

"That's a matter for the inspector's report."

"The report'll be nothing but lies."

MacIntyre drained his whiskey, stretched to place the glass on the desk. He righted himself, grunting, and said, "Son, I'm going to have to insist. I can't have you speaking like this about an officer of the Crown. There's allowances can be made on account of your situation, but if you're not willing to take my advice, then I can't help you. Think on it. You've seen it now, what's out there: men like Noone, the Native Police, they're all that's keeping us safe. These natives . . . they've the Devil in them, Tommy, they're naught but killers and thieves. If you still don't believe me, ask John. Wasn't two months ago he caught a nigger dragging two dead white boys at the end of a rope, right across his own bloody land! They'd been cut up and burned and all manner of things. Probably aiming to eat them once he got back to camp. That's what we're dealing with. There ain't no other way."

Tommy sat very still. The room leaned slightly. Air emptied from his lungs.

"Two dead *white boys*?" he croaked. "Dragged on the end of a rope?"

"That's what he told me. Weren't but a pair of young boundary riders from down Dubbo way. You understand what I'm telling you now?"

"What . . . what happened to him? The native Sullivan caught?"

"Bastard had a bloody revolver, Tommy. What d'you reckon John did?"

Tommy was nodding repeatedly. More of a tremor than a nod, and his face contorting somewhere between laughter and a most terrible grief.

"Dubbo," he repeated. "From down Dubbo way."

"Aye . . . look, are you alright there, son? You've gone a wee bit pale. Get you another water, something stronger maybe? When was the last time you ate?"

Tommy went to stand but couldn't. His arm buckled beneath him and he fell back into the chair. The glass slipped and shattered on the flagstoned floor. On the second attempt he managed to stand and he lunged across the room. MacIntyre was calling to him but Tommy fell against the door. He took hold of the handle, then paused, and when he spoke it took him everything to keep his voice steady and low:

"That day Ma came to see you, when she asked for your help—did you tell him about her? Sullivan? Did you tell him she was here?"

MacIntyre nodded. "I might have mentioned it when I saw him but—"

Tommy opened the door. It clattered against the wall. The noise echoed through the courthouse and jerked the guard to attention and pulled the clerk from his seat. Tommy barreled out into the main hall. MacIntyre was shouting but Tommy didn't hear him, his attention fixed instead on the bright shaft of sunlight falling through the front door and the whistling from the prisoner that squirmed into his head, a strange and eerie ditty, trilling up and down. He broke into a scrambled run, fleeing for the doors, reeled blindly into the light. With his hand raised against the glare he staggered along the front path, past the stocks and the sound of whip cracks and the screams of dying men . . . and women screaming also, babies crying, gunshot after gunshot and bodies falling down, down, down.

"You ready for that drink now, are ya? Get yerself a bloody drink!"

Father on the verandah, three holes in his chest. Drag marks where he'd crawled bleeding up the steps. He'd gone out into the yard to confront them, but it couldn't have been Joseph he'd confronted because Joseph was already dead. Sullivan had caught him and put him in the ground, long before the mustering, before the sales, before sending that note to Father, before hearing about Mother's betrayal. It was Sullivan. Sullivan had come to the house that day. The bastard had come to collect.

"Him and your mother had no right carrying on the way they did. Bloody well turned on me in the end. Lack of basic gratitude, of well-earned respect."

Locke would have been with him. Same as the first time, over by the cattle yards. Father with his carbine and at least one of them armed, carrying Joseph's revolver, wouldn't have known it was Father's old gun. They didn't even know Joseph. He was new, they'd never met him: just another native they'd caught on their station, the only one they'd found after bringing in Noone. Then things had become heated and Father was too slow, three shots in him before he could react, and Mother on the verandah wondering what was wrong; they chased her to the bedroom and picked her off too, no other reason than to silence her, no other base intent.

"Was she raped? Well, how was she lying? What did they see?"

Mary in the bedroom now, hiding beneath the bed. Might have seen Locke and Sullivan, heard their voices. A five-shot, not a six-shot: only one ball left.

"Has she spoke? But she's alive? You're sure?"

The dogs barking and lunging when they came back outside: Locke runs them through with his sword. Same quick thrust as he did in the bush, in and then out, flush in the neck, but not before one of them clamps their jaws on his hand.

"Bloody big snake with dog tooth that bugger."

And how quickly those dogs were cremated, how quickly the bodies were put in the ground. Sullivan reluctant to send for Noone until the house had been cleared, covering his tracks as he went. He'd expected the brothers that night but hadn't known what they would do, so he'd sent the watchman to meet them just in case. He wasn't a permanent sentry. He was only there for them.

"The boss says get their guns so I got to get your guns."

Noone had known. He'd known all along. No footprints, no evidence, neither Mother nor Mary touched. Two horses left behind, the house not ransacked.

"Strange for a man to be ambushed when he was already armed."

So Sullivan had to pay him. And he'd fixed it so Billy and Tommy would come. Making them complicit in the lie and in the deed, offering them their lives back and drawing them so close they wouldn't question him again.

"John has his own reasons for making you his boy."

Joseph, Arthur, the Kurrong: all were innocent. Sullivan had been behind everything, twisting the murder to his own ends. An excuse to clear his station and the surrounding lands, to finish the Kurrong altogether, see the last of them burn. Noone and Locke in his pocket, Tommy and Billy too. All done on their testimony, in their family's name. MacIntyre had judged it correctly, but he'd judged the wrong side.

"They've the Devil in them, Tommy, they're naught but killers and thieves."

Tommy stopped in the middle of the road, clutching his stomach, his mouth open in a long and empty howl. He arched his back and gazed pleadingly at the sky, the clouds, at whatever lay above, then trudged up the road to Beau and fell against him, his head on his rib cage, feeling the strength of him, the warmth. He un-hitched the reins, dragged himself into the saddle, and circled the horse around. Gaunt faces watching him, in windows, in doorways. As he walked Beau toward the edge of town, he saw a girl step from the shadows in front of Song's Hardware Store. She stood at the railing and spoke his name, but Tommy did not turn as he passed. He couldn't bear to look at her. The way she'd said it—innocently, tenderly—it hadn't sounded like his name at all.

Ahead the sun was falling in the west, and in the low light the earth and sky and all before him was red. He kicked on and rode right into it. Into the redness. Into the sun.

36

From the darkness of the empty hillside a lone horse and rider emerged into the half-light cast by the homestead. Every lantern burning, as they had been long ago, when Tommy first rode up here, Mary slumped in his saddle and strapped to his shirtfront. Now he approached slowly, patiently, walking Beau directly to the staircase, then dismounting and leading him into the shadowy recess beneath the verandah, where he tied him to one of the struts. Whispered to him gently. His hand on his neck, his forehead alongside, as if in prayer to the horse. He backed out of the recess. Made his way up the stairs. Memories of having stood here telling Sullivan his family had been killed, Sullivan nodding sympathetically, then hoisting Mary into his arms. Her little limbs dangling. The bunches in her hair. And Sullivan all the while assuring them that they'd done the right thing bringing her, that Mary would be looked after, that Weeks would take care of her now.

Through the door and into the hall, the house quiet, not even the staff about. He trailed his hand along the green wallpaper, its texture like fur, and fingered the ornate picture frames fringed in golden weave. He paused at the drawing room and listened, then eased open the door. Empty. A low fire burning. The furniture and the ornaments and the strange spectacle of Mrs. Sullivan's tree. It all seemed ridiculous. Like trappings of a lie. So many lies spoken right here in this room, every word almost—nothing anyone had told him had come close to being true.

In the atrium he cocked an ear and considered the silent house. Filthy and disheveled and dark from the sun, his wild eyes roaming, assessing the terrain. His attention settled on the parlor door. A low hum of voices, a sudden burst of laughter inside. Tommy flinched. Billy was in there, with Sullivan and at least one of Locke or Noone. Tommy's jaw set. Breathing through his nose. His unfocused gaze slid off the parlor door and fixed itself somewhere on the wall, until the parlor erupted again and his eyes hardened and he set off walking for the stairs.

In Mary's doorway he stood wondering whether she'd ever been in this room at all. No sign of her remained. The linen clean and white, the furniture neatly arranged, ready for some other guest. Sullivan had carried her up here and laid her down and knew all along it would be her deathbed. Now it was like she'd never lived. For all Mrs. Sullivan's praying, for all the promises they had made, the only aim had been to keep her from talking until Tommy and Billy were gone.

He backed out of the doorway and went along the corridor, the light from the sconces rippling as he passed. Into his and Billy's bedroom, their two beds neatly made, the curtains drawn, a square of hall light angled across the floor. At the foot of his bed was a pile of clean clothing, his clothing, the same he had been wearing when they first rode in, and then later, when they'd returned from . . . returned from . . . Timidly he lifted the corner of the shirt. As you would a shroud. His trousers were under there. His old greenhide belt. His father had worn that shirt once, those same trousers, had even cut the belt with his knife. Tommy looked himself over, at Sullivan's gaudy rags. He stepped into the room, closed the door, began to strip. A difficulty unbuttoning the shirt, a tremor in his hands. Stiffly he dressed, pulling on his moleskins, slipping his bare feet into his boots, cinching his belt tight. Like stepping back into himself, for all that meant. He'd asked the maid to burn these clothes but was grateful that she'd not. They were about the only rightful possessions he owned in this world.

On his belly he groped the dusty floor beneath his bed, retrieved the rifle hidden there, the small stash of powder, caps and balls, then sat on the bed and cleaned the rifle meticulously with the discarded shirt. Working in darkness, only a strip of light beneath the door, feeling his way from firing pin to muzzle to trigger to stock. Absently he stared at Billy's bed, imagined he could see his brother bundled beneath the blankets and hear the ticking in his breathing when he slept. Once that sound had made Tommy feel comforted, safe. Once Billy had crawled from that bed and climbed into this, the two of them back-to-back, as they'd always been. Once they had been brothers. Once.

Tommy tossed aside the shirt. Turned the rifle on its butt, tipped the powder into the barrel then loaded, rodded, and capped that one single shot. Briskly he stood, threw open the door, and marched away down the corridor, gripping the rifle by its forestock, shoulders rolling, a long determined stride and his eyes so fixed on the carpet runner before him that as he rounded the landing and came down the stairs he did not see Benjamin, the houseboy, crossing the atrium carrying a crystal carafe of wine; not until Tommy was on the final few steps and the two of them were only yards apart. Both paused. Benjamin cradling the carafe in his hands, his eyes on the rifle; Tommy suspended midstep. Slowly he advanced. Benjamin's eyes darted between Tommy and the service corridor behind him, the kitchens, the back door, the yard.

"It's okay," Tommy whispered. "Please—put down the wine."

Benjamin watched him warily. Tommy gestured for him to lower the carafe and finally he crouched and placed it on the floor, not once taking his eyes from Tommy's face. Fully staring at him. Not even blinking, it seemed. Tommy faltered in his gaze, everything it said about him, everything he'd done. He swapped the rifle to his left hand and offered his right for Benjamin to shake. The houseboy glanced at the hand but otherwise didn't move. Tommy's hand fell. He stepped aside and motioned toward the back of the house. Still Benjamin only stared.

"Go," Tommy begged, waving. "Go now, please."

The old man shook his head and walked unhurried out of the atrium and along the service corridor, and Tommy heard the back door slap against the frame. He took a long breath. Unsettled by the exchange. The row of animal heads were watching him, their empty glassy eyes. He bent and took a swig of wine, then another, wiped his mouth on his sleeve. The voices in the parlor grew louder and Tommy moved toward the door. Switched the rifle to his right hand, finger tensed on the trigger guard, and with his left took hold of the doorknob. The brass cool in his grip. Standing inches from the paneled door. Noone's voice stalled him. So close and clear through the wood. Tommy began trembling, his body suddenly inert and very weak. He couldn't move. Couldn't do what needed to be done. Desperately he closed his eyes and searched for his parents, their faces, Mary's too, but there was nothing, they were lost to him, like he'd forgotten his own blood. Only a memory of how he'd found them: Father slack-jawed and ashen, that fly on his eyeball; Mother half-scalped; Mary bleeding out on the bedroom floor. And so many others, so many killings, so many dead. The memories rouletting through him and Tommy's hand losing its grip on the doorknob and his feet shuffling backward and his face wrought with the pain of knowing that all of it, all of it, had been in some way his fault.

"Boy! Where's my fucking wine!"

Tommy's eyes snapped open. He flung wide the parlor door. Striding across the room, sighting Sullivan down the rifle, his aim square on the squatter's chest, until his thighs butted the desk edge and the muzzle pinned Sullivan to his seat. Quickly Sullivan settled himself. The surprise slid from his face. Flushed in the cheeks but he allowed a smile to creep and the fingers of his right hand to drum lightly on the desk.

"Now, then, son, don't be foolish. Whatever this is, we'll straighten it out."

Tommy stepped back a pace. Glanced at Noone and Billy in the two wingback chairs. Billy openmouthed, while Noone had steepled his fingers and watched like a punter at a show. On the corner of the desk before him was a small stack of crumpled banknotes and a leather money pouch, and though Sullivan looked imploringly toward him, it was Billy who rose and asked, "What the hell you doing?"

"Sit down, Billy."

"Not until you say what this is about."

"He knows what this is about. Sit down."

"I would do as your brother suggests," Noone said. "Besides myself, he's the only one in this room who is armed."

"Hell, Edmund," Sullivan said. "That's no help."

Billy lowered himself back into his chair. Noone arched an eyebrow playfully.

"You must have expected this, John. There is always a reckoning. It just seems that yours might have come earlier than either of us thought."

Tommy jabbed the rifle toward Sullivan. "Say it, you bastard. Say what you did."

"Quite the day you've had, Tommy. First the girl, now this."

"Just . . . fucking say it."

"Son, you're making a bloody big mistake here. All I've ever done is look out for you and your brother, your sister too, while she was alive . . ."

"You killed them. I know you did. Killed them with Joseph's gun."

"What's that now?" Billy asked.

"He came down the house, Billy. Him, not Joseph, and not the bloody Kurrong. He'd found Joseph with them bodies, killed him, took the old five-shot, had it on him when he came. MacIntyre as good as told me. All of it was him."

Sullivan raised a finger theatrically. "Hold up now, hold up. I seem to remember two boys rode up here a little while back saying it was *niggers* that had done 'em all in. Said they'd seen it with their own eyes. Swore to it, even. Begging for my help."

"Them testimonies were false and you know it."

"Well, then, we've all been misled. A dozen myalls, you two told us. Right here in this room. The inspector was a witness. Signed in your own hand."

The rifle muzzle was sagging. Some weight to keep

raised. Tommy hefted it repeatedly and his wounded hand ached. A tremble setting in. Sweat beaded on his forehead and his mind was losing the order of things. All he'd seen so clearly was now mired in fog. He pulled back his shoulders, stiffened, steeled himself again.

"Who was it shot them, you or Locke?"

"Make up your bloody mind, son. Joseph, myalls, me . . . now it's Locke?"

"Tommy, please," Billy said quietly. "You ain't making no sense."

"Might be he's got a fever," Sullivan said. "Could be the rot's set into that hand. Here, put down the rifle, I'll send a boy for Weeks."

"MacIntyre told me . . . told me . . ."

"Ah, that man's a drunk and a fraud. Doesn't know what bloody day it is, let alone about anything else."

"You never sent for Shanklin. Two telegrams went to him, one after the next."

"Telegrams? What you saying about telegrams? I wasn't even here, Tommy—I was out there dispersing . . . with you."

"Weeks sent the second one. On your word. Because Mary saw you. She knew."

Sullivan laughed and threw up his hands. "The boy's been drinking himself, I reckon."

"Why'd you do it? The money? Over a few mangy fucking cows?"

"The why is irrelevant," Noone said. "Either you want him dead or don't you."

"Shut your mouth, Edmund, for Christ's bloody sake."

"I'm not the enemy here, John. This was your doing from the start. You underestimated him. He's the only one capable of seeing through the ruse."

A silence settled over them. "It's not true," Billy said. "It can't be—"

Sullivan flung back his chair and came lunging for the rifle, and on reflex Tommy fired. Eyes closed as he pulled the trigger, staggering with the kick of it, the report booming around the room, then his eyes were open again and the smoke was swirling and Sullivan was collapsing backward, clutching at his chest. Blood gathered between his fat fingers. Steadily it came. Seeping through the gaps and from underneath his palm, and Sullivan wide-eyed and coughing and gawping around the room. He lifted his hand, peeked under it, the frayed edges of his clothing encircling the ragged wound. He groaned, closed his hand, eyes shifting from Billy to Noone, but neither of them moved from their seats. Billy cupped his mouth and seemed frozen in the pose; Noone met the squatter's stare with an indulgent smile, a strange kind of reverie broken only by Tommy fumbling in his pocket for another ball.

"Can't let you do that, Tommy."

"I got to make sure."

"That's not my concern."

"It ain't up to you."

"I'm afraid this time it is."

Noone opened his longcoat to reveal the ornate silver revolver Tommy had once held. He let the coat fall closed again. Tommy gave up on the ball and Sullivan began grunting horribly, blood and spittle foaming through his teeth, urging Noone to draw.

"You shot him," Billy mumbled. "Christ, Tommy— what have you done?"

"Ma went to see MacIntyre about the patrols. This bastard killed them for it. That and the money Daddy owed. We told him it was Joseph and he used it for his own ends. He's always wanted the Kurrong gone."

Billy stood. He motioned to Sullivan, who was gargling each breath. "But . . . look at the fucking state of him. What are we going to do now?"

"Didn't you hear what I just said?"

Billy was shaking his head. Eyes damp and fearful. He looked at Tommy again. "You're a bloody dead man. You've just noosed your own neck. Likely mine too."

"Alright, that's enough," Noone said, sighing. He clapped his hands on his knees and rose from the chair, scooped the money from the desk and deposited it inside the folds of his coat. "Entertaining as all this is, I'm afraid we must call it a night."

"You ain't no different," Tommy said. "You're just as bad as him."

Noone drew his revolver, inspected the cylinder, turning it idly, cartridges in each chamber, a steady clicking sound. "The work we do out here cannot be arbitrary, Tommy. I must have rightful cause. The law demands its justification, and your testimonies were mine. You were my warrant, you and Billy—don't you see?"

He snapped the cylinder into position and aimed the revolver at Tommy's head. Sullivan grunted forcefully. The breath wheezing out of him. His shirt soaked in blood.

"It's a shame, of course, since I've come to like you a great deal. A fine young man, great potential in you, particularly in a country where the young come slithering from their mothers as brainless and spineless as shits. There are not many who would have dared take their revenge in such a way. I applaud you for it. Bravo, Tommy. Bravo. But sadly your actions here have spoiled your own value, since the testimony of a murderer counts for naught in the eyes of the law. And I certainly cannot have you recanting. All our good work these past weeks would be undone."

Noone blurred behind the revolver. Only the shape of him there. Tommy said, "If you kill me, your warrant's gone."

He ratcheted back the hammer. "Your testimony will suffice."

Sullivan growling rabidly, the words strangled in his throat.

"You'll have to account for shooting me. Say what I've done."

"I'll say the blacks got you. It'll be grist to the mill."

"They saw me today in Bewley, everyone, all over town."

Noone hesitated, lowered the revolver, looked irritably around the room. As if replaying Tommy's visit to determine whether this was true. There was movement in the doorway. All three of them turned: Mrs. Sullivan standing there in her nightgown, clutching herself with her thin bare arms.

"And what about me, Mr. Noone? Do you plan on killing me too?"

Noone shrugged and fiddled the revolver restlessly in his hands. "Truthfully, in such circumstances, I find that killing everyone usually works out for the best."

She ghosted into the room and contemplated Sullivan across the desk. His eyes rolled toward her and stayed there. He was hardly moving now. Only his eyes and his chest when he breathed. His mouth hung open. A vacant palsied stare. His face looked jaundiced, and there were irregular pauses in the rhythm of each breath.

"Let the boys go," she said quietly. "What harm can they do?"

Noone gestured toward her husband. "There's the harm."

"It sounds as though they were perfectly justified. Are you paid?"

"I am."

"Then I'd suggest you leave too."

She didn't turn around. Watching Sullivan expire. Noone rolled his tongue in his mouth and glowered at them each in turn. A great frustration in him. As if weighing whether to simply shoot them all. A round in each head and it would be done with; he could walk straight out the front door. Nobody would accuse him. Nobody would dare.

"Please, Mr. Noone. Allow me this courtesy."

"Very well. I'll wait in the hall."

He left without acknowledging either of the boys, ducking through the doorway and striding into the atrium, where his footsteps abruptly stopped. Mrs. Sullivan glanced over her shoulder. Her eyes found Tommy's and she pulled her lips tight. "I'm so sorry. Truly, I knew nothing about any of it. I honestly thought we were trying to help."

"You want me to fetch the doctor?" Billy asked her.

"No, no, there's no need. Go on to bed, the pair of you. Tomorrow's a new day."

She turned to face Sullivan again, then perched on the edge of one of the chairs. Hands folded in her lap, back straight. "There now, John. Hush. It'll all be over soon."

The brothers left the room. Tommy eased the door closed on the latch. Noone was in the center of the atrium drinking wine from the carafe, and when he saw them he beckoned for them to come. They wouldn't. Neither moved. Noone holstered his revolver and offered the carafe, swept his other hand through the air in something like a bow. Tommy and Billy exchanged a look. They had no choice, in truth. Timidly they walked toward him and Noone kept the carafe out-held. Billy was first to take it. He swallowed a tentative sip. Then Tommy, then Billy again, who handed it back to Noone. And for a while they simply stood there, passing the wine around, like three old comrades drinking in that vast white vaulted hall.

When they were finished Noone placed the carafe on the floor and stood regarding the two brothers for a very long time.

"She's right, of course. Mrs. Sullivan. Whites can be so complicated to kill. Too many questions are asked, too much of a fuss made. Hence our current predicament: how to explain tonight's events. Of course, we can always blame the natives, there must be one about. The houseboy, perhaps. He with the downcast face."

"No," Tommy said. "Not him. I'll stand for what I did."

"How very noble of you, Tommy. But you're a fool to trade your life. Besides, as I have already told you, I cannot allow your testimony to be compromised, and so"—Noone nodded sharply, as if the solution had just crystallized in his mind—"here is my proposal. It is the only one I will make. Reject it and I'll shoot the pair of you right here where you stand."

He peered down at each of them. Neither could hold the stare.

"Tommy will leave the district. This very night. Ride south and never return. Billy will remain behind. Ordinarily I'd banish the pair of you, but this way I'll have a surety: each brother the other's keeper, as the good book says. If either of you talks, if Billy leaves, or Tommy returns, if there's so much as a letter in the mail, I will kill the both of you and your families and anyone else you hold dear. There will be no warning. One day you will simply look upon my face and know what the other has done. Do you understand?"

Both nodded, their eyes still downturned. Noone took Tommy's rifle from him and inspected the weapon disdainfully, like he knew not what it was. He gestured to the entrance hallway, the front door. Tommy turned to Billy but Billy's eyes were on the floorboards and he wouldn't look up, scowling like he was still trying to fathom what had just occurred. Tommy pitied him. His brother was a fool. He'd taken Sullivan at his word despite knowing his word was false. Greed and pride had got him, had been in him his whole life. Now he stared dumbly at the floor and Tommy knew he was only thinking about himself, about how he'd get by once Sullivan died. Not their own family or the Kurrong or all else they had done. He probably blamed Tommy for ruining things; despite everything, he still wouldn't consider it justified.

Billy came at him and Tommy flinched, then stood stiffly in his brother's embrace. Billy's arms were wrapped around him, his cheek against Tommy's cheek, holding him so tightly he couldn't fill a breath. Slowly Tommy melted. His hands crept up Billy's back. He stretched onto his toes to match his brother's height and was struck by the thickness of him, like holding Father in his arms, must have been years since the two of them had hugged. He felt his eyes filling. Billy whispered in Tommy's ear but his mouth was too close to make out what he said. The meaning was clear enough. He was saying a final good-bye. Tommy turned his head onto Billy's shoulder, then Billy gave him a sudden squeeze, loosened his grip, pressed his lips against Tommy's cheek, kissed him roughly, and was gone. He didn't look back once. Took two stairs with each stride, then ran around the landing and along to their bedroom. Tommy stood there sniffing, watching his brother go, crying in front of Noone but he cared little for what Noone thought of him now. Tommy hated him. The man had ruined his life. It crossed his mind that he should try and kill him also, but just the idea of it seemed impossible: Noone would never die.

The parlor door clicked open. Tommy sniffed and dragged a hand over his face, then turned to see Mrs. Sullivan emerge from the room. She closed the door softly and walked to the staircase, paused, and looked at them, her face untroubled, calm.

"He'll be found in the morning, I expect. I'm going to bed now. Good night."

Noone inclined his head. "Good night, Mrs. Sullivan."

"Not anymore," she said, her mouth ticking briefly

in a smile. She climbed the first few stairs, then paused. "Mr. Noone, since you're still here—I wonder if perhaps you'd attend to the formalities. The official explanations, a plausible chain of events, whatever you feel is best."

"We were just discussing that very thing. It is already in hand."

"You'll be rewarded for your troubles, of course."

"Of course."

"Suicide, I was thinking."

"No, suicide is messy, and a dishonorable way to go. You wouldn't welcome the taint. I think the best thing for all of us would be to find the man responsible for John's murder, attempt to arrest him, then kill him when he resists."

Tommy looked at him, aghast. Mrs. Sullivan said, "You have someone in mind?"

Noone surveyed the atrium, the staircase, the entire house.

"Tell me, Mrs. Sullivan, where does Raymond Locke sleep these days?"

37

They came down the steps together, Noone's long-coat flaring, Tommy struggling to keep pace at his side. Neither spoke. Tommy felt utterly defeated by the man. At the bottom of the stairs he ducked under the recess, then emerged with Beau and found Noone waiting. "Walk with me to the camp," Noone said.

"No."

"Indulge me. It's a fine night for taking the air. After all that excitement I'd say we would both benefit. And I'm not really asking, Tommy."

Tommy took a breath, led Beau onto the track, and they set off down the hill. An easy pace, a gentle stroll. After a short distance Noone seemed to remember that he was carrying Tommy's rifle; he tossed it into the darkness and it was lost among the scrub.

"Quite the scalp you've just taken," Noone said. "Shooting John Sullivan is not the same as shooting most other men."

"He's not so different."

"You don't think so? When word gets out there will be no little uproar."

"That's only 'cause people don't know what he is."

"People know exactly what he is," Noone said, laughing. "Why do you think he's so revered?"

"Well, you never seemed too bothered by him. Didn't even care he was dead."

"Oh, there are plenty more John Sullivans on the frontier, Tommy. And this one had run his course. With the Kurrong finished he'd have been no use to me, but what's worse is I think the fool had a notion the two of us were friends. I'd have been obliged to him socially, called upon for petty favors. No—you have done me a service. I'm thankful the man's gone."

They walked in silence awhile. Out of the glow cast by the house and into the dark no-man's-land between there and the workers' camp. Barely the light to see by, to pick out their next step, blindly crunching gravel underfoot. Noone a dark and formless shadow at Tommy's side, such that his voice came from the darkness, as if the darkness itself spoke.

"I suppose you consider my terms unfair? Forcing you to leave?"

"I was planning on it anyway."

"Without your brother?"

He sniffed. "Either way."

"And yet you are still angry with me? You hold me to blame?"

"For what?"

"That's what I'm asking you."

"I don't know."

"You don't know what you feel?"

"I don't feel nothing about you at all."

There was hesitation before Noone spoke again: "Of course, it's only natural to be angry when you've been duped. Consider, though, that since those who have wronged you will both soon be dead, and I have allowed you and your brother to live, it's really a rather satisfactory outcome from your point of view. About the best you could have hoped for, I would say. You should be pleased. There are plenty of positives to be found."

"What fucking positives?"

"Come now, Tommy. You must broaden your mind. You have got away with murder tonight. There aren't many men can say the same."

"You can. You lot do it all the bloody time."

"Ah, but that is different. We do not kill anyone: we *disperse*."

"Doesn't matter what you call it."

"Of course it does! That is all these things ever come down to, is it not, a legal sleight of hand? What is murder? How is it defined? Who gets to decide? Every law, every custom, every rule by which we live is made up by someone, conjured from thin air, then written down and by some sort of magic enacted into law. It is so malleable, Tommy. It is so unfair. The biggest myth in the world is that the law applies equally to all men—well, no, actually the biggest myth in the world is that God exists, but then even that amounts to the same thing: a made-up story written down and taken as His holy law. It is all the same parlor trick. There is no such thing as right and wrong. The only question is the individual's willingness to act. The rest is veneer, formality, perception . . . words."

"Course there's a difference between right and wrong."

"I disagree."

"You would."

"I assure you I am not alone."

"So you don't feel nothing about the things you've done?"

"Guilt, regret, conscience—they're redundant emotions, unnecessary after the fact. No, the decision must be taken beforehand: there is always an alternative path. We tell ourselves that we have no choice, when the very opposite is true: there is always another choice. Consider your own situation. You do not regret killing John, I assume, because you believe it was warranted, yet the dispersal of the Kurrong weighs heavily, I can tell. What is the difference? That you now know the Kurrong were not responsible for your family's murder, but back then you thought they were? Really? I don't believe there weren't doubts, or that at some point before we rode in there you didn't realize Joseph wasn't our only aim. Yet you participated. You still chose to—"

"You said if I didn't you'd burn me against a tree."

"So there you have it. You were faced with a choice and you acted. There is too much hand-wringing in the world these days, when the truth is, no one ever *really* feels remorse. At night in their beds or on their knees to pray, they chunter about regret and feel at peace. It is a charade. If they truly regretted something—if you were truly remorseful about what you've done, you would fall to your knees and ask to be shot. Or else you'd ride into town and confess and insist on being hanged. But you won't. No one ever does."

"I told MacIntyre what happened. He said we'd done nothing wrong."

"Well, quite. Because the law is on our side. What we did to the Kurrong was necessary, Tommy, and it's happening all over this land. In Tasmania the natives have all but disappeared. The guilt is collective, the responsibility shared. In a hundred years no one will even remember what happened here and certainly no one will care. History is forgetting. Afterward we write the account, the account becomes truth, and we tell ourselves it has always been this way, that others were responsible, that there was nothing we could have done."

"They're still dead," Tommy said. "All those people. That doesn't change."

Noone sighed. "As will you be one day, Tommy. As will I. So ask yourself, really, what fucking difference does any of this make?"

The camp emerged from the darkness. A ramshackle warren of barns and slab huts, lit by a low fire and shrouded in thin smoke. Shadows of men crossing back and forth, the shouting and the laughter, the quarrels and the cheers. Locke was in there somewhere. Chewing, spitting, arguing, eating his final meal.

They came to where the track forked, and paused.

"What'll you do to him?" Tommy asked. "Locke—what'll you do?"

Noone looked puzzled. "Kill him—what else?"

"How, I mean? How'll you do it?"

"I don't know. I suppose that depends on him."

"You won't try and arrest him?"

"No, Tommy. I won't. What would be the use?"

Tommy peered between the buildings, into the camp. Noone said, "If you want, you can come with me. I can't allow you a weapon but you're welcome to watch. I expect it will give us both some satisfaction. A mutual parting gift."

"You won't let me do it? What if I gave you my word?"

Noone inclined his head and considered him proudly. "Well now, look at you, Tommy. Look how much you've grown."

He tied Beau to a railing and followed Noone into camp, watched by men leaning in doorways or slouched on the bare ground. Some were armed, here and there a pistol sticking out of their belts or a knife hilt protruding from their boots. Noone strode on, oblivious; Tommy hurried along behind. Marching between the huts and into the very center of the camp, where a group of men sat around a fire. Tommy scanned their faces as he neared. Locke wasn't with them but he saw the watchman, Jessop, drinking from a bottle with his lank side hair hanging over his face. It occurred to Tommy that they might kill him also, and maybe Weeks if he was around, anyone who'd been involved, and nothing about that impulse felt wrong.

"Yeah? Fuck d'you want?" one of the stockmen asked.

"Good evening, gentlemen. I am looking for Raymond Locke."

There was a titter of laughter when Noone spoke.

"Who's asking?" the same stockman replied.

"Noone."

A tremor went through them. All eyes on the ground. The stockman swallowed nervously, then pointed at a candlelit slab hut across the little yard. "He's sleeping," he said.

"Excellent."

"He done something, like?" another man asked.

"Oh, yes," Noone said, turning a smile upon the group. "Indeed he has. Seems he and Mr. Sullivan had a disagreement earlier tonight. Locke was demanding more pay. For himself, you understand. John wouldn't give it, wouldn't cut all your wages to benefit just one man. Well, Locke wasn't happy. He considered himself a special case. He threatened John—as you will know, Locke just loves his threats—but John is not a man easily moved. Locke shot him. Shot him sitting in his chair. So unfortunately, gentlemen, thanks to your own headman, it seems you're all probably soon to be out of work."

"Fucking hell."

"That stupid bald cunt."

"Kill the bastard for all I fucking care."

Chatter broke out between them. Noone left them talking around the fire. Tommy followed him across the empty yard. When he glanced back at the men they were all watching, some standing, though none had made a move to come.

The hut was small. It had a railing and a narrow front deck and two windows either side of the door. Two rooms: one in darkness, the other flickering in candlelight. As they neared, Noone held out a hand in warning, then stepped quietly onto the decking and peered in through each window. He turned to Tommy and smiled. The smile was full and very wide. Noone nodded for Tommy to come closer, then he eased open the front door. Through the gap Tommy saw into the lit room, the soles of Locke's boots and his legs splayed apart on the bed. He was sleeping. Noone opened the door fully and rested it against the wall. Tommy stepped onto the porch behind him. A clear view of Locke now, slumped sideways, his piebald head hanging, his mouth open, his breathing thick and loud. Noone stood there appraising him. He drew his bowie knife slowly from his belt, then walked into the room. At the sound of him coming, Locke stirred. His eyes flickered, then snapped open and he jerked himself awake. Too late. Noone was upon him. He thrust the knife hilt-deep into Locke's side. Locke gasped and sat upright, an endless intake of air. "Hello, monkey man," Noone said, then he withdrew the knife and Locke collapsed back onto the bed. He lay there panting. His hand groped for Noone's face. Noone took his wrist and wiped his blade clean on Locke's sleeve. Locke watched the knife wide-eyed, blood pumping from his side.

"If you have questions, you should ask them. I doubt he'll last very long."

Tommy came forward, into the room, inching to the bedside. Locke's eyes rolled toward him. "Fuck," the overseer was slurring. "Fuck, fuck, fuck."

"Who was it?" Tommy said. "You or Sullivan? Who killed them?"

Locke frowned at Tommy like he could hardly see him there.

"You went to the house to kill them, you bastard. You had—"

"No," Locke said. "Talk. Come out . . . carbine . . . full of grog."

"Who shot him? You?"

Locke shook his head. "John."

"And you just fucking stood there."

"I only . . . I only did the dogs."

Noone erupted in laughter. "You and your dogs, Raymond!"

"John give back the revolver, said one ball left but . . . had to use me sword."

"So there you have it," Noone said, speaking to Tommy but staring at Locke. "The great McBride mystery has finally been solved, though I think you already knew. So long, then, Tommy. It's time for you to go now. Raymond and I are going to have a little fun before he takes his final leave."

Tommy didn't move. Locke gazed at him desperately. Noone perched on the side of the bed and muttered, "On you go, Tommy. Remember our terms."

Locke blinked slowly and looked away. Hopeless. Resigned. Tommy turned and left the room. He paused in the front doorway and saw Noone hunched over Locke's body, toying with the knife in his hand. He was talking to him gently, as if comforting an old friend. Locke groaned pitifully. Tommy came out of the hut and set off walking across the yard, toward the men still gathered around the fire. Locke screamed. Tommy stalled and the watching men flinched and one cupped his mouth with his hand. Tommy walked on. He rounded the campfire and felt the men's stares as he passed, until Locke screamed again and they recoiled and averted their eyes.

A peculiar agony in the sounds he was making. A peculiar kind of pain.

. . .

In the scant moonlight Tommy followed the trail through the trees and the clearing with the watchman's hut. Retracing the path he and Billy once took, Mary strapped bleeding to his front. Now he rode alone through the same bush and across the barren wasteland that led to the boundary trees, picking his way carefully between the boulders and termite mounds and unconsciously searching for the pair of Moses bushes in which he and his brother had hidden. Anything to hold on to. Anything that was real. His memories of his family were all he carried with him, but the memories felt as flimsy as dreams. He was hollow. Hollow and bereft. As Beau struggled to keep his footing on the shingle and scree, Tommy imagined him falling and pinning him to the ground, imagined the two of them lying out here wounded until it was time. Like that woman from Bewley who'd been found half-eaten—a bad death, Ma had said. Tommy would have taken that. He would have taken a bad death now. It seemed all the same to him. Bad life, bad death—was there any difference between the two? What lay before him was no kind of life, running from Noone for the rest of his days. He was heading for Glendale because there was nowhere else he knew, but then what? Where did he go at sunup? If he didn't leave, he and Billy were dead; Tommy didn't doubt Noone would keep his word. He was oddly principled in that way. Locke had had it coming since that first night in the scrubs, when he'd threatened Noone with a gun. Now look at him. Look at how he'd screamed.

In the blue gums Tommy dismounted and led Beau by the reins, picking a route through the trees. These same trees in which they'd once chased a dingo or emu—they'd never been sure. What if they hadn't? What if they'd gone south to hunt instead? Would all this still have happened? Would anything have changed?

In the trees he heard the rustle of creatures moving through the branches, possums or flying foxes going about their lives, utterly indifferent to his. They didn't notice his suffering. They didn't care. After all that had happened, life carried on. Tommy was realizing this now. He had lost everything. So many people had died. It was nothing. The world watched on impassively. It barely even blinked.

When Tommy mounted up again, Beau seemed to sense they were on McBride land, and quickened his pace for home. Tommy gave him the reins and let him carry him, and they were almost at a gallop as they crossed the final fields. The dark husks of the buildings came into view and Tommy let out a deep moan. He had not been back here since the burial. The pitch of the house roof, the outline of the stables and sheds, the empty skeleton of the stockyard rails. As they neared, he mapped the scrubland behind the house, searching out the two mounds of broken earth and the little white markers at their heads. He believed he could see them. Even in this darkness, from so far away. He watched and he watched, his attention so fixed on finding those graves that he missed the little campfire burning outside the bunkhouse door.

He was alongside the stockyard when he saw it: he slowed Beau to walking and moved cautiously across the patch of open ground, before halting at the edge of the yard. A small fire. Little more than a single flame and its surrounding glow. One log, maybe. The kind of fire meant to go unseen. The bunkhouse doors were open but there was no one around. Must have heard Tommy coming and hid. He checked the other buildings. They stood silent and empty in the gloom. The house with its verandah, the stables, the sheds: these makings of a life he recognized but no longer owned. He pulled himself back out of it. Someone else was here. He had no weapon but it didn't matter—with one kick of Beau's flank he could be gone.

"Show yourself or I start shooting. That's my barn you're hiding in."

There was movement in the bunkhouse doorway. Tommy braced himself, ready to flee. A figure stepped into the fireside glow. Tall and lean, wild-haired and bearded—Tommy's breath caught in his throat, his chest tightened, he scrambled down from the saddle and ran across the yard and threw himself into Arthur's embrace, the old man's body warm against his, enveloping him, his hand cradling the back of Tommy's head, stroking him gently, and Tommy was weeping, weeping, so hard he could barely stand, pouring it all out of him, everything that had happened, everything he had, and all the while Arthur whispering, "I've got you now, Tommy. I've got you now."

Gippsland, Victoria

1904

38

After lunch he sits alone on the verandah, looking over the leafy gully, drinking his coffee and having a smoke, his hat beside him on the bench. Still in his work clothes, the shirtsleeves rolled, his stockinged feet crossed before him on the deck, and his blue eyes narrowed in a squint that never leaves, even in the shade. Fair-haired and stubbled, the stubble gray and gold, hints of red when it's long. Beside his outstretched feet a black-and-white sheepdog lies sleeping; her ears twitch as he draws on the cigarette, then the eyes open irritably when he sighs out an exhale.

"That's me told," he says, smiling. "But it's my bloody deck you're on."

The dog closes her eyes again, and he laughs and shakes his head, gazes out over the gully, over his land.

The selection is spread across a meandering hillside, cut only by the east-west track running close to the house, then continuing all the way down to the creek far below. Once, he'd worried that the creek was too far away, that he'd have to find a means of pumping his water uphill, but in fact the hillside is riddled with trickling streams, either on the surface or just beneath, and he's never been short of water here. It has taken some getting used to—the seasons running backward, not pining for the next rainfall. Still gets dry in the summer, but the fodder is generally lush and plentiful, and by rotating the paddocks his cattle hardly know the taste of grain. Free to roam, bellowing happily, no idea how it feels to starve. Only after the fires of ninety-eight was there ever any trouble, but the grass recovered quickly enough. He'd only just arrived here and it had seemed so arbitrary that he was spared. Not everyone had been as lucky. Closer to town whole houses had been razed, cattle burned, yet the worst of it had missed him by a mile.

From his verandah the view stretches over the tops of the trees and across to the other side of the gully, the land undulating all around, rarely ever flat. White parakeets are squabbling in the treetops, hopping between the branches, screeching at each other—talking, he supposes—before one will take flight and another will follow and they'll circle around and land again, and the argument will start up anew.

"Worse than us two," he tells the dog. "Least you and me don't fight over a seat."

She doesn't acknowledge him. Tess, he has named her, after the woman in the book. He watches her sleeping, or pretending to sleep, then turns his attention to the parakeets again. He never tires of them, the birds; on a morning the bush is alive with their singing, kookaburras and lyrebirds, whipbirds and bowerbirds, all of them at it, performing almost, competing to be heard.

He exhales one last draw, then crushes the cigarette in the soil bucket at the side of the bench, sips the coffee in his left hand. A skewed grip on the handle, thumb and forefingers only, but well practiced and firm. He swallows and sighs. He is never happier than sitting out here, looking over his land, listening to the birds and the distant cattle, his work done, a drink in his hand. This is his entertainment; this is his life. On an evening he'll do the same, red wine instead of coffee, brandy maybe, sometimes a whiskey but not often; he's never been able to stomach the taste of rum. He'll sit through the twilight, watching the sun go down, watching the flying foxes, then stay on into the darkness, his face lit by the glow of a cigarette, Tess with her head in his lap or snoozing at his feet. When he's finished he'll go back inside and read a book before bed, filling his head with stories to keep away the dreams. That's when the memories get him. They come for him still. Some nights he wakes sweating and horror-filled and gasping at the air, whirling on the room like the walls are closing in. He daren't sleep again after that. So it's back to the verandah, wait for the dawn.

Now he groans as he stands and shuffles to the rail. He has his father's body, broad and tall, that same stiffness in his gait. He leans against the railing, drinks his coffee, scanning the gully east to west. Beside him, Tess stirs, lifts her head from the boards and pushes herself to her feet, stiff as him just about. She squeezes between his shins and the balustrades and restlessly circles his legs, then pauses looking west and snatches a couple of warning barks.

"You hear something?" he asks her, and Tess gives another volley in reply. "Alright, that'll do. Don't worry yourself. If it's anyone it'll only be Alf."

He looks to the west but can't see anything, no sign of Alf's wagon behind the bushes and trees. No jangling sound, either, but the mail coach is two days overdue, and no one else ever comes.

Might have brought his *Queenslanders*. News from up north.

He drains the coffee and goes inside, leaving Tess standing guard at the rail. Through the little living room and into the kitchen, where he puts a pot of fresh water on the stove to boil, then digs around the sparse pantry and comes up with a crust of bread and a couple of slices of salted beef. He combines them in a sandwich and weighs the offering in his hand. It's all there is—he's never been much of a host. The store this afternoon, then. Get some supper in.

When the coffee is made he carries the two cups in his hands and the towel-wrapped sandwich wedged under his arm, and goes out onto the verandah again. Now the mail coach is visible, the old Cobb & Co. wagon coming slowly along the track, big wheels turning, a four-team of horses and Alf floating above the hedgerow, hunched on his box. No passengers today, no luggage on the roof—means he might stop and talk. Tess barks again and though he scowls at her, he knows why she's upset.

"Ah, quit your whining. I'm not so bad these days. Besides, Alf's the only bloody visitor we get."

He hobbles down the steps and along the narrow footpath that leads through the long grass to the road, Tess right beside him, tight to his legs. There are gateposts, but no gate—he always intended hanging one, but found he had no need. He leans on one of the posts and watches Alf come. The coachman sees him and waves. With the coffees in his hands, he can only respond with a nod.

"Thought you'd forgotten us," he says as the coach pulls up on the track.

"Had to do a run to Bendigo. Never like going out there."

Alf ties off the reins, swivels on the box, clambers down. The horses are panting and covered in dust, and now that it's stationary, the coach creaks like it breathes. Alf brushes himself down, removes his hat, scrubs his face, and comes up smiling. An old-looking man, if not exactly old. Long, graying hair and sunburned skin, lines around the eyes, but the eyes themselves still keen.

"Howya, young Robert?" he says warmly.

"Howya, Alf?" He holds up the coffees. "Time for a stop?"

"Glad of it. Been out since dawn. That trough got anything in?"

"Help yourself. Filled it yesterday. Just in case."

"Ah, you're a good man, a good man."

While Alf unshackles the horses from the harness, Tess darts about excitedly, her tongue hanging, snapping the odd bark at their guest.

"He's not brought you anything. Something for me, though, maybe?"

"Aye, there is," Alf says, leading the horses to the trough. "Got a bundle of them *Queenslanders* for you in the back there. Still don't know what you're doing reading some other bugger's news."

Alf comes back from the trough, accepts the coffee, raises the cup in salute, and takes a tentative sip, blowing on the surface to cool it down.

"Thanks for this, Bobby—much obliged."

The coachman flops onto the wagon steps and lets out a sigh from his bones. He notices the sandwich and his eyebrows raise hopefully, then when it's offered he grabs it, unwraps the towel, takes a bite, and closes his eyes as he chews.

"You're no bloody baker, but by, she must have been a pretty cow."

"Prettier than you're used to, that's for damn sure."

"Ain't that the truth," Alf says, laughing. "Ain't that the bloody truth."

He stands by the gatepost with his coffee, watching Alf eat.

"I already told you, anyway. It's the cattle prices I get them for."

Alf squints up at him. "What that now?"

"The *Queenslanders*. For the market reports."

"Ah, don't worry about it, Bobby. I'm only having you on."

He nods and sips his coffee and bends to tickle Tess behind her ear. When Alf has finished his sandwich he dabs his mouth with the towel and hands it back.

"First-class that. First-class. So, then, what news from Sleepy Gully here?"

"No news. You know us. Working. Same as always."

"Stock keeping well?"

"Aye, they'll be right. Can't but help it round here."

"Well, I'm glad to hear it," Alf says. He takes another drink. "Been out much?"

"Such as?"

"Anywhere, Bobby. You seen anyone else since last I came by?"

"Course I have. Heading to town this very afternoon."

"Good. It ain't healthy a man living out here on his own."

"I ain't on my own."

Alf looks at Tess. "A woman, I'm talking about. Hell, beef like that, I'd marry you. Better yet, might trade the missus for one of them pretty cows."

"That keen to be rid of you, is she?"

"Good-looking fella like you, she'd be keener than

the cow!" Alf starts laughing, a phlegmy rattle that catches in his throat. He clears it, spits, drains the coffee, and passes back the cup. "Right then," he says, standing. "Let's see about them papers."

"No rush, Alf."

"Aye well, some of us have work to do."

"You mean sitting on your arse, telling them horses to pull?"

Alf feigns outrage. "Thirty miles I've done since sunup. Anyway, all I ever see you doing's waiting on that porch."

"Lunchtime."

Alf is smiling at him. "It's always bloody lunchtime round here." He opens the coach door, leans inside, rummages through the boxes and bundles of papers, then straightens, holding a small parcel of *Queenslander* journals, bound in brown string. "There y'are. Bloody northerners. Wouldn't welcome but one of the bastards down here."

He takes the journals from Alf and tucks them under his arm. "That's your own countrymen you're talking about. We're all under the same flag now."

"Well, I never agreed to it. Flag or no bloody flag. It's all boongs and chinks up there is what I heard. Be giving 'em the bloody vote next. Back in the old days they had the right idea about it, used to shoot the buggers on sight, none of this Protector of Aborigines bull crap. Anyway, these new laws'll sort 'em out. Send 'em back where they came from, I say—hold up now, what's bit your arse?"

He is still standing with the journals under his arm, the mugs dangling from his fingers, but all trace of a smile is gone. He attempts one now but fails.

"Nothing. Thanks for these. Anyway, best be getting on."

"Bloody hell, Bobby. You've not taken offense?"

"Course not. Too much coffee, need a piss. You manage with the team?"

"Aye, I'll manage with the team . . . just, I didn't mean nothing."

"I know. I need a piss, that's all it is. Come on, Tess. Come on, girl."

He hurries away, Tess running ahead of him, uphill along the path, but forces himself to turn and wave at Alf, now rehitching his horses to the coach. Alf returns the wave slowly, sadly, and he continues on to the house, doesn't look back again. Not sure he can keep it hidden, the guilt and grief stirred up by Alf's words and these bloody news journals he cannot bring himself to quit. He closes the front door behind him, tosses the *Queenslanders* on the coffee table, slumps down into the armchair, and holds his head in both hands.

He should have said something, spoken up against Alf, but then Alf's his only visitor, his only means of news from home. He stares at the topmost journal, that word *Queenslander*, and hates himself for it, his need to know, his inability to leave the past where it belongs, his fear that he'll open those pages and find a story about himself, his family's murder, the massacre that followed; his fear that the lies he has spent a lifetime telling will one day be untold.

39

The ride into town only takes half an hour, less if he pushes Lady any quicker than a walk. Which he rarely does; she can move when she has to, whether in the paddocks or on the road, but both prefer not to hurry, they're well suited that way. It isn't always so. Before Lady he had a gelding that reminded him of Beau, but there was none of Beau's temperament in that horse. Made him realize he hadn't appreciated how special Beau was. But then Beau was his first, he wasn't to know. So he'd sold off the gelding and bought Lady instead, hazel-colored coat, a gentle way about her. "A proper lady this one," the trader had told him. The name stuck. That was four years ago. He doesn't like to think about a time when she'll be gone.

The road twists through hilly bushland, then drops

into town, giving a view of the whole place as he rides in. It's not much, really. One of everything just about. Baker, butcher, general store. There's a pub and some tearooms and an iron-walled shed they call a town hall. All on the one street, houses scattered around, spreading up into the hills. The same creek that flows through his selection also winds through the town; they've tried to make a feature of it, built a hump-backed bridge, a bandstand, there's a park with flower beds and a paved walking path. It's nice here, he supposes. He's lived in worse places since leaving Glendale.

Although, can he really claim to live here? That he belongs? Certainly he's at home on his own land, but even after six years he's something of an outsider in town. Not that he's unwelcome—the fires of ninety-eight had seen to that. From his hillside he'd seen the smoke cloud coming, read its movement, read the wind, knew it was headed for town. He'd ridden like a madman to warn them, come tearing in along the road to find plenty still oblivious, going about their business, no clue what was coming their way. He'd carried water from the creek, stood with them shoulder to shoulder in the face of the fire. Then afterward, the bulk of the town mercifully spared, others not so lucky, he had done what he could to help. They'd all been grateful. He wasn't a stranger anymore. Despite the lingering suspicion and disapproval at how he lived, this man Robert Thompson—a name he'd taken from a headstone in a town called St. George—was an alright bloke after all. Gently, he pulled away again. Kept to himself on his farm. He has a story all worked out but doesn't like to tell it. It's easier not to have to. Easier on his own.

But they're friendly enough. They pass the time and wave or touch their hats when they see him riding in. Today is no different. He smiles and does the same. He walks Lady in the direction of the general store, but then notices that the baker's wife is serving and dismounts outside the bakery instead. He tethers Lady to the rail, takes off his hat as he walks in through the door.

"Well now, Bobby, isn't this a nice surprise."

She is around his own age, blond-haired, green-eyed, sharply featured, and attractive despite a billowing apron and a day's work in her face. She smiles wearily and fidgets as he approaches the counter, touching her clothing, her hair. They often do this, the women in town. He is thirty-three years old and unmarried, and they don't get many newcomers here.

"Hello, Emily, you keeping well?"

"Oh, you know. Too hot with the oven. You alright up there, are you?"

"Aye, we're fine. Running short, though. Couple of loaves if you would."

She looks around the shop with a pained grimace. The shelves behind her are bare. A few meat pies and pastries in the cabinet but that's all.

"It's the end of the day, Bobby. Bread's all gone. If I knew when you were coming, I'd have kept some back. You only have to ask."

"Don't worry. Just two of them pies, maybe. Still warm, are they?"

She shakes her head pityingly, then laughs. "Not your day, I don't think."

He laughs too. "Ah, give 'em here. Be lovely if you've made them anyway."

Her cheeks flush a little deeper. She wraps and bags the pies. He watches her fondly, this woman he barely knows, enjoys the two of them flirting like this, the effect it has on her, on him. He is aware that women talk about him, that they watch him through the windows as he walks down the street, and are all the more curious for how little he reveals.

"It's just not healthy, a man living all alone like that."

"He's got that native up there with him. A woman now, I heard."

"Well, that would explain it. Man like that should be married to a nice white girl, not chasing after some black."

"And children. Should be a father by his age."

"Exactly. To look at him you'd think there'd be a litter running around!"

In fact, there had been a woman, once. He had met her in Melbourne, on one of his visits—he has business there a couple of times a year. A waitress by the name of Anne; she had served him his tea. Fair-skinned, red-haired, freckles on her arms and cheeks. They had briefly spoken, then he found himself returning to the tearooms the following day, knowing it was a mistake but allowing himself to make it all the same. He had allowed himself so little. He thought maybe she was worth the risk.

Six months later Anne came out to live with him. He'd intended marriage, but she was back in Melbourne within eight weeks. The isolation unnerved her; he wouldn't let her change things, wouldn't change himself. The stolen nights they'd shared in the city, their carefree conversations, were replaced with anxiety and questions about his family, his childhood, his past.

"Whatever happened I'll still love you," she once told him, her damp eyes pleading, her palm against his cheek.

"No you won't," he said, brushing her away and heading back out to the fields.

The force of his dreams had been a shock to her: they had never come for him in Melbourne, in her lodgings or his hotel room. She saw the very worst of him, the screaming and the sweating and the horror in his face, and knew there was something rotten within. He could see it frightened her: how could they be married when she was scared of her man?

In many ways he was relieved. They traveled cordially back to the city, side by side in the dray. She had hardly met anyone in town—hadn't wanted to introduce herself until they were properly wed—so there was no need for explanations to be made. Another small blessing. He doesn't believe he deserves to be happy, not in that way at least. He has become reconciled to it now, considers it a fair price to pay; more than fair, in fact.

But then . . . the way the baker's wife looks at him, the way she twists her hair.

After the bakery he visits the general store, then packs his provisions into the saddlebags and crosses the road to the pub. A single-story shack, two rooms out back, too small to call itself a hotel. The place is known as Mickey's, after the Irishman behind the bar. His name is Jack but no one uses it: Mick, or Mickey, he is called.

He lays his hand on the door and hesitates. He knows what will be waiting for him inside. But then he also knows how towns like this work—if he doesn't show his face, he'll find himself excluded for good. There might come a time when he needs these people. The goodwill from the fires will only last so long. Were it not for that, he would probably be a pariah by now. It's a delicate line he treads.

There are a handful of drinkers. They turn to watch him come in. A pause, then his name ripples gruffly around the smoke-filled room, the greeting passing like an echo between the men: "Bobby . . . Bobby . . . Bobby."

He nods and says their names in reply, walking between the tables to the bar, where he acknowledges the few men huddled there before sitting down on a stool. Mick brings him a pot of beer—save a few dusty liquors, beer is all they have. The glass drips with condensation. He touches the foam to his lips and drinks.

"Had Old Alf in here earlier. Off the coach there, you know?"

He nods wearily. Mick standing over him, watching him drink.

"Said he called by your place. Said you might be coming down."

"Well, here I am."

"Aye," Mick says. He is a tall man, white hair, face like wind-beaten stone. He glances around and leans in close. "Said you got all touchy and ran off up the house. Something about boongs and chinks, he said."

He takes a long drink and swallows. "I needed a piss, Mick, if it's all the same to you."

"That's not how Alf tells it."

"Alf can tell it however he likes."

He sees off the beer and sets the glass on the mat. "Another?" Mick asks him.

"Aye, alright."

While he's waiting he glances along the bar and behind him at the room. Men sit in small groups, some alone, one facedown on the table, asleep. He knows most of them; they all know him. Think they do anyway. He has told them the story about his wounded hand, how he was holding a fence post on a station out east when the mallet came down too soon. He doesn't give the name of the station, or any of the others he's worked. Tells them he's originally from Sydney, since most people are, and nobody questions him now. They all have their stories anyway: none of them moved here clean.

Mick brings the beer, places it before him, stands back, and folds his arms.

"You know, Bobby, people don't like hearing things like that from Alf. Makes them nervous. Reminds them what you've got living with you up there. On your own you're a good bloke, you know we all think it. Welcome in here anytime. But this thing you've got for the natives . . . it's not right, Bobby; it's just not right."

He sips contemplatively at his beer. The others along the bar are listening.

"I don't have a thing for the natives."

"All the same, you let them stop on your land."

"Land's half his. I ain't letting nothing."

"Which is even bloody worse! Listen, there's people in this town got long memories as far as the blacks is concerned. They just don't want them around. You allow one in and there'll be dozens in no time—isn't there a woman now, I heard?"

He is staring dead ahead as he drinks. "I wouldn't know about that, Mick."

"Well, all I can do is warn you. And anyway, what's this Alf says about you reading *Queenslander*s? Wasn't you from Sydney, you said?"

"Cattle prices," he says flatly. He takes a sip, then throws back the rest of the beer and lowers the glass to the mat. "Surprised Alf never mentioned that too."

"I don't think he meant nothing, Bobby."

"Plenty to say all the same."

"Ah, he was only passing the time."

He stands and reaches into his pocket, picks out the change, lays it on the bar. The barman is watching him worriedly. "Stay and have another," he says.

"Best be getting back, Mick. Maybe next time."

The barman sniffs and looks away. "Aye, suit your-self. See you again."

"See you again."

As he walks to the door he returns their mumbled good-byes, pushes out into the sunshine, and for a moment stands there squinting and waiting for his eyes to settle, his body tense, his jaw set. Slowly he unclenches. Shakes himself down, replaces his hat. He crosses the street to his horse and catches the baker's wife watching him through the window glass. She busies herself behind the counter, then pretends to notice him only now. They exchange a smile and a wave before he climbs into his saddle and clicks Lady on, the pies Emily has made for him bouncing lightly in his bag. He doesn't look behind to see if she's still watching, but a part of him hopes that she is.

40

He sits at the table, reading while he eats. He has fried some potatoes in the skillet and warmed the pie in the stove. He imagines Emily making it, kneading the pastry with her hands, then scolds himself for doing so; imagines the baker instead: his big hairy fingers, his chin like a toad's. The thought never sticks. She filters back in like sunlight through leaves. What if she was with him now, at this table? What if she had kneaded, filled, and cooked the pie right here in this room? What if he took her off the baker and to hell with everyone else?

He concentrates on the journals. Flicking the pages with his left hand, forking the pie into his mouth with his right, just enough light from the lantern to see. He's been reading *The Queenslander* for many years now, after coming across a copy in the barbershop in town. No one knew how it had got there; he'd leafed through the first few pages, then Willis had said if he wanted to, he could take the journal home.

"You're the only one that's ever looked twice at it, Bobby," he'd said, laughing. "And the bloody thing's been in here over a year!"

So he'd taken it home and read it, and there in black and white he had seen his brother's name. A small entry in the announcements: a child, a girl, their fourth, Suzanna she was called. He'd shaken worse than from any fever, then he'd cried like no man should. He was an uncle. Four times over. Billy was married, a father: "grazier," the notice said. He reckoned the dates: by the time he'd read the announcement the child was eighteen months old. He hadn't slept at all that night, stayed out on the verandah drinking, imagining his brother's life. Three other children, a home, a wife. He pictured them at Glendale, but there was nothing to say he was still there. Might have taken another selection in the district, might even have taken Broken Ridge. Either way, Billy had moved on, made something of himself. Just like he always said he would.

Since then the *Queenslander*s have become a ritual: a newsagent in Melbourne orders them for him and they arrive in sporadic batches throughout the year. At first it was torture. Like a man searching for his own death notice, he would pick through the pages, anxious for news, for any name he recognized, any mention of Billy or even himself. There was rarely anything. The state was too big, the journal's coverage too wide. Once there was a piece about the closure of the Lawton saleyards, which was no surprise, but just reading the name brought plenty back. Bewley came up occasionally, and there was regular reader correspondence with titles such as "The Problem with the Blacks." Nothing more about Billy. Nothing about his family or Glendale. And then one day he turned the page onto a story about Noone.

They had made him police commissioner, the article said, for the entire state force. A talented and gifted naval officer, former chief inspector of the Native Police, where his pioneering work opened swaths of the interior for pastoral use, the man responsible for solving the murder of prominent squatter John Sullivan by the outlaw Raymond Locke, renowned administrator, politician, respected botanist and anthropologist, patron of the arts . . . on and on it went. And now he had command over the entire territory, all of Queensland was his.

He'd cut out the article and kept it. A reminder: never go back.

He eats the pie slowly, turns the pages one by one. Despite his wobble earlier, he's much better with the journals these days. Can even get some pleasure from reading about home—not his home, specifically, but the land that's in his bones. He'll see drawings or paintings of that vast and endless scrub, the red soil and the spinifex, and he'll imagine himself standing there, the heat, the silence, the smell. It all comes back to him. He doubts it will ever fade. But he doesn't like to linger there, can't stay in his memories too long. They only ever lead in one direction. So he'll turn the page quickly, and move on.

Nothing in this latest batch of journals catches his eye. He is onto the third volume by the time the meal is done and he decides to leave the remaining three for later. He scrapes the last of the pastry with his fork, then dabs up the crumbs with his thumb, sucks them off the end, could lick the plate just about. Bless you, sweetheart, he thinks to himself, then shakes his head and sighs. What's wrong with him today?

While he smokes he finishes the third *Queenslander*, then sets the journal aside. He sits back in the chair, the wood creaks. The clock is ticking in the living room and he wonders at the time. After seven, certainly: it's fully dark outside. Probably too late for a visit but he wants to take over the second pie. They'll have already eaten but it'll keep, and he feels an urge to give the thing away. Prove to himself he's not smitten. He laughs just at the thought of it. Smitten with a pie.

Tess is waiting for him on the back porch. As if she's read his mind. Maybe she has: the two of them are telepathic in a way he's never been with a dog. His father would have said he's too close to her, but what else can he do? She's not just another work-dog, though at least he doesn't let her into the house. Some rules you cannot shake.

"Just going over their place," he tells her, pulling on his boots. "You can come if you want to, but you'll be outside there the same as you are here."

Tess follows. With the pie in his hands and his dog at his heels, he sets off walking across the rear yard with its fowl house and struggling veggie patch, through a gate, and out into the fields. A mile to get there, but the terrain is uneven and difficult in the dark. There's no proper track. Only the flattened horse trail beaten out over the years, a constant passing back and forth between the two houses. Now it's mainly he who does the journey. His legs are stronger, younger. Perhaps his need is greater too.

A lantern is burning on the porch. He quickens his pace down the final slope, toward a house little different from his own. They had built both places together, same materials, same design, lived in an improvised humpy to begin with, then the first house while the second was built. They had nothing but the land and the land was enough. He can still remember the feeling. His giddiness at putting down roots.

Tess announces their arrival. He comes up the steps, balances the pie in one hand, and is about to knock when a woman's voice calls through the door, "Bobby? That you?"

"Aye, Rosie. It's me."

She opens up and smiles at him, notices the pie. "What's this?"

"Brought you some supper."

She touches his arm. "Thanks, love, but we've et."

"I thought so. Bloody good, though. You don't want it, I will."

She laughs. Her cheeks are plump, her eyes shine. She has short braided hair and dark skin whose lines show her age. Not that he knows it. You never like to ask. In fact, he knows very little about her, doesn't even know how she came to be here: one day she wasn't, then the next day she was. Which was fine. He liked her instantly. There's a fondness between them like nephew and aunt.

"He awake still?"

A voice from inside calls: "Course I'm bloody awake!"

Rosie smiles indulgently, steps aside to let him pass. She takes the pie, then crouches to ruffle Tess on her neck and under her chin. The dog sniffs the pie and Rosie singsongs to her, "You want a piece, do you? You want a piece of this?"

He walks through, into the living room. Arthur is sitting in his chair. The old man smiles at him. "Hello, Tommy," he says.

The sound of his name stalls him. Comes like the glimpse of a ghost. He looks over his shoulder, toward the front door, where Rosie is still playing with Tess, doesn't seem to have heard.

Arthur waves a hand dismissively. "Don't worry, her hearing's going. She'll think I said Bobby, they sound about the same."

Tommy sits in the other armchair, angled toward Arthur, the fire between them, though it's not much of one. A spindle of a flame from a clutch of dead logs, but Arthur likes a fire every night. Could be the middle of summer and he'd want one lit; keep away bad spirits, signal the end of the day. Old habits: Arthur hasn't changed much in all this time. Small things. Age leaving its mark. His knotted gray hair still hangs about his face, but the face is thin and haggard and the beard is all gray now. His body too is thin and shrunken: the best of his strength has left him, but he's not decrepit yet. He moves just as easily as he always did, no sign of aches and pains, and he gets out in the fields with Tommy, feeding, droving, mustering the stock. It's perhaps in the eyes that Tommy notices it most, his age, his decline: they are often laced with redness, damp and hesitant, quick to tear. Arthur is still just as full of himself but the eyes give him away. He is frightened, Tommy has concluded. He can see the end.

"Brought you a pie," Tommy tells him. "From the baker's in town."

"I'll bet you did. That pretty wife of his serve you?"

He slaps Arthur on the knee. "How d'you know she's pretty?"

"You've talked about her," Arthur says, shrugging. "And you're a bloke."

Arthur doesn't go into town anymore. There's nothing for him there, he says. In the beginning they'd visited together and people assumed he was Tommy's boy; Tommy corrected them but nothing improved. Arthur saw where it was headed. He'd seen it all his life. If they were going to make it out here, he'd need to be invisible, to disappear. So one night over supper Arthur said to act in town like he didn't exist: "I've not lost nothing by it. Your world's not my world."

Tommy protested but that's what they did, and soon Tommy found himself tolerated, then accepted in town, while up here he and Arthur carved out a life for themselves, at first just the two of them and now with Rosie, all on their own terms.

"Aye, well, she's married, so that's the end of it."

"It's never been the end of it," Arthur says. "Everything changes sometime."

"Not everything."

"Oh, yeah?"

"Took some shit on your account in the pub again. And from bloody Alf."

"How does he know about us?"

Tommy shrugs. "Someone'll have told him."

"Ah, fuck 'em," Arthur says, laughing. "You know I don't care."

Rosie comes through with the pie. She has left Tess outside on the porch.

"Don't care about what now?"

"Them buggers in town," Arthur says, and Rosie blows out incredulously as she passes through the room and into the kitchen.

"You want anything?" she calls.

"Tea maybe."

"Bobby, I meant!"

"I'll take a tea."

Rosie clatters the pot on the stove and they both settle back in their chairs.

"Alf bring them papers, did he?" Arthur asks. "That why you've come?"

"Can't I pay a visit now?"

"Only saw you this morning. Sick of looking at your bloody face."

Arthur is grinning. Tommy's laugh trails off in a sigh. "Aye, he brought them. Nothing so far. I've still got three to go."

"Give you much trouble this time?"

"Only on account of what Alf said. Not from the papers yet."

"Glad to hear it. Never known a man spend so much money on making himself unhappy. I don't know why you still bother, I really don't."

"Yes you do."

"Aye, well. It's time you let it go."

Rosie comes in juggling three cups of tea. She drags a little stool between the armchairs and puts two of the cups on top, hesitates with the third in her hand.

Arthur asks, "Give us a minute, love?"

"Right you are," she says brightly. "I'll go and play with the dog."

When she's gone they sit in silence, listening to her outside, that singsong voice she uses with Tess. Tommy reaches for his tea but it's scalding. He puts it back down on the stool.

"Tommy, listen," Arthur says quietly, urgently. "Stop with them bloody papers. Get on with the baker's wife, or any other woman you like. Twenty years is long enough. It's more than long enough."

Tommy is leaning forward on his elbows, his head hanging low. He looks up at Arthur and asks him, his voice weak, barely forming the word: "How?"

Arthur considers him a long time with those damp red eyes.

"I've told you this already: I can't forgive you. There's only you can do that."

"Like it's so easy."

"It's not meant to be easy. It should be bloody hard. But that don't mean you can't try. You were fourteen. You only did what was needed to survive."

"How are you so sure?"

"Because I know you. I've known you your whole bloody life. What happened up there wasn't your doing—there's men done worse and moved on just fine."

"That doesn't make it alright."

"I never said it did."

"You talking about Billy? Or Daddy?"

"I'm talking about all of 'em. Every bugger out there. Me included. You've seen it for yourself."

"That was different."

"In your eyes, maybe. This country . . . people have been fighting since the first boat came, before that even, the whole world's crooked these days. We each do what we have to to make it through." He taps his chest, his heart. "It's what's in here that counts."

Tommy shakes his head. "You know it's not that simple."

"Mate, there's plenty of people headed to hell, blacks as well as whites, but you ain't one of them. You'll be up there with your family. God'll see you right."

Tommy frowns at him. "Don't act like you believe that horseshit."

"Hey—I'm a Mission boy. I'm the closest you've got to a priest!"

Both men laugh weakly. It fades and Arthur reaches for his tea and slurps it, watching Tommy over the rim.

"Billy wouldn't make it," Tommy says. "He'd never be let in."

Arthur shrugs. "That's his lookout. You and him ain't the same."

Tommy picks up his tea, leans back in the chair.

"You know, I'd be the one that would have to write him. If ever we were to speak again. He has no idea where we are."

"I thought there was no letters, you said."

"He has to die one day. Noone. I keep checking the death pages."

"Well, that's something else you need to quit."

"Can't help it, though a part of me doubts it'll ever happen."

"You wouldn't want to risk it before that?"

"Billy's got a family. He'd go after them first. Anyway, what's the point? He won't have changed that much. He'll still be what he was."

"Aye. And he'll still be your brother."

He shakes his head. "I think about it sometimes. But me and Billy are done."

Tommy agrees to stay for supper. They each have a small slice of the pie, then the three of them sit around the kitchen table, talking and drinking until late. He's back to being Bobby again—somehow Arthur never slips. And even if he did, he doubts Rosie would bat an eye. She must know there's something about him, about the two of them, their past; Arthur might have told her everything by now. He wouldn't blame him. He knows the harm keeping such secrets can do.

In darkness he stumbles his way back across the fields, Tess alongside him, the moon lighting their way. A cow bellows as they pass and he mumbles for it to quiet down, but fondly, like hushing a child or pet. He doesn't mistreat his cattle, won't whip them or beat them or mishandle them like in the old days. He has a theory that it helps with the taste of the beef, but he keeps it to himself. And that's not really why he does it. He keeps that to himself too.

The house peels from the shadows. Tess runs on ahead. She's waiting for him when he reaches the gate, sitting there patiently, her head cocked; he leans over and flicks the latch and the gate swings open to let her through. Across the yard and onto the back porch, where he takes off his boots and kneels down to say good night, scuffing Tess around her jaw, stroking her head and back. Her tongue lolls happily. Like she's smiling, almost. "See you at sunup," he tells her, rising and going in through the door to the kitchen, where his dinner plate and the pile of *Queenslanders* are still on the table from before. He lights the lantern, pours himself a whiskey, sits down in the chair, and slides the next journal from the top of the pile. On the cover is an illustration of a man fishing, happily casting his line into a river at the bottom of a deep red gorge. Looks a bit like Wallabys, Tommy thinks. He lights a cigarette. Sits there smoking and staring at that cover a long time. He takes a sip of the whiskey. His eyes flick to the other *Queenslanders*, then back to the man fishing: he stubs out his cigarette, picks up the journal, and carefully returns it to the top of the pile.

He stands. Blows out the lantern, scrapes back the chair, carries the whiskey through the house and out the front door, where he finds Tess waiting for him beside the verandah bench.

"How did you know, eh?" he asks her, rubbing her head. "How did you know?"

He sits down on the bench, lights another cigarette. Tess hops up beside him and lays her head in his lap. He drinks, he smokes. The darkness of the gully around him, the shapes of the trees, the shadows of his land. Everywhere is shadow, shades of black and gray, the hillside and the house upon it, the pitch of its roof and the hollow of the verandah and within it the outline of a man sitting with his dog, and the single red dot of his cigarette end, glowing when he inhales.

Author's Note

The characters, events, and most of the locations in this novel are fictitious, but all are rooted in historical fact. The Queensland Native Police operated from the colony's formation in 1859 until the early years of the twentieth century, and for his comprehensive study of all aspects of the force, I am grateful to Jonathan Richards's *The Secret War: A True History of Queensland's Native Police* (University of Queensland Press). Reading *Blood on the Wattle: Massacres and Maltreatment of Aboriginal Australians Since 1788, 3rd ed.* (New Holland Publishers), by Bruce Elder, provided the first spark for this story, and the book was a helpful source throughout. The epigraph is taken from a digitized version of the original *Queenslander* edition, accessed via Trove (http://nla.gov.au/nla.news-page2531550), a valuable online resource offered by the National Library of Australia. All errors or inaccuracies in the novel are my own.

Acknowledgments

Thank you to: my agent Lucy Luck and all at C+W; Anna Stein at ICM Partners; my editors Terry Karten and Laura Macaulay, and all at HarperCollins and Pushkin Press; my tutors and course mates at UEA, particularly Andrew Cowan, Helen Cross, Malachi McIntosh, and Jean McNeil; my family for their support and encouragement; and above all Sarah, for everything.

About the Author

Paul Howarth was born and grew up in Great Britain before moving to Melbourne in his late twenties. He lived in Australia for more than six years, gained dual citizenship in 2012, and now lives in Norwich, United Kingdom, with his family. In 2015, he received a master's degree from the University of East Anglia's creative writing program, the most prestigious course of its kind in the UK, and was awarded the Malcolm Bradbury Scholarship.

THE NEW LUXURY IN READING

We hope you enjoyed reading
our new, comfortable print size and found it
an experience you would like to repeat.

Well – you're in luck!

HarperLuxe offers the finest in fiction and
nonfiction books in this same larger print size and
paperback format. Light and easy to read, HarperLuxe
paperbacks are for book lovers who want to see
what they are reading without the strain.

For a full listing of titles and
new releases to come, please visit our website:

www.HarperLuxe.com